FREE TO FALL

Also by Lauren Miller
Parallel

FREE

TO

FALL

LAUREN MILLER

HARPER TEEN
An Imprint of HarperCollinsPublishers

*In loving memory of my Granny Bea, who would've
surely been committed for APD*

HarperTeen is an imprint of HarperCollins Publishers.

Free to Fall
Copyright © 2014 by Lauren Miller
All rights reserved. Printed in the United States of America.
No part of this book may be used or reproduced in any manner
whatsoever without written permission except in the case of brief
quotations embodied in critical articles and reviews. For information
address HarperCollins Children's Books, a division of HarperCollins
Publishers, 10 East 53rd Street, New York, NY 10022.
www.epicreads.com

Library of Congress Cataloging-in-Publication Data
Miller, Lauren (Lauren McBrayer), 1980–
    Free to fall / Lauren Miller. — First edition.
        pages cm
    Summary: "In a near-future world where everyone is controlled by
their smartphones, sixteen-year-old Rory Vaughn suddenly begins
listening to the voice within—which kids are taught to ignore—and
discovers a terrible plot at the heart of the corporation that makes the
devices"— Provided by publisher.
    ISBN 978-0-06-219980-5 (hardback)
    [1. Boarding schools—Fiction. 2. Schools—Fiction. 3. Smartphones—
Fiction. 4. Love—Fiction. 5. Science fiction.] I. Title.
PZ7.M6227Fre 2014   2013047725
[Fic]—dc23   CIP
                                                              AC

Typography by Sarah Nichole Kaufman
14 15 16 17 18 LP / RRDH 10 9 8 7 6 5 4 3 2 1
❖
First Edition

1

IT CAME IN A PLAIN WHITE ENVELOPE, which made both more and less of its significance. More, because their decision was printed in ink, on thick cotton paper, which felt a little like they'd carved it in stone. Less, because there was nothing about that nondescript rectangle to imply that there was life-changing information inside. The envelope arrived a month after my sixteenth birthday, on an otherwise unmemorable Wednesday afternoon in April. Nineteen and a half hours later it bore an impressive coffee stain and was still unopened.

"Just read it," Beck said from behind his camera. I heard the rapid fire of his shutter as he held down the release button, his lens angled up at the slanted glass roof. It was lunchtime on Thursday, and we were spending our free period where we always did, in the living room at the Seattle public library, which looked nothing at all like a living room or a library and more like a cross between a greenhouse and a steel cage. It was quarter after one already, which meant we'd probably be late for fifth period again, but neither of us was in a rush to get back. Beck wanted more pictures, and I was too distracted to think about AP Psych.

"I already know what it says," I replied, turning the envelope over in my hands. "It's thin. I didn't get in."

"All the more reason to open it." Beck pointed his camera at the girl behind the register at the coffee cart. The lens extended as he zoomed in on her face. My best friend was mildly obsessed with the coffee-stand girl, who was clearly not the least bit interested in the gangly teenage boy who was semi-stalking her.

"If I know what it says, there's no *reason* to open it," I said petulantly.

"Seriously?" Beck said, finally looking me in the eyes. I shrugged. Beck plucked the envelope from my hands and tore it open.

"Hey!" I shrieked, reaching for it. But Beck was already unfolding the letter. A button-size lapel pin slipped from the crease of the letter and onto the floor. I stared as it rolled a few inches and fell on its side. *Why would they send a pin unless . . .*

"Dear Ms. Vaughn," I heard Beck say. "We are delighted to inform you that you have been accepted into the Theden Academy Class of 2032. Blah, blah, blah, the rest doesn't matter because YOU GOT IN!"

"Shh," hissed the woman across from us, her face pinched in an annoyed glare. She gestured at her tablet. "This is a *library.*" Without looking at her, Beck pointed his camera at her face and held down the shutter release. "Stop that!" she snapped.

I reached for the fallen lapel pin. It was round and gold and looked like something my grandfather might've worn. Then again, I never knew either of my grandfathers so I'm not exactly an authority on their taste in accessories. I slipped the pin into the pocket of my jacket, keeping my fingers on it for safekeeping. Beck was still snapping pictures.

"Please excuse my friend," I said to the woman apologetically, handing Beck his bag. "He didn't take his meds today."

"This is true," Beck said solemnly. I yanked his arm and pulled him toward the exit.

It wasn't until we were outside, standing under the Fifth Avenue overhang and feeling the sideways spray of cold, misty rain on our foreheads, that it finally registered: I'd gotten in, which meant I was going. The Theden application process was rigorous, but the attendance process was easy: If you were offered and accepted a spot in the incoming class, they took care of everything else. Travel, lodging, tuition, food. All of it paid for by Theden's thirty-billion-dollar endowment.

"Let me have it," I said, taking the letter from Beck's hand. Needing to see it for myself.

"I knew you'd get in."

"Yeah, right."

"Rory, you've been taking college classes since eighth grade. You edit Panopticon entries because their historical

3

inaccuracies bug you."

"I did that *once!*"

Beck raised an eyebrow.

"Linked pages count as one entry," I argued.

"Whatever. All I'm saying is that if there were ever a shoe-in for smart-kid school, it's you."

But Theden was so much more than smart-kid school. The two-year college prep program—the only of its kind in the country—guaranteed its alumni a free ride to the college of their choice and an executive-level job right after. All you had to do was graduate. Which, from what I'd read, was no small feat. And that was assuming you could even get in. The entire school was only two hundred and eighty-eight kids, occupying sixty acres in a tiny town in western Massachusetts. I'd practically memorized the brochure. "The Theden student knows with unwavering certitude that he belongs in our program," the first page read, "yet is wise enough to recognize that he is not the best judge of his own capabilities. Thus, the Theden student eagerly submits to the rigor of our application process." Rigor was right. Four one-thousand-word timed essays, an IQ test, two psychological exams, three teacher recommendations, and one excruciatingly cryptic interview with a member of the admissions committee. It was intense, but then again, getting a degree from Theden was like being handed a golden ticket to life. Had it not been free I couldn't have applied, but it was, and so I did, unceremoniously, without telling anyone but my dad and Beck. I didn't have an "unwavering certitude" that I belonged at Theden, just a nagging feeling that I might.

"Your umbrella," I reminded Beck as he stepped out into the rain.

"Eh. Leave it. It was busted anyway."

"You can't just leave your umbrella, Beck."

"Why not? Because I absolutely need to possess a four-dollar umbrella with two broken spokes?" He tilted his head back and stuck out his tongue. "Plus I'm not sure this cloud spit even counts as rain."

"You're just too lazy to walk over there."

Beck pulled out his handheld, a refurbed Gemini 4. "Lux, am I being lazy right now?"

"I don't know," Lux replied in a voice that sounded just like Beck's. The decision-making app came with a pre-installed voice, but nobody used it. It was so much cooler to hear your own. "I do know that your umbrella is located at the Fourth Avenue entrance. It would take approximately two minutes and twenty seconds to retrieve it at your average walking pace. Would you like to go there now?"

"Nope," Beck said cheerfully, pocketing his Gemini as he stepped out into the rain.

"I'll get it," I muttered. I tucked the letter under my coat and dashed down Madison. Not that I really cared if Beck left his umbrella. But Lux knew how cheap the umbrella was, how close we were to school, how late we were already going to be to fifth period—and yet it still suggested that Beck go back and get it, which meant it might be really important that he did.

Of course, the jerk didn't wait for me, and in the time it took me to go back for his umbrella, the spit rain stopped. I contemplated running to catch up with him, but I was wearing shitty-traction Toms and didn't want to ruin my elation about Theden by wiping out on the sidewalk. So I stuck my earbuds in and tapped over to my playlist, letting Lux pick the tracks.

I caught up with Beck a few blocks from school, stopped on the sidewalk, grinning at the image on his viewfinder. He held the camera out for me to see. It was a woman, obviously homeless, her sunken eyes looking straight at the camera. *I don't want your money,* her cardboard sign read. *Just look at me, so I know I exist.* The words and her expression were arresting on their own, but they weren't what made the photograph so compelling. It was the people in the foreground, the passersby, eyes glued to their phones as they hurried to wherever they were going at lunch hour, completely oblivious to the woman with the sign. "A cop made her move about a minute after I got here," Beck said. He elbowed me, making a point. "Good thing I ditched the umbrella, right?"

"A small price to pay for a shot like that," I allowed.

"I could make a whole series of photos just like it," Beck said excitedly as we picked up our pace. We were already three minutes late for class. I pulled out my Gemini to check our ETA. Ninety-two seconds until we reached campus, another thirty-three for me to get to AP Psych. I was still consulting my screen when I heard Beck say, "I mean, it's not like it'd be hard to find people who are being ignored by a bunch of idiots on their handhelds." As if on cue, I tripped on an uneven patch of sidewalk. He just looked at me. "Really? You need to track our progress down to the millisecond? We'll get there when we get there, Rory. Or we won't."

Beck had a very ambivalent relationship with his hand-held. He used one, of course, but only for calls and texts. I, on the other hand, used my Gemini for everything. My calendar, my assignments, my Forum page, my playlists and books— I wanted all of it at my fingertips, always. And, of course, I wanted Lux, which kept my life running smoothly. I consulted the app at least a thousand times a day. What should I wear? Where should I sit? Who should I ask to Sadie Hawkins? Every decision that could possibly matter, and most that probably didn't. Except Theden. I hadn't asked Lux whether I should apply because I was too afraid the answer would be no.

We split from each other when we got back to school, and I headed to Psych. I was scrolling through my newsfeed as I walked, so I didn't see Hershey Clements until I almost ran into her.

"You're Rory, right?" She was standing outside my class-room door, her dark hair pulled back off her face and twisted into one of those artful knots you see in magazines but can never replicate yourself. She was wearing eye shadow but no mascara, and dark pink lip gloss. Enough makeup to be intimidating without hiding the fact that she didn't need to be wearing any at all. She was gorgeous. And really tan. Hershey's parents had taken her to Dubai for spring break (a fact I knew because she had, inexplicably, friended me on Forum, despite the fact that we'd never had an actual conversation, subjecting me to her incessant status updating while she was away) and she'd returned last Monday with a henna anklet and a caramel-colored glow, a reminder to the rest of us how pale and poor and uncultured we were.

"Um, hi," I said. She seemed to be studying me, or sizing me up, maybe. What did she want? She had to want *something*. Hershey Clements would not be waiting for me in the hall-way unless there was something in it for her. Girls like her did not talk to girls like me. I wasn't an outcast or anything, but with an I'm-too-cool-to-be-cool boy for a BFF and no real girl friends (having a dead mom and no sisters really screwed me over in the female-bonding department), I wasn't even on the periphery of Hershey's crowd. Still, the whole I'm-not-sure-I-know-your-name routine was total BS. She knew who I was. We'd had at least two classes together every year since sixth grade.

"I have to admit, I was a little taken aback when I saw your name," she said then. "I mean, I knew you were smart and all, but I assumed it was because you were, like, obsessed with studying and crap." *Huh?* I was lost, and Hershey could tell. "I saw you got into Theden," she said, rolling her eyes like I was an idiot for not keeping up.

"You did?" I'd just opened the letter twenty minutes ago

8

and hadn't posted it anywhere yet. Had Beck put it on Forum?

"Duh. The app updates every day. A week after they send the letter, they put your name on the admitted list."

"What app?"

Hershey sighed heavily, as if it was stressful for her to be interacting with such an imbecile. She pulled her handheld from the back pocket of her denim mini. "The Theden app," she explained, tapping a little tree icon that matched the design on the lapel pin in my pocket. She held her phone up for me to see.

"Wait, why do you have—?" Something gold glinted on the inside of her wrist. The Theden pin. She'd pinned it on the cuff of her cashmere blazer. Suddenly I understood. I met her gaze. "You got in too."

"Don't look so surprised," she retorted.

"I'm not surprised," I lied.

"Whatever. It's fine. I'm pretty sure my grandmother bought my way in anyway. That's how my dad got in. Hey, lemme see your phone."

She reached around me, grabbing my Gemini from the back pocket of my jeans. She touched its share button to hers. "There," she said, handing the phone back to me. "You have my number. We should be friends now." As if it were a given that I *wanted* to be friends with her. Then she spun on her heels, pulled open our classroom door, and sauntered inside.

2

IT WAS AN ETERNITY TO AUGUST. There were days when it felt like it would never come, that time had actually slowed down and would eventually stop. It didn't help that my ordinarily laid-back father had become cloyingly nostalgic and sentimental, gazing at me over the dinner table like the dad character in a sappy wedding movie. My stepmom wasn't any better.

Thankfully, they both worked full-time, my dad at his latest construction site and my stepmom for a chocolate shop in Beacon Hill, so I was on my own during the day. I spent nearly every afternoon with Beck, accompanying him on whatever photo assignment his mentor-of-the-week had given him. Beck was in the national apprenticeship program, which meant he'd intern in his chosen field for the next two summers then go straight into the workforce after high school, trading college for a two-year federally subsidized internship. When he got his last assignment of the summer—to chronicle a day in the life of someone living in Nickelsville, Seattle's last remaining tent city—Beck just about exploded with excitement.

It was the evening before my departure, and we'd been hanging out among the fuchsia tarps all day. It was after seven already, and Beck had thousands of pictures of his subject, a homeless man named Al whose left leg stopped just above his knee. The light was starting to fade now, and I was no longer as comfortable as I'd been midday. I'd turned Lux on silent, but the words PROCEED TO A SAFER NEIGHBORHOOD were blinking on my screen.

"Wasn't your assignment a *day* in the life?" I asked Beck in a low voice. "Not a night in the life? We should head back downtown."

"During the golden hour?" Beck had his camera to his eye and was rapidly shooting as Al built a small fire in a metal bucket by his tent. "Rory, look at the sky. This is a photographer's wet dream."

I wrinkled my nose. "Gross."

"If you need to go, you can," he said, his face still behind his lens. "I know you have that dinner with your dad." I was leaving early the next morning, and my dad was taking me out for a going-away dinner at Serious Pie, just the two of us. I'd told him it was more than fine for my stepmom to come with us, but he insisted we go alone, assuring me her feelings wouldn't be hurt. I doubted this but was happy to have him to myself on my last night at home. Kari was great for my dad, but I could relate to her even less than I could to him, which is to say, not at all.

"I don't want to leave you down here alone," I told Beck, my voice even quieter than before.

"I'll be fine," Beck said, finally lowering his camera and looking at me. "The light will be gone in another thirty minutes or so anyway. And he's here." He pointed at the uniformed cop sitting in his car across the street.

"Okay," I said, still uncertain. There was a reason Lux kept people like us out of neighborhoods like this (if you even could call a homeless encampment a "neighborhood"). "But will you at least launch Lux? I'll feel better if I know it's running."

"Nope," Beck replied pleasantly, lifting his camera back to his eye.

I sighed, knowing I wouldn't win this argument. It was a waste of breath to even ask.

This was how Beck rolled. Untethered to technology. He liked trusting his instinct, going with his gut. He said that's what made him an artist. But I knew better. It wasn't his gut that he trusted. It was the Doubt.

He started hearing the voice when we were kids. A bunch of us heard it back then. A whisper in our heads that instructed us and assured us and made us believe the impossible, urging us to the left when reason pointed to the right. The so-called "whisper within" wasn't a new phenomenon—it'd been around as long as people had—but neuroscience had only recently pinned it down. For centuries people thought it was a good thing, a form of psychic intuition. Some even said it was God's voice. Now we knew that the inner voice was nothing more than a glitch in the brain's circuitry, something to do with "synaptic pruning" and the development of the frontal lobe. Renaming it the Doubt was a marketing strategy, part of a big public service campaign sponsored by the drug company that developed the pill to suppress it. The name was supposed to remind people what the voice really was. The enemy of reason. In kids, it was nothing to worry about, a temporary by-product of a crucial phase in the brain's development that would go away once you were old enough to ignore it. But in adults, it was the symptom of a neurological disorder that, if left untreated, would progress until you could no longer make rational decisions.

The marketing campaign did what it was supposed to do, I guess. People were appropriately freaked out. I was in fifth grade then and hearing the voice all the time. Once we started learning suppression techniques—how to drown out the Doubt with noise and entertainment, how to distract your brain with other thoughts, stuff like that—I heard it less and less, and eventually it went quiet. It was like that for most kids. Something you outgrew, like a stutter or being scared of the dark.

Except sometimes you didn't, and you were labeled "hyperimaginative" and given low-dose antipsychotics until you didn't hear it anymore. That is, unless you were Beck and refused to accept both the label and the pharmaceutical antidote, in which case the Doubt stuck around, chiming in at random moments, causing your otherwise rational brain to question itself for no apparent reason other than the fact that

that's what the Doubt did. I worried about him, what it would mean for his future if he got a permanent diagnosis, but I also knew how stubborn he was. There was no telling Beck what to do. Especially not while he was taking pictures.

"Oh, hey, wait a sec," I heard him say as I started toward the bus stop across the street. When I turned back around, he was digging in his pocket. "Your going-away present," he said, holding out a small plastic box with a snap lid. I recognized the distinctive uppercase *G* etched into the top. The Gnosis logo. I was mildly obsessed with Gnosis and its gadgets, which, besides being slick and stylish and technologically unparalleled, were made out of recycled materials and completely biodegradable. "They're the gel earbuds you wanted," Beck explained as I snapped open the lid. I'd been eyeing them for months but couldn't rationalize wasting a hundred bucks on headphones. "And before you tell me I shouldn't have spent the money, I didn't," Beck added before I could protest. "They were part of the swag bag from that fashion shoot I helped with last month."

I grinned. "Best gift ever," I said, squeezing Beck's arm.

"Now you can geek out even more over your playlists," Beck teased. He was into music too, but not like I was.

"And hear you better when you call me," I said, slipping my gift into my ears. The earbuds slid down my ear canal like melted wax. I could barely feel them once they were in.

"Assuming you're not too busy to answer."

"Hey. I'll never be too busy for you."

He smiled. "Take care of yourself, Ro," he said then, slinging an arm around my shoulders. "And just remember, if you fail out, you can always come home and be my assistant."

"Yeah, thanks," I said, elbowing him in the stomach. "And to think, I was worried I'd miss you." When he met my gaze, he smiled, but his eyes were sad.

"I'll miss you too, Ro."

I flung my arms around his neck and hugged him, hard, then headed for the bus stop again, blinking back tears.

"Okay, spit it out," I said to my dad. "You're obviously prepping for some big flight-from-the-nest moment over there. Let's hear it." We'd just split the last slice of fennel sausage pizza, and I was perusing the dessert menu, contemplating a root beer float even though I was pretty sure that Lux would tell me to skip it. Across the table my dad was twisting his red cloth napkin like he was nervous about something. I braced myself for a sappy speech. He reached for something on the booth beside him.

"It's from your mother," I heard him say as he set a small box and an even smaller envelope on the table in front of me. My dessert menu was forgotten when I saw the gift.

The only thing I had of my mother's was a blanket. According to my dad, she worked on it every day of her pregnancy, determined to finish it before I was born. The design, hand sewn in pink yarn, was a series of squares, each bigger than the one beside it, that followed a particular mathematical sequence and fit together to form one rectangle. The squares were connected by yellow quarter circles made with even tinier stitches than the squares, which ran together to form a golden spiral that extended beyond the confines of the rectangle. At the two ends of the spiral, there were little orange cross-stitches, marking the beginning and the end. It was a strange choice for a little girl's blanket, but I loved it. Maybe my mother knew that her little girl would never be into flowers or butterflies. Maybe she somehow sensed that I'd prefer the structure and predictability and mathematical completeness of a Fibonacci tile.

I never could ask her, because she died when I was born, two days before her nineteenth birthday. I was premature and there were complications, so the doctors had to do a C-section, and I guess a vein in her leg got blocked, and the clot went to her lungs. "Pulmonary thromboembolism" was the phrase on her death certificate, which I found in a box in my dad's closet when I was nine, on Christmas Eve. I'd been looking for hidden presents.

I stared at the box, and then at him. "What do you mean it's from Mom?"

"She asked me to give it to you." He tugged at his beard, clearly uncomfortable.

"*When* did she ask you to give it to me?" I meant *When did she make the request?* but my dad misunderstood.

"The day you left for Theden," he said carefully.

"What? I don't understand. How could she have possibly known that I'd—"

16

"She went there too, Rory."

"Wait, *what*? Mom went to *Theden*?" I stared at him, stunned, as he nodded. "But you went to high school together. You got married the day you graduated. You always said—"

"I know, sweetheart. It was what your mom wanted. She didn't want you to know about Theden unless you decided on your own to go there."

"And whatever's in that box?"

"I was supposed to destroy it, and the card, too, if you didn't go."

I sat back in my chair, my eyes on the box. It was light blue with a white lid and it didn't look new. One of the corners was bashed in, and the cardboard was peeling in a couple of places. The envelope was the kind that comes with floral bouquets, not bigger than a business card. "What's in it?" I asked.

"I don't know," my dad replied. "She asked me not to open it and I haven't. It's been in a safety deposit box at Northwest Bank since two days after you were born."

I reached for the envelope first. The front was blank, but when I picked it up, I saw handwriting on the back. My mom had written my name, in blue ink, right along the seam of the flap. I recognized her handwriting from the tag she'd pinned to my baby blanket, which I kept in a little zippered pouch on my nightstand. *Aurora*. I hated my name, the hardness of the *r*'s, but in my mom's loopy script, it looked so feminine and delicate, so unlike its typewritten form. I touched my finger to my tongue and then pressed it onto the tip of the cursive capital *A*. The ink bled a little, and when I pulled my finger away, there was a faint blue stain on my skin. It seemed impossible, that the same blue that had been in my mother's pen, a pen that she'd held and written with when she was very much alive, was now on my finger. I felt tears creeping toward the corners of my eyes, and I blinked them away.

Writing in ink along the edge of an envelope's flap is like sealing it with wax. If it's been opened, you can tell because the tops of the letters don't line up exactly with the bottoms. These were unbroken. Is that why my mom had written my name where she had, to let me know that the words inside were meant for only me? My heart lifted just a little at the thought.

"Are you going to open it?" my dad asked. He was, I realized, as curious as I was about its contents. I slipped the envelope into my bag.

"Not yet," I said, and reached for the box. The gift I would open now; the note I would save until I was alone.

The box was lighter than I expected it to be, and when I picked it up off the table, I heard a sliding rattle as its contents slipped to one side. I took a breath and lifted the lid. Inside was a silver cable chain with a thick rectangular pendant. My dad smiled when I pulled it from the box.

"I thought that might be what it was," he said. "She didn't have it on when she d—" He choked a little, his eyes dropping to the table. "When you were born. I always wondered what she'd done with it."

"This was hers?" I asked.

He nodded.

"She came back from Theden with it," he said.

I palmed the pendant, studying the odd symbol etched into its surface. It looked kind of like a fishhook with the number thirteen beneath it. Her graduation year. "What is it?" I asked.

Dad shrugged. "I always assumed it was some school thing," he said. "Your mom never said. But she treasured that necklace. I'm not sure I ever saw her take it off."

I set the pendant back in the box. "I'm so confused, Dad. Why would Mom ask you to lie to me?"

He hesitated for so long, I wondered if he was going to respond at all.

"Something happened to your mom at Theden," he said finally. "She was different when she came back."

"Different how?"

"The Aviana I grew up with was ambitious, for one thing. Not in a bad way. She just had these big dreams, you know? When she got into Theden, I figured that was it. She'd go, and she wouldn't come back. And that was okay. I loved her. I just wanted her to be happy."

"And was she?" I asked. "Happy?"

"I thought so. She had all these new friends and was always going on about her classes. When she didn't come home for Christmas our senior year, I resigned myself to the fact that I probably wouldn't see her again. Your grandparents were gone by then, so she didn't have much of a reason to come back." His brow furrowed. "But then, about a week before she was supposed to graduate, she showed up at my house and told me she'd dropped out. She said she'd changed her mind about college. Didn't want to go anymore. She said she wanted to start a family instead. Then she asked me to marry her."

I stared at him. This bore no resemblance to the love story I'd heard growing up. Two high school sweethearts who eloped in the Kings County Courthouse on graduation day and honeymooned in a camping tent. That version made sense. This one didn't. My dad could tell what I was thinking.

"Your mother was impulsive," he replied. "Irresistibly impulsive. And I was powerless to refuse her." He smiled and signaled for our waiter. But he hadn't given me the answer I was looking for. He may have explained why *he'd* gotten married at eighteen, but not why my mother had wanted to, or, more important, why she would've dropped out of the most prestigious high school in the country just shy of graduation. Why she would've given up her future for something that could've waited.

"And that's it? That's the whole story?"

Dad looked hesitant, like he didn't want to say yes but couldn't in good conscience say no. "Your mom, she was unlike anyone I'd ever met," he said finally. "She had this . . . quality about her. An inner calm. Even when we were kids. She didn't worry about stuff the way the rest of us did. It was like she was immune to it almost." He paused, and the thought *I did not inherit that* shot through my head. His eyes were sad when he continued. "When she showed up at my house that day, she seemed . . . shaken. But when I'd ask her about it, she'd shut down."

"What could've happened to her?" I asked.

"I've asked myself that question a thousand times," Dad replied. "Wishing I'd pressed her more to find out. But I thought I had time. I didn't think she'd . . ."

The unspoken word hung heavily between us. He didn't think she'd *die*. But she had, just eight months later.

"But *something* happened," I said. "Something must've."

Eventually Dad nodded. "Something must've," he said.

3

"PEANUTS OR PRETZELS?"

"Pretzels." Hershey held out her hand without looking up. We were midair, side by side in first class (thank you, Theden), and I was waiting for her to fall asleep so I could finally open the card from my mom, but my companion was completely immersed in one of the many gossip magazines she'd downloaded to her tablet. I hadn't slept the night before, thinking about that little paper rectangle, wondering what it said, hoping it would answer the shit storm of questions in my head.

"Sir? Peanuts or pretzels?" The flight attendant had moved on to the man across the aisle from me.

"Peanuts," he mumbled, and the flight attendant reached into her cart.

"Uh, actually, would you mind having pretzels instead?" The man, Hershey, and the flight attendant all looked at me. "I'm allergic to peanuts," I explained.

"There was no allergy listed on the manifest," the flight attendant said accusingly. "Cindy!" she called down the aisle. "Is there an allergy on the manifest?" Cindy consulted her tablet then came running toward us, tripping over a man's foot and nearly face-planting in the process. I heard Hershey snort.

"Aurora Vaughn, 3B. Peanuts."

Our flight attendant's expression went from accusing to five-alarm fire. She started snatching peanut packages from passengers in neighboring rows.

"Sorry," I said to the guy across the aisle.

"So what would happen if you ate one?" Hershey asked me as the flight attendant handed me a bag of pretzels.

"I'm not sure," I said. "I had a pretty bad reaction to a peanut butter cracker when I was three. A woman at my daycare had to use an EpiPen."

"Does it freak you out?" Hershey asked. "Knowing that you're one poor snacking choice away from death?"

I looked at her. *Seriously? Who said things like that?*

"No," I said, reaching for my earphones. "I don't even think about it." I didn't need to. Lux analyzed ingredient lists, tracked allergic reactions and food-borne illnesses in other users who consumed the same foods, *and* alerted you if someone in your immediate vicinity was either allergic to something you were eating or eating something you were allergic to. The only time I had to be cautious about it was in confined spaces with no network access. In other words, on planes. I slipped in the earbuds and turned up the volume.

A few minutes later Hershey flung off her seat belt and stood up. "I have to pee," she announced, dropping her tablet on my lap and stepping over me into the aisle. As soon as she was gone, I yanked out my earbuds and pulled the envelope from my bag. Careful not to rip the paper, I slid my nail under the flap and gently tugged it open.

The card inside was made of soft cotton paper, the kind they didn't make anymore. My brain registered the number of handwritten lines before my heart did, and when my heart caught up, it sunk. There were only three.

I formed them free, and free they must remain
Till they enthrall themselves;
I else must change their nature.

I turned the card over, but the other side was blank. So much for answering my questions. This had raised a hundred more.

"What's that?" Hershey was back. I hadn't seen her walk up.

"Nothing," I said quickly, and tried to slip the card back into my bag. But Hershey snatched it. Her eyes skimmed over the words. "Weird," she declared, handing it back to me as she settled into her seat. "What's it a quote from?"

"I dunno. It's from my mom." As soon as I said it, I regretted it. I did not want to talk about my mom with Hershey.

"Did it come with a note?"

I shook my head. This *was* the note. Instinctively, I reached for the pendant around my neck. It was surprisingly heavy on my collarbone.

I saw Hershey open her browser to GoSearch. "Read it to me again," she said.

"'I formed them free, and free they must remain—'" I said, and paused, puzzling over the words I'd just read as Hershey typed them. *Who* formed *who* free? "'Till they enthrall them—'"

Hershey interrupted me. "It's from *Paradise Lost*," she said. "Book Three, lines one twenty-four to one twenty-six."

"Is that a play?" I'd heard of *Paradise Lost* but knew nothing about it.

"A poem," Hershey replied. "A super long and super boring poem published in 1667." Her eyes skimmed the text on her screen. "Oh my god, shoot me now. Is this even English?"

"Who wrote it?"

"John Milton," she said, tapping the thumbnail of his photo to enlarge it. She zoomed in on his eyelids. "A man in desperate need of blepharoplasty."

Hershey clicked back to her magazines, bored already. I pulled up the Panopticon entry for *Paradise Lost* on my own tablet and began to read. *The poem, considered one of the greatest literary works in the English language, retells the Biblical story of Adam and Eve's expulsion from the Garden of Eden.* I tapped a link for a full text version of the poem and my eyes glazed over almost as quickly as Hershey's had. None of the books we'd read in class were anything like this. Public school curriculum focused on contemporary lit, novels that had been written in the last twenty years. Was this the kind of stuff they read at Theden? Panic fluttered behind my ribs. What if I couldn't keep up?

I closed my eyes and leaned back against the headrest. *Please, God, don't let me fail,* I said silently.

You won't fail.

My head jerked. I hadn't heard the Doubt since the summer before seventh grade. I remembered the effect it'd had on me back then, the peaceful feeling that settled over me after it spoke. This was the opposite experience. I was rattled and unsettled and all those other words that mean not at all okay. The Doubt was for unstable people and artists and little kids. Not, as the application packet had made explicitly clear, for Theden students. The psychologist who'd conducted my psych eval asked at least three times when I'd last heard the voice, relenting only when she was satisfied that it'd been more than three years. If the members of the admissions committee knew what I'd just heard, my time at Theden would be over before it started. That was part of what made my new school different. You couldn't just be smart. You had to be "psychologically impervious." Immune to crazy.

It's just nerves, I told myself. Lots of perfectly sane adults heard the Doubt when they were stressed. But telling myself this only intensified my anxiety.

"We should order matching comforters," I heard Hershey say. She'd moved on from her magazines and was now scrolling through the Anthropologie lookbook. "Otherwise we'll end up with that whole hodgepodge, mismatched, pretending-to-be-eclectic dorm room cliché. What do you think of this one?"

I still didn't understand how we'd ended up living together. According to our acceptance packet, roommate assignments were done by a computer program that matched students based on their personalities and interests. Since Hershey and I had exactly nothing in common, I had to assume the program was flawed.

I blinked and tried to focus on the neon paisley pattern on her screen. It was hideous.

"Why don't we wait and see what the room looks like first?" I suggested.

Hershey gave me a pitying look. "I won't make you pay for it, if that's what you're worried about."

"It's not that," I said evenly. "I'd just prefer something that doesn't make my eyes feel like someone has poured bleach on them."

"How about we repurpose some old denim and stitch it together with hemp?"

I ignored her jab and went back to my tablet.

Paradise Lost was still on my screen, so I scrolled up to the beginning and began to wade through it, forcing myself to read every word. I absorbed none of it, but the task occupied my mind for the rest of the flight. It was a trick I'd learned in elementary school. As long as your brain was busy, the Doubt couldn't speak.

Our flight landed in Boston fifteen minutes ahead of schedule. If we hurried, we could catch the earlier bus to campus, assuming we didn't have to wait for our bags. As we speed-walked to baggage claim, I launched my travel monitor and tracked our suitcases as they made their way from the belly of the plane to the carousel. They got there thirty seconds after we did.

My heart-shaped lock was busted, as if whoever inspected my bag hadn't even bothered with the key that hung next to it. The sleeve of a T-shirt was pushing out through the opening, dirty from the conveyer belt. I wouldn't have locked it at all, but the zipper track was warped, causing one of the sliders to inch away from the other, leaving an open gap. Lux had recommended that I use a twist tie, but I'd used the lock instead. Beck had given it to me on my thirteenth birthday as part of a vintage diary set. I never wrote in the notebook, but I adored the heart-shaped lock. I sighed and slipped the broken lock into my pocket as Hershey struggled to lift her gargantuan Louis Vuitton from the carousel. Served me right for ignoring Lux.

"The two-thirty shuttle to Theden Academy campus departs in three minutes," our handhelds declared in unison. We hurried to the pick-up spot. The driver waved us over.

"Just in time," he said as we boarded, marking our names off on his tablet. Hershey immediately pulled out her Gemini to post a status update. I knew Beck would be waiting for mine, but my thoughts were too jumbled to formulate a pithy post.

I looked around at my new classmates. Nothing about them screamed gifted. They were just a bunch of sixteen-year-olds on their handhelds. I felt a wave of disappointment. I'd been so worried about feeling out of my league that I hadn't considered that the alternative might be worse.

Hershey was on Forum for most of the two-hour ride to campus. I put my earbuds in and stared out the window, watching as the buildings got farther and farther apart until there was nothing but trees and rock. Giant slabs of granite lined the roads as we cut through mountain, the sunlight a deeper gold than I'd ever seen it. Apart from the network towers—made to look like trees, but much too perfect-looking to fool anyone—there were none of the trappings of modernity that Seattle's nature parks were known for. No assisted sidewalks. No solar-powered trolleys. It was as if time had given up on these woods or accepted its own inconsequence. My cheek pressed against the window, I let my eyes unfocus and blur. By the time we descended into the Connecticut River valley, I was asleep.

"Rory." Hershey nudged me with her elbow. "We're here."

My eyes sprung open just as the bus passed through the campus gates. I spun in my seat, watching as the wrought-iron rungs moved back into place behind us, sealing us off from the rest of the world. It was more for show than security; the stone wall stopped just a few feet from the gate. Still, it was imposing, the smooth stone columns, the iron gate, the high arch with ornamental scrolls. And in the center of the arch-way, the tree-shaped Theden seal, identical to the design on the lapel pin clasped to the tongue of my sneaker.

The driveway was long and paved with something smooth and gray that definitely wasn't asphalt. Towering elms, evenly staggered along the sides of the road, formed a high canopy of green above us. Beyond them, the ground sloped up and the light disappeared into thick, overcrowded woods.

The driveway curved to the left and there it was: Theden Academy. A dozen redbrick buildings enclosing an interior courtyard that was still out of sight. I knew from Panopticon that these were the original structures built by Theden's founders in 1781, and that the academy's architecture was considered one of the best examples of the Federal style. What I didn't know was the effect the whole would have on me when we rounded that corner, the Appalachian Mountains coming into view just as the buildings did, the forest like a cocoon around them.

"Wow," Hershey whispered, uncharacteristically un-blasé.

We were silent as the bus pulled into the large parking lot marked FACULTY and double-parked behind a row of BMWs. The spaces were labeled with engraved bronze placards on thick wrought-iron posts.

"That's Dean Atwater," Hershey said, pointing at the tall, silver-haired man striding across the lawn, his hands loosely in the pockets of his pressed khaki pants. "I recognize him from my dad's photos."

Our driver cut the engine as Dean Atwater boarded the bus.

He had a kindly, grandfatherly quality, with the commanding presence of a prep school dean. He smiled broadly in greeting as he surveyed our faces. His eyes hung on mine for a few seconds, something like recognition flashing there. My heart sped up. Had he known my mom? I knew how much I resembled her. Our coloring was different, but we had the same wavy hair, the same smattering of freckles across our cheeks, the same heart-shaped face and almond-shaped eyes. My dad said I was taller than she'd been, but you couldn't tell that from pictures. I looked so little like him that my stepmom once joked that Mom had just cloned herself, but my dad snapped at her for being insensitive and she never said it again.

"You're here!" Dean Atwater declared, pumping his fist in the air. The seats around me erupted into cheers and whistles. The old man laughed. "Time has no doubt been crawling for each of you since the day you received your acceptance letters. I can assure you, it will speed up now. Before you know it, you will be graduating and wondering where the last two years went." He smiled. "Or, in my case, the last twenty-five."

Twenty-five years. He *had* to have known my mom. I touched my mom's pendant, feeling the engraving under my fingertips.

"The upperclassmen returned to campus last week," the dean continued. "So we'll all gather at six this evening in the rotunda for an opening assembly, followed by our annual welcome dinner. Until then, you're on your own. You'll find your dormitory assignments under the 'housing' tab in your Theden app. That's also where you'll find a list of important campus phone numbers—the registrar, my office, the psych line. . . ." *The psych line.* I swallowed hard. "And your campus key. Our locks are tied to your handhelds," he explained. "Your key will get you through the main door of each academic building and into your assigned rooms." Around me, people scrambled for their phones. "I suggest you spend the next few hours getting acquainted with one another and our campus. I'll see you all again at six." He gave us a little wave and stepped back down off the bus.

"My dad told me it was like this," Hershey whispered, closing out of Forum and tapping the little Theden icon on her screen. Around us, kids were checking their housing assignments and talking excitedly. No one had gotten up yet.

"Like what?" I asked.

"Totally free. A super-late curfew, no dorm check-ins, no dress code. Basically, no rules. You can pretty much do whatever you want."

"Really?" Prep schools were notorious for their rules. I'd figured Theden would be even stricter than most.

"Uh-huh. A 'privilege of prudence' or some crap." She leaned against me and held her Gemini up for a selfie. "Perf," she said when she saw it, then promptly uploaded it to Forum. My Gemini buzzed.

The photo "roomie BFFs!" has been added to your timeline by @HersheyClements.

The photo was horrendous. My forehead was shining and my bangs were split down the middle and my smile looked more like a grimace. But there was no way to delete it now that she'd posted it, and no way to untag myself either.

"Lovely," I muttered, gathering my things. My handheld buzzed again.

@BeckAmbrose: had a nightmare u moved 3,000 miles away and became "roomie BFFs" w HC.

Hershey heard me laugh. "What's so funny?" she asked.

"Nothing," I lied, dropping my handheld into my bag. "Come on, roomie," I said, nudging her forward. "Let's find our room."

Theden's two hundred and eighty-eight students all lived in the same building, Athenian Hall, a V-shaped structure on the north end of campus. Our room was on the second floor of the girls' wing and looked more like a fancy hotel room than a dorm. There were two double beds, matching mahogany desks and dressers, two walk-in closets, and an electronic fireplace. But no light fixtures. When I didn't see any in the ceiling, I looked around for lamps. The brightness in the room had to be coming from somewhere, and there weren't any windows. But there wasn't a single light source that I could see.

Hershey had picked up the small black remote sitting on the bed she'd claimed as hers. There was an identical remote on my bed, with three rows of buttons on the front and the distinctive Gnosis logo on the back. Hershey started at the top and worked her way down, pressing every button. First the room got brighter, then dimmer, until it was completely dark save for the wall connected to the door, which glowed a warm amber. Hershey's face lit up. "PHOLED wallpaper!" She pressed another button and the wall became a TV screen. Another, and we were looking at the dashboard of her Gemini. Another, and the screen split into two screens. "Turn your side on," she told me, pointing at the remote on my bed. "The button labeled LINK." When I pressed it, my Gemini dashboard popped up next to hers.

I'd heard that Gnosis had developed wallpaper made up of PHOLEDs—the display technology used in most of its devices— but I didn't think it'd been released yet. I walked over and touched the wallpaper with my fingertips. It was smooth and cool under my skin, and when I pulled my hand away there were faint fingerprint smudges there. I wiped them away with the hem of my T-shirt.

Hershey tossed her remote onto the bed. "Let's take a walk. I want coffee."

"Good call. The dining hall has an all-day snack cart. I saw it on—"

"Lame," Hershey declared. "It's only a ten-minute walk to downtown. Eight if we take the unauthorized scenic route, which we totally are." She pulled a tube of lip gloss and a mirrored compact from her bag. She slid the tube across her lips then pursed them in a sultry pout. "C'mon," she said, snapping the compact shut. "Let's go."

The "unauthorized scenic route" involved trespassing through a private cemetery east of campus, which was marked, appropriately, PRIVATE PROPERTY—NO TRESPASSING. Despite the midday sunshine, I was creeped out. The moss-covered headstones were oversize and weathered with centuries of age. I shivered in the humid heat.

"Which way?" I asked impatiently, eager to get out of there. Whoever owned this place had hung that no trespassing sign for a reason. And they'd put a giant statue of a very angry-looking angel in the center of the cemetery, his long stone finger pointing toward the exit, to emphasize the point.

"I dunno," Hershey said, squinting at her Gemini. "I lost service."

"Can we please just go back? I'd prefer not to get arrested on my first day here." I was attempting to sound more annoyed than freaked out, but the truth was I was both.

Hershey rolled her eyes. "Relax. The town green is just on the other side of those woods." Her eyes scanned the trees. "I think." She held her Gemini up, searching for a signal. "So much for the 'everywhere network,'" she said.

"It's not a shortcut if we get lost," I pointed out.

"God, Rory, would you just chill out? Here"—she reached into her bag and pulled out two airplane bottles of Baileys, tossing one to me—"that'll help." She twisted the cap off the other one and chugged its contents. "Ugh." She shuddered, wiping her mouth with the back of her hand. "I hate Baileys. But I couldn't reach the vodka."

"I'm not drinking this," I said, handing it back to her. "The assembly starts in an hour."

Hershey sighed. "Look, Rory, I'm not suggesting you get wasted and take an exam. It's our first day, and we've got nothing to do but listen to a bunch of self-congratulatory and ultimately forgettable speeches about how great we are, and how great Theden is, and how much greater we'll all be when we graduate from here. The onus is on us to live deep, to suck all the marrow out of life. No one's gonna do it for us." She held the mini bottle back out, waving it a little until I took it. I'm not sure why I did; maybe it was the shock of hearing Hershey use the word *onus* correctly, or the fact that she'd casually quoted Thoreau. Or maybe it was just that her words had struck a chord. I applied to Theden because I wanted my life to change, but so far the only thing different about my life was its location. And that wasn't enough.

I unscrewed the cap and took a tiny sip. Hershey grinned and held up her own empty bottle. "To sucking the marrow out of life," she declared.

I raised my bottle to hers. "And topping it off with Irish cream."

We laughed, but as we clinked, my eyes caught the epigraph on a headstone a few feet away and the laugh got lodged in my throat.

BE SOBER, BE VIGILANT;

BECAUSE YOUR ADVERSARY THE DEVIL, AS A

ROARING LION, WALKETH ABOUT,

SEEKING WHOM HE MAY DEVOUR.—1 PETER 5:8

The hair on my forearms prickled. I brought the bottle back to my lips, but this time only pretended to sip it. Hershey had already turned and was heading toward the trees, so I quickly emptied the contents of the bottle on the grass and hurried to catch up.

"So where are we going?" I asked, falling in stride with her.

"Café Paradiso," she replied. "It's on the river. Used to be a mill or something."

I pulled out my Gemini to check the reviews on its Forum page, but I still didn't have service. "This whole place is a dead zone," I said. Beside me, Hershey chortled.

"Fitting, right?" She tossed her bag over the rusty chain-link fence that stood between us and the trees, and began to climb. "Ouch!" A broken link had snagged the hem of her dress, scratching her thigh.

"You okay?"

"I'm fine." She cleared the fence then jumped. "You coming?"

I made my way over, careful to avoid the broken link. There was an embankment on the other side that led into a denser patch of woods. Hershey scampered up the grassy hill and disappeared into the trees. "I see buildings," she called. "We're close." I followed her up, sliding in my sandals. It was several degrees cooler up there, dense leaves blocking the sun. A few steps later, I heard the river roaring up ahead.

Café Paradiso was in a wooden building on the corner of State and Main, painted fire-engine red and set apart from the others. I had service again, so I pulled up the café's Forum page. Its rating was one and a half stars.

"There's another coffee shop a few blocks down," I said, pulling up the page for River City Beans, voted "Best Coffee in the Valley" by the *Berkshire Gazette*. I wasn't a snob about much, but I was a Seattle native, after all. "It's got way better reviews."

"Yeah, that's the place Lux recommended," Hershey replied, striding toward Paradiso.

I sighed and followed her.

A bell above the door jangled as we stepped inside. It was split-level, with the counter at ground level and seating space in a loft above it, overlooking the river. For a place with thousands of bad reviews, it was awfully packed. I didn't see a single empty table. When we stepped up to the counter, I understood why. There was a laminated sign stuck to the register that read IF YOU LIKE US, LEAVE US A REALLY CRAPPY REVIEW ON FORUM. SHOW IT TO US, AND YOUR NEXT DRINK IS ON US!

"You didn't fall for it," I heard a male voice say. "Or you just like shitty coffee." I looked up. The guy behind the counter was about our age, and he might've been cute were it not for the tattoos covering his bare arms and peeking out from the collar of his white V-neck T-shirt. I didn't have anything against tattoos in general—Beck had a *hanja* character behind his left ear—but this guy had that whole my-diffuse-body-art-makes-me-countercultural-and-thus-cooler-than-you vibe about him. The Mohawk on his head didn't help.

"I was brought against my will," I said, and the boy smiled. His eyes, pinned on mine, were dark brown, almost black, his pupils shiny like wet paint. "Let me guess—first-years at the academy?" There was something dismissive in his tone, as if our affiliation with Theden was a mark against us.

"I'm Hershey, and this is Rory," Hershey said, stepping up to the counter. "Maybe you can show us around sometime." The boy didn't respond. "Cool ink," she cooed, touching her fingers to his forearm. There were lines of text drawn there, each one in different handwriting. They looked like lines of poetry or quotes from books. The writing was small and I definitely wasn't about to lean in for a closer look, so it was hard to be sure. "What's your name?" she asked him.

"North." His eyes still hadn't left mine. They were doing that rapid back-and-forth thing that eyes do when they're studying something. Or, in this case, someone. Heat sprung to my cheeks. I cleared my throat and looked past him to the chalkboard menu. Beside me, Hershey pulled out her Gemini.

"Don't tell me you're gonna let that thing order for you," he said, his gaze finally shifting from me to Hershey.

"Never," Hershey replied. She scrolled down to the very

last entry on Lux's recommendation list. "I'll have the coconut latte," she announced. "Lux promises I'll hate it."

This was her thing, I'd learned. Doing the thing Lux said not to.

"I'm experimental," Hershey added, and smiled. North swallowed a laugh.

He turned back to me. "So what about you?" he asked. His voice was teasing. "Do you like to experiment?"

I blushed and hated myself for it. "I'll have a vanilla cappuccino," I said, glancing at my phone out of habit, even though I knew without looking what Lux would have me order. It was always the same.

"Okay, first, that's the worst order ever," North replied. "We roast our own beans, and everything is single origin, so if you're gonna have coffee, don't kill it with vanilla. Second, if you like sweet stuff, our spiced matcha latte is a way better choice."

"I'll have a vanilla cappuccino," I repeated. "I don't like tea."

North shrugged. "Your call," he said, punching in our orders. We scanned our handhelds to pay and moved to the other end of the counter to wait for our drinks.

"I'm totally going to hook up with him," Hershey whispered, barely out of his earshot.

"Ew." I made a face, but inside I felt a surge of envy. Not because I had any desire whatsoever to hook up with the smug, tatted-up barista, but because Hershey was the kind of girl who could. I glanced over at North as he steamed the milk for our drinks. The espresso machine he was using looked like an antique. It had to be the noisiest and least efficient way to make a cappuccino ever.

"One coconut latte, and one vanilla cappuccino," North declared, setting two paper cups on the counter. His expression was neutral, but his mouth looked funny, like he was biting the inside of his cheeks to keep from smiling. I smiled politely and reached for the cup with *VC* scrawled on the side in black marker. No printed drink stickers here. I felt like I was in a time warp. Hershey took a sip of hers and shuddered.

"Ugh. Gross." She smiled at North. "Perfect."

"Happy to disgust you," he replied, then glanced at me. "Yours okay?"

"I'm sure it's fine," I said, and took a sip.

The second it hit my tongue, I knew what he'd done. The fiery bite of the cayenne laced with the ginger. He'd made me the matcha drink. I hadn't been kidding; I didn't like tea. And I hated ginger. But this wasn't like any tea I'd had before, and mixed with all the other ingredients, the ginger was kind of the best thing I'd ever tasted. I took another sip before I realized North was watching me. It was too late to pretend I hated it. Still, I refused to acknowledge the told-you-so look on his face.

"Well?" he prompted.

"This is a really crappy cappuccino," I deadpanned.

North let out a laugh, and his whole face lit up with it.

"To be clear, the fact that I'm drinking this doesn't prove your point," I told him.

"My point?"

I rolled my eyes. "That I shouldn't let my handheld make decisions for me. You thought I missed that not-too-subtle subtext?"

"An Academy girl? I'd never sell you that short."

"Even without Lux, I never would've ordered this," I pointed out. "I hate two of the four ingredients."

"Ah, but there are *seven* ingredients. And so what if you hate two of them? The fact that I hate Russian dressing doesn't diminish my enjoyment of a good Reuben sandwich. Ours is amazing, by the way."

"We're talking about sandwiches now?"

North pressed a button on the espresso machine and the steamer shot out a short burst of hot air, blowing a piece of hair in my face. I pushed it away irritably. There was something unnerving about this boy, and I didn't like feeling unnerved.

I started to say something else, but he'd turned and headed back to the register.

"Flirt much?"

I jumped. I'd completely forgotten Hershey was standing there.

"I was *not* flirting with him," I retorted, glancing over my shoulder to make sure North hadn't heard her. He was busy with the next customer.

"Whatever. Can we go now? I want to change before the assembly." I started to remind her that this little expedition had been her idea, but she was already halfway to the door.

4

BACK AT OUR ROOM, Hershey changed into an off-white minidress and bronze flats, and pulled her hair into a sleek low ponytail. I looked about twelve years old standing next to her in my navy sundress and espadrilles. I fought the creeping, sinking disappointment that kept wrapping itself around my ribcage. Of all the roommates I could've been matched with, I'd ended up with her.

We made it to the auditorium a few minutes before the assembly was supposed to start. While Hershey went to get our name tags, I stood near the entrance, taking it all in. The pictures I'd seen hadn't done the room justice. The ceiling was painted to look like a summer sky and rose into a steeply pitched dome. The floor was polished marble and was inset with the Theden logo.

A lanky blond guy in seersucker pants and a navy blazer stepped up beside me. His hair was parted and combed flat, and he was wearing penny loafers. Like, with actual pennies in them.

"Hey," he said, extending his hand. "I'm Liam." Even though his preppy getup would've relegated him to the social fringes back home, I could tell that he was popular here. Maybe it was his posture or the confidence in his smile. Or the fact that people kept calling out his name and slapping his back as they passed.

"I'm Rory," I said, caught off guard by the attention and the hand-shaking. No one my age had ever shaken my hand before. Then again I'd never stood in a room that looked like this one either. Liam's palm was rough and callused against mine, but his fingernails were neatly clipped and buffed to a shine, like he'd gotten a manicure. The rest of his appearance followed this rough versus polished pattern. He was dressed like he belonged on a sailboat, but there was a scar at his hair-line and the bluish-yellow remnants of a bruise beneath his right eye. Sports wounds, I guessed, since Liam had both a water polo pin and a rugby pin stuck to his blazer.

"So what do you think of Theden so far?" he asked. "It's a little surreal, right?"

"A little?"

Liam smiled. "It's easier to get used to than you'd think," he said. "I grew up on the south side of Boston. Less than a hundred miles from here, but it feels like a world away."

The south side of Boston? I'd been expecting him to say Nantucket or Martha's Vineyard or some other place where rich kids were hatched and groomed. "So you weren't a legacy?" I asked.

"Hell, no. Whatever the opposite of being a legacy is, I was that. You?"

"My mom went here," I told him, feeling like an impostor. It was true, but it didn't mean what he thought it did. My only connection to this place was a woman I never knew who, for reasons I'd probably never understand, didn't even want me to know she'd gone here.

Hershey came up behind me and slipped her arm through mine. "Who's your friend?" she asked, sizing Liam up.

"I'm Liam," he said. His eyes slid down her legs as he extended his hand.

"Hershey," she replied, not bothering to shake it. She turned to me. "We should go in," she said. "I don't want to sit in the back."

"You can sit with me if you want," Liam said. "I've got seats down front."

"Great." Hershey flashed a plastic smile. "Lead the way."

"So what's his story?" she whispered as we made our way toward the auditorium. "Is he as boring as he looks?"

"He's nice," I hissed.

"We can go around the side," Liam said as we stepped inside the auditorium. The rotunda was impressive, but this was breathtaking. The heptagonal room was lit by crystal chandeliers, and its marble walls were framed on all sides by rows and rows of gold pipes. I'd read that there were more than fourteen thousand of them, making the Theden Organ one of the largest in the world, and the only one of its size that was still operational.

I tilted my head back, taking it all in, as we made our way down the far left aisle to the second row, which was blocked off with orange tape and a sign that said RESERVED FOR STUDENT COUNCIL MEMBERS. Liam lifted the tape and gestured for us to sit.

"You're sure it's okay for us to sit here?" I asked.

"A perk of being class president," he said, crumpling the sign in his hands.

The row in front of us was occupied by faculty. When we sat down, the woman on the end turned her head. She had flawless black skin and one of those stylish Afros that only the excessively attractive can pull off. She was striking, with sharp cheekbones and deep-set green eyes that locked on mine and didn't budge. I smiled. She didn't smile back.

"Just in time," I heard Liam say. I looked up and saw Dean Atwater approaching the podium. He didn't wait for the room to get quiet before he began to speak.

"You are here because you have two things your peers back home do not," he declared, his words reverberating off the pipe-lined walls. "Qualities known by Ancient Greeks as *ethos* and *egkrateia*." He overenunciated the Greek for emphasis. "Character and strength of will. Here you will put those qualities to work in the pursuit of something more noble. *Sophia*. Wisdom." He gripped the podium now, leaning forward a little. "But wisdom is not for the faint of heart. Not all of you will complete our program. Not all of you are meant to."

I looked at my hands, the anxiety I'd felt on the plane rushing back. My mother didn't have what it took. Maybe I didn't either. I was the daughter of a high school dropout and a general contractor. What made me think I could even keep up?

"I know what you're thinking," Dean Atwater said then, as if he'd read my mind. But he was gazing past me, into the center of the crowd. "You're second-guessing your fitness for this program. You're questioning our decision to let you in. Could the admissions committee have made a mistake?" The crowd twittered with nervous laughter. Dean Atwater smiled, his face kind. "Let me assure you, students"—he looked directly at me—"your presence here is no accident."

It was meant to be comforting, but I squirmed in my seat.

The dean's gaze shifted again. "Now, for some housekeeping matters. Each of you has been assigned to one of twelve small sections. Section members share a faculty advisor and will meet together daily for a reasoning skills intensive, which you'll learn more about tomorrow. Your section assignments will appear along with your course schedule under the 'academics' tab in the Theden app." There was much rustling as people pulled their handhelds from purses and pockets. "I said *will* appear," Dean Atwater added with a knowing smile. "When you're dismissed for dinner. We've got one more announcement first. Please welcome your student-body president, Liam Stone."

The room erupted in whistles and applause as Liam joined

Dean Atwater at the podium. "On behalf of the student council," Liam's voice boomed into the mic. "I'm happy to announce that a date has been chosen for this year's Masquerade Ball. Mark your calendars for September 7." The room erupted into loud cheers. "For you first-years—the Masquerade Ball is a black-tie fundraiser for all alumni and current students. As is tradition, a shop in town will provide the tuxes and dresses, and we'll all be given masks to wear. Though, as we second-years can attest, the word *mask* is a bit of a misnomer. They're more like gigantic papier-mâché heads, most of them more than three hundred years old and worth more than your parents can afford." He grinned. "In other words, make it an idiocy-free evening, guys."

Dean Atwater chuckled as he took back the mic. He looked over at Liam. "Anything else, Liam?"

"No, sir."

"Well, then," Dean Atwater said, clapping his hands together. "Let's eat!"

Sleep came easily that night, partly from physical exhaustion, and partly because I'd eaten so much lobster and steak that all the blood in my body had rushed from my head to my stomach, draining me of whatever mental energy I had left. I drifted off with the silver pendant between my thumb and index finger, wondering if they'd served surf 'n' turf at the welcome dinner nineteen years ago and whether my mom had felt as out of place then as I had tonight, but I awoke later with a start, my hand still pressed to my collarbone. My chest was heaving a little beneath it. I'd been having a nightmare—running somewhere, or from someone—but the details slipped away from me as soon as my eyes adjusted to the dark. I listened for Hershey's breathing, worried that I'd cried out and woken her. But the room was quiet. I slid my hand under my pillow, feeling for my Gemini, and blinked as my screen lit up: 3:03 A.M. Still rattled from the dream I couldn't remember, I tiptoed to the bathroom for some water, using my handheld as a flashlight. As I passed my roommate's bed, I realized that the tiptoeing was unnecessary. Hershey wasn't in it.

I quickly sent her a text: where r u??

Half a second later, her handheld lit up in the dark. She'd left it on her nightstand. I picked up her Gemini and erased my text.

I lay awake for a while after that, wondering where Hershey had gone. It was stupid, but I felt a pang of disappointment that she hadn't invited me to go with her. Not that I would've gone, but still. When an hour passed and she still wasn't back, I started to worry. *You're not your roommate's keeper,* I told myself, forcing myself to go back to sleep.

It wasn't even light yet when I woke up again, jolted awake by the screaming chorus of a This Is August Jones song. Hershey's alarm. She fumbled for her Gemini, knocking it off the nightstand in the process. "Sorry," she mumbled, then pulled her pillow over her head and promptly fell back asleep. Her alarm was still going off. Any relief I felt about the fact that she wasn't dead in the woods somewhere was overshadowed by the immense irritation of having my eardrums accosted by excruciatingly crappy pop music at 5:45 in the morning.

"Hershey!" I barked.

"Fine," she grumbled. She slid her hand along the floor, feeling for her Gemini. It took her another thirty seconds to actually turn it off. By the time she did, we were both wide-awake. I rolled onto my side. I'd seen Hershey wash her face before we went to bed, but she had mascara smudges around her eyes now.

"Five forty-five? Seriously?"

Hershey rubbed her eyes. "I may have forgotten that my phone readjusted itself for the time difference."

I burst out laughing.

"I was tired when I set it," she said irritably. I expected her to elaborate, to boast about her late-night escapades or at least hint that she'd snuck out, but she turned away from me, toward the opposite wall.

"How'd you sleep?" I asked, giving her another opportunity. She didn't take it.

"Great," she replied. Her Gemini lit up again as she launched Forum.

I watched her back for a moment, wondering what other secrets my roommate was keeping, and why.

5

A SMALL CROWD WAS GATHERED at the doorway to my first class. There was a sign next to it that read ELECTRONIC DEVICES MUST BE LEFT OUTSIDE. NO EXCEPTIONS, with a cubby station beneath it. I figured no one wanted to abandon their phones until they absolutely had to, but when I got closer, I noticed that none of my classmates were looking at their screens. They were all staring into our classroom, which was still out of my view. I moved toward the door and peered inside.

The room was the most hi-tech I'd ever seen. Every wall was a screen, and instead of desks, there were twelve egg-shaped units that reminded me of those sleeping compartments they had on luxury airlines, except that those are made of gray plastic and these were made of something shimmery and translucent and almost wet-looking. "Even without a bell, you all can still be late," our teacher said, then stepped into view. It was the woman I'd seen at the assembly yesterday. When I saw

Dr. E. Tarsus on my schedule, I'd pictured a man, an older white one, with gray hair and thick glasses. This woman was the total inverse of that. Standing still, she had the countenance of an eagle, her shoulders broad and her posture perfect. But when she moved—as she did now, toward the front wall, with purpose—she reminded me of a jungle cat, the sharp, angular edges of her shoulders and hips visible beneath her clothes.

She taught Plato Practicum, the official name for the practical reasoning intensive Dean Atwater mentioned at the assembly and the only class on my schedule that met every single day. She was also my advisor, so I wanted to make a good impression.

As we filed into her classroom, milling around and looking generally uncertain (*do we stand next to the pods? inside them?*), Dr. Tarsus stepped up to the front wall and wrote with her index finger, her words appearing like chalk on the wall's surface. Instantly the wall transformed into an old-fashioned chalkboard, and she was writing in chalk. I knew it wasn't actually a chalkboard, just a rectangle of interactive wallpaper resembling one, but the texture was so reminiscent of the real thing that for a split second I wondered if somehow it was. *The beginning is the most important part of the work,* she wrote in impeccable script. *Plato,* The Republic, *book two.*

"Pick one," she said, turning to face us now. She gestured to the egg-shaped compartments. I went for one in the middle.

"You should see a small square in the center of your screen," Dr. Tarsus said as I sat down in my pod's metal chair. I felt it adjust beneath and behind me, sliding forward a few inches and conforming to the curve of my spine. "Press your thumb firmly into the box," Dr. Tarsus instructed. "Your terminal will activate." The screen she was referring to was oblong and rounded outward like the nose of an airplane. When I touched my thumb to the little box, the door to the compartment slid shut, sealing me inside. Within seconds, the surface I'd touched and the walls around me had become completely transparent, like glass. I could see my classmates in the row in front of me, the walls of their enclosures as invisible as mine. Dr. Tarsus was perched atop a stool at the front of the room.

She stood and began to make her way around the room as she spoke. "As Dean Atwater explained yesterday, this program is unique in its focus. You're here to gain knowledge, yes. To learn the who and the what and the where and the why of literature, history, mathematics, psychology, and science. But you're also here to pursue something that is far more valuable than knowledge, and much harder to attain." She paused for effect. "*Phronesis*," she said then. "Prudence. Wisdom in action. The ability to live well."

Something in me grabbed ahold of this idea. Wisdom in action. *I want that.* The conviction that I'd made the very best choice, without having to ask an app on my handheld to be sure. When left on my own, I waffled and wavered, second-guessing my decisions before I even made them. It was the reason I'd always sucked at sports. And gardening. And art. It was the reason I used Lux for nearly every choice I made, from the mundane to the major. I craved the assurance that I was on the right track, headed somewhere that mattered.

I knew what Beck would say. That prudent genius was an oxymoron. That the greatest athletes and the most talented artists and the most brilliant thinkers went with their gut. But wasn't that exactly what Dr. Tarsus was offering? A gut I could trust.

Don't exchange the truth for a lie.

My whole body stiffened, bracing against the voice. Hearing it once was one thing. A fluke. But here it was again, less than twenty-four hours later, cryptic and eerie and even louder than it had been the day before. Dread pooled in the pit of my stomach as I swallowed. Hard.

Chill, I told myself firmly. The Doubt wasn't anything to panic over unless you couldn't turn it off, like that French girl in the Middle Ages who let herself be burned at the stake. So I'd heard it a couple of times. It didn't have to be a big deal. If I ignored it, the way I'd been taught, it'd eventually go away, the way it had when I was a kid.

Dr. Tarsus was still talking. I started repeating her words in my head to drown out the Doubt's, which were replaying like an echo in my mind. "The ancient Greek philosophers, and Aristotle in particular, understood that *phronesis* could not be attained in a vacuum," she was saying. "Or a classroom for that matter. They believed that *phronesis* had to be hard-won through personal experience." She pulled a tiny remote from her skirt pocket and typed on its screen. The walls of our pods instantly turned opaque. I realized now that the pods were soundproof and that her voice had been coming through tiny speakers above me. "The simulations we do in this practicum will provide that experience," she said, and my screen lit up. Grateful for the distraction, I focused intently on the image on my screen. It was a ground-level shot of Nob Hill in San Francisco. I'd never been there, but I recognized the steep hill and cable-car track from movies and TV. The image shifted, and I realized that it wasn't a photograph but video footage shot from the point of view of a pedestrian waiting with several others at a trolley stop. The camera must've been on a pair of glasses, or mounted between the guy's eyes, because I was seeing whatever he saw as he looked around, glanced at his handheld, even bent to tie his shoe—a men's Converse One Star.

"Our simulations will differ in format, but the way in which we interact as a class will generally remain the same," Dr. Tarsus went on. "The booths you're in are equipped with audio technology designed to facilitate our discussions. You can hear me, obviously. But I can only hear one of you at a time. The booths are wired to record your audible responses and broadcast them over the speakers in the order they were received, and I'll respond—or not—as I see fit. There is no need to wait until you've been called on, and no risk that you'll interrupt one another. Speak when you have something to say. If the discussion stalls, I will begin addressing my questions to specific students, in which case the responses of other students will be recorded and delayed until the person I've called on has responded." She paused, and I imagined her glancing around the room. Were the walls opaque on her side, or could she see us? I kept a pleasant smile on my face just in case. "Any questions?" she asked. I shook my head, eyes riveted to my screen. A family with three kids and a baby in a stroller had gotten a wheel caught on the trolley track. "Excellent," Dr. Tarsus said. "Let's begin."

Immediately the audio from the video switched on. I could now hear the chatter of the people on the street, car noises, a jackhammer pounding on asphalt nearby. And a baby crying. The baby in the stroller caught on the track. The parents still hadn't gotten the wheel unstuck, and they seemed to be having trouble getting the baby out. Next to me, an obese man in sweat shorts and a T-shirt fiddled with his waistband. Somewhere in the distance, a cable car rang its bell. Dr. Tarsus had called this a simulation, so I assumed these details were important and paid attention to all of them. But what were we being tested on?

The cable car sounded its bell, much louder this time. Much closer. Instinctively, my head turned in the direction of the sound, and when it did, my view shifted. I blinked. Was I controlling the camera? I turned my head the opposite way, and the camera moved with me. I felt the headrest against the back of my skull and realized that it must have motion sensors. I'd just started to move my feet—wondering if I could get the guy with the camera to walk—when I heard the bell a third time, so loud this time my head whipped to the right. The cable car had crested the hill and was now barreling down it.

Toward the baby in the stroller.

Just then the screen froze and Dr. Tarsus's voice came through the speakers. "Here are the facts. The wheel of the stroller you see is caught in the track in such a way that it cannot be removed without dismantling the entire stroller, which, with the proper tools, would take four and a half minutes. The cable car careening toward it has just experienced brake failure. Unless stopped, the cable car will hit the stroller in forty-two seconds, traveling at sixty miles per hour. The baby inside the stroller is buckled into a seat belt that has jammed." Her voice was dispassionate, almost bored, as if she were describing the weather. "If the trolley hits the stroller," she continued, "the angle of impact will cause the trolley to jump its track, killing at least five passengers on board, including two children, and two pedestrians. The baby and its parents, who will refuse to leave the stroller's side, will also be killed, along with their three other children, who will be crushed when the trolley flips over. The only way to prevent this outcome is to force a crash before the trolley reaches forty miles an hour. The trolley is currently traveling at thirty miles an hour." I felt my eyes go wide with horror. I knew that what we were seeing wasn't actually *real*, but still. The scenario reminded me of the morality quizzes Beck was always taking online. Except in those, I couldn't hear the baby whose life was at stake or see its parents' desperate faces.

"The man next to you weighs four hundred and eighty-four pounds," Dr. Tarsus continued. "He is both blind and deaf.

You, a third-year medical student, are his caretaker, and he will go wherever you lead him. If he were to walk across the track in the next ten seconds, the trolley would hit him going thirty-two miles an hour and would come to a stop just before reaching the stroller. In light of the choices available to you, what is the most prudent thing to do?" A few seconds later my screen unfroze and I was back in the action again. I turned my body to the right and was now facing the fat man next to me, who was clearly waiting for my cue. The trolley blared its horn again. I glanced back at the parents pulling frantically at their baby's stroller. Could I convince them to move away from the track? One look at their desperate, panicked faces, and I had my answer. It was pointless to try.

I scanned the rest of the scene for another option. Across the track, there was a hot dog cart, with a vendor in a striped hat behind it. The cart was on wheels. Did it weigh as much as the fat man? I had no idea, but I doubted it. I whipped my head back around toward the stroller. Could I help them get it unstuck? I moved my feet like I was running in place and instantly the camera was moving. I was sprinting toward them. Seconds later I was at their side.

The wheel was pinned in the groove between the steel rails. Instead of pulling up on it, I tried pushing it. The wheel turned, and the stroller moved a few inches.

"Push the stroller that way!" I cried, forgetting for a second that the people I was yelling at were computer generated. Could they even hear me? But they seemed to. They immediately stood and started pushing the stroller down the track. I dashed back to the hot dog cart. If it weighed less than the fat man, then it wouldn't slow the trolley down as quickly, but it would at least do something, and if the parents could get the stroller far enough down the track, maybe it'd stop before it reached them. I had to try. I couldn't lead a deaf and blind man into the path of an oncoming train.

"Help me push this cart!" I yelled at the vendor.

"No way!" he shouted back. I grabbed the cart's handle and yanked it. It wouldn't budge.

Crap. According to the timer at the bottom of my screen, twenty-one seconds had already passed. The trolley was zooming toward us. I had to do something. Fast.

I whirled around, looking for something I could put in the trolley's way, but there was nothing. Just the fat man and the stroller.

And me.

As the timer raced toward forty, I ran to the center of the track and squeezed my eyes shut, bracing for the impact. Of course, I didn't feel any. Just the sound of a buzzer as the simulation ended. I opened one eye. On my screen were the words DEATH TOLL: 2. My "body" lay crumpled and bloody beneath the trolley. The baby's father was also dead, pinned under the trolley's grill. When my body wasn't enough to stop it, he'd tried to help. His wife and baby and two other kids were all still alive. As was the fat man, who stood by the tracks, oblivious to it all.

The screen blinked black, and then a list appeared on the screen. The class roster, twelve of us, ranked by death toll. There were seven people who'd done better than I had, with a death toll of only one. The fat man. Their grades set the curve, pushing mine to the middle. The others hadn't intervened at all, and the trolley had killed the family with the baby, just as Tarsus had said that it would. My hands unclenched and my shoulders relaxed. Being in the middle of the curve had its benefits. I wouldn't get singled out. The pod walls became transparent again and I could see Tarsus at the front of the room.

"As with all the simulations we'll do in this class," came Tarsus's voice through my speakers, "the goal of this exercise was what economists and social scientists call 'net positive impact.' Those of you who chose to sacrifice the fat man achieved this result. Of the players in the scenario, he had the lowest utility value. Blind, deaf, and overweight, he contributed very little to the well-being of society. The prudent course of action, then, was to use this man to stop the train. Of the options available to you, that was the only one that yielded a net positive impact."

"Why was it net positive?" someone asked. "I mean, yeah, it was the best option available, but a person still died."

"Ah," said Tarsus. "Excellent point. A person did die. However, that person was a blight on society. A drain on social resources. His death, then, was actually a gain for society as a whole."

I physically recoiled. Because he was disabled and over-weight, the poor man's death was a *gain*?

"This simulation is based on an old ethics hypothetical called, aptly, the trolley problem. I use it every year on the first day of class, and every year my students are roughly split into two groups—those who sacrifice the fat man and those who do nothing." She paused and looked directly at my pod. "This year, however, one of you got creative."

Creative isn't bad, I told myself. *Creative is—*

"Rory," she said, and my whole body went taut. So much for not getting singled out. "You tried to stop the cart with your own body. Of everyone in this scenario, you had the highest utility value, followed by the baby's father, a prominent ven-ture capitalist, who you also killed." Her tone was scathing. I shrunk down in my seat. "Do you have a hero complex?"

It sounded like a rhetorical question, so it took me a second to realize she was actually asking me. "Uh, n-no," I stammered. "I just—"

"Heroism is narcissism in disguise," she declared, cutting me off. "And narcissists are incapable of the objectivity that prudence requires. So if you want to prove that you're wor-thy of being here, I suggest you tame that self-admiration with haste." She flicked her eyes away from my pod and moved on. She didn't look in my direction for the remainder of the class period. *Worthy of being here.* She'd hit my fear on the head.

I had to hustle to get across campus for my second-period class. Our teacher was standing on a chair when I arrived, fiddling with the string of paper lanterns he'd hung from the ceiling. His classroom looked like a classroom should, with rows of metal desks and a single screen on the front wall. The only not-in-public-school-anymore aspect of his room was the handheld dock built into the upper right corner of each desk. I docked my Gemini and my name turned from red to green on the class roster projected onto the screen.

"Welcome to Cognitive Psychology," our teacher said when everyone was seated. "I'm Mr. Rudman. But you guys can call me Rudd." He was young, mid-twenties I guessed, and in his hipster horn-rimmed glasses and sneakers wasn't nearly as intimidating as Dr. Tarsus. He was cute, in a Seattle tech-geek sort of way. An older, more brainy version of the kind of guy I was used to from back home. The familiarity was disarming. I relaxed a little in my seat.

"In this class, we will look at how people perceive, remember, think, speak, and solve problems," Rudd explained. "We'll study how the healthy brain operates, what its limitations are, and how those limitations, if exaggerated, can lead to psychosis." He punched a button on his handheld and the wall behind him lit up with a sign-up sheet. The left-hand column contained a list of twenty-four mental illnesses, in alphabetical order, from Acute Stress Disorder to Trichotillomania. The right-hand column was blank. I glanced down at my desk and noticed that my Gemini was lit up with the same image.

"Topic choices for your first term paper," Rudd explained. "Due in five weeks. Simply put your name down next to the disorder you'd like to study and tap 'confirm.' And don't fret: If you're feeling indecisive or indifferent, there's an auto-select button at the bottom of your screens that'll let you use Lux to decide." He tapped his screen once more and the topic list went green. "Happy picking."

I scanned the list from the bottom up. "Akratic Paracusia Disorder (APD)," the third topic from the top, caught my eye.

Choose that one.

The voice was unequivocal, a quiet scream. Twice in two hours. My insides went taut as the words of a nursery rhyme I'd sung as a child sprung to mind, an incessant refrain in my head. *Watch out, little girl, for the Doubt, watch out, watch out, watch out.*

Beads of sweat popped up along my hairline. I hadn't heard the voice since my eleventh birthday and now I'd heard it three times in less than twenty-four hours. I gave my head a firm shake to clear it. *Don't make this a big deal. Just let Lux decide and be done with it.*

I tapped the auto-select button and my name appeared in gray next to "Claustrophobia." All I had to do was press CON-FIRM. My eyes darted back to topic number three. The space next to it was still blank.

Choose that one.

It was ironic, the Doubt telling me to choose the Doubt. That's what APD was. The medical term for adults who listened to the inner voice. I knew because I'd heard Beck's parents use it. It was the diagnosis they were so desperate to avoid.

When we were kids, Beck's parents would tease him about the voice he heard, asking what the Doubt wanted for dinner, whether the Doubt liked chocolate ice cream, if the Doubt wanted milk with its cookie, to which Beck would patiently respond that the Doubt wasn't a person, but a spirit, and spirits couldn't eat because spirits didn't have bodies. When we got older, and the rest of us began to ignore the voice, his parents stopped laughing. He was ushered to a psychiatrist who prescribed the antipsychotic Evoxa and recommended that Beck double up on extracurriculars and spend more time interacting online to keep his mind occupied. Beck ignored his advice, and the voice kept talking. He told his parents he didn't hear it anymore, just so they'd leave him alone, but I knew they still worried. I didn't know enough about the disorder to understand why.

My finger hovered over the CONFIRM button, my name still in gray next to "Claustrophobia." What made choosing APD as my research topic so irrational? It had to be, because that's what the Doubt did, by definition: It hijacked your thoughts, making you doubt what your rational mind knew to be true. Curious, I scrolled down to see where APD appeared on Lux's recommendation list.

It was at the very bottom.

"Thirty seconds!" Rudd announced. The list was filling up fast.

Choose that one.

I'm not listening to the Doubt, I told myself. *I'm protecting myself from it.* Knowledge was power, after all. Before I could think twice, I typed my name next to topic number three and tapped CONFIRM.

6

"THE FOOL IS DESTINED TO REPEAT HISTORY. The wise man has the wit to avoid it."

My history teacher, a wiry white-haired man in his seventies, was giving an overview of our coursework for the semester, but I was only half listening. While everyone else was dutifully scrolling through the syllabus, I was on Panopticon, my mind whirling but not registering any coherent thought. I'd read the entry for APD before, but it had different significance now.

> **Akratic Paracusia Disorder:** *from the ancient Greek* akrasia *"lacking command over oneself" and* para + acusia *"beyond hearing." A* **psychiatric disorder** *characterized by persistent* **arational auditory hallucinations** *expressed as a single voice. The voice, known colloquially as "the Doubt," is commonly heard by healthy prepubescent children and believed to coincide with the rapid* **synaptic growth** *of the*

frontal cortex *that occurs in early adolescence. The postpubescent presence of the voice, however, indicates a predisposition for Akratic Paracusia Disorder, or APD. Diagnosis is based on observed behavior and the patient's reported experiences.*

Although the specific cause of the disorder is unknown, factors that increase the risk of developing the disorder include a family history of APD or extended periods of high stress, emotional changes, or isolation from one's peers. If caught early, APD can be treated with **antipsychotic medication**. *Without pharmaceutical intervention, the akratic brain quickly degenerates, resulting in self-destructive behavior and, eventually,* **dementia**.

Our teacher stepped into my sightline.

"Any questions?" he asked pointedly, looking directly at me. I gave my head a tiny shake, lowering my tablet onto my lap. He nodded and moved on. I closed out of Panopticon and pulled up my history syllabus, but I still couldn't concentrate. My vision blurred and all I could see were the words *predisposition* and *degenerate* and *dementia* over and over on the page.

I'd spent so much time worrying about Beck's mental health. Should I have been nervous about my own? Half an hour after resolving to ignore the Doubt, I'd done exactly what it'd told me to do. *That's not why I did it,* I reminded myself. *I had perfectly rational reasons for picking APD as my topic.* Still, the fact that I was hearing the voice at all had me completely unhinged. My mind was jumpy and frantic, like a frog caught in a jar. Third period passed in a blur of words I didn't hear. I had to get this under control, fast.

I wasn't hungry, but I went to lunch anyway, trailing behind a group of girls from my history class who seemed to know one another from summer camp. Someone had opened the dining hall windows, and the noise from inside reverberated off the courtyard walls.

Hershey waved me over when I walked in. She was at the salad bar, heaping lettuce onto a dark metal plate. From the smile on her face, it seemed the morning's foul mood had lifted.

"I am obsessed with these plates," she said when I walked up.

I reached for one. It was so cold it made my fingers throb. I turned it over in my hands, wondering what it was made of, and saw a thick, shimmery, uppercase G etched into its surface. My eyes flicked to the plate dispenser and saw another G there. Gnosis hadn't just donated the classroom gadgets; they'd stocked the dining hall too.

Hershey had moved from the lettuce to the cucumbers. I followed along behind her, mechanically dropping toppings onto my plate. The produce on the salad bar was bright and colorful and fresh, certified organic and sourced from a nearby farm, but I wasn't hungry for it. The Doubt had stolen my appetite.

"You think he's single?" I heard Hershey ask. I followed

her gaze. Rudd had just emerged from the hot-food line.

"He's a teacher."

"He's not *my* teacher," Hershey replied, nudging me with her hip. "And he's not wearing a ring."

She waggled her eyebrows and headed to the pasta bar while I looked for a place to sit. Back home, I never ate in the lunchroom. Beck and I always spent our free period off campus, opting out of the social hierarchy. Standing there alone with my tray, I remembered why. I shifted awkwardly from one foot to the other. There weren't any empty tables.

"C'mon," Hershey said behind me, sauntering past me with her tray.

We sat at a table by the window with two girls from Hershey's section, Rachel and Isabel, and the three of them gossiped about the other members of their section and their faculty adviser's fashion sense while I picked at my salad.

"Ugh, you're so good," I heard Isabel say. She had pale blond hair and wore glasses that I'm pretty sure cost more than my whole wardrobe. "I suck at food," she explained, gesturing at the half-eaten cheeseburger on her place, wedged between a pile of French fries and a mountain of mac and cheese. "I'm eleven pounds over Lux's recommended weight," she said. "Which I know I should loathe and feel motivated to do something about, but I just don't *care* that much, you know? I like the way I look. And the way fries taste." She eyed my salad. "Meanwhile, I'll bet you picked that without even asking Lux. Which is why you're, like, half my size."

I was about to tell her that I actually hated salad when I heard Hershey mutter, "Help, I think I just fell asleep," under her breath.

"Hey, girls." Liam smiled affably as he slid into an empty seat next to me. "How's the first day going?"

"Swell," replied Hershey, managing to sound both bored and sarcastic. Liam was undeterred.

"Who are your advisers?" he asked. "I'll give you the dirt."

"The dirt?"

Liam smiled conspiratorially. "You'd be surprised. Some of our faculty—"

"Showing these young women the ropes, Liam?"

Liam straightened his shoulders at the sound of the dean's voice, sitting taller in his seat. Dean Atwater had come up behind us. Hershey smirked. She'd obviously seen him coming and hadn't said anything.

"Trying my best," said Liam easily, his eyes on Hershey.

"Not that this one needs your help," Dean Atwater said. I glanced at Hershey, expecting some clever response, but she was staring openly at me. So were the other girls. I looked up at Dean Atwater. He was looking at me, too. "You're our only Hepta this year," he said when I met his gaze.

Hepta. It was the Greek prefix for the number seven. I'd looked it up in the student handbook when I saw it in my acceptance letter, in a box labeled "academic designation." It meant I had a natural aptitude for all seven liberal arts subjects. I'd just assumed it was a common thing at Theden.

"Our class didn't have one," Liam said, not even attempting to keep the surprise out of his voice.

"Neither did the class before," Dean Atwater added. "Which makes Rory quite exceptional." He put his hand on my shoulder. Hershey's eyes narrowed.

"Oh," I said, because I didn't know what to say. I kept my face neutral, but my insides soared. *Quite exceptional.* Here. At Theden. Dean Atwater gave me a knowing smile. "You didn't let history deter you. I commend you for that."

He gave my shoulder a squeeze and walked off.

"Wow," said Isabel, peering at me through her navy frames. "My older brother was a Hexa, and my dad acted like *that* was a big deal." She and the other girl had been ignoring me before, but now they regarded me with a mix of curiosity and reverence. Hershey's gaze was sharper than that. She was stuck on the history comment, trying to figure out what it meant.

So was I.

"Yeah, most Theden kids are Pentas," Liam said, a slight edge in his voice that hadn't been there before. "An aptitude for five." I guessed by his attitude that Liam was a Hexa. An aptitude for six.

The table was quiet for a few seconds. All eyes still on me.

Then Hershey pushed back her chair and stood up. "I'll see you guys later," she said, then turned and sauntered out. Liam watched her go.

The other girl, Rachel, rolled her eyes at Hershey's retreating figure. "Envy is so public school," she said. "I, for one, think it's cool that you're a Hepta." Her smile seemed genuine, so I returned it.

"Thanks," I said. "I'm not sure I understand what it means, or why it—"

Liam cut me off. "It means you were born for this."

"Born for what?" I asked.

He looked at me like the answer was obvious. "For greatness," he said.

I left lunch even more determined to silence the Doubt. If I was a Hepta, then surely my brain was capable of overriding whatever little synaptic misfire was causing me to hear it in the first place.

"I need caffeine," I told Lux as I made my way across the courtyard after my last class. The fact that it was the first day of school hadn't stopped my teachers from piling on the homework.

"The coffee cart in the dining hall is open until nine," came Lux's reply. Instantly its recommendations popped on screen, a vanilla cappuccino at the top of the list. But the line for the coffee cart already was spilling out onto the dining hall steps. I slipped my phone in my bag and started toward it, then stopped. I could get downtown and back in the time it would take to wait for my drink. Plus, I'd avoid having to make small talk with the perfectly nice but painfully chatty girls from my history class who were clustered at the end of the line.

I set off for River City Beans, the place Lux had recommended the day before. What I really wanted was that matcha concoction I'd had at Paradiso, but there was no way I was showing up there two days in a row. Or giving North the satisfaction of ordering his drink.

I skipped the cemetery this time, taking the street route instead, through a quiet residential neighborhood and across a natural footbridge that traversed the narrow part of the river. The wind picked up, rustling the trees, and I shivered, wishing I'd brought a sweater. As I turned down Main Street, the sun disappeared behind a blue-black cloud. There were several more rolling in across the mountains, darkening the sky. It rained all the time in Seattle, but we didn't get thunderstorms like this.

I was looking over my shoulder at the clouds as I reached for the door handle at River City Beans and gave it a tug. The door didn't budge.

CLOSED ON MONDAYS read the sign on the window.

So much for trusting yesterday's advice.

For a second I debated heading back to campus before the storm, but as the sky lit up with lightning, I decided against it. Paradiso was just two blocks down, and I could tell from here that its lights were on. I'd wait it out there.

As I pushed open the door, I saw North working the espresso machine. At the jingle of the bell, he looked up. My eyes fell to my feet, feeling silly for being there, for coming alone.

"Hey," North called. "Couldn't stay away?" When I lifted my gaze to meet his, he smiled. His whole face changed when he did. His eyes were dancing a little, and there was no trace of yesterday's smirkiness.

"Something like that," I replied, as thunder rumbled behind me. I shivered and stepped further inside.

"Vanilla cappuccino?" North teased, already reaching for the canister of matcha. He had an earbud in his ear, connected by a wire to a white matchbook-size device clipped to the belt loop of his jeans. I'd seen pictures of old MP3 players and guessed that's what it was.

"What're you listening to?" I asked.

"Cardamon's Couch," replied North over the hiss of the steamer. "They're a local band. He slipped the bud out of his ear and held it out for me. I had to lean over the counter a little to get it up to my ear. "My friend Nick is on mandolin. His brother's the steel guitar."

It took me a second to orient myself in the song, which had an unusual chord structure and a jarringly despondent tone. But then it all came together, all at once: the soulful lyrics, the haunting melody, the guttural steel guitar, and the feverish mandolin. There were other sounds too, sounds I couldn't place, eerie rumbles and clangs and whines. I put my palm over the earbud and closed my eyes, letting the music drown everything else out. When the chorus ended, I handed the earbud back to North.

"They're awesome," I said, pulling out my handheld and

typing in the name. "You said Cardamon's Couch, right? I want to put them on my playlist."

The band's artist profile page popped up on my screen. They had no user rankings and a sales ranking in the seven digits. "Oh," I said, jumping to the obvious explanation for their obscurity. "They're new."

North shook his head. "Nope. Third album."

I scrolled down and saw that he was right. Their first was released four years before. "I don't get it," I said, puzzled. "Why is nobody listening to them? They're different, but they're not *that* different. And a lot closer to the stuff I like than most of what Lux recommends."

"Lux doesn't care what you like," North pointed out. "Lux cares about what you'll buy."

"But aren't those the same thing?"

"Hardly. You buy stuff you don't like all the time. You just don't realize it because you're too busy telling yourself you love it to justify the fact that you bought it. Hey, can you snap?"

I'd been bracing for another lesson on the perils of app-assisted living, so the question threw me. "What?"

"Can you snap?" he repeated. "Your fingers." He snapped his.

"Can't everybody snap?" I asked him.

"You'd be surprised," he replied, pouring soy milk into a metal beaker. He nodded at my hand. "Let me hear yours."

"Is there a point to this?"

"Yes," he replied. "Now, snap."

I snapped. He grinned. "Now that," he said, "is an excellent snap." He flicked on the steamer.

"And why, exactly, are you so interested in my snapping skills?" I asked as I touched my handheld to the register's scanner to pay for my drink. It didn't beep, so I tried again, waving my Gemini a little in front of the sensor. Still no beep.

"It's on me," North said over the hiss of the steamer. "Well, as long as you take it to go."

"You're bribing me to leave?"

He flicked a switch and the hissing stopped. "Nope. I'm bribing you to come with me."

My stomach fluttered just a little. "Come with you where?"

He glanced past me out the cafe's bay window. A girl with a shaved head and a Paradiso T-shirt was quickly turning the hand crank to close it as lightning flickered menacingly on the other side. "You'll see," North said mysteriously, pouring milk into a paper cup with circular precision. With a few flicks of his wrist, he drew a perfect leaf in the foam. My eyes slid up his forearm to the words tattooed there. Only one line was legible at this angle. *Who is the third who walks always beside you?* There was no attribution, nothing to indicate whether it was something he had written or a line he'd taken from somewhere else.

"It's T. S. Eliot," North said. My head jerked up.

"I didn't mean to—"

"It's tattooed on my forearm," North said, handing me my drink. "It's meant to be read. But not right now, because we

76

have to go." He snapped a lid onto my cup.

"It's about to start raining," I pointed out.

"So we should hurry," he said, giving his apron strings a tug. The girl who'd just been at the window had joined him behind the counter. North handed her his apron.

"You better hustle," she told him. "It's already raining on the mountain."

"Just in time." His eyes were bright with excitement. "Wait here," he instructed me. "I'll be right back." Without pausing for my reply, he ducked into the kitchen.

"How do you know North?" the girl asked when he was gone.

"I don't," I said. "Uh, do you know where he's going?"

"Do you have the key to the bottom cabinet?" North had reemerged with a backpack on one shoulder and a hoodie over his arm. The girl nodded, then slipped a key off her key ring and tossed it to him. He caught it easily. "Hand me your bag," he told me.

I shook my head. "I can't. I have homework to do."

"We'll be gone less than an hour," North said, lifting my bag off my shoulder. "Your stuff will be fine." I glanced at my Gemini, peeking out from my bag's side pocket. "Unless, of course, you can't go without your leash . . ." He looked at me, eyebrows raised, baiting me. I opened my mouth to tell him that I wasn't going wherever he wanted to take me and I didn't care if that made me lame. But he cut me off.

"I'm meeting the guys from Cardamon's Couch to record

some music," he explained in a low voice. "And we need someone who can snap. Another friend of ours was supposed to do it, but she got called into work. We were gonna just do it without, but then you came in, and you're such a stellar snapper. . . ." Outside, there was a loud crack of thunder. He looked past me, out the window. "Look, no big deal if you don't want to come," he said, sliding his arm through the other strap of his backpack. "I get that you barely know me. But I've got to get going, so . . ." He wasn't going to try to convince me.

I looked over my shoulder at the darkening sky, wavering. He was right, I barely knew him. And I had homework to do. But that song I'd heard was *really* good. And I was curious. About the band. About him.

I met his gaze. "How much does this snapping gig pay?"

He grinned. "Free matcha for life."

I handed him my bag, then looked at the girl with the shaved head. "I know your loyalty is probably to him, but if I'm not back in ninety minutes, call the police."

7

A CEILING OF HEAVY STORM CLOUDS had settled over the valley. With each crack of thunder, I expected them to burst open, but the rain held off.

"Where are we going?" I called to North as we crossed into the woods, having to shout a little over the rustling trees. My stomach twisted in nervous little knots. I wasn't good at spontaneity. Or surprises.

"The cemetery," he replied, stopping to help me down the hill.

"The *cemetery*?"

"I'll explain when we get inside," he said, lifting my cup from my hands. I went down the hill sideways, careful not to slip, and waited for him at the chain-link fence Hershey and I had climbed over the day before. North stooped down next to me and reached under a raised part at the bottom of the fence, setting my cup on the other side. The way the grass was matted, I knew he'd done this before.

"Inside?" I asked, looking around. "Inside where?"

He pointed at the small square building at the center of the cemetery. It was built into the side of a hill, so its roof was covered with grass and its entrance was only partially in view. There was an apple tree directly in front of it, like the one on the pin stuck to my shoe, planted in a square plot of grass the same size as the building, surrounded on all sides by the cemetery's stone sidewalk. "The rain's gonna start any second, so unless you want to get soaked . . ." He clasped his fingers together, making a little platform, and nodded at my foot. I put a hand on his shoulder and stepped up.

It started coming down just as North dropped inside the fence. "C'mon," he said, grabbing my free hand. We sprinted across the grass toward the entrance, weaving around head-stones. The air smelled like wet stone. I kept my eyes on the ground as we darted past the statue of the angry angel in the center of the cemetery, avoiding his menacing gaze.

We were both laughing as North unlocked the structure's gated door and we stepped inside the narrow overhang. With his guitar on his back, North had to stand away from the wall behind him, which left less than a foot between his chest and mine. My limbs were electric with his nearness.

"Now what?" I asked, keeping my voice light, as if I were used to being in tiny semi-enclosed spaces with boys I barely knew. I brushed my hair out of my eyes, but a strand fell back down. North reached for it, twisting it gently before tucking it behind my ear. My bottom lip quivered a little when his fingers

80

brushed my cheek. I bit down on it, hard, reminding myself he was a complete stranger.

"Now we go inside," he said. He leaned into the granite wall beside us, and it retracted then slid smoothly aside.

I did a double take. "How did you . . . ?"

"It's a lever and pulley system," North explained, gesturing for me to follow him inside. "The stone's actually sliding down, not over." The inner chamber was dark even with the door open, so I moved carefully, not wanting to walk into anything. To my surprise, the air inside wasn't heavy or dank like I expected it to be, but smelled fresh, like the room had just been cleaned. I heard a soft thud and the sound of a zipper. A few seconds later, the room lit up.

North's backpack lay open on top of the marble coffin in the center of the room, next to an LED lantern. The walls and floor were marble too, and the ceiling was covered in gold leaf. The room was much bigger than I expected it to be, nearly as large as my dorm room, and empty save for the coffin and the low ledge that lined the walls. A bench for mourners, I supposed.

"This is a mausoleum," I pointed out.

"No wonder they let you into the academy," North teased. He started lifting things out of his backpack. A thin silver laptop. A tiny black microphone, no bigger than a button. Two metal coffee canisters. A thick rusty chain. A plastic Baggie of coins. Outside, rain pounded on dry earth.

I tried again. "You record music in someone's internment space?"

He raised an eyebrow. "Internment space. Nice use of a vocab word, Rory." It was the first time he'd said my name. I liked the way it sounded on his lips. The *r*'s rolled just a little, not like he was trying to roll them. It was just the way he talked.

Just then there was commotion outside, and the stone door slid open. Three soaking wet guys tumbled in out of the rain. They were laughing and cursing at the same time.

"Rory, meet Nick, Adam, and Brent," North said, pointing them out. "Aka, Cardamon's Couch. Guys, meet our snapper."

"Hey," they said in unison, dropping their instrument cases onto the marble.

"Holy crap, it's pouring," Brent said, shaking the rain out of his hair. He looked younger than the other two, younger than me even, and his red curls were the exact same shade as Nick's.

"I told you guys to leave when you heard thunder," North said.

"Yeah, but genius here said it had to be a thunder *clap*, not a rumble," Nick replied, punching Adam in the shoulder.

"I didn't want to schlep all the way out here if it wasn't going to actually rain," Adam said defensively, shrugging out of his wet jacket. He tossed it onto the coffin. It landed with a wet slap. I shuddered. "Don't worry, no one's buried there," he assured me.

"How do you know?" I asked him.

"North opened it."

I gaped at North. "You opened it?"

North shrugged. "I figured if it wasn't sealed, there couldn't be a body inside. The lid is really light," he said, putting his hands under the rim and lifting it a little. "No way it's actually marble."

"So why would they put a coffin in here if they weren't going to put a body in it?"

"Good question," Nick said, unzipping his mandolin case. "Better one: Why put a building with perfect acoustics in a graveyard?"

"Ah. So that's why you come here to play."

"It's better than a recording studio," Adam replied, tugging open the large rectangular case at his feet. "And it's free."

"But why the need for rain?" I asked.

"It masks the sound," North explained. "Plus, it's the only time we can be sure no one will be out here. It's a private cemetery, so technically we're trespassing. Fortunately, only a crazy person would come to a graveyard in a thunderstorm." He grinned.

I knew I should be worried about getting caught, arrested even, and what it would mean for my future at Theden, but I told myself the odds of that actually happening were slim. Thunder and lightning were crashing just seconds apart, which meant the storm was right over us, and the rain was coming down so hard, it sounded like we were standing under a waterfall. North was right; no one in their right mind would venture out here now. I could start worrying about consequences when we left.

Nick had started to strum his mandolin. The instrument had to be at least a hundred years old, but it was in perfect condition, not a single scratch in its veneer. I was watching his fingers dancing effortlessly over the strings when the others joined in. Adam on a bongo drum, Brent on an upright bass. Even just riffing like that, they were awesome.

"Okay," North said, setting his laptop and the mic down on the floor in the center of the little circle we'd formed. "Which one do you want to do first?" he asked Nick.

"The chain in the small can," Nick replied. "With a snap on the five beat."

North looked up at me. "Just count it out in your head," he said. "One, two, three, four, *snap*. Over and over." I nodded, suddenly nervous I'd screw it up.

The guys tinkered with their instruments as North got the chain and the canister from the top of the coffin and knelt on the floor by his laptop.

"'No Vacancy,'" Nick said when everyone was ready, and the others nodded. "One, two, three—" And they all started to play. I was so taken with the instant fury of their fingers and hands that I almost forgot to snap, but North caught my eye just in time. He, meanwhile, was dropping the chain in the canister and picking it up again. I closed my eyes so I could focus on my snapping and immediately got lost in the music. The snaps came instinctively then. I didn't even have to count them out.

They played three songs, and there were snaps in two of

them. North used the coins in the cans, and the chain on the marble, each combination becoming its own instrument, integral to the whole. Something inside me stirred and moved as I listened to the last song, the one without any snaps, watching North's face from behind my lowered lashes. This music was better than anything on my playlist. It baffled me that these guys could be so off the radar.

"That's a wrap," North said when they were finished. My heart sank a little. I didn't want it to end.

The guys said their good-byes and cleared out as quickly as they'd come, leaving North and me alone again.

"So, you're their sound engineer?" I asked as North slid his laptop back into the front pocket of his backpack.

"Basically. They used to record at a studio in Boston, but it was expensive, and the end result wasn't any better than what we were getting here. So I bought some sound software and some mics and started doing their stuff myself."

"But you seem so antitechnology."

He laughed. "Antitechnology? Hardly. Anti-handing-over-my-autonomy-to-a-two-by-four-inch-rectangle? Yes."

"So you don't use one?"

"A handheld?" He hesitated for a sec then shook his head. "I can't use a Gemini without using its interface."

"And you're anti-Gemini because . . . ?"

"Because I know how it works," he said, then switched off the lantern. The rain had stopped, but the sun was nowhere to be found. I felt my muscles twitch as the anxiety I'd been putting off rushed back in. I practically leaped to my feet.

"I should go," I said quickly, moving toward the entrance. "I didn't realize how late it was."

"You still don't know how late it is," North pointed out.

"Yes, thank you," I said irritably, sliding just a little on the slick grass as I stepped outside. North caught me by the elbow, and my whole body felt it.

"So I have to make a quick stop," he said as we set off back toward the fence. He was keeping both his voice and his head down now, moving quickly and quietly. His caution only intensified my rising panic. *What was I thinking, coming out here like this?* I so easily could've gotten caught. Not to mention the mountain of homework I'd just blown off. On the first day of school, no less. The dean's welcome speech came barreling back. *Wisdom is not for the faint of heart,* he said. *Not all of you will complete our program. Not all of you are meant to.*

"You game?" I heard North say.

"What?"

"I asked if you wanted to come with me to pick up my hard drive. The shop's just down the street from Paradiso. It's cool, they have tons of old—"

I cut him off. "I have to get back. I need to get my stuff and get back to campus."

"Ah. The nightingale returns to her cage," said North.

"Theden is hardly a cage," I retorted.

86

"I wasn't talking about your school." North made a little rectangle with his thumb and index finger and then jerked toward it, as if yanked by a magnet or a leash.

I rolled my eyes, refusing his help as I climbed back over the fence, holding my empty cup with my teeth. A jagged link scratched a line down my forearm, but I didn't react. He hopped over easily, landing lightly on the other side. I walked ahead of him as we made our way back downtown, in a hurry to check my phone. As long as no one had been looking for me, I was probably okay.

"Well, thanks for coming with me," North said when we reached Paradiso's door. "I'd walk you back to campus, but—"

"I'll be fine," I said quickly.

There was an awkward second or two where we just stood there, looking at each other in the near-dark, North with his backpack, his thumbs hooked in his belt loops, me clutching my empty cup with both hands. My brain was yelling at me to get back to campus, but my feet were rooted in place. Then North smiled and started to say something, but I cut him off.

"I probably won't be able to hang out again for a while," I told him. "Things are gonna get busy with school, and I need to focus. Theden is really intense." I needed to say it, to remind myself, but as soon as the words were out, I realized how bitchy I sounded. "Sorry," I said quickly. "It's just that—"

"I wasn't aware that I'd asked to hang out with you again," he said with a smirk. I felt myself flush. "But thanks for letting me know." He turned and headed off down the sidewalk, whistling as he walked.

Hershey was perched on my desk in our bedroom, waiting for me.

"Where were you?" she demanded.

"Library." It was the obvious choice for an alibi, since there was no risk that Hershey had been there. I'd decided on my way back not to tell her where I'd been. She had her secrets. Why shouldn't I have some of my own? I dropped my bag on the floor by my desk and my eye caught the Café Paradiso logo on a half-crumpled napkin inside. I nudged the bag under my desk with my foot. "Why?" I asked, keeping my face neutral. "Were you looking for me?"

"Only for the past two hours," Hershey replied, still studying me with narrowed eyes. "You weren't showing up on Forum."

"My phone was on private," I said with a shrug, which was true. North had toggled the switch before locking it in the cabinet.

"Well, it would've been nice to send me a text," Hershey said, her tone telling me that the inquisition was over. "I was worried about you."

I'd stepped into our closet, so she didn't see me make a face. I highly doubted that my roommate's interest in my whereabouts had anything to do with my well-being. More like she was worried she was missing out on something. I stepped out of my mud-splattered shoes and into a clean pair, exchanging my damp cardigan for a jacket.

"Sorry," I told her when I stepped back out. "Next time, I will." It was a promise I could keep, because next time @ *the library* wouldn't be a lie. Unless I wanted to end up a dropout like my mom, I had to get my head in the game. I was already working out how late I'd have to stay up to finish the homework I'd blown off during my little graveyard excursion. "Ready to eat?" I asked Hershey. Dinner started at six and it was already ten after.

"I wish I had your discipline," she said, linking her arm through mine as we stepped into the hall. "You work *so hard*." I resisted the urge to make another face, since this time Hershey could see me. I'd wondered when she'd bring up the Hepta thing, and this was clearly her segue into it. She'd minimize its significance by emphasizing my effort. But she didn't go where I thought she would. "Doesn't the stress ever get to you?" she asked instead. "The pressure, the expectation. I'll bet the risk of a nervous breakdown is nearly doubled for someone like you."

My mind catapulted to the voice I'd heard earlier. "Someone like me?"

"You know." Hershey waved her hand. "Overachievers. The stressed-out type."

"I'm not on the verge of a breakdown," I said evenly. "Sorry to disappoint."

"Rory, calm down," Hershey said with a tinny laugh, giving

my elbow a squeeze. "I was trying to give you a compliment. You're a rock star. I just wondered if it ever got to you."

"Not so far," I said. My voice was brittle.

We'd reached the stairwell, so I dropped Hershey's elbow and moved ahead of her, down the stairs. The hall below was more crowded than ours had been, a long stream of second-year girls en route to the dining hall. I joined the current, picking up the pace to get some distance from Hershey.

The girls in front of me were walking in a huddle, watching a video clip on one of their handhelds. The screen was out of view, but I could hear the audio and immediately recognized the voice. It belonged to Griffin Payne, the CEO of Gnosis, and a man whose voice was almost as ubiquitous as his face.

"Our lucky beta testers will receive their Gemini Golds next week," he was saying. "And the device will officially go on sale six weeks from today." Gnosis had been hyping its new handheld for more than a year but hadn't yet announced its release. That explained the video. Gnosis didn't pay for ads or ad time, instead relying on viral videos like this one to spread the news about their newest products. "And just in case your eyes weren't green enough with envy already"—Griffin paused for effect—"I give you: the Gemini Gold."

The girls in front of me all reacted.

"Oooh, *adore*," one of them said.

The girl next to her made a face. "You're joking, right? It's so cheesy." Over her shoulder I caught a glimpse of it, a little gold rectangle, no bigger than a matchbook."

"I'm with Amy," a third one said. "I like it."

"Maybe it's a metaphor," the girl on the end said. "Symbolism disguised as aesthetics." The other three turned their heads to look at her. She was wearing ill-fitting jeans and was much less put together than they were, bookish bordering on owlish in her round glasses and pageboy haircut. But they seemed to revere her.

"Leave it to Nora to make an academic exercise out of it," the girl on the end said, but she sounded more envious than mocking. This was the difference between Theden and every other high school, I realized. Here, intelligence was social currency.

"A metaphor for what?" Amy asked.

"Blind veneration," replied Nora, her owlishness suiting her now. "From the golden calf narrative." The others gave her blank looks. "In the Bible? We read it in Ancient Lit last year."

"Hey, I'll worship at the altar of my Gemini anytime," Amy said flippantly. "In Lux I trust."

"And last I checked, Lux couldn't send plagues on people for their disobedience," the first girl chimed in. "So there's that."

I wanted Nora to respond, to elaborate on what she meant, because I could tell there was more to it, but we'd reached the dining hall, and as the crowd funneled through the double doors, I fell behind. As we shuffled in, I looked to see what Beck was up to. The Forum map showed him at Bartell Drugs on Fourth Avenue downtown. His most recent status was near the top of my newsfeed, posted eleven seconds ago.

@BeckAmbrose: u really had to ask? #yesplease #thereisasanta

Beneath it was a screenshot of his in-box. He'd blurred out every text but one.

@Gnosis: Congratulations, @BeckAmbrose, you have been randomly selected to participate in the beta test for the new Gemini Gold! Reply "yes" to accept.

"You've got to be kidding me," I muttered. That the kid who once let a horse pee on his Gemini (on purpose, for a photo) would get the new model months before the rest of us was some sort of sick karmic joke.

I immediately called him. He picked up on the first ring.

"You're so jealous right now," he said, all smug.

"It's so unfair," I pouted. "I would be such a better beta tester."

"No way," Beck replied. "You're way too biased." He was probably right about that.

"So when do you get it?" I asked

"Next week, I think," Beck said. "I have to sign about a hundred nondisclosure forms first. The whole thing's a little Willy Wonka. This thing better do my laundry for me with all the hype. Hey, hold on a sec." I heard fragments of a muffled conversation, then Beck was back. "Hey, Ro, I'll call you later. I'm in line for the flu vac, and some old dude just totally cut. I gotta show him who's boss."

"Good luck with that," I said with a laugh.

"Ohmygod, I want that man to do bad things to me," I heard Hershey say. She was on my heels, the Griffin Payne video playing on her screen. He was demonstrating the features of the tiny golden device, which was clipped to a band on his wrist like an old watch.

"Ew, gross," I replied, making a face. "He's old enough to be your father!"

"Barely," Hershey said, stepping past me into the dining hall.

"Rory!" Rachel called from the serving line. She was standing with Isabel, who turned and waved us over.

As we joined them in line, I felt something I'd never felt in the lunchroom back home, which is probably why Beck and I never ate in it.

I felt like I belonged.

8

"CAN I ASK YOU SOMETHING?"

"Sure," I said, without looking up. Hershey and I were back in our room, doing homework on our beds. In theory, anyway. Hershey had the TV on, and I was staring blankly at my history textbook, thinking about how a certain someone's face looked in the flickering light of the lantern that afternoon.

"At lunch, when the dean came to our table, he said you hadn't let history deter you. What did he mean?"

I kept my eyes on my screen. "Beats me," I said, and rolled over onto my stomach, away from her.

On the bed next to me, my handheld buzzed. I reached for it, grateful for the distraction. It was a text from an unknown number, and there was no message, just a little paper clip symbol signaling an attachment. I tapped it, and my screen went white. A few seconds later something red flashed on screen.

A pi sign came into focus, and I watched as it circled my screen before stopping at the bottom left corner. A dozen other

Greek letters followed it, popping on-screen in little red bursts then circling one another before falling into three horizontal lines.

Η παρουσία σας ζητείται κάτω από την αριστερή πλευρά του Αρχαγγέλου Μιχαήλ στις έντεκα απόψε.
Η επιλογή είναι δική σας. Ελάτε *μόνοι*. Πείτε κανείς.

My name appeared, and the Greek text beneath it morphed into English.

Aurora Aviana Vaughn,
Your presence is requested beneath the left wing of the Archangel Michael at eleven o'clock tonight.
The choice is yours. Come alone. Tell no one.

Within seconds, the words disappeared and my screen went dark. When I tapped my screen, I was back to my in-box. The message from the unknown sender was gone, along with the attachment accompanying it. The hairs on my arms stood on end.

Go.

Well, that confirmed it. The Doubt was indeed bat-shit crazy, just like science said. The left wing of the Archangel had to mean the sculpture in the cemetery. Like hell I was going to a graveyard by myself at eleven o'clock at night. An hour after curfew. Especially without knowing who had invited me.

Go.

I shoved in my earbuds. If the voice wouldn't shut up, I'd drown it out.

But as it got later, I started to waver. Whoever sent the message knew my whole name. That eliminated Forum stalkers and total strangers, since my Forum page only said Rory, and nobody—not even my dad—called me Aurora. The Greek letters, the formalness of the language. It had to be something school related. I'd read about Theden's invite-only campus clubs in the campus brochure but just assumed you had to be a legacy to get in. Then again, I was a legacy. And my class's only Hepta. Plus, it wasn't like the message was threatening. There was no demand. Just a request. *The choice is yours.*

I grabbed my handheld to query Lux, but I stopped when I remembered the text's instructions. *Tell no one.* Did an app on my phone count? It's not like whoever sent that text would know if I consulted Lux about it. Then again, whoever sent that text had somehow remotely erased it. Maybe they would know. Maybe it was a test.

There was only one way to find out.

"I'm tired," I announced, pulling back the covers of my bed. The only way I'd get out of the room without having to explain myself to Hershey was if she was asleep.

"You still have your clothes on," Hershey pointed out.

"Yeah. I do that sometimes." I slid underneath the covers and reached for the light. "Good night."

"Night," Hershey replied. Still watching TV. I squeezed my

eyes shut and waited. She had to be tired. She'd hardly slept last night.

It felt like an eternity before I heard the TV go off. Then Hershey was in the bathroom brushing her teeth. I stole a glance at my handheld. It was ten twenty-nine. I had less than thirty minutes to get out of there. When the water turned off, I slid my Gemini under the covers and deepened my breathing. A few seconds later, the whole room went dark. I lay there and listened. Eventually Hershey's breath steadied. She was asleep.

As quietly as I could, I slid out of bed, grabbed my boots, and slipped out the door.

I reached the cemetery's wrought-iron gate at ten fifty-eight. I'd been prepared to hop the fence again, but to my surprise, the gate was slightly ajar. Whoever orchestrated this had a key.

The cemetery was deserted and dark. I didn't even have the moon to guide me; the sky was black except for a few greenish clouds, remnants of the afternoon's storm. I pulled my handheld from my pocket and switched on its light. The last thing I wanted to do was trip over a headstone and face-plant on some dead guy's grave.

As I approached the meeting spot, I checked the time. The words NO SERVICE were blinking at the top of my screen. My breath hitched a little. What was I doing? It was an hour after curfew on my first day of classes and I was in the middle of a cemetery, again, responding to a cryptic, anonymous invitation. I looked up at the angel. The first time I saw him, I thought his hand was pointing at the exit, but now I saw that it was pointing at the sky. Why did he look so angry? Weren't angels supposed to look . . . angelic?

"Aurora Aviana Vaughn," a voice said out of the darkness, and the hairs on the back of my neck prickled. It was unnatural, mechanical-sounding, but clearly male. Whoever had spoken was using a voice distortion app.

I turned slowly, forcing myself to stay calm as I prepared to meet the owner of this voice. It had come from at least ten yards away, so I could still make a run for it. But the figure before me was completely shrouded in a hooded black robe. It hung over his face, hiding both it and the handheld he was using as a mic, and the fabric brushed the ground as he approached me. He stopped several feet from me and held out his arm. His hand was covered by a long velvet glove and held a blindfold made of the same fabric. He expected me to let him *blindfold* me? Was he nuts?

"If you want to accept our invitation, you have to put this on," he said, his voice buzzing just a little when he spoke. He took a step forward, and the white rubber tip of a sneaker peeked out beneath his robe. He saw it too, and shuffled a little to hide it, stumbling in the process and cursing under his breath. I swallowed a giggle, no longer afraid. This wasn't the grim reaper. He was just a guy in a costume using a voice distortion app. This whole scenario was probably part of some club's hazing ritual, just like I'd thought.

"Okay," I said simply, and turned around so he could tie it

on. The velvet was soft on my skin and smelled like patchouli.

"Open your mouth," he instructed.

"Why?" I asked, or started to, when I felt velvet brush my lips and tasted cherry on my tongue. He'd put something in my mouth. A thin square of plastic, it felt like, but as I tried to push it out with my teeth, it dissolved. "What was that?" I tried to ask, but couldn't form the words. Within seconds, the world went black.

My body tensed the moment I came to. I was sitting upright, as if I'd been awake the whole time, my butt on something hard. Stone steps, I soon realized, in a massive circular arena. It reminded me of the pictures of the Odeon of Herodes Atticus in my history textbook. How long had I been out? There was no arena of this size anywhere near campus that I knew of. I inhaled deeply, trying to get my bearings, and was surprised at how cold the air was in my chest. I felt something heavy on my head and reached for it. It was the hood of a velvet robe like the one my captor had worn. The fabric hung past my fingertips and pooled on the floor beneath me.

Just then there was a flash of light below as a U-shaped ring of torches caught fire around the perimeter of the center stage, casting a flickering glow that barely reached the bottom row of steps. This place really was huge. I looked up at the sky, but there was no sky. Only darkness, like a void.

I looked to my left and could now see several other figures, also in hooded robes, scattered among the steps. I looked to my right and saw five more. They were sitting, motionless, but their heads were moving, like mine, side to side and up and down, scanning the massive room. I jumped as a loud gong reverberated off the stone. It was impossible to tell where the sound had come from, but it filled the arena with its brassy clang. The gong sounded again, and I saw movement below. Figures emerged from the base of the arena onto the center stage. They were robed, but instead of hoods, they were wearing heads of some sort. Elaborate papier-mâché contraptions that sat on their shoulders, exactly how Liam had described the masks for the Masquerade Ball, adorned with bits of real fur and feathers and skin.

I felt my lungs fill with cold air and relief. If these people had the school's masks, they weren't crazy killers. They were associated with Theden like I thought, which meant that I was okay. Feeling my pulse slow, I watched the figures move around the stage, as if performing some odd, silent dance. Then I heard a voice. It sounded female, but I couldn't be sure because it was distorted like the hooded figure's had been. It was coming through speakers behind and above me, and it reverberated off the walls.

"All these at thy command," the voice declared. "To come and play before thee." In choreographed unison, the figures with the animal masks all sunk to their knees as two more figures emerged. Their masks were human—one male, the other female—and resembled ancient Greek sculptures, with sharp features and blank eyes. I leaned forward to get a better look as another voice spoke, this one deeper and more eerie than the last.

"All is not theirs, it seems!" a voice boomed as the gong struck a third time and yet another figure emerged. It had the same black robe as the others, but its mask was twice as large and about five times as ominous. It was the head of a giant serpent, with layers of scales that looked arrestingly real. "Envious commands, invented with design to keep them low." Were these words from a play? The way the serpent delivered them, I thought they might be.

As the serpent figure made its way to a platform at the center of the stage, the male and female figures bowed their unmoving faces in reverence. When he reached the platform, he spread his arms wide, his robe flaring out like a dragon's wings. "Welcome," he said, looking up at us now. "We are glad you have come." I wondered whether the voice actually belonged to the person in the serpent's mask or if we were simply meant to believe that it was. As the voice spoke, the serpent revolved slowly, like a ballerina in an old music box. Behind him, his mask rose into a reptilian hood, like a cobra preparing to strike, and stretched down the wearer's back like the horny tail of a dragon, fanning out behind him at the floor. Even at this distance I could see how intricate the design was, layers and layers of textured papier-mâché with gold leaf outlining each pointy scale.

"There are some who received tonight's invitation but were too afraid, or blind, to accept it. You who have come felt drawn—perhaps without knowing why, or how—to join us. The Greeks called this instinct *nous*. Intuition. Few have it. Your presence here suggests that you do." I squirmed in my seat. It wasn't intuition that brought me here; it was the Doubt. My eyes, now fully adjusted to the flickering dim light, quickly scanned the circle, counting the figures seated on the steps. There were fourteen. Envy flickered inside my chest. They were drawn here by instinct while I'd been chided by a figment in my head.

"Now there is another choice to be made," the serpent said out of the silence. "You have accepted the invitation to know more, and while the full truth must remain obscured for a while longer, we can tell you this: You are being evaluated for membership into a sacred alliance of gifted minds. The next few weeks are a test."

My heart was beating wildly again, out of excitement now instead of fear. The masks, the torches, the archaic speech. This wasn't freaking Junior Beta. This was a legit secret society.

The serpent paused again as the figures on the stage rose to their feet. The two humans flanked the reptile while the other animals began to climb the arena's steps. The figure in the lion mask was directly below me, his painted mesh eyes tilted up toward mine.

"The time has come to choose," the deep voice went on. The lion stopped on the step just beneath me, its eyes at mine, and held out its gloved hands. There was an oversize playing card in each palm. "If you'd like to continue your candidacy, take the card on the right," the voice boomed. "And speak of this to no one. You will hear from us again at the appropriate time." I leaned forward to get a better look. The image was faded but exquisitely rendered, the card a mini painted canvas. The naked woman in the center held a staff in each of her outstretched hands and was hovering above the Earth, encircled by a textured green wreath. Below her were various animal creatures, their upturned faces strikingly similar to the masks I saw onstage. The voice continued. "If, on the other hand, you would prefer not to proceed with the evaluation process, choose the card on the left. No questions will be asked." I slid my eyes over to the lion's other hand. There was less to see on this card, just a single figure, a teenaged boy in a feathered plume hat. He looked like some sort of medieval peddler, a knapsack over his shoulder and a thorny white rose in his fist.

Choose today whom you will serve.

For the first time, my stomach didn't sink when I heard the voice. Instead it lifted a little. Maybe the voice wasn't the Doubt after all, but intuition, like the serpent said. His words had kindled something within me. I wanted to be whoever these people thought I was.

The arena was completely quiet as the candidates considered their choices. I felt the lion watching me even though I couldn't see his eyes. "Take your time," the serpent instructed. But I didn't need any. I reached for the card on the right.

The lion nodded slightly then quickly withdrew his left hand, the card disappearing into the folds of his robe. With his right hand he took my elbow and turned me around so I was facing away from him, and then he tapped my lips with his fingertips. I opened my mouth and felt the thin strip on my tongue again. "I knew you'd get in," the lion whispered then. He wasn't using the distortion app this time, and I recognized his voice immediately. It was Liam.

My awareness returned suddenly, all at once. *Liam!* The lion was Liam. It felt like a major discovery, but of course he'd given his identity away on purpose. He'd wanted me to know.

I was back in my room, sitting upright in my bed, my boots still on my feet. The hooded robe was gone, and there was a stiff paper card in my right hand. My eyes darted to Hershey's bed. It was empty. Had she snuck out again or had she been in that arena too?

I looked down at the card in my hands. I could barely make it out in the dark. Soundlessly, I unlaced my boots and crawled back under the covers, pulling my mom's blanket over me like a tent. If I heard the door unlock, I'd pretend I was asleep.

I held my Gemini up to the card. Unlike the two Liam had offered me earlier, this one wasn't painted in color. It was a single *Z* printed in shiny black ink with the number thirty-two beneath it. My graduation year. My heart was pounding as I ran my fingers over the ink. The symbol and number were different, but the design was identical to the one on my mom's silver pendant.

She was in the society too.

My GoSearch for "secret society at Theden" didn't produce any results. It seemed impossible, but there wasn't a single hit with the words anywhere near one another. I tried "ancient alliance Theden" also to no avail. When I removed the reference to Theden, I got millions of hits. Pages dedicated to conspiracy theories about the Illuminati and the Freemasons and Skull and Bones at Yale, unofficial rosters of past members, even fan pages on Forum. But as soon as I narrowed my search, I came up cold. Whatever this "sacred alliance" was, it was completely off the grid. I felt myself smiling at my screen. A *real* secret society. How cool was that?

I started a text to Beck then quickly erased it. Yes, it was unlikely they could see my texts, but I didn't want to take any chances.

"Please let me get in," I whispered in the dark, palming the pendant like a good luck charm. Then I squeezed my eyes shut and tried to will myself to sleep. Too wired to relax, I started running through the numbers of the Fibonacci sequence in my head. My favorite sleep trick. The math nerd version of counting sheep. I'd been doing it for years, anytime I was tired but couldn't turn my mind off: 0, 1, 1, 2, 3, 5, 8, 13, 21, 34, 55, 89, 144, 233, 377, 610, 987, 1,597 . . . At some point my brain gave up and I fell asleep.

9

I DIDN'T HEAR HERSHEY COME IN, but she was back in her bed when I woke up the next morning. She was still asleep when I got out of the shower, so I went to breakfast alone. Liam was at the waffle station when I walked in. He pretended not to see me, but it was so obvious he did.

"Mornin'," he said casually as I stepped up beside him and ladled batter into the grooved ceramic plates.

"So many questions."

"They'll all be answered," he replied in a low voice, spreading butter onto his steaming waffle. "*If* you get in."

"Last night you said you knew I would. Now you're saying I might not?"

"I'm saying you have to be evaluated," he replied. "All the candidates do. And until the council vets you—"

"The council?"

Liam winced. "Forget you heard that. Listen, Rory, I know it's exciting and confusing and a lot to take in. I was in your shoes a year ago. I know exactly how it feels. But you have to respect the process. And I can't break my vows."

"Can you at least tell me how I got chosen? Is it because I'm a Hepta?"

"That's not the only reason," Liam replied. "But it's the reason you got the Zeta."

"The Z on the card?"

Liam nodded. "Every candidate is assigned a Greek letter," he explained, glancing behind us to make sure no one was in earshot. "Zeta has a numerical value of seven, so they always give it to a Hepta. If you get in, it'll become your society name," he explained, reaching for a bottle of maple syrup. "The letter and your class year. It keeps the membership list completely anonymous." I didn't know the alphabet well enough to know which letter was on my mom's pendant, but I could easily find out.

"What's yours?" I asked.

His expression darkened. "Look, Rory, I can't talk to you about this. I've already said too much."

"Is the secrecy really necessary?" I whined. "And what about the people who picked the card on the left last night? They know about the society and have no incentive to keep it to themselves."

"Person, singular," Liam corrected. "There was only one." He nodded toward a kid sitting two tables away. I recognized him from my comp sci class. "That tab we put on your tongues was something called ZIP," he explained, keeping his voice low. "It inhibits an enzyme in the brain that enables you to remember stuff. If we'd given you a stronger second dose, your memories of the tomb wouldn't have stuck."

"That's what he got?" I asked, still watching the boy. He was spooning oatmeal in his mouth, his eyes vacant, like he was still half-asleep.

The corners of Liam's mouth turned up in a little impish grin. "Along with a tiny dose of Rohypnol."

"You *roofied* him?"

Liam rolled his eyes. "Hardly. It was the prescription kind, and just enough to make him think that any memory fragments he has left are from a dream." Liam pulled out his Gemini, which was lit up with a new text. "I gotta go," he told me. "We can talk later. But not about this," he warned. "I mean it, Rory. No more questions."

"Fine," I said. "But can you at least tell me if Hershey was there? Last question, I promise."

"Hershey?" He let out a single, biting laugh. "No. Hershey was most definitely not there."

"You're acting like it was ridiculous for me to even ask," I scoffed as he stepped past me.

He didn't look back. "That's because it was."

I developed a routine that week, one I told myself I'd stick with until exams. Every day after my last class I'd stop at the dining hall's coffee cart for a vanilla cappuccino then head to the library to do homework. It kept me from falling behind, but mostly it kept me from going back to Paradiso to see North, which is what I thought about doing every afternoon at four o'clock when I'd get a craving for a matcha latte and start rationalizing a quick walk downtown. *It wouldn't be to see North,* I'd assure myself. *He's probably not even working.* But every day I'd remind myself that I knew better, and I'd decide against it. If I wanted to excel at Theden, I had to stay focused. I couldn't get distracted, especially not by a townie who would never understand why I cared so much about academics anyway.

My brain, apparently, hadn't gotten the message. We'd talked about the perils of distraction in practicum that morning and I'd zoned out halfway through wondering whether North had tattoos anywhere other than his arms.

Excellent.

At least the Doubt had finally shut back off. I hadn't heard it since that moment in the arena. I hadn't heard from the society again either—whatever their "evaluation" was, it didn't seem to have started yet. Which was good, because I was barely sleeping as it was. Despite the fact that we had enough homework to fill every waking hour between classes, there were a bunch of on-campus activities that first week that we were "strongly encouraged" to attend. Wednesday was the first-year bonfire and marshmallow roast, Thursday was the first pep rally, and this afternoon was a sign-up fair for intramural sports. I'd gone to the first two but was skipping the last one. I was all about joining, but the idea of playing softball or ultimate Frisbee on a regular basis made me want to pluck my eyeballs out.

"We should get Thai food tonight," Hershey said as we bussed our trays after lunch. We were with Isabel and Rachel again. The four of us had started sitting together at every meal and hanging out in the common room at night. Izzy was self-deprecating and smart and struggled with her weight. Rachel was fearless and funny and had an opinion about everything. I liked them both a lot. But their bank accounts were in the realm of Hershey's, and mine most definitely was not. We'd gone out for pizza after the pep rally and gotten Indian take-out on Tuesday night. Both times Hershey had ordered for us—white truffle pizza and 24-karat dosa, both ridiculously expensive—and both times we'd split the check four ways. I didn't have to consult Lux to know I couldn't afford this trend.

"Yum," Isabel declared. "I'm in."

"Me too," Rachel chimed in.

Hershey arched an eyebrow at me.

"Sure," I said, swallowing a sigh. I knew I could just ask Hershey to pay my share—she'd offered when we'd gotten the take-out—but I didn't want to. I told myself it was because I didn't think it was fair to her, but the truth was I didn't want to remind the other girls how different I was from them. And by different, I meant not rich.

It was an odd thing, being at a school that gave a free ride to all its students and being in the socioeconomic minority. Pretty much everyone at Theden was wealthy. And not just my-parents-are-doctors-and-lawyers wealthy. My classmates had serious money, the kind that went back generations and would be waiting for them in trust funds when they turned eighteen. It was tempting to assume their money had gotten them in—after all, that's what Hershey thought about herself—until you heard them speak. They were exceptionally, dauntingly intelligent.

Hershey wasn't in our room when I got back that afternoon, so I dropped my bag and wandered outside. There were tables set up on the sidewalk and music blaring from speakers on the lawn. Kids in intramural T-shirts were holding sign-up sheets and handing out candy.

Avoiding the fray, I pulled out my phone and headed away from the courtyard, toward the practice fields. I hadn't checked my newsfeed since breakfast, so there was a lot to catch up on. At 1:53 p.m. PST Beck had posted a selfie of himself standing next to a glossy print of a boat passing under Ballard Bridge with the status *I thought I was at an art gallery. apparently not.* I tapped the comment button and wrote, *ooh, that'd be perfect for my closet.*

Beck didn't reply right away, so I kept scrolling down, skimming statuses, until suddenly it got colder and the glare on my screen disappeared. I looked up and saw a rust-colored canopy above me. I'd crossed into the woods. Now that I was paying attention, I could hear the crinkle of leaves brushing against one another and the distant rush of the river and, if I listened really closely, the sound of my classmates in the quad. I clicked out of my newsfeed and over to my newest playlist, sliding down the volume before I pressed play so I could still hear the rustle of the trees.

I stayed out of the cemetery, walking alongside the fence instead, toward the polo fields and the stables where the team kept its horses. The girls' field hockey team was playing a scrimmage on the practice field, so I sat on the hill to watch. If I kept my eyes on the ball as it shot from stick to stick, I could almost not think about North.

My Gemini buzzed just as the whistle blew at the end of the scrimmage. The sun was beginning its descent beyond the horizon, taking the afternoon's warmth with it. It would be dark soon.

@HersheyClements: what r u doing?

Watching FH scrimmage, I typed. Omitting *avoiding you* and *thinking about North.*

@HersheyClements: get ur ass back here. we r going to din. Xo

"We're leaving in sixty seconds," she announced when I came through the door. "We have to eat early because Izzy wants to digest before bed." Our dress fittings for the Masquerade Ball were the next day, and Izzy had been dieting all week so she could fit into a smaller size. According to Lux she was still seven pounds over her recommended weight, which seemed crazy to me. She was curvy, not fat, and her waist was tiny. I had my own anxieties about tomorrow's fittings. With zero boobs, short legs, and a body like a ruler, I wasn't a girl who looked good in formal wear. At homecoming the year before, I could've passed as a fourth-grader playing dress-up. Likely the reason I didn't have a date.

"I'll meet you guys downtown," I said, stepping past Hershey into our room. "I'm gonna take a shower first."

She sighed like I'd just ruined the entire evening.

"Izzy's fitting is at nine tomorrow," she said. "Which means we need to be finished eating by eight forty-five so she has a full twelve hours to de-bloat."

"Well, *we* feel disgusting and want to take a shower," I replied. "So you can either wait for me, or I can meet you guys there." I knew she wouldn't offer to wait.

"Whatever," she said, grabbing my Gemini from my hand. "It's Thaiphoon on Drake Street." With uncanny speed, she added the restaurant to my planner and pinned the location on my map. "Here." She handed the handheld back to me and sauntered out.

I switched my location status to private, then quickly showered and changed into my one pair of semi-expensive jeans (a going-away present from my stepmom) and a silk T-shirt I found at my favorite thrift store in Seattle. It was a little low-cut, so I switched my mom's pendant to a longer chain that would lay heavy on my collar, keeping me from flashing my decidedly unsexy bra every time I leaned forward. I'd seen

Hershey wear a hoodie as though it was a blazer, so I tried that, cuffing the sleeves and letting it hang open, the hood tucked inside the back collar. Twenty minutes and two impatient texts from Hershey later, I was on my way out the door. The sun had dipped below the mountains, so I opted for the street route this time, passing through the imposing campus gates before turning onto Academy Drive, a straight shot to the west end of downtown.

The restaurant was a block north of Café Paradiso, which meant unless I wanted to take some crazy back-alley route behind it, I'd have to walk past the café's entrance. As I approached the propped open door, butterflies nipped at my chest. "You're being ridiculous," I muttered under my breath. Still, I kept my head down as I passed by the café, pretending to be absorbed in a text. Really I was just typing the words *ridiculous ridiculous ridiculous* over and over in my notepad.

"Hey."

I choked on my gum then tripped on nothing. North caught me by the elbow as my Gemini clattered onto the sidewalk, bouncing a little on its rubber corners. My gum was stuck to the cement.

"Easy there," he said. He bent to pick up my handheld. Heat flooded my cheeks as I saw him glance at my screen. "I think adorable is a better fit," he said, handing it back to me. He smelled like bar soap and Earl Grey tea. "Cool hoodie."

"I'm on my way to dinner," I blurted out. My eyelids were firing like a camera shutter, *blink blink blink blink*

blink. The scent, his nearness, these things had come out of nowhere. It was taking me a second to recover. I put my hands in my pockets and tried to look blasé. "Thaiphoon." I pointed at the sign ahead, as if he might not believe me. "I should probably—" *Go* was the word that came next, but it got caught in my throat somewhere as our eyes met. There it was again. That feeling of familiarity. Like I knew him better than I did.

"Do you *really* want to eat overpriced, small-portioned vegan Thai food right now?" he asked.

"I sense you have a better idea," I said wryly. He smiled.

"I do. An underpriced, oversized, Italian meatball sub."

"The boy who drinks matcha and uses stevia eats meatball subs?"

"Hell, yeah," North replied. "And because you have a skeptical look on your face, your acceptance of my offer just became mandatory." He lifted my Gemini from my hand. "What's your password?" he asked.

"I'm not telling you my password!"

"Fine. Enter it yourself then." He handed it back to me.

"And why am I doing this?" I asked as I punched out the numbers.

"Necessary precautions," he said when I handed it back to him. "We can't have all your throngs of Forum followers finding out about Theden's best-kept secret. Giovanni might raise his prices on us." He blinked in surprise. "Your handheld's already in private mode."

"Why is that so astounding?"

"Because you're a Forum girl," he replied. "The whole point of the platform is to facilitate the constant narration of your all-important life. What will your followers think if they don't know where you are at all times? How will you possibly stay relevant?"

I made a face. "Are you always this cynical?"

"Yes." He handed my Gemini back to me. "Why'd you go private?"

"My roommate was bugging me. Why is your laptop ginormous?" I pointed at his messenger bag. It wouldn't close, his computer was so big.

"It's an antique," he replied. "I was actually on my way to a repair shop a few blocks down. You mind coming with, then we'll get the subs?"

I was already sending Hershey a text. Not feeling well. :(Gonna skip dinner.

"Your roommate?" North asked with a nod at my screen. I nodded back.

"The girl with me the day we met," I said, toggling the vibrate switch to off before slipping my Gemini into my back pocket. I preferred to save my butt from the text storm that was sure to ensue. "Yeah, I remember her. She's pretty hard to forget." North was looking the other way, readjusting his shoulder strap, so I couldn't see his face. "We should get going," he said then. "Shop closes at seven."

I nodded, suddenly self-conscious. Memorable was

something I was not. I was the girl who blended into the background, easy to forget.

The repair shop was tucked into an alley, its entrance hidden behind a nondescript brick wall, and wasn't the fancy electronics shop I was expecting. It was cramped and crowded with dated gadgets and gizmos and some random jewelry that appeared to be for sale but didn't have price tags.

"Hey, NP," the girl behind the counter said, looking up from the Gemini in her hands. She was my age, maybe younger, and punk pretty, with hot-pink bobbed hair and a platinum-studded button nose.

"Noelle, this is Rory," North said. "She goes to the Academy. Rory, this is Noelle. Her grandfather owns this place."

"Hi," I said.

"Wow, you go to Theden?" Noelle asked. "That's so cool. I just started my application. Any tips?"

"I'm still surprised they let me in," I admitted. "I'm sure you'll get in too," I told her, because that's what people say, when really I was thinking that whoever did her psych eval would make something of her decision to dye her hair pink and put holes in her nose. Nobody at Theden looked like that.

"So what's wrong with it?" she asked North, picking up his clunky silver laptop. The overhead light glinted off the surface of a gold locket in the glass cabinet below, drawing my eye. It was dove shaped with a tiny hinge on the left side. There was a tiny blue gem at the bird's eye and silver etching at its wing. It looked so out of place among the other, bulkier pieces, so delicate and feminine amid the heap of gold watches and gray plastic video consoles.

"Hard drive's fried," I heard North say. My eyes were still on the locket. "I'd toss the thing, but I'm sort of attached. Think Ivan can fix it?"

"He can fix anything." Noelle slipped the laptop into a padded ziplock bag then began typing out a claim ticket. She knew North's contact info from memory. "You need a loaner in the meantime?" she asked, swiveling the touchscreen for North to sign. "Oh, wait, you have, like, seven other computers."

"Nine, actually," North said with a grin.

It took a sec for this to register. "You own *nine* computers? Do you collect them or something?" I asked.

"Old computers are sort of a hobby of mine," North said as he lifted his bag back on his shoulder. "So you'll call me when it's ready?" he asked Noelle.

"Yep," she said, reaching for her Gemini.

"Good luck with your Theden app," I told her.

"Thanks," she said distractedly, already back to her handheld. North pulled the door open for me and I stepped outside into the alley.

"And now," he said as he joined me on the pavement, "dinner." He pointed at the green awning next door. GIOVANNI'S was printed in peeling white letters.

I was expecting a fast-food place, but Giovanni's was a sit-down restaurant with a handful of white-clothed tables. Giovanni himself was in the kitchen. He greeted North with a bear hug that left a tomato sauce stain on the back of North's T-shirt and quickly went to work on our sandwiches, which, North explained, weren't on the menu. He used to eat at Giovanni's when he was a kid, and Giovanni noticed that North never ate his spaghetti. He'd pick the meatballs off and put them between two pieces of garlic bread, then douse the whole thing in marinara. So one day Giovanni brought out North's creation just the way the little boy liked it and had been making it for him ever since.

"So you grew up here?" I asked as we headed out, our sandwiches in a bag under North's arm.

"Boston," North replied, leading the way down the narrow alley behind Main Street. "But we used to visit here a lot to see my aunt. She owns Paradiso," he explained. "She hardly ever comes in anymore, though."

"And your parents . . . ?"

"My dad's still in Boston," he said. "Trying to pretend his only son isn't a high school dropout. My mom died when I was three."

Suddenly it made sense. The familiarity. He had a dead mom too. With all the technology out there to prevent accidents and cure illnesses, we momless were a rare breed. I was the only kid at Roosevelt without one, and probably the only kid at Theden, too. I wanted to tell North I was like him, but the words got lodged in my throat.

"Why'd you drop out of school?" I asked instead.

He glanced back at me. "School just wasn't my thing."

"So now you just make coffee?"

His eyes clouded. "I'm sorry I fall short of your standards."

"I didn't mean it that way," I said quickly, flushing. "You don't fall short of my standards. I don't even have standards."

"A girl like you should have standards." He was wearing that amused smile again. "High ones." He'd stopped in front of the back entrance to Paradiso. There was another door right beside it, made of metal instead of glass. "That is, as long as said standards do not prevent you from having dinner with an older, just-makes-coffee-for-a-living high school dropout in his empty apartment," North said, twisting the knob on the metal door.

The words *empty apartment* reverberated in my head. "Exactly how old is he?" I asked as I stepped past him, trying to sound coy and not totally freaked out by the idea. Inside the door was a flight of stairs going up. North closed the door behind us and turned both bolts.

"Seventeen," he said, starting up the stairs. My legs felt weak beneath me as I followed him up. I'd never even been in a boy's bedroom—except Beck's, and Beck didn't count.

There was a second door at the landing, with a doorbell button next to the knob and two deadbolts in the frame. North unlocked the door, using a different key on each bolt and a third one for the knob. *What was with all the locks?*

I didn't need Lux to tell me I didn't belong here. I should've been with my classmates, if not at Thaiphoon with Hershey

120

and the girls, then back on campus in the dining hall, eating roasted sea bass and Swiss chard and talking about string theory or Jane Austen. But *should* didn't matter much right then, because doing what I was supposed to do would mean missing out on this.

"After you," North said, pushing the door open.

10

THE FRONT DOOR OPENED into the living room, which wasn't actually a room but just a couch, a coffee table, and an overstuffed bookshelf sandwiched between a tiny kitchen and an even tinier sleeping area.

"So you live alone?" I asked as I followed North into the kitchen. I figured he had to, since there was only one twin-size bed.

He nodded as he unwrapped our sandwiches. "This place came with Paradiso's lease. When I started talking about moving out here for good, my aunt offered to let me live up here for free." He took a bite of his sub. Marinara sauce dribbled down his chin. I examined my own sandwich, wishing I had a knife and fork. "Just go for it," North said. "There's no un-messy way to do it. But after your first taste, you won't care."

He was right. The ingredients by themselves were pretty unremarkable, but somehow together they became oh-my-gosh-you-have-to-try-this delicious. I wished for a second that Lux were running so I could mark this sandwich a favorite. Then again, Giovanni's meatball sandwich, like North's matcha latte, wasn't on anybody's menu, so its flavor profile couldn't be cross-referenced against my consumption history or added to my preference hierarchy.

"Wanna watch a movie?" North asked, his voice muffled with meatball.

I quickly dabbed at the corners of my mouth. "You have a box?"

"Not a GoBox, but a laptop with a DVD player and a bunch of DVDs." He pointed at the bottom row of the bookshelf, which was lined with plastic cases instead of books. "Pick one."

I walked over and scanned the titles. *Rudy, Rocky, Bull Durham, Hoosiers.* "These are all old sports movies," I pointed out.

"Oh, but they're so much more than that," replied North. "Have you seen any of them?"

I shook my head. "Which is your favorite?" North thought for a second then grinned. "Sit," he instructed. "I'll put it on. I don't want you to know anything about it going in." He went to the shelf and grabbed a case I hadn't gotten to yet then kept his back to me so I couldn't see the title.

I pulled my handheld from my pocket to check the time. I had six texts from Hershey, the most recent of which she'd sent three minutes ago and was written in all caps.

@HersheyClements: WHERE ARE U?!?!

I quickly checked her location. Drake and Main. She was still at the restaurant.

"Your roommate again?" North asked.

"Uh-huh. I'm telling her I'm at the library so she'll leave me alone."

"Don't lie. Not over text, anyway. Just don't answer."

"She won't know I'm lying," I told him. "I'm private right now."

"Doesn't matter. Your location is hidden from the outside world, but your Gemini still knows your GPS coordinates. And even if Lux isn't running, it's logging it."

"How do you know?"

"Because it says so in the terms of use."

"You've read the terms of use?"

North raised his eyebrows. "You haven't?"

"Oh, come on. Nobody reads the terms of use."

He shook his head. "You realize how whacked that is, right? You let Lux make decisions for you and you don't even know how it makes them?"

I ignored this. "Okay, let's say you're right—"

"Which I am."

"And Lux does know where I am right now. Why does it matter if I lie about it?"

"Because Lux uses a slicing algorithm," North replied. "Which means it's designed to detect patterns in events based only on narrow glimpses of a user's experience. Let's say you've been identified by Lux as a person who lies only when she feels guilty or when she's trying not to hurt someone's feelings or when she's doing something she knows she probably shouldn't be doing, like, I dunno, hanging out in some older guy's apartment." I saw the hint of a smile. "If you lie about where you are right now, then Lux will gather whatever data it can about this situation—including your location coordinates—and redirect you away from situations like this in the future. And I, for one, don't want that to happen."

It sounded a little conspiracy-theory paranoid to me, but the truth was I had no idea how Lux worked. Every time I got a pop-up box with a privacy notice or an update to the terms of use, I just hit "accept."

I set my Gemini facedown on the coffee table and looked over at North. "So are we watching the movie or what?"

"So what'd you think?" North asked when the credits began to roll.

"It was . . . interesting," I said.

"So you hated it."

"No! I liked it. It's just— I'm not sure how I'm supposed to feel about it, that's all. The voice in Ray's head was supposed to be the Doubt, right? So are we supposed to feel sorry for him?"

North made a sound like a laugh. "You're supposed to feel moved. Inspired."

I felt myself squirm. The story *was* inspiring, that was the problem. Its message made me uneasy. The main character hears this voice in his head saying "If you build it, he will come," so he decides to build a baseball diamond in his cornfield, and all these dead baseball players show up to play in it. Besides being totally random (why exactly were these baseball players just hanging around, looking for someplace to play?), I found it super irritating that we were supposed to buy that the guy just automatically knows what the voice means. The phrase is cryptic and totally vague and yet Ray somehow understands that "If you build it, he will come" means "Build a baseball diamond in your cornfield"? Yeah. Okay. I can totally see how he'd figure that out.

"It was just . . . implausible," I said carefully, not wanting to totally tear into North's favorite movie.

"Says who?"

I looked at him. "Um, me? A voice in his head told him to build a *baseball diamond.* In a *cornfield.*"

"And look what happened," North replied. "He saved his farm. Made peace with his father. Brought people joy. Think of where he would've ended up if he hadn't listened."

I started to point out that losing one's farm might be preferable to losing one's mind, but I stopped when I saw North glance over at the wooden cuckoo clock on the wall. It was quarter to nine already.

"I should go," I said quickly, before he could suggest it, and got to my feet. "Thanks for the sandwich. And the movie."

"We should do it again sometime," North said as he followed me to the door. "Now that I know that you're more of a

Rocky girl. No dead dudes or un-embodied voices in that one. Just stubbornness and punching."

"Perfect," I said, and stepped over the threshold onto the landing. I expected him to come out with me, but when I turned back around, he'd stepped farther back into his apartment, his body tucked behind the open door. I swallowed my disappointment. "Bye," I said, giving him a little wave before turning away.

"Hey, Rory?"

"Yes?" *Thank God* shot through my head as I spun on my toes to face him. Maybe actually kissing him would put an end to all the thinking about it. My heart was drumming in my chest as I looked up at him, channeling a girl who knew how to be kissed. I wasn't actually; the only boyfriend I'd ever had was in ninth grade and kissing him was like kissing a fish, all pinched lips and closed mouths.

"Don't mention that we hung out to Hershey, okay?"

My heart felt like someone had squeezed it. She was so unforgettable that he remembered her name. I was certain I hadn't said it.

"Sure." My voice sounded flat.

"It's nothing personal, it's just—"

"It's fine," I said, flashing a smile. "I get it." Before the moment got any more awkward, I turned and descended the stairs. Halfway down, I heard his door close.

He's a private person, I told myself as I walked back to campus. "Or he's completely embarrassed to be associated with you," I muttered.

When I got to the courtyard, my eyes scanned the windows until I got to my own. The light was on. Hershey was still awake. With a sigh, I pulled out my Gemini to let myself in the main door. There was a new text on my screen.

BLOCKED NUMBER

A man built a rectangular house.

His windows all faced south.

What color was the bear outside?

As soon as I tapped the message, another one appeared:

You have thirty seconds to respond.

Instantly my heart was racing. It was from the society; it had to be. Part of their evaluation. But the question made no sense. What did the shape of the man's house have to do with the color of the bear he saw? I felt myself start to panic. Was it a trick question? How could I possibly know what color the bear was unless I knew what *kind* of bear it was, and how could I know what kind it was unless I knew where the—

Suddenly it clicked. *His windows all faced south.* The house was in the North Pole. The bear was a polar bear. To the man, it would look white. I quickly typed my answer. Within seconds I got another text.

Well done, Zeta.

My breath whistled through my teeth as I let go of the breath I was holding. One down. How many more of these would there be?

Still jittery with adrenaline, I went to the common room for some tea. There was a group of second-years playing Scrabble on the couches, so I sat at one of the long study tables instead. An hour later I was still there, hunched over my screen, working through the hardest word puzzles I could find, the chamomile cold in my cup. Next time I heard from the society, I'd be ready.

I woke to the sound of a finger tapping a screen and the whoosh sound of e-pages turning. Hershey was sitting cross-legged on her bed, flipping through *Vogue* on her tablet. She'd been asleep when I finally made it back to our room at midnight, saving me from the inevitable inquisition. Or, rather, postponing it until now.

"If you didn't want to come with us, you should've just said that from the beginning," she said the moment I opened my eyes.

"I stopped by the public library and got sidetracked," I told her, rubbing my eyes. I'd never actually been in the redbrick building downtown, but I'd read that it was open until eleven on Fridays and Saturdays, and based upon what Hershey already thought of me, it wasn't a stretch for her to believe that's where I'd choose to spend a Friday night.

Hershey was an excellent reader of people so I was fully

prepared for her to call bullshit on my act. But she just sighed. "I worry about you, Rory. You're working too hard." *Relative to you, everyone is,* my brain shot back. Hershey hadn't set foot in the library since we arrived on campus, and I hadn't once seen her study. She tossed her tablet aside. "But I get it," she said. "I just missed you, is all."

I softened. Why was I so critical of her? Sure, she had her flaws and sometimes she said things that made me want to tear my skin off, but she was completely inclusive. She was making an effort to be my friend and I was treating her like crap.

"We should go soon," Hershey said, scooting off her bed. "We don't want to be late for our fitting."

We took the street route downtown. Hershey was walking fast, so I pulled out my handheld to double-check our appointment time. We were both scheduled for ten o'clock, and it was only 9:45. At this rate, we'd be ten minutes early.

The shop was on the south end of Main Street, which was good because it meant we wouldn't have to pass by Paradiso on the way. I still hadn't decided how to feel about North's don't-tell-Hershey-about-us comment, but I certainly wasn't about to go strolling by with her the very next day. He'd think I was doing it on purpose to make some sort of point.

"Your destination is on your left," Lux announced as we arrived in front of a shop with a frosted glass door. Through the display window, I saw racks and racks of brightly colored gowns, each covered in clear plastic, and a girl from my section on the tailor block. There was another one waiting in a chair nearby. "Your appointment is in eleven minutes."

"Perf," Hershey declared. "We have time for a coffee." She set off down the sidewalk toward Paradiso.

"Why don't we try River City Beans?" I suggested, hurrying to catch up with her. The only thing worse than walking by with Hershey was walking in with her.

"Because Paradiso is right here," I heard Hershey say. She stepped up to the café's bay window and smiled. "And so is he."

Hershey pulled the door open and sauntered inside. North looked up when the bell jingled, his eyes locking with mine. He held my gaze for a second then flicked his eyes to Hershey. No smile, no greeting, not an iota of recognition in his eyes. I fought disappointment. "Hey, Rory," came a female voice. It was the girl with the shaved head I'd met the day I went to the cemetery with North. We hadn't exchanged names, so North must've told her mine.

I angled my body toward her so North was out of my sightline. If he was going to ignore me, I was happy to reciprocate. "Can I get a medium vanilla cap?" I asked her. "Triple shot."

"And for you?" she asked Hershey.

"Just black coffee," Hershey replied. "A large." I expected Hershey to turn her attention back to North—from her comment at the door, I assumed that's why we came—but she didn't. "How do you know her?" Hershey asked me as the girl went to work on our drinks.

"I came in on my way to the library last night," I said

vaguely. Then, as casually and disinterestedly as I could muster, "Isn't that the guy you thought was so hot?"

"Not hot," Hershey corrected. "Mildly sexy. And that was only because I was jet-lagged and tired and not thinking straight." She glanced over her shoulder at North. I could see him out of the far corner of my eye, washing the milk canisters at the sink. "So," her voice was louder now, as if she were broadcasting whatever she was about to say, "Did I tell you I'm seeing someone?"

So that explained the late night sneak-outs. I tried to look surprised. "You are?"

Hershey nodded dramatically. "It's kind of scandalous," she said. "So we're keeping it a secret. But the chemistry is *intense*." She glanced back at North again. Clearly to see if he was listening. He wasn't looking at us, but I knew he'd heard her. Everyone in the café had. She was a hot girl using her outside voice to talk about hooking up. People paid attention to that.

"Does he go to Theden?" I asked.

Hershey gave me a mysterious smile.

"Your appointment starts in two minutes," I heard Lux say as the girl with the shaved head put our drinks on the bar.

I took a sip of mine and smiled. "Yum. So much better than the matcha drink I had last time." It was childish, and not even much of a jab, but I couldn't help it. I saw Hershey glance at North again as she reached for her coffee.

"Are you really seeing someone?" I asked Hershey when

we were back on the sidewalk.

"I use the term *seeing* loosely," she said, looping her arm through mine. "Hooking up with in varied and unconventional places is more accurate." I was intrigued and mildly grossed out. How unconventional were we talking here? Against my will, my mind leaped to the dream I'd spent the morning trying to forget. North and I, on the floor of the mausoleum, in the rain. All at once I was fuming, and the more I thought about the way he'd just treated me, the angrier I got. He's sweet as can be to me when we're alone and acts like he doesn't know me when Hershey's around? God, it was so *transparent*. And offensive. He obviously didn't want me to tell Hershey that we'd hung out because he was trying to keep his options open. I was most irritated at myself for agreeing to keep it a secret. I should've said, *Here's a better idea, asshole: Let's not hang out at all.*

"So which will it be?" I heard the shop owner ask, interrupting the who-do-you-think-you-are speech I was giving North in my head. I'd tried on six dresses, five that Lux had chosen for me and one that Hershey had picked, gowns that belonged on celebrities, not sixteen-year-old nobodies with knobby knees and crappy posture, but I still couldn't decide. Hershey had gone with the first dress she'd put on, a floor-length red sheath with a plunging neckline and a thigh-high slit up the side. I thought the shop owner was going to have a coronary when Hershey came out of the dressing room in it.

"Um," I said for about the nine hundredth time. The dress I had on was pretty. Black and strapless and simple. I started to tell her I'd just take this one when Hershey piped up.

"She'll take the Dior," she said, pointing at the green taffeta ball gown on the rack beside me. It was the one she'd picked out for me, a dress I never would've chosen for myself—bright and big with jewels on the bodice and layers and layers of crinoline underneath. But it fit, and the color made me look decidedly less pasty than normal, so I nodded my assent.

As I was pulling on my jeans, my Gemini buzzed.

New Forum message!

@KatePribulsky: sorry for before. will explain l8r. can u come over tonight?

I didn't recognize the name so I zoomed in on the profile pic. Shaved head, pierced nose. It was the girl who worked with North. Since she clearly didn't have anything to apologize for, the message had to be from him.

To my great annoyance, my heart fluttered at the thought. So pathetic.

I punched out can't tonight then blocked @KatePribulsky from my account.

11

THE FOLLOWING FRIDAY, after a particularly brutal beating in practicum, I slipped into my seat in Cog Psych and audibly exhaled. Not only was the Masquerade Ball tomorrow, but I had a two-day break from the Beast. Aka, Dr. Tarsus.

Her class continued to be fifty-five minutes of unadulterated hell every morning. It wasn't the subject matter I hated, or the format. Just her. Anytime I tried to participate in class, I got hammered for it. My comments were "short-sighted" or "misguided" or "woefully off the mark." When I stayed quiet, she blasted me for not participating. I couldn't win.

I docked my Gemini and pulled out my tablet to sync up. We'd been moving through the physical architecture of the brain, and today we were supposed to cover the frontal lobe. But the screen at the front of the room was dark. Rudd was coming around with his handheld, stopping at each desk. Witty and approachable, Kyle Rudman was the anti-Tarsus, and by far my favorite teacher.

"Were we supposed to start on chapter three?" someone asked in a panicked voice.

"Nope," Rudd replied as he stepped up to my desk. "We've still got another two days on chapter two. We're just taking a time-out to talk about your research projects." He reached for my handheld. "Hey, Rory. You've got APD, right?"

My mouth went dry. I knew he was asking about my topic, but the way he phrased it stirred the little well of fear at the base of my spine. I hadn't heard the voice since that moment in the arena, but I kept thinking about it. I was seriously questioning my choice of paper topics, wishing I'd trusted Lux after all. Every time I started reading a journal article or a scholarly paper, the nagging uncertainty would creep back in. I'd catch myself questioning the science, trying to poke holes in the research—which, by the way, was a lot less conclusive than I'd been taught to believe. There were theories about how the elimination of synaptic connections in the frontal lobe could cause auditory hallucinations, but no real proof, a fact that every science textbook—and teacher—I'd ever had had completely glossed over. There were moments when I felt certain that there was more to the Doubt than the research let on. Was this why Lux had steered me away from picking APD as my topic? Did the app somehow know that I'd react like this? That in itself was alarming. Virtually every source I'd found talked about the fact that there were some people who were predisposed to hear the voice and less capable of blocking it out. Was I one of them?

"Rory?"

"Uh, yeah," I said. "APD." Rudd punched a button on his handheld and a new icon appeared on my screen. It was red with the letters DPH in the center and had a little lock symbol at the upper right corner.

"You've all been given limited access to the Department of Public Health's medical records database," Rudd said as he returned to the front of the room. "Your login has been coded to the research topic you selected, allowing you to review the med records for patients who suffered from the mental illness you're studying." He picked up his tablet off his desk and tapped the DPH icon. The app launched on the screen at the front of the room. "Now, I know what some of you are thinking," he deadpanned as he logged himself in. "You're hoping this means you'll be able to prove once and for all that your frenemy is a certified nut job. But, alas, your access is limited to *dead* crazies, and this particular database is anonymous anyway, which means the only identifying information you'll have are gender, ethnic origin, and birth and death dates." He made a face of mock disappointment, and we all laughed.

Once inside the database, Rudd gave us a brief tutorial on how to search by diagnosis and how to filter our results. "The point here is for you to play sleuth. To look for clues as to how the pathology you're studying affects a patient's wellness, to find patterns and consistencies among different patients, and to reason through the trajectory from diagnosis to death. What are the pivot points? How could healthcare policy be improved to give sufferers of your illness a better quality of life?"

Seeing how the Doubt had ruined people's lives would no doubt help silence my inner skeptic. Sign me up.

The girls were already in the dining hall when I got to lunch. Izzy was at the salad bar, studying her screen. "It just says cucumbers," she said as I walked up. "Does that mean I can have an unlimited amount of them?" She looked at me for the answer. She'd been using Lux to help her diet for the Ball and was a half a pound from her goal.

"I think so?"

"Excellent," she said, dumping the entire container onto her plate.

I grabbed a tray and slid down the counter. I was scrolling through the ingredients in the Chinese chicken salad when I felt someone beside me.

"You coming to the match tomorrow?" I heard Liam say.

"Uh—" I assumed he was talking about water polo, but it would never have occurred to me to go to a match. I could count the number of sporting events I'd attended in my life on one hand.

Liam saw the look on my face and laughed. "I'll take that as a no."

"I'm not much of a sports person," I said apologetically.

"Well, since you said no to my first question, you're not allowed to say no to my second one."

"Uh-oh," I said, eyeing him with mock suspicion.

"Be my date to the Ball."

I heard the word *ball* and for a second I thought he was still talking about water polo.

"Wait, the Masquerade Ball?"

"Is there another one I don't know about?" he teased. A few seconds passed as I just stood there, too stunned to hold up my end of the conversation. *Liam was asking me out?* My self-concept wasn't that bad, but guys like Liam didn't typically go for girls like me. Then again, my experience with guys like Liam was pretty limited. I glanced past him and saw Hershey at the soup station, watching us.

"Sure," I said finally. "I'll go with you."

Liam grinned.

"Awesome. I'll see you tomorrow."

As soon as he walked off, Hershey walked over. "What was *that* about?" she asked, setting her tray down next to mine and reaching for a pair of metal tongs.

"Liam asked me to the Ball," I blurted out.

"Look at you," she said, nudging me with her hip. "Are you gonna hook up with him?"

"No! I mean, he just asked me. My brain's not there yet."

"Well, put your brain there," Hershey pressed. "Either you can imagine hooking up with him or you can't."

How could I want to hook up with Liam when every time I heard the words *hook* and *up* in the same sentence, my brain catapulted to North?

"I guess I can," I allowed. "Maybe."

"So you like him."

"I think he's a nice guy," I clarified.

"Don't mistake calculation for kindness, Rory," she said, snapping her tongs at my face like a crocodile's jaw. Then she laughed and slid her tray down the bar.

The Grand Rotunda had been barricaded all week, and when I passed through its doors Saturday night, I understood why. The room's austere marble surfaces were hidden behind elaborate set pieces that seemed to be growing out of the walls instead of sitting in front of them.

"I can't get over how incredible you look," Liam said as he held the door open, his voice echoing inside his lion mask.

"It's the dress," I told him. *And the fact that my face is completely hidden,* I wanted to add. Our masks had been hand-delivered in layers and layers of tissue paper to our dorm rooms on Thursday afternoon. When I saw Hershey's and mine, I knew I'd been right. They were exactly the masks the society members had worn. But up close they were even more spectacular than they'd appeared to me then. I'd been given a peacock, its elongated beak made of smooth yellow lacquer, with textured white stripes above and below the eyeholes that felt like they were made of leather, and close to a hundred tiny curled feathers on the crown. The fanlike crest of iridescent blue-green feathers was a separate piece, attached with stiff wire to a bejeweled hair comb. Hershey's jaguar mask was less striking but just as beautiful, with wet-looking black fur that felt like it had come from an actual jungle cat. It was hard to believe these pieces were nearly three hundred years old. Aside from a few small patches of matted fur and one bent feather, the masks were in perfect condition.

"It's the girl *in* the dress," Liam corrected. He was wearing the lion's head again, and in the light I was struck by how real it looked, from the thick, caramel-colored mane to the fuzzy triangular nose and downturned black mouth. "The only way you could look better," Liam added, giving my hand a squeeze, "was if that mask wasn't hiding your beautiful face."

It was a cheesy thing to say, but he sounded like he meant it, so I let myself beam. It's not like anyone could see it.

"Whoa," I heard Liam say beside me. It was more of a grunt, really, as though the word had escaped without him meaning for it to. It was hard to follow his gaze since I couldn't see his eyes, but there was no mistaking what had prompted the reaction.

Hershey was standing a few yards in front of us, next to a smoking volcano, talking to a man in a brown bear's head. A cloud of dry ice billowed around her, rustling the bottom of her red dress. Knowing Hershey, she'd probably picked the spot just for the effect. She'd wrapped her bare arms in black leather shoelaces and shaded her shoulders with streaks of kohl eyeliner, blurring the line between mask and skin. *Whoa* was right.

"Oh, look, there's Hershey," I said casually, as if Liam and I hadn't both been staring at her for the last ten seconds. I watched as she put her hand on the bear's forearm and he shook it off. Who was under that mask? There was something familiar about his posture, but I couldn't place him. Was that her mystery boy? If so, there was clearly trouble in hookup land. I could tell from his body language that he did not want to be having whatever conversation they were having. I took a step toward her, but Liam caught my arm. "Let's dance," he said, moving into my sightline. I was struck again by how real his mask looked, right down to the fan of whiskers.

"Uh, okay," I replied, not at all sure I could do that in this dress—or these heels. I gripped Liam's hand to steady myself as he led me to the center of the dance floor.

"I can see you back there," Liam said as he wrapped his arms around my waist. "Analyzing me with those impenetrable blue eyes."

"Analyzing you, huh?" In reality, I was too consumed by the awkwardness of trying to slow dance with a giant mask on my head to be analyzing anything, but he didn't need to know that.

"You were doing it when we met," Liam replied. "I was trying to be all cute and charming, and your eyes weren't giving anything away. The whole time I'm thinking, *So does this girl like me or not?* I've been asking myself the same question ever since."

He paused as if he was waiting for my answer. I faltered. What was I supposed to say? I did like him, in the regular sense of the word. But the way he meant it? Until Hershey interrogated me about it yesterday, I hadn't even considered the idea.

"What's not to like?" I said lightly. "I—"

"We have a lot in common, you know," Liam said, cutting me off. "We were both stuck in a cage of mediocrity," he said. "Yours was in Seattle, mine was in Boston. And now we're here. On our way to somewhere much, much better."

I bristled. Yes, there were times when I felt like an outsider back home. And there were moments when I wanted nothing more than to escape. But it hadn't been a cage, and the life my dad and Kari were living wasn't *mediocre*. Who appointed Liam the judge of lives, anyway?

He could sense my reaction. "That didn't come out right," he said quickly. "All I meant is that we'd make a great team." He gave my hips a light squeeze. "That is, if you can stand me." Through the painted mesh of the lion's mouth, I saw him chewing self-consciously on his bottom lip, and I realized that his confidence was an affectation, like the penny loafers and the popped collar. Part of the persona he'd worked so hard to adopt. Behind the mask was a kid from a crappy neighborhood wearing someone else's clothes. I softened.

"Hmm . . ." I teased. "Does it require me to attend sporting events? Because that just might be too much."

"I think we could come to an arrangement," he said with a laugh.

"Here's an idea," I said lightly. "I'll come watch you hurl

yourself around in the water if you'll spill all those society secrets you're keeping."

"That I can't do," he replied in a low voice. "Not until you get in."

"Ooh, 'until' not 'unless.' Does that mean I've been upgraded from an 'if' to a 'when'?"

Liam leaned in so our masks were touching, the opening for his mouth pressed against the mesh at my ear. "You're a Hepta," he said. His hands were heavy on my hips. "It's always been yours to lose."

"No pressure," I joked. But my mouth was turned away from him and he didn't hear me.

"C'mon," he said then, letting go of my hips and reaching for my hand.

"Where are we going?" I asked as he led me through the crowd. The rotunda was now packed with way more alumni than current students. The alums were easy to spot because they were wearing much smaller, newer masks that covered only their eyes, party gifts they were given on the way in. I spotted the guy in the bear mask talking to a group of recent grads, but I didn't see Hershey anywhere.

"Hey! Stone! Get your ass over here!" Liam's water polo teammates were beckoning for him. He waved them away and kept moving toward the stairs that led up to the rotunda balconies. But instead of going up, he went around to the underside of the staircase. There was an old phone booth under there, the kind with an accordion door. Liam slid it open and turned around to face me, lifting my mask from my shoulders in one fluid motion before tugging off his own.

"What are you doing?" I asked.

"This," he said, and pulled me inside the narrow space. I stumbled in my heels, but Liam caught me and gently pressed his lips against mine. The accordion door sprung shut behind us, nudging me farther into him.

I ignored the ache in my chest as he kissed me. I would not think about North right now. I would not picture him in his tomato-stained T-shirt, sitting on his worn-out couch surrounded by obsolete technology and dog-eared paperbacks, Mohawked and tattooed and completely adorable. Liam was nice, and he was smart, and he wasn't embarrassed to be associated with me. These were not insignificant traits.

I put my palms on his chest and kissed him back. But when I felt his tongue brush my lips, I pulled away. "We should get back to the party," I said, fumbling for the door behind me.

He started to protest, but I already had the door open. "I'll meet you back out there," I said, not meeting his gaze. "I'm just gonna run to the bathroom." I felt him reach for my hand, but I was already halfway out the door.

"Rory."

Please don't ask me why. I don't want to lie to you, and I can't tell you the truth. I can't tell you that the whole time we were kissing, I was wishing you were someone else.

"Hm?"

"Your mask," he said, and handed it to me. He was still

standing in the booth and had to hold the door open to keep it from springing shut between us.

"Thanks," I said brightly. "See you in a second." I had no idea where the ladies' room was, but I strode with purpose back into the main room as if I did. When I didn't immediately see it, I hurried toward the stairs on the other side of the rotunda, to the balcony above. *What was I doing? Hiding?*

There was a man on the steps, all muscle and dressed in black like a security guard. I hesitated when I saw him, expecting him to tell me I couldn't be up there. But he just looked me over and stepped aside to let me pass. When I reached the landing, I went to the railing, wrapping my palms around it. The gold plating was cool on my skin. I spotted Liam below me and instinctively stepped back into the shadows.

"They never think to look up," a voice behind me said. Griffin Payne—*the* Griffin Payne, CEO of Gnosis, Griffin Payne—was leaning against a marble column, a shiny Gemini Gold in his hand. His mask, black and feathered with a pointed beak, was pushed off his face, and his smile was friendly. "Every year I come up here, and I'm always amazed—not so much as a glance."

"You've conditioned them to look down," I said, with a nod at the Gold in his hand. My mask bobbed a little, knocking against my collarbone.

He laughed. "I suppose that's true." He stepped forward and extended his hand. "I'm Griffin, by the way." Like everyone in America didn't know who he was.

"Rory," I said, quickly wiping my palm on my dress before shaking his hand, hoping the sweat wouldn't stain. As we shook hands, I noticed his ring. It was bulky, like a class ring, but instead of a gemstone there were four symbols in Arabic, or maybe Hebrew. I thought of the Greek letter on my pendant, but these were clearly different.

"You get to play God up here," Griffin said then, stepping up to the railing. "Silently judging everyone below. Take that guy, for instance"—he pointed down at one of Liam's friends, a kid whose wild, shaggy hair was sticking up through the blowhole of his orca mask—"he's gonna regret that do. He thinks it's cool now, but he'll look back at his class photo and wonder what in the hell he was thinking."

I giggled.

"Oh, this isn't just a guess," Griffin assured me. "I know from personal experience. If you're ever in need of a serious gut-busting bout of hilarity, just take a stroll down the fourth floor of Adams Hall. Fifth picture down. I'm the guy with the white-boy Afro. It ain't pretty."

I giggled again. On TV Griffin seemed so . . . intense. But in person he was laid-back and funny.

"What year did you grad—?" I was interrupted by the sound of footsteps.

"There you are," a voice boomed.

Griffin and I both turned. The man's face was hidden inside the head of a bald eagle, but his voice had given him away. It was Dean Atwater.

"Hiding again?" the dean asked as he strode toward us, his voice echoing a little in his mask.

"Not very well, apparently," Griffin replied. Dean Atwater chuckled then turned to me. Each eye was two concentric circles, shiny and black inside of white, and though I knew they had to be transparent on his end, they were opaque on mine. I saw no trace of the man inside.

"You look wonderful tonight, Rory. Though I'd encourage you to spend time at the party, not above it." His tone was light but it felt like an indictment.

"Yes, of course," I said quickly. "I was on my way back down." I turned to Griffin. "It was very nice to meet you, Mr. Payne." He'd introduced himself as Griffin, but I felt weird calling him that in front of the dean.

Griffin smiled kindly. "The pleasure was mine."

I gave them both an awkward little wave then headed toward the stairs, gripping my dress in both hands so as not to trip over it.

"Rory!" I heard Griffin call. I turned back around. "Keep us in mind when internship time rolls around," he said. "I'll look out for your application."

I bobbed my head. "Will do," I called back. "Thank you!"

Beaming, I made my way down the steps. An internship with Gnosis meant a very good shot at a *job* at Gnosis.

I stopped on the last step to scan the room. Liam was still with his friends, and didn't seem to be looking for me. I didn't see Hershey or the guy in the bear mask. I slipped my phone from my clutch and raised it to my lips. "Should I date Liam Stone?" I asked Lux.

"You'd make a good match" came Lux's reply. I brought the phone back to my lips, ready to ask about North, when I realized I couldn't. North didn't use Lux, so he didn't have a profile for the app to analyze. If I wanted to assess our compatibility, I'd have to do it myself.

There was a commotion behind me as Griffin and Dean Atwater descended the steps, the man in black at Griffin's elbow. I stepped aside to let them pass, and pulled out my Gemini. Griffin had topped *Forbes* magazine's "40 Under 40" list last year, so I knew he had to be in his thirties, which meant there was at least a chance he'd been in my mom's class. Panopticon had my answer:

At sixteen, Payne was admitted into Theden Academy, an exclusive preparatory school in the Berkshires of western Massachusetts. He graduated from Theden Academy in 2013 and interned that summer in Gnosis's research and development department. He returned to Gnosis as Director of Product Design after graduating from Harvard College in 2017.

2013. He was in my mom's class.

Needing to see for myself, I left the rotunda through the side door and went straight to Adams Hall. To my surprise, the main entrance was unlocked. Except for the faint green glow of the emergency lights, the building was pitch-black. Using my phone's flashlight, I mounted the steps to the fourth floor.

The walls were lined with Theden class photos. The official kind, shot in black-and-white, with a placard proclaiming the year. I stopped at the first one. The image was grainy and the students' clothing was more conservative than what we wore, but otherwise it looked how my class photo might, smiling teenagers in dressy clothes lined up on risers in front of the Grand Rotunda. CLASS OF 1954, the placard at the bottom declared. I kept moving down the hall, counting the frames. The years jumped around. They weren't in any particular order.

Griffin's class was exactly where he said it'd be, fifth one down. He stood in the center of the group, smiling broadly, his hair looking like he'd stuck his fingers in an old electrical socket. I slid my light down to the bottom of the frame, looking for the placard with the class year.

CLASS OF 2013.

My light jumped wildly from corner to corner as I looked for my mom, too impatient to scan the rows one by one. The students were all wearing short sleeves, which means the photo could've been taken in the early fall or late spring. If it was the latter, my mom may have already been gone.

It was my own face that caught my eye. Standing right next to Griffin in the center of the photo, the very last place I looked. Of course it wasn't my face, it was hers, but a stranger wouldn't have been able to tell the difference. Her eyes, her cheekbones, the shape of her nose. They were my features on a taller, more willowy frame. Our coloring was different—she was auburn and olive, while I was chestnut and fair—but you couldn't tell that in black-and-white. I could see my face reflected in the glass between us, painted with Hershey's makeup, and it looked less like mine than the girl's in this old photograph did. Stepping closer, I pressed my hand to the glass, not caring about fingerprints, just wanting to connect to the girl on the other side.

I stood there for a few moments, trying to step into the moment the photograph had captured. My mom, standing with her classmates, smiling a confident smile. There was no trace of uncertainty in her eyes, no hint of what would come next. If she was struggling at Theden, this photo didn't show it.

My Gemini lit up in the dark.

@LiamStone: where r u?

I sighed audibly. I couldn't hide out in this dark hallway forever. I snapped a few pics of the class photo with my Gemini, but my built-in flash created a glare on the glass. Without the flash, I couldn't see the photo at all. The best I could do was hold my handheld at an angle and move in tight on my mom. The shot I ended up with was a close-up of just her. The blue Forum icon popped on screen: *Post photo to your wall?*

My finger hovered above my screen. I posted everything

to Forum. But this photo couldn't be summarized in some pithy caption. I tapped the word NO and the pop-up box disappeared. Instead I called Beck, the only person other than my dad who would understand what finding the photo meant to me without me having to explain it.

"Hey," he said, picking up on the second ring. "Aren't you supposed to be at that fancy dance of yours?"

"I am," I replied. "But I just found this picture of my mom, and I—"

"Text it to me," he said.

I heard a ding through the phone as my message popped up on his screen. I was looking at it on my end too.

"Wow," he said. "She looks just like you."

"I know, right?"

"You send it to your dad?"

"Not yet," I said, but the truth was, I wasn't sure I was going to. I knew how hard it was for him to look at pictures of her. "Well, I should probably get back to the party."

"I'm glad you found it," Beck said.

"Me too."

I walked slowly back to the rotunda, across the grass this time, my heels sinking in the soft ground with each step, thinking about the girl in that photograph. She was a complete enigma to me. She'd walked across this same lawn, yet it felt to me like she'd inhabited a separate universe. Would she ever be more to me than a face that looked like mine?

Liam signaled for me the moment I entered the rotunda.

He was standing with a group of faculty members in various reptilian masks. I looked for the serpent mask but didn't see it.

I pretended not to see Liam and looked for Griffin. He was easy to spot: Surrounded by a group of aging alumni on the far side of the room, Griffin was talking animatedly with his hands. I caught the word *empire* on his lips.

"Hey," Liam called, coming toward me. "Where'd you go?"

"I was looking for Hershey," I lied. "Have you seen her?"

"Not in a while," Liam replied. "Wanna dance?"

He held out his hand and in my mind I decided to take it. To dance with him, to try to enjoy myself. But then I looked down at the hand he held out to me. How different it was from the hand that caught me when I tripped on the sidewalk last week. That one was cracked and stained and caked with coffee grounds, the nails bitten down to the quick. And when it had caught my arm, I'd felt it down my spine.

"I have to go," I said suddenly.

"Go where?" Liam asked, looking confused.

"I just have to go."

Liam said something after that, but I didn't hear it. I was already at the door. I knew I should still be mad at North for how he treated me in front of Hershey, and I was. So mad I could punch him in the face. But that anger did nothing to quell my sudden need to see him.

I stopped by the dorms to drop off my mask and get a jacket, worrying for a sec that Hershey would be there, passed out or puking. But our room was empty. Feeling my confidence wane just a bit, I dug through Hershey's drawers in search of her stash of airplane alcohol. But she'd either finished it or hidden it well; all I found was a half-empty mini bottle of Kahlúa. I downed the rest of it, gargled some mouthwash, and left.

It was late and dark and cold, and I was missing the most important event of the fall semester. But I didn't care. I wanted to see North. And now that I let myself want it, I *really* wanted it. I felt it on my skin, in the back of my throat, underneath my ribs. As I walked, I rehearsed what I would say. I'd be casual. I'd joke that I couldn't live another day without seeing *Rocky*. Then he'd apologize for the way he acted last weekend, promise me it'd never happen again. The whole encounter unfolded so smoothly in my head that I was genuinely surprised when I stepped up to the café's bay window and didn't see him inside.

Without thinking, I kept walking. Around the building and through the door and up the stairs to North's landing where I rapped my knuckles against his cold metal door without a second's hesitation. The door couldn't open fast enough.

Until it did.

My stomach, and all the excitement that had been bubbling up in my chest, crashed to my knees when I saw the look on North's face.

"What are you doing here?" he said in a low voice, stepping into the crack between the door and its frame.

"I, uh . . . ," Mortified, I dropped my eyes to the ground. There was a parcel there, wrapped in brown paper, addressed to Norvin Pascal. I saw North see it too. He bent quickly to pick it up. My eyes went to the space where he'd been standing, my gaze pulled into his living room by the flash of red I saw there.

Hershey's dress was draped across his couch.

North straightened up, blocking my view again. "You should go," he said quietly.

Dumbly, I nodded. *Why is Hershey's dress on your couch?* my insides were screaming. But my brain knew. It'd already put the pieces in place. This was why North hadn't wanted me to tell anyone we'd hung out. Why Hershey had wanted to go by Paradiso that morning, and why North had acted so weird when we did. He was the guy Hershey was hooking up with. Her secret scandalous fling.

"I can explain," he said then, even quieter now.

"No need," I said, anger burning my throat. "I get it." I wanted to spin on my heels and stomp out, but the stairs and my stilettos were a dangerous combination. So I simply turned and walked down carefully, praying that he couldn't see me shaking. A second later I heard the door click shut.

12

I TOOK A LONG SIP OF THE COFFEE I'd smuggled into the stacks, lukewarm now. You could bring drinks into the library's main study lounge, but I wanted to be alone today, so I was at a desk in the stacks, eating cereal from a plastic Baggie, drinking weak dining hall coffee, and blinking back tears.

I tried again to focus on my screen, my eyes burning with fatigue. I'd fallen asleep quickly the night before after practically running back to my room, but I'd woken up again when Hershey crept in just after midnight and was still awake when everyone else began trickling back to the dorms a little before one. After that, sleep eluded me. I stared at the ceiling as the hours dragged by until finally, at six, I got up and went here. Except for a quick dining hall run when it opened at eight, I'd been in this chair all day, trying to work on my cog psych paper but mostly thinking about North. I felt like such an idiot. We'd hung out twice, both times alone, and both times he'd kept it completely platonic. I couldn't even be mad at him. He couldn't have made it clearer if he'd tried.

Ding! A pop-up box appeared on my screen: *You will be logged out due to inactivity in sixty seconds.*

I sighed and tapped CONTINUE. How long had I been staring at these same search results? I was clicking through health files of patients with akratic paracusia, looking for subtle connections between them, but all I was finding were not-so-subtle ones. It was the same story over and over. Previously sane person starts hearing a voice in her head. Person starts adhering to the voice's commands. Person engages in increasingly irrational, self-sacrificing behavior. Suddenly she's quitting her job or giving all her money away or inviting ex-cons to dinner. Family members freak and intervene. Person resists medication. Person's life falls apart.

After that, one of two things always happened. Either the person was forced into treatment by a concerned family member or simply fell off the grid. It wasn't clear where people in this second category went, but the entries in their medical files just stopped. No annual physicals, no checkups, no routine immunizations. They're unemployable without these things, so it's not as if they're off leading normal, productive lives. I couldn't help but think of the photographs Beck took that day in Tent City, images of men with wild eyes and women with vacant ones. Had they heard the Doubt? Had it led them over the edge?

My handheld buzzed with a text.

@HersheyClements: where r u? im starving. meet at the dh?

I fired back a reply without thinking: already ate. studying.

I wasn't angry with Hershey. I didn't have a right to be. She didn't know that North and I had hung out. But I couldn't act as if nothing had happened, either. So I was avoiding her, at least for now.

My handheld buzzed again.

@NathanKrinsky: Come by the café. Pls. There's something u need to c.

The profile pic belonged to another one of North's coworkers, a guy I'd seen mopping the floors.

My chest fluttered and I hated myself for it. No, I would *not* come by the café. Not today, not ever. I started to punch out a reply but thought better of it. Instead I blocked @NathanKrinsky and buried my handheld in my bag.

Unfortunately, there was no block function in my brain. I couldn't stop myself from replaying those horrific, mortifying moments in my head, the look on North's face when he saw me, and worse, the sight of Hershey's dress on his couch when he bent down to get that package at his door. It struck me now that he'd seemed, at least for a second, more concerned about the package than he had about my presence. Why?

I pictured the brown parcel in my head. Addressed to Norvin Pascal at North's address. *Was Norvin his real name?*

When I searched the name on Forum, only one page popped up. My breath snagged in my throat when I saw the profile pic. Even without enlarging it, I knew it was of North.

In disbelief, I scrolled through his profile. All that stuff about Forum being an "invisible cage"? It was bullshit. He was on all the time. And his status updates were gross.

@NorvinPascal: When people say they're having a good hair day, all I can think is "Sometimes you have bad hair days??" And I wonder what that's like. #rockthehawk #blessed

I almost barfed on my screen.

With another annoying ding, the DPH pop-up box reappeared, blocking my view of North's page and snapping me out of my stupor. I had work to do. *It* mattered. This other crap didn't.

I tapped my screen to stay logged in then scrolled back up to the top of my list to remind myself what I was looking at. I'd decided to explore environmental triggers of APD first, so I'd narrowed my results to females in the Pacific Northwest. Next I'd sort by age. As I was tapping the "18–24" button, I accidentally hit the "Sort by Date" tab. The results automatically resorted by death date, putting the oldest files on top.

I scrolled down, skimming stats, debating whether to open some of these older cases or go back to the newer ones, when one file in particular caught my eye.

Birth Date: April 13, 1995.
Gender: Female
Date of Death: March 21, 2014

It was the birth date that got my attention first. My mom's birthday. My dad and I celebrated it every year with cake and ice cream at the diner in Belltown where he took her on their first date. But it was the death date that made the hair on the back of my neck prickle. It was a day we also commemorated with cake. *My* birthday.

Heart pounding, I clicked the link for the full file. The words on the screen ran together as I sped to the bottom of the page. The last entry was dated March 21, 2014. I clicked on it and audibly gasped. It was stamped with the logo of the University of Washington Medical Center, the hospital where I was born. As I scrolled down, my eyes grabbed ahold of words and phrases as my brain struggled to make sense of them.

Patient presented with severe labor pains after twenty-two hours of active labor at home. Ultrasound consistent with fetal post-maturity syndrome and acute oligohydramnios. Patient underwent an emergency cesarean section and delivered a 3.2 kg female. Immediately following the procedure, patient began exhibiting signs of respiratory distress and lost consciousness. CT scan revealed large thromboembolism in right lung. Patient was pronounced dead at 16:05. Cause of death: pulmonary thromboembolism.

My thoughts stalled as I read and reread the words *pulmonary thromboembolism*, over and over. This was my mom's medical file. It had to be. The birthday, the death date, the baby delivered by cesarean section at UW hospital, the particular cause of death. All of it lined up. But this patient had APD.

My brain, normally so practical, refused to accept the evidence in front of it. There must've been some other eighteen-year-old girl who delivered a baby by emergency C-section at UW hospital on my birthday and then died from a blood clot. Or maybe my mom's file had just been miscoded with the APD diagnosis and showed up in my search results by mistake.

Or my mom was crazy.

All my fears about my own sanity swelled to the surface. I knew from my research that if my mom had APD, then my own risk for developing the disorder was three times the average. Suddenly I saw all my uncertainty about the Doubt in a new light. It wasn't healthy skepticism. It was neurosis. People with APD didn't think they were sick.

My pulse was drumming in my ears as I scrolled back up to the top of my mom's file and clicked on the first entry. Forcing myself to read slowly, I moved through the file methodically, starting with the entry from her birth in 1995, going over yearly checkups and sick visits, a broken ankle at age seven, stitches for a busted elbow at nine, an appendectomy at fourteen. Normal kid stuff. No mention of voices or mental illness or any psychological issues at all. I felt myself begin to relax. Maybe her file had been miscoded, like I'd thought. Maybe she didn't have APD after all.

I was midway through an entry dated April 2013 when I saw the words that removed any doubt whose file it was. *Theden Health Center.* The paragraphs that followed were a depressing description of a very disturbed young woman who was on the brink of failing out of school. It was a psych eval, signed by a Dr. K. Hildebrand, and at the bottom was a tentative diagnosis: *Behavior symptomatic of acute akratic paracusia and personality disorder.* The next entry, signed by the same doctor, was dated two weeks later and summarized test results from more than a dozen neurological and psychiatric exams, confirming the doctor's initial diagnosis. At the bottom was the doctor's prognosis: *Non-curative. Institutionalization recommended.*

The next entry was a link to a "Notice of Expulsion" dated May 1, 2013. *Student no longer meets the psychological requirements for enrollment.* The document was signed by Dr. Hildebrand and Dean Atwater.

My mom didn't drop out of Theden. They'd kicked her out.

Reeling, I went back to the very last entry in my mom's

file, the report from the day she died, and read it more closely. I didn't know many of the medical terms I saw, but I could piece together what had happened based on what I already knew from my dad. My mom went into labor nearly three weeks early, and there were complications. They needed to do a C-section. A blood clot had formed in her leg, traveled to her lungs, and she was dead.

Before the pop-box reappeared again, I slid my finger to the top of my tablet and pressed the PRINT SCREEN button, saving the image of that final entry to my photobox, then I clicked over to look at it there. Then my eyes lost focus as I stared, unblinking, at my screen. Minutes, maybe an hour, passed as I sat there, not moving, not really thinking, just staring. When the pop-box reappeared again, I let the system log me out.

13

"TOMORROW, THEN," Liam said, his voice at my shoulder.

I kept my eyes on my tablet. It was the night before day two of fall midterms, and the library's central reading room was packed. I'd deliberately chosen a corner table so I could be alone, but the water polo team had claimed the one behind me, and Liam's seat backed up to mine. Right now he was tilted back in his chair, balancing on two legs as he twirled a stylus with his fingers. He'd asked me out at least twenty times in the past month, and each time I'd politely turned him down. If he were anyone else, I would've told him straight out to stop asking, but he was a society member and I didn't know how much sway he had over tap decisions. I was pretty sure that made me gross and calculating, but I wasn't about to let Liam keep me from getting in. I'd gotten eight more word puzzle texts, the most recent just the night before, and I'd solved all eight.

"Rory." I could hear him smiling. "I'm willing to beg."

"I can't tomorrow," I said.

"Saturday, then."

"Let's talk about it after midterms," I said. It would be so much easier if he'd just get the picture here and let it go. But for some reason he seemed determined that we date.

I contemplated moving to the stacks, but I'd come without a jacket and it was freezing out, which meant the stacks would be an icebox. The crackle from the fireplace in the center of the reading room made it cozy, and the coziness was calming. Calming was good, since I was hovering on the brink of a major panic attack about our second day of exams. Day one was the left-brain subjects—calculus, comp sci, and Chinese. Tomorrow would be a thousand times worse: lit, history, cog psych, and the test I was dreading the most, our practicum performance exam. There was no way to prepare for it, which had me unhinged. I had no idea what to expect. No one did. The exam changed dramatically from year to year, so the second-years weren't any help either.

One of Liam's water polo buddies whispered something that the others found hilarious, and the table erupted into laughter. They were amped up on caffeine and sugar and getting more and more boisterous, and I was getting more and more nervous that I wasn't prepared for the next day's tests. I'd spent the past fourteen nights in the library, not leaving until well after midnight, despite Lux's insistence that I needed at least eight hours of sleep.

Out of the corner of my eye I saw Izzy enter the reading

room and scan the tables for somewhere to sit. A few seconds later she was heading toward me. Quickly, I started packing up my things. I'd studied with her a few times over the past couple of weeks, and every time we'd talked more than we'd worked.

"Oh, no, you're leaving already?"

I jumped just a little, as if she'd surprised me. I hated faking it, but our midterm scores were a huge part of our grade and if I wanted to do well, I couldn't spend the rest of the night chatting about movies or makeup or the caloric value of the vending machine granola bars.

"Hey!" I said. "Yeah, Hershey and I are going to study together back in the room." Internally, I winced. This wasn't even remotely true. Hershey and I hadn't *ever* studied together, and we certainly didn't have plans to do it that night. As if it would mitigate the lie, I tacked on something true. "She hates the library."

"Hershey *studies*?" Liam piped up. His teammates snickered.

"See you guys later," I said, and walked out.

It was freezing outside and it was starting to sprinkle. I sprinted to the dorms, raindrops stinging my face, and was heaving by the time I got to our room. Hershey was at her desk, hunched over her tablet. I assumed she was studying, until I heard her sob.

"Hershey?" She didn't react. I wondered if she'd even heard me. I dropped my bag onto my bed and moved toward her. She was really crying, her fists clenching and unclenching at her sides. I touched her shoulder and she looked up. Her face was puffy and red. "What's wrong?"

"I'm going to fail," she said, sobbing. Her voice was hoarse and raw. "Today was a disaster, and tomorrow—I haven't even been doing the reading, Rory. Not at all. I thought—God, I don't know what I thought. That I could just float by, the way I always have, I guess." She shook her head.

"You're not going to fail," I said lamely, because that's what friends say, and because that's what we were, as complicated as our relationship had become.

"You think I deserve it," she said then. Her eyes welled up with fresh tears. "My grandmother will hate me," she whispered. "My parents. Oh God, my parents." She pressed her palms to her face and said something else, but her words weren't intelligible.

Help her.

Ever since finding out about my mom's illness, I'd been stressing about hearing the Doubt again, afraid of what it would mean for me. Now it had spoken and I wasn't scared of anything. I was pissed off. I'd already decided to help Hershey half a second before the voice spoke. Now if I did it, I'd be listening to the Doubt.

I looked at Hershey. She was five inches taller than I was, but she looked so small sitting there, her shoulders hunched and shaking.

This isn't about you, I snapped at the voice, as if it could hear me, then I put my hand on Hershey's arm.

"I'll help you study," I said. My roommate dropped her hands and looked at me, blinking her swollen eyes in surprise.

"What about *your* exams?"

Hershey and I were on alternate schedules, which meant her second-day tests were the ones I'd already taken. Not a single subject overlapped.

I shrugged. "I'll be fine," I said, and tried to believe it. Yes, Hershey had gotten herself into this, and maybe she did deserve it, but I couldn't let her fail out.

She grabbed my hand and squeezed it. "Thank you," she said. Her eyes were glossy with gratitude and hope.

We started with comp sci, Hershey's strong suit, and then moved to calc, mine. She was as unprepared as she said, but was a fast learner and grasped concepts quickly. Still, there was a lot of material to cover, and as the night drew on, we both began to drag.

At 3:30, we went down to the common room for vending machine coffee. Liam was there, practicing for his history oral exam. I angled my body away from him, keeping my eyes on my screen as I launched Lux. I changed my projected bedtime from midnight to four o'clock tomorrow afternoon, selected the "energy" and "stamina" filters, and then touched my sensor to the vending machine. A paper cup dropped down, followed by a stream of steaming black liquid.

"What'd you get?" Hershey asked.

"No idea," I replied, lifting the cup from the tray. "I let Lux decide." I took a sip. It was thick and strong. "A red-eye, tastes like. With stevia instead of sugar."

"Done." Hershey typed in her order then touched her Gemini to the vending machine. A second cup dropped down. I kept my back to Liam as we waited for the cup to fill.

I saw her eyes flick from me to him. "Did something happen between you guys?" she asked. "You cooled on him pretty quickly after your big date."

"Liam and I are fine," I insisted. "We're just better as friends."

"If you say so," she said, reaching for her coffee. "I still think there's something you're not telling me." My cheeks burned as the image of Hershey's dress slung over North's couch popped into my mind. Yes, there was something I wasn't telling her, but it had nothing to do with Liam.

"We should get back to studying." I picked up a lid for my cup and turned toward the door.

"Hey, Rory?"

"Hm?" I turned back around.

Hershey was looking down at her cup, her eyes hidden by a wall of dark hair. "Why are you doing this?"

"Doing what?"

"Helping me."

I answered instinctively. "Because you're my friend."

Hershey grabbed my hand and squeezed it. Her voice broke as she whispered something in reply. It was too quiet for me to make out, and I didn't want to ask her to repeat it. But I kept replaying the moment as we ran through calc problems and her Chinese vocab list. It sounded like *I'm sorry.*

We didn't sleep. At seven in the morning we were still at it, but I could tell that Hershey was no longer panicking. She was ready. Maybe not for an A+ performance, but she'd pass. I, on the other hand, was screwed. It wasn't like I hadn't studied for my day-two exams at all, but I'd been relying on a final night-before push. Not to mention a solid six hours of sleep. Now here I was, an hour before my first test, queasy from the late-night coffee and so tired that my eyes felt like I'd soaked them in bleach and hung them in the desert to dry. I would've cried had I not been too dehydrated to produce tears.

I showered and put on a sweaterdress, hoping the outfit would perk me up a little, but I didn't have the energy to dry my hair, so I twisted it into a knot and clipped it. Hershey was humming as she brushed her cheeks with bronzer, the bags under her eyes hidden behind concealer.

"I'm almost ready," she said, catching my eyes in the mirror. "Want to grab a quick breakfast?" I knew food was a good idea, but I couldn't imagine actually consuming it. My stomach was fizzy and sour, and the last thing I wanted to do right then was put something in it.

"I think I'll wait," I told her. "Get something after my practicum exam." *Which starts in twenty-two minutes,* my mind was screaming. I slung my bag over my shoulder and started for the door.

"Just so you know," Hershey said behind me. "I know why you really helped me."

I turned back around. "What?"

"It was the Doubt." Her voice was soft, but it echoed like a scream.

My brain stalled. *How could she possibly know?* My next thought was more practical. *Don't get defensive.*

"The Doubt?" I said with what I hoped was a quizzical smile. The effort hurt my face. "You think I hear the *Doubt*?"

"Well, I know your mom did," she replied, sounding very sure.

I took a step back. "Excuse me?"

"I know your mom heard the Doubt."

I stared at her. "Who told you that?"

"No one," she said quickly. "I just figured it out." *She's lying* shot through my head. There's no way she could've known about my mom. So who told her? Who else knew?

She seemed self-conscious now, as if this moment wasn't unfolding the way she played it out in her head. Then again Hershey wasn't exactly the type to think this sort of thing through before launching into it. "I mean, I'm not going to *tell* anyone—"

"I can't talk about this right now," I told her, turning away. "I have to go. Good luck on your tests."

I pulled our door open and stepped into the hall, letting the old mahogany door shut behind me. Just before it closed, I glanced back and caught Hershey's eye. "I don't hear it," I said, as convincingly as I could. The door closed before she could reply, but she didn't need to. I could tell from her face that she didn't believe me.

14

"TODAY, YOU GET TO PLAY GOD," I heard Tarsus say. Up until that moment I'd been distracted, replaying the conversation I'd just had with Hershey. When she'd said, *Play God*, she'd gotten my attention.

The screen in my pod lit up with a still shot of a giant wooden platform floating in the middle of a sparkling turquoise sea. Rolling green hills rose up on the island behind it, and the beach was beautiful white powder, nothing like the gray-brown sand on the Washington coast. Vertical logs rising out of the water formed a little footbridge from the beach to the platform, which was at least a hundred yards offshore. The dock itself was empty except for a pyramid of wooden crates stacked one on top of the other.

"In sixty seconds the dock on your screen will be crowded with celebrants" came Dr. Tarsus's voice through my speakers. "It's independence day on this island, and natives and tourists alike will gather for a fireworks display. The dock's capacity is two hundred and fifty people. When the fireworks begin, there will be more than three times that many there."

The image on my screen zoomed in so I was looking more closely at the crates. "These twelve crates are filled with more than two tons of aerial display fireworks. The fireworks are all 'pre-scribbed,' which means that an electrical match was attached to each shell before the fireworks were loaded into the crate. In thirteen minutes one of these fireworks will explode, setting off a chain reaction that will destroy the dock and kill everyone on it.

"Your job is to decide who lives and who dies," Tarsus said then, as the platform was instantly populated with people. It was so crowded, I didn't see an inch of open space. "Using your hands, you will be able to zoom in on individuals, and if you double-tap their bodies, you'll see key details about them. Where they're from, how old they are, what they do for a living. This information is there to assist you in your decision-making. As always, your grades will be based on net social impact—the fewer high-value people who die, the better your mark will be."

My eyes jumped around the platform, taking it all in. There were people of all races, from all walks of life, it seemed. There were clues, I saw, to help us know where to begin. Expensive sunglasses, designer sun hats. The tourists. No doubt the highest-value people on the dock. A pit formed in my stomach. I didn't want to do this.

"You'll only be able to move one person at a time," Tarsus

said. "To move someone, simply hold your finger on their body until it begins to blink, then slide your finger to wherever you want them to go. Once you've initiated an evacuation, you'll be able to move on to the next evacuee."

My heart started to pound as a countdown clock popped up on my screen, showing thirteen minutes and ten seconds.

"Oh, and one more thing," Tarsus said. "There are hefty deductions for injuries and deaths that *you* cause. It's better for someone to die in the explosion than at your hand. Good luck, students. You may begin."

And just like that, the audio clicked on and the clock started to run.

Hurry, I told myself. *You have to hurry.* But I was frozen, eyes glued to the group of young native children at the center of the dock. There had to be at least a hundred of them, all shoeless and wearing flowered headbands and sashes, laughing as they waited for the fireworks to begin, their voices carrying above the rest. I double-tapped one.

Male. 8 yrs. Indo-Fijian descent. IQ 75. Unskilled.

The pit in my stomach swelled. He was such a cute kid, with a wide, toothless smile. But I'd learned enough in class to know that his utility value was low. Every person, thing, action, and outcome had one. A number from −1 to 1 that represented their net impact on society. Like the father in the simulation we'd done on the first day of class—the PhD I'd let die—some people were worth more than others, and if I wanted to do well on this exam, I'd have to evacuate those people first. Then, if there was time, maybe I could save the kids.

I wanted to save them all.

Could I somehow identify the faulty firework before it blew? No. Tarsus had said there were more than two tons of explosives in that crate. Besides, I wouldn't know what to look for anyway. My eyes darted to the clock. There were only twelve minutes and thirty seconds left and more than seven hundred and fifty people to get off that dock. *Hurry,* I told myself again.

But as I lifted my hand to the screen, it stopped me, with just a single word.

Wait.

I reacted. *"Wait?"* I clasped my hand over my mouth. I hadn't meant to say it out loud. Our pods were wired with cameras and speakers, and I had no doubt that Tarsus had them going now. *Wait?* I demanded again, silently this time. The voice spoke again.

Wait.

The advice, so clearly and unmistakably irrational, snapped me into action. I needed to do exactly the opposite of what the Doubt had instructed. I needed to hurry the hell up.

Scanning the crowd, I double-tapped a youngish man with a Rolex on his wrist.

Male. 29 yrs. American, Norwegian descent. IQ 156. Hedge fund manager.

I knew how to do the analysis, still I resisted the valuing that had to be done. *Just get him off the platform,* I told myself. I held my finger to his head until he began to blink, and then I slid him toward the footbridge. No, the water was faster. With a flick of my wrist, I tossed him into the ocean. As soon as I did, he began to swim toward shore.

Buoyed by the progress, I held my finger to a girl nearby. I didn't have time to check their stats. I'd have to assess their value just by looking at them. It was gross, but we'd learned enough in class to know what to look for. How to size them up. This girl was wearing Chanel sunglasses and a tailored linen sundress, and there was a giant diamond on her finger. From the way she was smiling at the native kids, I pegged her for a philanthropic socialite, someone with the means to do a lot of good. Quickly, I slid her toward the water and she began to swim toward shore.

I started moving faster now, without second-guessing myself, hurling people into the water as fast as I could. Seven minutes in, I'd saved two hundred and ninety-eight people. Number two hundred and ninety-nine set me back. It was a thirty-something man in seersucker shorts with tiny anchors on them. Since it looked like he belonged on a boat, I was shocked when he flailed his arms as soon as he hit the water and quickly sunk beneath the surface. My death toll ticked from 0 to 1.

Crap. I hadn't thought about people who couldn't swim. I felt myself start to panic, but I pushed the panic away. The odds that someone who couldn't swim would go on vacation to a tropical island had to be slim. I couldn't reassess my strategy now. I kept moving, evacuating people into the water as fast as

I could. With only sixty seconds left, I'd gotten six hundred people off the dock and lost only that one.

With ten seconds left, the pit in my stomach returned. I hadn't been able to save a single native kid nor their young female teachers. *Maybe it won't explode,* I found myself thinking with only ten seconds left. Maybe the Doubt was right. Maybe the sim was a trick of some sort, and we were supposed to know that somehow and ignore the instructions we'd been given. I found myself hoping for this as the clock ticked toward zero.

But with two seconds remaining, the crates burst into flames. It took a full second for sound to kick in. A crackling sound then a *pop pop pop.* All at once there was smoke everywhere, black and then gray, with spurts of light as the fireworks went off. The platform disappeared in the cloud of smoke, but the bodies didn't. They were tossed in the air like rag dolls, the air thick with their screams. I squeezed my eyes shut, unable to watch it, and I kept them closed until the sound stopped. I should've kept them shut even longer. The image of the aftermath was far worse than the explosion had been. Limbs and trunks floating among charred wood. Bodies on fire in the sea.

I swallowed hard and tasted bile. *It's not real,* I reminded myself. Still, I cast my eyes down, not wanting to see anymore.

"Congratulations, Rory," I heard Dr. Tarsus say through my speakers. "With the lowest net social impact and a death toll of only one hundred and eighty-eight, you got the highest grade in the class." I raised my eyes to my screen and saw our class roster there. My name was at the top. The name beneath me had a death toll that was nearly double mine. "The rest of you checked the stats on every person you saved. Rory relied on her rational instincts and had a far better result."

It was the nicest thing Tarsus had ever said to me.

Pride yanked at the corners of my mouth. I'd done it. I'd gotten the highest grade in the class and defeated the Doubt in the process. Okay, so maybe *defeated* was a little strong, but I'd finally answered the question that had been poking at the back of my mind since the first time I heard it. *Could I trust it?* The rational answer had always been no, but still I'd wondered. Now I knew. If I'd listened to the Doubt during the simulation, I would've failed my exam. And if it'd been real life, eight hundred people would be dead, instead of only one hundred and eighty-eight.

One hundred and eighty-eight people were dead. And just like that, my good mood evaporated, and I was back on that dock with those smiling, doomed kids.

It wasn't real, I told myself again as I pushed through Hamilton Hall's double doors into the bright October sun. It had to *seem* real in order to trigger all the reactive neural activity we were supposed to know how to suppress. Still, I couldn't stop thinking about the children I'd left behind. Their giggles as they crowded around their teachers, *ooh*ing and *aah*ing at the sky's display. It was their little bodies that flew through the air when the crate exploded. Their screams that surged then went silent when their burned flesh sunk below the surface of the sea.

Casualties were inevitable in a situation like that. I knew that. There was no way to identify the flawed firework or move the heavy crates, no time to even try. It was a given that the dock would explode. The only variable was how many people would be standing on it when it did. Of course, it wasn't just a numbers game—Dr. Tarsus had made that clear. Our bystanders were valued by the software, ranked in order of importance. I'd gotten the best score not because I'd left the fewest number of people on the dock but because the ones I'd left weren't considered as valuable as the ones I'd gotten off.

"It's an effed-up concept," I said to Liam at lunch. He'd planted himself at our table without an invitation, taking Izzy's seat. She was dyslexic, so she got extra time for her exams. "People are assigned *values*? As if some lives matter more than others?"

"They do. And you don't disagree."

I looked him in the eye. "Yes, I do. I completely do."

"Okay," he said, leaning back in his chair. "A trainful of convicted murderers is speeding toward a bus full of Nobel Prize winners. You can either derail the train or knock the bus into a ravine. If you do nothing, everyone will die." He popped a piece of cauliflower in his mouth and looked at me. "Choose."

Hershey looked up from her tablet. She'd been cramming for calculus since the lunch period started, barely touching her tomato soup. "I'd save the murderers."

I gaped at her. I knew she was just saying it to get a reaction out of us, but still. "You guys are both sick."

But Hershey looked thoughtful. "In Liam's world, you kill the murderers because you've assigned them a negative utility value. But maybe there's another way to look at it. Maybe you save the murderers because of their redemption value."

Liam raised his eyebrows. "Their *what*?"

Hershey chewed on her lip, thinking. "They know they're murderers, right? So they don't expect to be saved. They expect whoever is deciding to save the Nobel winners instead. So if the opposite happens . . . I dunno." She sounded self-conscious. "Maybe it changes them, and maybe other negative-utility-value people are changed just hearing about it. Maybe they're redeemed somehow. And maybe the net effect on society is greater than if you'd saved the good guys."

"Or maybe they'll just kill more people because, you know, they're *murderers*." Liam said it like Hershey's idea was the dumbest in the world.

"You're a jackass," Hershey snapped. She turned to me. "What do you think?"

"I think the whole premise is flawed. First of all, it's a completely unrealistic scenario. Why are all these murderers on a train in the first place? Where are they going? And why is there a bus full of Nobel Prize winners—I mean, c'mon, really? They're on a *bus*? Stuck on the track?"

"Just because it's an unlikely scenario doesn't make it a

useless hypothetical," Liam replied. "The point is to see how you'd reason through the possible outcomes."

"But I have no control over the outcomes," I argued. "And I never would! The idea that I could be sitting in a room somewhere with a button that would let me decide who lives and who dies—"

"People make those kinds of decisions all the time," Liam said.

"Oh, yeah? Who are these button pushers? I'd like to meet one," I said sarcastically.

Liam gave me a patronizing look. "That hypo on your exam, the people on the dock. Where'd it happen in real life?"

"Huh?"

"Tarsus bases her sims on real-life events," he replied. "That's her big pitch for why they're so useful." As he said it, I remembered Tarsus telling us that on the first day of class. I'd forgotten. Somewhere in the back of my mind I heard the sound of those little kids screaming as their bodies were blown to bits. Those were real kids somewhere? My stomach clenched and unclenched like a fist. Why had I been so quick to abandon them? So what if their utility value was the lowest on that dock? They were *children*.

It took some effort to put the image of that exploding dock out of my mind after that, but I managed to do it long enough to take my last two midterms. By the time 4:30 rolled around, my brain felt like oatmeal.

"To you!" Hershey shouted when I opened our door, a

bottle of sparkling cider in her hand. "For saving my ass."

I smiled and stepped inside. "I take it you passed?"

"An A and two Bs," she said proudly. "As long as I didn't totally bomb lit yesterday, I'm golden." She poured some cider for me, and we clinked cups and drank.

"No stolen champagne?" I teased.

"New leaf," Hershey replied, refilling her cup. "From now on I will only pilfer nonalcoholic beverages." We giggled and sipped our cider. "Seriously, though. Thank you." Hershey's eyes were shining as she looked at me. "I didn't deserve your help," she said.

"Hersh, that's not—"

She held up her hand, stopping me. "I didn't. And had it been me, I would've let you fail. And don't say I wouldn't have, because trust me, I would've. So now I owe you, and I'm going to do whatever it takes to make it up to you. Okay?" Her eyes were earnest, almost pleading, as if it were important to her that I accept.

I nodded.

She smiled. "Good. I'll start by doing your makeup." She set the bottle down on her desk and gestured to her chair. "Sit."

15

VILLAGE PIZZA WAS PACKED when we walked in. Rachel and Izzy had gotten there early and scored a booth by the window. We shrugged out of our coats and slid in next to them. "We've deemed this a no-thinking weekend," Izzy announced. "So we're auto-ordering."

"No argument here," Hershey replied, handing Rachel her Gemini. "My brain is fried." Rachel touched each of our handhelds to the scanner on the wall, and a few seconds later our order popped up on the screen. "Anybody good here?" Hershey asked, craning her neck to scan the crowded room.

"Eh," Rachel replied with a disinterested shrug. "Mostly townies."

"Your boyfriend is here," Hershey announced. I thought she was talking to Izzy, but she was looking at me. I followed her gaze. North was at the take-out counter, paying cash for a large pizza. I quickly looked away.

"You mean *your* boyfriend," I corrected, keeping my voice light.

Rachel turned to look. "He's the guy?"

Hershey made a face. "He is most definitely *not* the guy. But he has a thing for Rory. You should see the way he flirts with her."

Annoyance shot through me. I didn't want to rock the boat with Hershey since we were getting along so well, but this charade was a little much.

"If you don't want to talk about your hookup, that's fine," I said evenly. "But please don't make crap like that up just to cover it up."

Hershey blinked, stunned. "Wait, you think I'm hooking up with *North*?"

She looked so surprised that I faltered. "Aren't you?"

"No!" she replied. *Then what were you doing at his apartment with your dress off?* I almost fired back. But I didn't want to let on that I knew, or explain why I was at his apartment that night. Not in front of Rachel and Izzy.

"Two Hansen's, a lemonade, and a diet Z Cola," our waitress said, passing out our drinks. Instead of putting my napkin on the table, she handed it to me, folded once in half. I noticed the handwriting inside right away.

I need to talk to you. It's important.—N. P.

185

I quickly crumpled up the napkin and shoved it into my pocket. The other girls were discussing the ingredients lists on their soda cans and didn't notice. I turned my own can in my hands and wondered what North could possibly *need* to say to me. If whatever it was was so important, why didn't he come over here and say it to my face, instead of sending me a cryptic napkin note? The answer, of course, had to be Hershey. What game was he playing here? What game was *she*? I watched her across the table as the four of us devoured our extra-large deep-dish, unanimously ignoring Lux's suggestion that we stop at two pieces each, and wondered.

Rachel and Izzy were meeting some guys on the debate team for brownies after dinner, but I was too stuffed and too tired to do anything but sleep, preferably for about a day and a half.

"You guys go ahead," I told them as we took turns swiping our handhelds to split the bill. "I've gotta go to bed."

"I'll go back with you," Hershey said. When it was my turn to pay, she waved my phone away and double-swiped hers. "My treat."

As we parted ways on the sidewalk, Hershey linked her arm through mine. As if on cue, we yawned in perfect unison then immediately lapsed into exhausted, slightly maniacal giggles.

"I'm so tired, I can barely feel my legs," Hershey said as we crossed the street to cut through the park, arms still linked.

"I'm so tired, I think I'm already asleep," I said.

We giggled again then fell into a comfortable silence. Just

as I was about to ask her about North, Hershey cleared her throat. "Can we talk about the voice?" she asked. I felt myself stiffen. Hershey had to have felt it too, which is probably why she didn't wait for my answer. "I've never heard it," she said before I could shut her down. "Even when I was little. I used to envy the kids that did."

"Why?"

Hershey looked thoughtful. "I figured I was missing out, I guess. Everyone would talk about being 'led' and feeling 'guided.' It seemed so . . . easy. To not have to weigh the options and decide for yourself. To be given the answers without having to take the test."

I almost laughed at the absurdity of it. *Easy?* Yeah, right. Listening to the Doubt meant completely setting yourself aside. Even as a kid, I'd understood that. The voice would whisper not to worry when reason said I should. It'd tell me to slow down when I needed to hurry, to be kind when I was angry, to listen when I so desperately wanted to be heard. "Guided" was the euphemism for being chastised and corrected and coaxed.

"I mean, obviously the answers are *wrong*," Hershey said then. "They have to be, right? It's not the Doubt unless it's irrational, so—"

I interrupted her. "It's not irrational. It's *a*rational." That had been the most surprising discovery in my APD research—other than finding out that my mom had it. The "irrational inkling" was another nickname for it, but the empirical evidence suggested that the voice was much less predictable than that.

"*A*rational?"

"Not rational or irrational," I explained. "Sort of outside the realm of reason, I guess."

She considered this. "Is it weird when it speaks to you?" she asked then.

"It's hard to remember," I lied. "It's been so long."

"Rory." Her voice was gentle but chiding. "I know you still hear it. Talk to me about it. I'm not going to tell anyone."

I looked over at her and hesitated, wavering. I hadn't planned on ever telling anyone about the voice, not my dad, not even Beck. And here I was about to spill it to Hershey, a girl with secrets of her own she insisted on keeping, a girl who hardly inspired a great deal of trust. There was no way that was a good idea. I should've asked her how she could possibly know what I'd barely admitted to myself, but I was too caught up in my response to wonder about the question.

Hershey kept pressing. "It told you to help me study, didn't it?"

I started to shake my head to deny it, but Hershey barreled on. "It's the only explanation. Why else would you do it? It's not like I had some compelling sob story to win you over. I blew off school. I deserved to fail."

"No, you didn't," I said, more for my own benefit than hers.

"Rory, come on," she said, swinging around in front of me to look me in the eye.

"The voice did tell me to help you," I said finally. "But

188

that's not why I did it. I helped you because you're my friend."
This was the truth. It struck me in that moment how disturbing that should be—that my mind and the Doubt's had been completely in sync.

Hershey burst into tears. Instinctively, I reached for her hand. It sat limply in mine as she cried.

"Hersh, it's really not a big deal," I said softly. "You needed help, I helped. It's not like it hurt me at all. I did fine on my tests."

"You don't understand," she said, shaking her head.

"So tell me. What's going on?"

She shook her head again. "I can't," she whispered. "You'd hate me."

For a second I forgot she didn't know anything about me and North. That had to be what she couldn't bring herself to tell me—that she was hooking up with the guy I liked. So I made it easy for her.

"Hershey, I already know."

Her eyes jerked up. "What?"

"Not the details, but I know something happened. I came by his apartment that night. I saw your dress on his floor."

Confusion flashed in her eyes. "Huh?"

"You and North," I said. "The night of the Masquerade Ball."

Finally it registered. "So *that's* why you thought we were hooking up!"

"If you weren't, why was your dress on his floor?"

"Because I puked on it," she replied. "I went to Paradiso thinking coffee would sober me up. Ugh, I could throw up again just thinking about it." She grimaced. "Anyway, North loaned me some clothes and gave me a bag for the dress. That was it. Really." I believed her, but it didn't completely make sense. If it was so innocent, why didn't North just tell me that when I showed up at his door? Instead he'd seemed so cagey, so concerned that Hershey would find out I was there. *I can explain,* he'd said. So why hadn't he? The wad of napkin felt like lead in my pocket. "So does he know you like him?" she asked.

"I don't like him," I said quickly.

"Mm-hm. Whatever. But he'd be lucky to have you." She slipped her arm through mine and laid her head on my shoulder. "I'm sorry I've been such a sucky friend," she said after a minute.

"You haven't been *that* bad," I said, squeezing her arm. I waited for her to laugh or make a joke, but she didn't. She was quiet after that.

We stayed like that the whole way back to campus, my hand on her arm, her head on my shoulder. *I've never had this,* I thought. Having a boy BFF has its perks—less drama, less gossip, more action movies—but I'd missed out on the sisterhood of girlfriends. The comfort of sameness. I'd envied other girls, their ease with one another, the way they occupied the same physical space, touching one another's hair and faces, clinging to arms and waists. With a boy, there had to be margin.

Distance. You couldn't hold hands or sit on laps or walk arm in arm like this. Unless, of course, you were more than friends, but Beck and I never were. With a pang I realized that I hadn't spoken to my best friend in weeks. We'd texted a few times, but he hadn't returned any of my calls. It wasn't entirely unlike him—he hated the phone—but still, it stung. We caught up with two girls from my pod in the courtyard. Dana and Maureen. They were carrying bags of movie theater popcorn and jumbo-size boxes of candy.

"What'd you guys see?" I asked as we fell in stride with them.

"*Sugar Sword Four*," Dana replied, making a face. "So bad."

"Serves us right for not asking Lux before spending twenty-three dollars on the fourth installment of a franchise about a girl who fights crime with candy," Maureen chimed in. "Then again, the only other choice at the theater downtown was a war movie. After our practicum midterm, I couldn't watch another explosion." She shuddered a little.

I felt the smile fade from my lips. Going out with Hershey had made me forget my practicum midterm, but the mention of it brought the horrible images rushing back. I'd gotten so caught up in celebrating my grades that I'd forgotten to search for the real incident online. Was Liam right? Was the scenario based on something that had actually happened? My stomach squeezed at the thought.

I waited until we were back in our room to start looking. "Want to watch *Forensic Force*?" Hershey asked from her bed.

I was lying across mine, typing the words "dock explosion faulty firework island" into GoSearch, and I didn't look up.

"Sure."

"What are you doing?" Hershey asked. In my peripheral vision, I could see her craning her neck to see my screen.

"Trying to find the news story Tarsus used for our practicum exam today."

"The people on the dock?"

I glanced at her and nodded.

Hershey looked at me like I'd said I wanted to rip my nails off with rusty pliers. "Why?"

"I just . . . want to know what really happened, I guess." I was barely acknowledging this to myself and definitely wouldn't admit it to Hershey, but the truth was, I was looking for absolution. In some weird and twisted way, if more people died in the real version than did in my simulation, I could let myself off the hook. If I'd done better for those people onscreen than they'd fared in life, maybe I'd stop feeling guilty about the ones I didn't save.

"Well, I think it's a bad idea," Hershey declared, aiming her handheld at the wallscreen. "Shitty things happen in the world. There's no use dwelling on them." She scrolled down to the most recent episode of *Forensic Force* and pressed play.

"I'm not dwelling," I muttered as I scanned the first page of search results. When I didn't see anything that looked remotely like our exam, the tension I'd been carrying around started to give way. Until I tapped over to the next page and was staring at an image identical to the scene I'd seen in class. The same green mountains in the distance, the same floating bridge leading to the same white sand beach, the same wooden crates of fireworks and crowded dock. It was a "before" photo, obviously, pre-explosion, when the platform was still intact. But it had to be from the same day. I double-tapped the photo and read the caption beneath it: INDEPENDENCE DAY CELEBRATION IN FIJI, OCTOBER 10, 2030.

Less than a week ago. The photo wasn't attached to an article, so I searched again, with the date this time. The top hit was a story from the day after, with the headline "Dock Accident Cuts Fiji Freedom Fest Short." I tapped my screen to open the page. I had to read the first paragraph three times before I understood what happened.

In a fortuitous accident, a floating platform holding a crowd of natives and tourists in Fiji collapsed on Sunday, dropping celebrants into the South Pacific Ocean just moments before the event's arsenal of fireworks exploded. With more than eight hundred in attendance for the island's annual Fiji Freedom Fest, it is believed that the weight on the dock moments before the collapse was nearly three times its posted limit.

"Thank God they broke the rules," John Smith, an American tourist on his honeymoon, remarked afterward. "If the dock hadn't collapsed, we all would've been standing on it when the fireworks blew."

Instead the wooden crates that held the more than
two tons of aerial-display fireworks caught fire just
as they sunk below the surface of the water, killing
hundreds of tropical fish but no humans.

I swallowed hard. In real life the dock had broken apart just moments before the fireworks caught fire. But I'd evacuated at least half of the weight by then, preventing the collapse and thus ensuring the explosion. The relief I should've felt that no real people had died was sucked away by a stilling reverence for the voice that had known how to save them.

The Doubt had been right.

If I hadn't done anything—if I'd only *waited*—every single person on that dock would've survived. But how could the voice have known that? The Doubt didn't belong to some external, omniscient force. It was an auditory hallucination my brain produced. But if that's all it was, then how could it have told me something I didn't know? Because there was no way I could've known that platform would collapse when it did.

I sat there, staring at my screen until it went dark, emotions rushing through me like river water. What was I supposed to do now?

I reached for the pendant around my neck, pinching it between finger and thumb. Is this what my mother had gone through, this same internal debate? In the end, she'd chosen to trust the voice, and look how it had ended for her. With a permanent diagnosis and a ticket back to Seattle.

"Find it?" I heard Hershey ask.

"The dock collapsed before the explosion," I told her, tossing my tablet onto her bed. She scanned the story then tossed it back.

"That's good news, right?"

When I didn't answer, Hershey looked at me. "What?" I hesitated. So long that she asked again. "Rory. What?"

"I heard the Doubt during the exam," I said finally, regretting it as soon as the words were out. But I needed to tell someone, and Beck wasn't there. He also hadn't returned yet another one of my voice messages, which my brain didn't have space to analyze at that moment. Hershey didn't react. She just picked up the remote to pause the TV.

"Okay," she said. "And?"

"And it told me to wait."

"To wait?"

"We were supposed to save as many people as possible," I explained in a hushed, hurried voice, even though we were alone in our room. "And I didn't know what to do. There were all these little kids . . . I just kind of froze. And then I panicked, because obviously the test was timed, and we didn't know when the dock would explode, just that it would."

"Ugh, your exam sounds so cool. Ours was so lame. But keep going."

"The point is I thought I had to hurry. Everyone did. How else were we supposed to get those people off the dock before it exploded? But the voice, it told me not to do anything. It said to wait. Which made no sense. Except—"

"The dock would've collapsed before the explosion," Hershey said. "You would've saved them all." She exhaled, her breath whistling through her teeth. "And there's no way your brain could've figured that out somehow?"

"No."

Hershey looked thoughtful. "So the Doubt, it—"

"It knew something I didn't," I said. "Which is impossible. Scientifically, empirically impossible."

"Yeah. You're right. So it must've just been a fluke, then." She was baiting me, because she could tell I didn't believe that.

I rolled over onto my back and looked up at the ceiling. "Do you think it's possible that the Doubt isn't as bad as people think?"

Hershey was quiet. I glanced over at her again. She was on her back too, staring at the ceiling. "But there's science," she said finally, but without her usual conviction. "Studies that prove that the Doubt isn't rational." She turned her head and met my gaze. "Right?"

There *were* studies. I'd read most of them. But as I'd pointed out in my research paper, none were particularly complete. The most famous one compared life outcomes between people like my mom and people like Hershey—people who professed to trust the Doubt and people who claimed never to have heard it—and concluded that the second group fared much better in terms of happiness, stability, and prosperity. It was a splashy headline, but it hardly said anything about the

Doubt itself. "I guess I'm just not convinced," I said finally. "But even that freaks me out, because that's probably how it started for my mom, too, and look what happened to her."

"What *did* happen to her?" Hershey asked.

"I don't really know," I admitted. "I know she started hearing the Doubt, and she saw a psychiatrist about it. It got pretty bad, I guess—her grades were suffering and stuff—and her doctor wanted to commit her. So they expelled her."

"Wow," Hershey said. "That's heavy."

I rolled onto my side, toward her. "Please don't say anything to anyone. About my mom, or what I heard today."

"I won't," she said. "I promise." But she didn't meet my gaze.

16

HERSHEY SPENT THE WEEKEND doing homework, venturing into the library for the first time all semester. I found her asleep on top of her tablet in the otherwise empty main reading room late Saturday afternoon, drooling on her calculus problem set. I curled up in one of the armchairs by the reading room's crackling fire and let her sleep while I waded through my lit reading.

I kept zoning out, thinking about North.

I wanted to believe Hershey's story about what happened, but it didn't completely make sense. If it was so innocent, why didn't North just tell me what was going on when I showed up at his door?

I was still wondering about it and debating my next move as I sat in practicum on Tuesday morning, half listening to Dr. Tarsus's lecture on prudence. Outside our classroom window, storm clouds were rolling in off the mountain.

"And while I'm loath to imply that it's simple," Tarsus was

saying, "I do think the formula is instructive." She wrote with her finger on the front wall, and an equation appeared there in green chalk.

$Pr = K/n * R * I$

"Prudence, Pr, is a function of n, the number of knowable facts, K, the number of known facts, R, the actor's inherent capacity for reason, and I, the actor's commitment to action." Tarsus paused and surveyed the room. "Questions?"

"Can you maybe do an example?" Dana asked, her voice echoing a little in my pod's headrest speakers.

"Certainly," our teacher replied, turning back to the wall. "Let's use a historical—"

"You're missing something," I blurted out. Tarsus's eyes darted my way. I clasped my hand over my mouth. "I'm sorry," I said quickly. "I didn't mean to—"

"By all means, Rory, enlighten me," she said, crossing her arms. "What have I left out?"

"Unknowable facts," I said weakly, wishing I'd just kept my mouth shut. It seemed so obvious to me, but Tarsus was looking at me like I'd said something unintelligible.

"I think perhaps you've misunderstood," Tarsus replied, her voice dripping with condescension. "The variable n represents all facts that *could* be known by the actor." She tapped the letter with her fingernail. "K, then, represents the number of those facts that *are* known by the actor. Thus, any 'unknown' facts are accounted for in—"

I interrupted her again, this time on purpose. Her tone was

really irritating me. I had the highest grade in her class and she was talking to me like I was an idiot. Plus, I felt sure of myself in a way I often didn't. Not in a cocky way. I just knew I was on to something. "Not *unknown*," I corrected. "Unknowable. As in, not susceptible to perception by the senses. Factors the actor cannot comprehend with reason alone."

Tarsus's expression darkened for a moment, then her lips curled into a sour smile. "Since I'd like to avoid wasting class time with this useless frolic, I suggest you and I continue this discussion after class." Without waiting for me to respond, she moved on.

When she dismissed us, I strode to her desk, angry enough to be bold. Tarsus looked at me with arched eyebrows. "You seem upset," she said.

"I'm not upset," I said. "I'm confused. When the syllabus said 'class participation encouraged,' I thought it meant you were willing to listen to what we had to say."

Tarsus smiled. "So your feelings are hurt, is that it?"

"No, my feelings are not hurt," I said, keeping my voice even. "I'd just like to understand why you were so quick to shut me down."

"Because I knew where the conversation was heading, and I was trying to help you, Rory. 'Unknowable facts'? Have you ever heard the expression 'You can't un-ring a bell?'" She cocked her head, examining me, her black eyes even more eagle-ish than usual.

"What bell are we talking about here?"

"There's no doubt that you're bright, Rory," she said in a knowing voice. "But your comments in class today were very concerning. Someone with your background ought to be careful about what she says."

"My background?" I asked, as though there was any doubt what she meant. Tarsus didn't bother elaborating.

"You know what the word *akratic* means, don't you?" she asked. "It's Greek for acting against one's better judgment. And while you're doing very well in this class, I saw you in our exam on Friday. You said the word *wait* out loud, as if you were talking to someone. Who could it have been?"

The boldness I'd felt just seconds before fluttered away, leaving only a pounding heart in my rib cage.

"No one," I said quickly. "I wasn't talking to anyone."

Tarsus cocked her head. "Are you sure about that?"

I knew I should just get out of there before I made things worse, but something was bothering me and I couldn't leave without an answer.

"What would've happened if I *had* waited?" I asked her, my voice wavering just a little. "If I'd left everybody on that dock."

Tarsus didn't hesitate. "You would have failed the exam."

"But in real life, the dock—"

"Collapsed. Yes, I know. But reason dictates that an overloaded dock should be evacuated to prevent collapse, not left as is in order to cause it." She was watching me closely. "So if you'd left all those people on the dock despite knowing that the crates would explode, then I would've had to assume that one of two things had occurred. Either you'd been paralyzed by indecision or blinded by an irrational impulse. Both would've been grounds for a failing grade."

"So you were trying to trick me," I said.

Tarsus's mouth curved into an icy smile. "Trick you? Now you sound paranoid. Perhaps a visit to the campus health center would do you some good. I can write you a referral if you'd like."

I swallowed, my throat like sandpaper. "What did I do to make you hate me so much?

Tarsus just laughed. "I don't care about you enough to hate you, Rory." She turned away then, having gotten the last word again. "Please close the door on your way out."

I somehow made it through history, but there was no way I could choke down lunch. So I changed into sweats and went for a run through the woods instead, letting the sound of leaves crunching beneath my sneakers drown out the cacophony of noises in my head. It started to drizzle as I was starting my third lap around the cemetery. Without thinking, I climbed over the fence and sprinted toward the mausoleum, cutting across the graves to get there faster. Other than the rhythmic sound of rain split-splatting on dry leaves, it was quiet as I approached. It wasn't until I'd slipped through the wrought-iron gate of the mausoleum that I heard the music.

I put my knuckles to the granite to knock, but that seemed

a little ridiculous, and it's not like they would've heard me any-way. So I took a breath and leaned the weight of my body into the stone the way I'd seen North do. The rock slid away.

I was expecting the whole band so I jumped a little when I saw only North. He was on the floor, leaning against the marble coffin, a laptop on his lap, its speakers blaring.

"Rory," he said as I stepped inside the tomb. There was surprise in his voice, and relief. He set his computer aside and scrambled to his feet.

"I got your note," I said.

"How'd you know I was here?" He moved toward me slowly, his eyes never leaving my face, as if he were afraid I might disappear.

"I didn't," I said. Then softer, "I just hoped you were." I shifted awkwardly from one foot to the other. "You said you could explain."

He nodded. "I can. But you should probably sit down." He gestured toward the mourner's bench behind us.

My stomach dipped. "Okay," I said, and sat.

He sat down next to me, angling his body toward mine so our knees were nearly touching. "I tried so many times to get in touch with you," he said, leaning forward on his elbows. His hair was wet from the rain. "But no matter whose account I used, you blocked me. I even thought about sneaking on cam-pus, but the school got a restraining order against me last year and—"

"Wait, *what*?"

He looked sheepish. "The guys and I broke into one of the buildings to record. The one with the organ and the gold dome."

"You broke into the Grand Rotunda? Didn't you know there'd be an alarm?"

"I disabled the alarm. They caught us when the canister blew."

"The canister?"

"We were using a huge canister of compressed air to play the pipes like a xylophone," North explained. "Or trying to. It exploded the first time we tried to let air out."

"Holy crap. Did they arrest you?"

"Just me," North replied. "I told the other guys to run." He saw the look on my face. "It sounds like a big deal, but I wasn't seventeen yet, so it was juvie court, and they let me plead it down to a misdemeanor that'll come off my record completely when I turn eighteen." His expression darkened. "The school sued me separately, though, and got the restraining order. I can't come within fifty feet of their property line." He smiled a little. "Not that you're not worth some jail time," he said, nudging my knees with his. Then his eyes got serious. "But a criminal record would destroy my career."

His *career*? It was an odd word choice for a guy who made coffee for a living.

He took an unsteady breath. "There are things you don't know about me, Rory," he said then, and my arms prickled with goose bumps. I inched back on the bench, drawing my knees to my chest. "And I want to tell you. It's just—" He stopped. His eyes were searching mine, jerking back and forth and back and forth like the sound bar on a decibel meter, and his back foot was jiggling like a jackhammer.

"It's just what?"

His eyes dropped to his knees. "I've never told anyone what I'm about to tell you. Literally, not a single person. So, it's just—" He lifted his eyes again. "Can I trust you, Rory?"

"Of course," I said, and reached for his hand. We both jumped a little when we touched, but I didn't pull away this time, and he turned his palm up to face mine. My heart was pounding like a drum.

"First," he began, "there was never anything going on between Hershey and me. What you saw that night wasn't what you thought you saw."

I nodded. "Hershey told me what happened."

"Yeah. I doubt she told you all of it." His voice was grim.

"So tell me the rest."

"The day we met, when I made you the matcha. That night, Hershey came back—late—just as we were closing. I think she was a little drunk."

The night of the welcome dinner. Hershey snuck out that night. She'd been drinking, too. The airplane bottles of Baileys and whatever else.

"What did she want?" I asked, even though I knew what she wanted. She'd made it clear that afternoon when we met North.

"She basically told me she was game for a no-strings-attached arrangement," North said. "I politely declined."

I couldn't help it. I giggled. "How'd she take that?"

"Not so well," North said with a laugh. For a second the heaviness of the moment lifted. "She said, and I quote, 'It's a long way down from here.'"

"She didn't!"

"Oh, yes. She did." North shook his head in disbelief. "I have to give her points for a healthy self-image." He shrugged a little. "I shouldn't have cared, I guess, but I felt bad about rejecting her and then immediately going after you. That's why I asked you not to say anything to her about us. I didn't want to rub it in her face that I was crazy about you."

"Crazy about me, huh?" I managed to sound teasing, but I felt lightheaded, like I might faint.

"I'll get to that in a minute," North said, squeezing my hand. "I need to get the rest of this out, first." I nodded. "Okay. So. The night of your dance she came into Paradiso for coffee, piss-drunk, then puked all over herself. She had puke splatter on her arms and was very worked up about getting it on her dress. So I told her she could get cleaned up at my place and sleep it off for a couple hours."

"Nice of you," I said.

"She was your roommate. And your friend, I thought." The way he said *I thought* made my stomach sink. Where was he going with this?

He took a breath before continuing. "While she was in the

shower, I got out her phone to text you. She'd just been on it, so it was still unlocked. When I clicked on her message pane, I saw an outgoing message to a blocked number attaching a document with your name on it."

I pulled my hand back. "What do you mean, a document with my name on it?"

"The file name. Well, technically it was your social security number, but I recognized it."

"Wait, *what*? You know my social security number?"

North took a breath. "Yes. And I can explain. But you need to know what was in this document first."

"You opened it?"

He nodded. "It was the fifth time she'd sent the document to that same blocked number, and each time the file size got bigger. I had a really bad feeling about it. And I was right."

I felt sick. "What do you mean?"

"It was a log," he said. "Like, a journal, with dates and times, but it was all stuff you'd done. Conversations she'd had with you." His voice got faster, more urgent, as he went on. "And there were references to audio files that weren't attached to the message, so while she was in the shower, I imaged her Gemini. You showed up right as I started, and I knew if Hershey heard you, she'd catch me."

I held up both hands, stopping him. "What do you mean, you 'imaged' her Gemini?"

"I made a copy of its contents," he explained. "So I could go through it after she'd left."

"I don't understand. How?"

North hesitated, his eyes doing the back-and-forth thing again. "I'm a hacker," he said finally, watching closely for my reaction. "I do that kind of thing for a living."

"A hacker," I repeated. Whatever I was expecting him to say, it wasn't that. "So, what, you get paid to break into people's handhelds?"

"Among other things. Look, Rory, I'm not going to try to rationalize it to you. I know it's illegal—"

"*Very* illegal." I wasn't trying to be judgy, but it came out that way. He slid back on the bench, away from me.

"Yes," North said, sounding more guarded now. "Very illegal. Which is why my clients pay me a lot of money for my services, and why no one but you knows what I really do."

"Which is what, exactly?" I asked.

"Most of my work relates to public image restoration," he said. "A person does something embarrassing, pictures end up online, and with Forum's ridiculous privacy policies, there's no way to take them down once they're up. Even if you hide the photos from your timeline, they're still there. Same with wall posts and status updates. They live forever." North shrugged. "So people pay me to remove them."

"Rich people."

"Very rich people. With a lot to lose. People who need my services but prefer that I not formally exist."

"So your Forum profile—"

"Is there in case anyone starts digging. My name is real, but nothing else. All the check-ins, the status updates, the Forum chats—all fake." He slid closer to me and took my hands. "I hid it from you because I didn't want you to think I was that guy. I wanted to be real with you. I wanted to just be me."

His breath smelled like coffee and breath mints. I kissed him right then, leaning forward so quickly my feet landed on his and our teeth knocked together before we found each other's lips.

We pulled away a few seconds later, both breathless, him from surprise and me from the exhilaration of what I'd just done.

"I confess to lying to you and I get that? I should hide stuff from you more often," he quipped.

I swatted him on the arm. "No. You shouldn't. You get a one-time pass, that's all."

"I'll take it," he said, and smiled. Then his brow furrowed, and the giddy joy I'd been feeling evaporated.

"I need to see that file," I said.

"Yes, you do." North pulled a clunky iPhone from his pocket. It was nearly twice the size of my Gemini. He tapped the cloud icon on his screen.

"Wait, how do you have service?" I asked him.

"I'm using Wi-Fi instead of the Li-Fi. It's the old commu-nications infrastructure, before VLC replaced cellular. Since I'm here so much, I installed an access point on the roof." He typed a few words onto his screen then handed it to me. He was quiet as I read.

By the end of the first page I thought I might puke. It was a log, like North had said, of everything I'd said and done since we arrived on campus, and every entry was written to make me sound unstable. I was "paranoid" that Dr. Tarsus hated me, "obsessed" with Lux, "evasive" about my mom's past, and "preoccupied" with my mom's necklace. Midway through the second page I stopped reading and closed my eyes.

North scooted over so he was next to me, and he put his arm around my shoulder. "Do you have any idea who she's been sending this to?"

I shook my head, at a loss. Someone in the secret society maybe? Could this be part of their evaluation? It seemed plausible that they'd ask roommates for dirt. But why would mine throw me under the bus like that?

My eyes were still closed when North kissed my tear-streaked cheek. His nose was cold, and feeling it on my face made me smile despite everything.

"I should go," I said reluctantly, handing back his phone. "I have class this afternoon, and I have to talk to Hershey."

"Are you going to tell her what you know?"

"I have to. But I won't mention you, don't worry," I assured him.

"Mention me all you want," North said, standing up. "Tell her I saw the log on her phone and opened it. Just as long as she doesn't know how I got the rest of it." He gave me his hands and tugged me to my feet. My body bumped against his and I felt it all down my spine.

"Thank you," I said, stepping back a little, putting some distance between us. If I stayed this close to him, there was no chance I would make it to my next class. "For finding the file, for showing it to me."

"You're welcome," he said, and slid open the mausoleum door. Then he pulled me to him and kissed me, a thousand slow kisses, in the rain.

Hershey was sprawled out on her bed doing homework when I got back after my last class.

"Hey!" she said, all smiles. "How was your day?"

My gut twisted, like a towel being wrung out.

"I know what you did," I spat, my voice tight, fully aware that I sounded like a sixth-grade girl.

Hershey's smile faded. "Huh?"

"I read what you've been writing about me."

Hershey went pale. "Rory. Oh, God. I can explain."

"Yes," I said, my voice like ice. "Please do."

Hershey took a shaky breath. "The day I got into Theden, I got a call from Dr. Tarsus. I thought she was just calling to congratulate me on getting in. But then she said she needed my help. That another girl from my school had been accepted, but she thought the admissions board had made a mistake, and she needed me to help her prove it." *Dr. Tarsus.* I put my palm on the surface of my desk to steady myself. It wasn't the secret society after all. It was much, much worse.

Wringing her hands, Hershey went on. "She said they

shouldn't have let you in because of your mom. Because she was 'akratic.'" Tears were rolling down Hershey's cheeks, leaving streaks in her bronzer. "She said we could force your dismissal by presenting evidence to the executive committee that you were unstable, but that I couldn't tell anyone what we were doing until she'd built her case. She said she'd make sure I had access to you, all I had to do was keep a log and record some conversations." Hershey gave her head a hard, angry shake. "I should've told her to go f—"

I cut her off. Her *should've*'s were useless to me. "So she knows I hear the Doubt," I said dully. "You were recording our conversation on Friday. That's why you kept asking me about the voice."

"No," Hershey said firmly. "No. I haven't written down or recorded a single thing since you helped me on Thursday night and won't ever again." She came toward me and reached for my hands, but I snatched them back. "Rory," she said, "I am so sorry I did this."

"Why did you?"

"I was flattered, I guess, that she'd ask for my help." She sounded ashamed. "And by the time that wore off, too envious of you to stop."

"You expect me to believe you did this because you *envied* me?" I let out a bitter laugh. "Wow, you must really think I'm an idiot."

"Of course I envied you, Rory. You were a freaking Hepta

212

and, worse, you didn't even *know* it. Everything came so easily to you."

"You've got to be kidding me. *Easy?* I worked my ass off to get here, and I've been working twice as hard ever since. And now you've taken all of it away from me." Something caught in my throat. I pressed my lips together to keep from crying.

Hershey put her hands on my shoulders. "Listen to me, Rory. I'll fix this. I'll tell her I won't do it anymore. Then I'll go to the dean. I promise you, I won't let her hang you out to—"

"Don't you get it?" I spat, shrugging away from her. "It's too late. You already gave her the rope."

I turned on my heels and walked out.

17

I WAS OUTSIDE PARADISO six minutes later, heaving from the run. I could feel my hair plastered to my forehead and could only imagine how crazy I must look. Sweatpants, no jacket in fifty-degree weather, nose red, eyes rimmed with the morning's mascara. Not exactly how I wanted North to see me. But too late, he already had.

He left a customer at the counter to meet me at the door.

"Hey," he said in a low voice. "How'd it go?"

"One of my teachers put her up to—" I stopped as my eyes landed on my lit teacher, who was watching me from the condiment station. North followed my gaze and lowered his voice even more. "Why don't you head up to my apartment?" he said, pressing his keys into my hand. "I get off at five." I slipped my Gemini from my back pocket to check the time. It was four-thirty.

"Okay," I said, closing my fingers around the keys. My teacher wasn't paying any attention to me now, but I felt the need to be stealthy. Maybe Tarsus wasn't the only faculty member who wanted me out. Plus North wasn't exactly citizen of the year. It didn't help either of us for us to be seen together.

As I mounted the steps to North's door, I toggled my privacy switch. I didn't want Hershey coming to find me here. I didn't want to hear her apology, partly because I was afraid I might forgive her.

I let myself into the apartment and locked the door behind me. Stepping out of my boots, I wandered over to North's bookshelf in bare feet.

I let my finger slide over broken spines as I scanned titles. There were some I'd heard of and a bunch I hadn't. Some were barcoded and covered in plastic, former library books, before libraries went completely electronic. Others were worn and water stained. The books on the very top shelf were hardbacks with tattered fabric covers, their titles etched in gold leafing instead of printed with ink.

The book on the end was shoved back slightly, recessed from the rest, so I reached for it to pull it forward. I started a little when I saw its title: *Paradise Lost* by John Milton.

I heard myself mumbling the words on the handwritten note my mom had left me. I hadn't realized I'd memorized them. *I formed them free, and free they must remain til they enthrall themselves; I else must change their nature.* I pulled the book from the shelf and turned it over in my hands. The pages were uneven and yellowed, and the edges of the fabric cover were frayed. Gingerly, I opened to the first page. The paper was dry and splotched with age.

Paradise Lost
A Poem in Twelve Books
The author John Milton
This Seventh Edition, Adorn'd with Sculptures
Printed in London, 1705

I'd never seen a book this old. Early editions were super rare. And expensive. Which, it struck me then, might not be a big deal for someone like North. How much would rich people pay to have their transgressions erased? A lot, I imagined. I grazed the page with my fingertips, not wanting to damage the delicate paper. Gently, I began to turn pages, one by one, not so much looking for the quote as taking in the book as a whole, its eerie oldness. When I got to the third page, I stopped. Instead of words, this page was a watercolor painting. The caption beneath it read:

HIM THE ALMIGHTY POWER
HURLD HEADLONG FLAMING FROM TH' ETHEREAL SKIE.

It was an excerpt from the text above, and with the image I could understand its meaning. God was casting an angel down from the sky. I turned more pages, looking for more pictures. There were many, each one stranger than the last and yet oddly familiar at the same time. When I got to Book Seven, I understood why. The caption beneath the illustration was:

GOD SAID,

LET TH' EARTH BRING FORTH FOUL LIVING IN HER KINDE,

CATTEL AND CREEPING THINGS, AND BEAST OF THE EARTH,

EACH IN THEIR KINDE.

It was a depiction of the creation of Earth. There was a lion in the center of the page, its head an exact replica of the mask Liam had worn to the Masquerade Ball, and a cluster of other animals lined up beside it, some with horns and others with antlers, some spotted, some striped, all startlingly familiar. I turned the page, looking for Adam and Eve. We'd read parts of Genesis at the beginning of the semester, so I knew they were created next. I didn't really need more confirmation, but I got it anyway. The faces of Adam and Eve I found two pages later matched the human masks I'd seen bowing to the serpent in the arena that night.

My eyes shot up to the ceiling in wordless thanks. This discovery felt purposeful, like I'd been led here, to this moment, to find these drawings, to make this connection. Both the note my mom had left me and the masks the secret society used were taken from this book. There had to be something more in these pages. Maybe a clue to what she was trying to tell me. I held the book against my chest and willed myself to find it.

There was a soft knock. "It's me" came North's voice

through the door. I was still holding the book when I let him in.

"Milton fan?" he asked with a nod at the book.

"I think I might be," I replied. "I'll let you know after I've read it."

"You want to borrow my copy?"

I looked at him in surprise. "Can I? It looks expensive."

He laughed, reaching around me to close the door. "It was. But I assume you're not planning to use it as a drink coaster. Of course you can borrow it. Books are meant to be read. On paper."

"How retro of you," I teased. North dropped his messenger bag and walked into the kitchen with a brown bag. As he opened the bag, my stomach growled in anticipation.

"Ham or turkey?" he asked.

"Turkey," I said, hopping up onto his single bar stool as he slid my choice across the kitchen counter. The sandwich was panini pressed, the cheese dripping out from between dark crusty toast.

I bit into it. It was even more delicious than it looked. I hungrily took another bite before I'd even swallowed the first. North reached for my wrist, turning it over in his hand.

"*Greedily she engorged without restraint*," he teased, pretending to etch the words into my skin.

I felt myself blush as I hurried to swallow. "I didn't have lunch!" I said between chews.

"It's a line from *Paradise Lost*," he said, laughing. "Describing the moment when Eve ate the fruit from the Tree of the Knowledge of Good and Evil."

"You know it well enough to *quote* it?"

"Well, that line in particular I remember because my aunt put it on the back of the first Paradiso T-shirt she ever had printed," replied North. "The name Café Paradiso is actually a shout-out to Milton. And Università del caffè in Italy where she learned to make coffee."

"'I formed them free, and free they must remain til they enthrall themselves; I else must change their nature,'" I recited. "Book three, lines one twenty-four through one twenty-six."

North's eyebrows shot up in surprise. "Impressive for a girl who hasn't read it."

"Do you know what it means?" I asked.

"I think so," he said. "It sounds like God talking about humanity's free will. By making man free, he allowed the fall to happen."

"The 'fall,'" I repeated. "The fall from what?"

"For Satan, it was a literal fall from heaven to hell. For man, it was getting expelled from Paradise." He flipped to the back of the book, to the final illustration. An angel who bore a striking resemblance to the statue in the cemetery was leading Adam and Eve out of Eden's gates. The caption beneath it read:

THEY HAND IN HAND WITH WANDRING STEPS AND SLOW,
THROUGH EDEN TOOK THIR SOLITARIE WAY.

"In both cases, the created were trying to become like the creator and enslaving themselves in the process," North explained, his voice all teacherly and cute. "That's what Milton meant by the word *enthrall*—in Old English, it meant 'to put in bondage.' At least, a—"

"Enslaving themselves to what?" I asked, too curious to feel stupid.

"Their pride, for one thing," North replied. "And their blindness. By believing the serpent's lies, Adam and Eve altered their worldview. They saw the world differently after that. They could no longer see it for what it really was." North smiled. "Thus beginning a perpetual cycle of shitty decisions."

"But shouldn't we be able to get past that?" I asked. "I mean, God gave humanity reason, right?"

"Reason didn't do Adam and Eve much good," North pointed out.

"But they didn't know what we know," I replied. "We've progressed so much since then. As society—and science—advances, shouldn't we eventually be able to see the world for what it really is again?"

"That's one view," North said.

"What's *your* view?"

North hesitated. "Have you ever heard the term noumenon?" he asked. "It's Greek. From the word *nous*, which basically means 'intuition.'"

Nous. It was the word the serpent had used in the arena. An eerie feeling rippled through me, almost like déjà vu.

"I've heard of nous," I said vaguely. "What does noumenon mean?"

"It's a type of knowledge that doesn't come from the senses," North replied. "Truths that exist beyond the observable world. Science insists that noumenon is a fiction, that there isn't anything that exists outside of the observable world. I think Adam and Eve made that same presumption when they ate that fruit. They thought they had all the facts. They couldn't see how little they saw."

They couldn't see how little they saw. It was the mistake I'd made in my practicum exam. Thinking I had all the facts. All at once I wanted to tell him about it.

"So every Theden student has to take something called the Plato Practicum," I said, forgetting my sandwich. "It's supposed to improve our practical reasoning skills through these simulated experiences. Kind of like virtual reality, I guess. We sit in these little pods, and the scenarios play out in 3D on a three-sixty screen."

"Cool," he said, and hopped up on the stool next to me. "What are the scenarios like?"

"Well, usually we're given a set of actors whose actions we're supposed to manipulate, and we're graded on our choices. For our midterm on Friday, we had to choose who to evacuate off a crowded dock before it blew up."

"What's the goal?" North asked.

"Net positive impact," I replied. "On society as a whole.

The person who gets the best outcome relative to the rest of the class sets the curve."

North nodded as if this made perfect sense. "So you're playing Lux."

I looked at him. "What?"

"What you just described—that's exactly what Lux does," North explained. "It manipulates individual users to achieve a net positive impact across all users."

"How do you know so much about Lux? From hacking?"

"I know a lot about Lux from hacking, yes, but I know what I just told you from reading the terms of use. Which, I'm guessing from the look on your face, you still haven't read."

"It really says all that?"

"In arcane, impossibly hard to decipher legalese, yes."

"So how does it work, exactly?"

"Well, Gnosis doesn't share its algorithm, obviously, and I can't see it because it's on the back end of their server. But presumably they've come up with their version of a net positive impact function. They store user data in something called a 'SWOT matrix'—basically it's this little four-box grid cataloging a person's strengths, weaknesses, op—"

I finished his sentence. "Opportunities and threats." North's eyebrows shot up in surprise. "That's what we're given in our practicum sims," I explained. "I thought SWOT was something our teacher made up."

"Nah, it's a business term that's been around for a while," North replied. "But Gnosis has taken it to a whole new level.

They use it to promote equilibrium—their word for lives that run smoothly. You should see some of their user profiles. The level of detail is insane. They have to be, I guess, for Lux to work the way it does. Every recommendation Lux makes comes from that grid."

All of a sudden I couldn't stop thinking about the moment when I'd chosen my cog psych research topic. Why had Lux put APD at the very bottom of its recommendation list? My mom's diagnosis was in her medical file, so Lux had to know that I had a predisposition for it. So why wasn't it at the top?

"I need to see mine."

North started to shake his head.

"Please, just show it to me. I won't tell anyone."

North hesitated for another minute then sighed. "Okay," he said finally. He balled up his cellophane wrapper and dropped it in the incinerator beneath his sink. "But only because you said please." I expected him to pick up the tablet on the kitchen table, but instead he came around the island and walked toward the closet by his bed. "You coming?" he called before disappearing inside. I hopped off my stool and hurried in after him. He was standing in front of a life-size poster of Five O'Clock Flood, quite possibly the worst band in the entire history of the world.

"Uh, you have a poster of Five O'Clock Flood," I said. "In your closet. I'm not sure where to start with that one."

"Oh, Norvin is a big F.O.F. fan," North deadpanned. He squatted on his heels, pulling out the tacks from the bottom corners of the poster, and the paper immediately rolled up, like a window shade. Where the poster had been was a narrow door in the wall with a finger sensor lock. "Welcome to my office," he said, rising to his feet. He slid the tacks into his pocket and touched his thumb to the lock. There was a beep as it deactivated.

"Holy hi-tech."

"Not really," North said, pushing the door open. "The closet was huge, so I partitioned some of it off and put up a cheap fiberglass wall. If someone wanted in, they could knock through it with their fist. Hey, grab the closet door, would you? And lock it."

I pulled the door shut and turned the knob lock, then followed North into the secret room. It was tiny, just big enough for a desk and ergo chair and two wallscreens. There was a stack of old laptops in the opposite corner, each on its own narrow shelf. North pulled out the chair for me to sit on then reached for the keyboard on his desk.

"You use a keyboard," I said.

"I do. When you have to type fast, touchpads are a bitch." He pressed the enter key and the wallscreens lit up. North reached for the black mouse next to the keyboard. It was big and bulky and hardly what I'd expect a hacker to use. North saw me looking at it and grinned. "What can I say? I'm old-fashioned."

I rolled the chair closer to the screen, eager to see real hacking in action. But North just clicked on a folder on his desktop then selected the file at the top of the list. "You ready for this?"

"Wait, my profile is on your *desktop*? So you've already—"

North looked sheepish. "I downloaded it the day I met you."

"Stalk much?"

"Okay, so maybe it's borderline creepy—"

"Borderline?"

"You gave me no choice!" he protested. "You were impossible to read. And I'm an excellent reader."

"A modest stalker," I retorted. But I was smiling. "How refreshing." My smile faded as North clicked open the document. There were four quadrants, like he'd said, and within each one was a list, the entries in type so tiny you'd need a magnifying glass to read it.

"From what I can tell, they rank the entries within each category, which means the stuff at the top is weighted heavier in the algorithm. Although I'm sure there are nuances, at a very basic level the app appears to be designed to move people away from their threats and toward their opportunities, taking into account their strengths and weaknesses. So, for example, if an opportunity would expose a highly ranked weakness, the opportunity would probably become a threat. Does that make sense?"

"I don't know," I said. "I can't really focus on anything you're saying because I'm trying to read my threats list. Can we zoom in?"

North clicked on the *T* quadrant and a new document

opened. This one looked like a spreadsheet. At the top was my social security number and date of birth. Below that was a list. My eyes went to the entry at the top: *Knowledge of her blood type.*

"I don't understand," I said slowly, staring at the screen. "I know my blood type. I'm A positive."

He pointed at the next entry on my threats list. "Do you know who that is?" It was a ten-digit string in a 3/2/4 pattern, obviously a social security number: 033-75-9595.

I shook my head. "I don't understand," I said again. "There's some person out there who's been identified as a 'threat' for me?"

"Not one person," North corrected. "Half a dozen." He pointed at the next five entries on the list. All social security numbers. The sandwich I'd just eaten felt like lead in my stomach.

"Who are these people?" I asked him. "Is there any way to find out?"

"Not without a Forum handle. The way Gnosis has encrypted its data, there's no way to search across all user profiles. It's a weird idiosyncrasy I haven't been able to crack. I can click through random profiles, but I can't pull up a particular one without knowing the user's handle."

"Okay, so move them over to my opportunities list then."

North started to shake his head. "Rory—"

I cut him off. "I didn't finish what I was telling you before. About my midterm."

"The dock," North said.

"The goal was to evacuate as many 'high-value' people as possible before these huge crates of fireworks exploded. When the timer started, I just froze. There were all these little kids there, natives, and I knew they were considered low value, but I couldn't stand the idea of leaving them to die. Then, all of a sudden, I heard a voice. Telling me to wait. Not to evacuate anyone. That's the way I took it, at least."

"This voice—"

"It was the Doubt," I said firmly. I didn't want to dance around it anymore. "It was the Doubt, and I ignored it, because that was the rational thing to do. But then I found out that the simulation was based on something that happened in Fiji last week. Except in real life, the dock didn't explode because it was over its weight limit. It collapsed into the water just as the firework blew. So if I'd waited, no one would've died."

North took a few seconds to process this. "I don't understand what this has to do with your Lux profile," he said finally.

"That wasn't the first time I'd heard the voice," I said. "It started the day I flew out here, on the plane. I was worried about Theden, and the voice promised me I wouldn't fail. I heard it again the next day. Twice. Once in practicum, then again when I was picking my research topic for cog psych. The Doubt told me to pick akratic paracusia disorder. APD. It's the medical term for people who listen to the Doubt. It's sort of a long story, but if I hadn't listened to the Doubt that day—if I'd trusted Lux instead—I never would've found out that my mom had it."

"Had," North repeated. I saw something in his eyes. Not hope, exactly, but something like it. The *you, too* I'd felt when he told me he'd lost his mom.

"She died when I was born," I said. Then, because I felt my voice breaking, I barreled on. As long as I was talking, I wouldn't cry. "She was nineteen. She was diagnosed with APD while she was here, actually. At Theden. They kicked her out because of it. And I'm thinking, Lux had to have known that, right? It was right there in her medical file. So why did it try to steer me away from picking APD as my research topic? What else has Lux decided to keep from me?"

"Lux hasn't *decided* anything, Rory," North retorted. "Lux is an app following an algorithm that some computer programmers wrote after some business people pretending to be social scientists decided they could 'optimize' society by making people's lives run more smoothly."

"Fine, but that algorithm has determined that there are six people out there who somehow have the potential to throw my life into chaos. It's weird, North. Really freaking weird. Who are these people and what does my *blood type* have to do with anything? If you were me, wouldn't you want to know?"

"Sure, but—"

I grabbed his arm. "So do it. Move them to my opportunities list. Lux is designed to move a person toward her opportunities, right? If those people are at the top of the list, then—"

He put his hand on mine. "I can't, Rory." He sighed. "Not

won't. Actually can't. What you're talking about would require access to Lux's back-end data, behind Gnosis's firewall. That's impossible, even for me. Trust me, I've tried."

Hot tears sprung to my eyes. I turned away from him. "So, basically, I'm powerless."

"You're far from powerless, Rory." I felt his hands on my waist. "You have a guide that's far better than Lux."

I spun around to face him. "You're telling me to trust *the Doubt*?" My voice was incredulous. Accusing.

"*I* do," he said softly.

"You— You hear it too?"

He nodded, his eyes searching mine. "Not every day or anything. But sometimes."

"Have you ever seen a doctor about it?"

North made a face. "Why, so they could numb me out on antipsychotics? No, thank you. My brain is fine the way it is." It was the same thing Beck always said.

"But what if we're . . . sick?" *Sick* was easier to say than *crazy*.

"Do you feel sick?" North asked.

"Well, no. But I've read the research, and—"

"Whose research are we talking about here?" he scoffed. "'Science' with a capital *S*? The same geniuses who said the Earth was the center of the universe?"

"Okay, so what is it then? If it's not a hallucination, where is the voice coming from?"

"People used to think it was the voice of God."

"But that's crazy," I said, then winced when I saw North's face. "Not crazy. I just meant, why would God give us the capacity to reason and then tell us not to use it?"

"Human rationality convinced Eve it was a good idea to eat forbidden fruit," North challenged.

"But what if the Doubt is the *other* voice?" I countered. "The snake."

North just looked at me. "Do you really believe that?"

I thought of everything I knew of the voice in my head. When it had spoken, what it had said. I thought of those little children on the dock, the ones the voice had tried to help me save. "No. I guess not. But I'm still not totally convinced I should trust it. Not all the time, anyway."

North flipped over his forearm and pointed to one of his tattoos. *A double-minded man is unstable in all his ways* it read, in simple block type. I touched the words with my fingertips. There was truth in them. Unstable was exactly how I felt. Not mentally, but somewhere in my chest, at the root of myself. "It's from the Bible," North said. "The Book of James."

There was a medical term for double-mindedness. *Dipsychos.* It was part of the pathology for akratic paracusia. "Of two minds" was how my textbook defined it. Reason and the Doubt at war in your brain.

"The point is, there will always be competing voices," I heard North say. "In your head and in the world. You can't spend your life caught between them."

I looked up at him. "You're telling me to choose."

"I know better than to tell you to do anything," North said, reaching around me to shut down his computer. "But if you don't decide, the world will choose for you."

18

I CALLED MY DAD on the walk back to campus, but he and Kari were at Mulleady's for trivia night, and with the background noise, I could barely hear him, so the conversation didn't last long. I wasn't sure what I was planning to say to him anyway. I wanted to ask about my blood type, to see if he had any clue how it could've possibly ended up at the very top of my Lux threat list, but obviously couldn't tell him why I was asking or what North had shown me or why I felt so rattled by what I'd seen.

I tried Beck next, but he didn't pick up.

Hershey wasn't in our room when I got there. It was already after ten, so I buried myself in bed and tried to relax under the weight of the covers. My mind was whizzing, whirling, and my body ached with tension I couldn't let go of. Over and over I heard North's voice. *If you don't decide, the world will choose for you.* It reminded me of something the Doubt said that night in the arena. *Choose today whom you will serve.* But I hadn't.

I was still wavering, hovering, between trusting the voice and wishing it'd leave me alone.

"I don't want to be double-minded," I said to my ceiling. Then I waited, as if I might get a reply. When none came, I rolled over onto my stomach, feeling silly for expecting one, and slipped my hand under my pillow. As I did, my fingers brushed paper. It was a piece of computer paper, folded several times. Like a note.

I unfolded the paper and lit my screen. I saw the words *Academic Achievement Report* first, then the columns of grades, then her name. Aviana Grace Jacobs. It was my mom's Theden transcript, stamped SPRING MIDTERM 2013 at the top. How the hell did it get under my pillow?

I studied it more closely now, grade by grade. A, A, A, A, A. All of them, As. How could that be? A psychiatrist had called her academic performance "dismal" two weeks before the date on this transcript. But these grades were far from dismal, they were *perfect*. It didn't make sense. Was that the point whoever had put this here was trying to make? Uneasy, I refolded the transcript and slipped it back under my pillow. "I'm so confused," I whispered in the dark, clutching my pendant. "What am I missing?"

Time passed. Hours, maybe. I was too tired to look. My achy, weary body warred with my brain, fighting for sleep. But my mind was spinning in relentless circles, keeping me awake. At some point, I pulled the blanket my mom had given me up over my shoulders and tried to envision myself running along the yellow path of the cross-stitched spiral, charging toward the center, the numbers of the Fibonacci sequence reverberating in my head: 0, 1, 1, 2, 3, 5, 8, 13, 21, 34, 55, 89, 144, 233, 377, 610, 987, 1,597. Behind my eyelids, the squares on my blanket became stone walls, and the spiral became an illuminated path in the dark. A trail I was following to the center, as if I knew I'd find something important there.

As I came around the last curve, I saw my mother. She was wearing the green sweater she'd had on in her senior class photo, her auburn hair loose around her shoulders the way I often wore mine. She smiled when she saw me, opening her arms wide.

"Mama," I cried, rushing toward her. I slipped my arms around her, pressing my face against her neck.

"Don't be deceived," she whispered into my hair. "Where the lie is, there is truth."

"What lie?" When she didn't answer me, I pulled back to look at her face, but her eyes were still and vacant. The eyes of a corpse.

With a gasp I stepped back, watching in horror as leafy branches pushed out of my mother's mouth and eyes and ears, as if there were a tree growing inside of her, overtaking her. I turned to run, but suddenly there were walls all around me, closing me in as the trunk of the tree swelled against me, filling the tiny space and crushing me between wood and stone.

I awoke with a start, ice-cold, my face beaded with sweat.

It was 3:33. Hershey's bed was still empty.

With my breath ragged from the dream, I went to the bathroom to splash some warm water on my face. It didn't help. Shivering, I stood blinking at my pale reflection in the mirror, my dark hair matted to my forehead. I looked like crap. Maybe Tarsus was right; maybe the stress was getting to me. Maybe this was the brink of a breakdown. Dreaming about one's decomposing mother was hardly an indicator of health.

I turned off the faucet then tapped off the light. As soon as the room went dark, my tablet lit up.

Don't be deceived, the voice whispered.

With a creeping, tingly feeling I walked toward my night-stand. The login box for the DPH medical records database was open on my screen. But I hadn't used the DPH app since I turned in my research paper. Two weeks before.

The hair on my arms stood on end as I tapped the user-name field, praying my login credentials were still active. My heart surged with relief when the landing page appeared.

I typed my mom's social security number into the search box and waited.

No matching entries.

I checked the number I'd typed. I'd gotten it right. I tried again.

No matching entries.

The beads of sweat were back. It was as if the entire file had disappeared.

Or been erased.

"And in sets the paranoia," I muttered. My dream had left me rattled, making me suspicious when there was no reason to be. My mom's file was one of the oldest I'd run across. It'd probably been deleted to free up storage space. I was the idiot who didn't think to download it. But I *had* taken a picture. A screenshot of the final page, the entry from the day my mom died. It wasn't the whole file, but it was something. I quickly pulled it up on my screen.

I moved through the phrases slowly this time, methodically, determined to understand each word. *Ultrasound consistent with fetal post-maturity and acute oligohydramnios.* I cut and pasted the entire phrase into GoSearch. The first hit was a link to an article in the *American Journal of Obstetrics* entitled "Management of Post-Term Pregnancy."

My eyes scanned the abstract of the article. *Fetal post-maturity syndrome refers to a fetus whose growth in the uterus after the due date has been restricted.*

It didn't make any sense. My parents were married on June 11. I was born exactly thirty-six weeks later, a month before my due date. With a salty sour feeling in the back of my throat, I went back to the screenshot and scanned it for evidence of my mom's due date, or some description of how many weeks along she was. There was nothing there.

Then my eyes caught the thumbnail image of an ultrasound

picture taken when my mom arrived at the hospital. I zoomed in with my fingers. When I did, my breath snagged in my throat.

GA: 43w6d.

I'd taken human anatomy as an elective in ninth grade, and there'd been a whole chapter in our textbook dedicated to fetal development, with ultrasound images just like this one. I knew all the acronyms. CRL meant crown-rump length. ABO had something to do with blood type. And GA stood for gestational age. If the fetus in this picture was forty-three weeks and six days old when this image was captured, then there was no way I'd been conceived on my parents' wedding night. My mom was already seven weeks pregnant by then.

Don't be deceived, the voice had said.

Suddenly the entry at the top of my Lux threats list came barreling back to me.

Knowledge of her blood type.

My eyes flew to the margin of the ultrasound photo.

Maternal ABO: A+

Fetal ABO: AB+

Blood type is genetic. Another fact I learned in human anatomy. If you know the type of a child and one of her parents, you can figure out the other parent's type. But I already knew that my dad's blood type was A positive, same as my mom's. He was a regular blood donor, so it was right there on the donor card in his wallet. There were exactly two possibilities for the offspring of double A positives: type A or type O. According to this ultrasound photo, I was neither of these.

My dad wasn't my dad. He couldn't be.

I switched my screen off, preferring to process this in the dark. The whites of my eyes were still visible in the glass, illuminated by a sliver of lamplight coming through the crack between the blinds and the windowsill. It had never entered my mind before that moment that my dad might not be my dad. Not once, in sixteen and a half years, not even after the bazillionth milkman joke. But, sitting there in the dark, letting the idea settle over me, it was as if I'd always known. And all at once it seemed impossible that I hadn't realized it before. We looked nothing alike. We were nothing alike. "I take after my mom," I'd always say, but that didn't explain the blackness of my hair or the blueness of my eyes or the fact that I had a cleft in my chin when neither of my parents did.

My chest burned like someone had fired a cannon through it. My poor dad. I understood now why my mom would let the pregnancy go so far past her due date; she needed my dad to think I was due later. Otherwise he wouldn't believe the baby was his.

I put my head on the bathroom counter, feeling its slick coolness on my skin. Who was my real father? Did he know that I existed, or had my mom lied to him, too?

When my screen lit up with a text, it was after six. I'd been sitting in the dark for hours, my thoughts like tennis balls shooting out of one of those practice machines. As long as I was thinking, I wasn't feeling, and I didn't want to feel this.

The message was from a blocked number, with an attachment. Another task from the society. But it wasn't a word puzzle this time.

Your task is to connect these nine dots. You must use straight, continuous lines.
You may not lift your finger once you have begun. You may not retrace a line you have already drawn.
What is the fewest number of lines necessary to complete this task?
You have two minutes to respond.

It seemed so straightforward. Five lines. That's what it took to hit every dot. But it seemed too easy. The society's puzzles were harder than this. But no matter what I did, I couldn't do it in less than five.

Don't you have eyes to see?

My body tensed, not with anxiety that I'd heard the voice, but with anger that its words were so completely useless. "Eyes to see *what*?" I shouted at my screen as the timer passed the one-minute mark.

And then, in a flash, out of nowhere, it seemed, the solution came to me. I'd been keeping my lines within the confines of the dots. If I swung my lines out wide, I could do it in four.

With twenty seconds left, I hit the number four and pressed send, then held my breath as I waited for a reply.

Well done, Zeta.

Gemini still in my hand, I closed my eyes and gave into the dulling fog. Dreamlessly, I slept.

19

I SLEPT THROUGH BREAKFAST and only barely made it to practicum. I thought I'd feel better after a couple more hours of sleep, but I woke up shivering and achy. Fortunately, Hershey either hadn't come back or had slipped in and out of the room without waking me, so at least I didn't have to deal with her on top of everything else.

We were working in teams in practicum, which was good because I was useless on my own. My head was pounding and my eye sockets felt like they were radiating heat. Meanwhile my brain was on a screaming loop: *My dad is not my dad! My dad is not my dad!*

"Rory, could you stay after class for a few moments, please?" Dr. Tarsus said at the end of the period. She phrased it as a question, as if I could refuse.

"Sure," I said, making my way to her desk as everyone else filed out.

"I hate to be the bearer of bad news," Tarsus said when we

were alone. "But as your adviser, I thought you should hear it from me first." She pinned her beady black eyes on mine. "Hershey Clements is no longer a student here."

The words didn't register. "What?"

Tarsus was watching me carefully. "She was taken to the health center early this morning for a psychiatric evaluation. Her doctors made the recommendation for dismissal a few hours ago."

I stared at her. "What's wrong with her?"

Tarsus pursed her lips. "I obviously can't share those details with you, Rory. But it appears that the stress of our rigorous academic program caused Hershey to become a bit . . . *confused*."

It was her word choice that tipped me off. If she'd said any other adjective, I might've believed her. But Hershey wasn't "confused" about anything.

"Trust me when I say it's in everyone's best interest— including yours—that she not be on campus anymore. Out of respect for Hershey's privacy, I'd ask that you'd leave it at that." *Trust her?* Not on my life.

"Where is she now?" I asked. "I want to talk to her."

"I strongly suggest that you focus your energy on your own well-being and let Hershey attend to hers." *How was it that the woman could make everything sound like a threat?*

I expected her to turn away then, the way she always did when she was finished with me, but she reached out and took hold of my necklace instead, examining it in her palm. I resisted the urge to step back, out of her reach, knowing how it would look to her if I did.

"Pythagoras's letter," she said, raising her eyes to meet mine.

I put on a bland smile, refusing to give her the satisfaction of a reaction. "Oh?"

"The upsilon," she replied, letting go of the pendant at last. "Pythagoras saw it as an emblem of the choice between the path of virtue and the path of vice. One leads to happiness, the other to self-annihilation." She cocked her head, the corners of her mouth turning up a little. "A fitting choice for someone like you."

"I have class," I said abruptly. "I'll see you tomorrow." Though I wanted to sprint from the room, I forced myself to walk until I made it to the courtyard. When I hit the grass, I broke into a run, charging toward the woods.

I arrived at Paradiso out of breath and light-headed, my eyes like little fireballs in my skull.

"You look awful," North said when he saw me, coming around the counter to meet me.

"Gee, thanks."

He put his palm on my forehead. "You have a fever."

"I do not," I said, pushing his hand out of the way and putting mine there instead. "I don't even feel hot."

"That's because your hand is as warm as your forehead, genius." I punched him in the arm and he laughed. "So what are you doing here?" he asked. "Don't you have class?"

243

"Hershey got kicked out of school."

North's mouth dropped. *"What?"*

"Dismissed for 'psychological reasons.' It's a complete load of crap, obviously. Tarsus just got rid of her because Hershey stood up to her."

"And Tarsus is who, again?"

"The teacher Hershey was spying for. She doesn't think I should be at Theden because of my mom. Hershey told me she was going to tell Tarsus she wouldn't do it anymore. I guess this is where that got her."

North looked skeptical. "Does this Tarsus woman really have the power to get Hershey kicked out like that? I'd think there'd be a whole process, doctors' signatures, stuff like that."

"That's why I need to see Hershey's psych eval," I told him. "Can you h—" I stopped myself before I said "hack" and lowered my voice. "Can you help me get it?"

"I'll try," North said. "She was at the campus health center?"

I nodded.

He glanced over his shoulder. "I should probably get back to work," he said apologetically. "Kate has the flu, so we're understaffed. But I get off at four and can look into the Hershey stuff then. You want to come over after your last class and we can do it together?"

"That would be great," I said, pulling out my handheld to check the time. "I should get going anyway. My calculus class started five minutes ago."

"Will you please stop at the drugstore first and get something for your fever? It'll take two minutes. I'd give you something, but Kate cleaned out our medicine drawer last night."

"You're worried about me," I said, and smiled.

"Nah. It's purely selfish. I want to be able to kiss you without infecting myself."

I punched him in the arm. He caught my fist and touched it to his lips. "I'll see you later," he said, then jogged backward toward the register, as if he didn't want to take his eyes off me. "Go get some medicine," he instructed, pointing at the door.

"Yes, sir," I said, giving him a little salute.

The drugstore was just at the corner, so I stopped in for a bottle of Tylenol and a Powerade. There was a crowd of people at the pharmacy window, lined up for the flu vaccine. *Crap.* I hadn't gotten mine yet. My dad had sent a text to remind me, but I'd just spaced, mostly because I'd never had to think about it before. At Roosevelt, the school nurse came around with a cart at the start of flu season. I'd seen something in the *Theden Herald* about a free flu clinic on campus, but obviously I hadn't followed through. And now I was paying for it.

"I guess Lux is good for some things," I muttered as I stood in the ridiculous line to pay. If I'd been syncing the app to my calendar like I normally did, Lux would've reminded me that I was due for my vaccine.

I took four Tylenol and pounded the Powerade, then tossed the empty bottle into a trash can on the green. It sunk into the bin without hitting the metal rims. In my head, I heard Beck doing his crowd-goes-wild sound and smiled.

It was just before seven in Seattle. Beck always left for school at 6:45. I turned off the sidewalk into the woods and dialed his number, resigned to the fact that I wasn't going to make it to calculus. One skipped class wouldn't kill me. I was sick after all.

Beck picked up on the third ring. "I've discovered the most perfect breakfast food ever invented."

"Hello to you, too," I said, the top layer of my anxiety melting away as soon as I heard his voice.

"Egg white frittata. It tastes like an omelet, but—" His voice got muffled as he took a bite. "You can eat it with your hands. While walking to school."

"A revelation," I said. "Hey, why haven't you returned any of my calls?"

"You've been busy," Beck said between bites.

"How would you know? You haven't called."

"Ah, but if I had, I would've gotten your voicemail, and that would've been inefficient." I had never, in our eight years of friendship, heard Beck use the word *inefficient*.

"Come again?"

"I had Lux schedule a call back. Since we haven't called you back yet, I can assume there hasn't been a good time."

I would've thought he was joking, but there wasn't a punch line. "You're using *Lux*?"

"I know. Your world is officially rocked right now. But part of the deal for the beta test was that we had to use all the pre-installed apps. Lux is even more integrated with the operating

246

system on the Gold, so it's hard not to. Not that I would try to avoid it now. How did I ever get by without it? I'm actually sort of pissed at you for not making me use it before."

That one was definitely a joke. I'd gone as far as offering to clean out Beck's locker if he'd commit to using Lux for a week, and he'd turned me down.

"Wait, so you're using it, and *liking* it?"

"What's not to like? My life is like a well-oiled machine. I haven't been late to school in a month, I'm a day ahead in all my classes, and I no longer get the shits after lunch." Beck used to insist on eating a ham and cheese sandwich from the coffee cart every day despite the fact that he's severely lactose intolerant. "It's amazing. I'm operating at, like, eight hundred and forty-eight percent. I don't even have to think anymore."

I don't even have to think. It'd never bothered me before, how little thinking Lux users had to do. How little thinking Lux users *wanted* to do. That's why we used the app, after all. It did the work for us. But when did decision-making become such a chore? I shivered, wrapping my bare arms around my rib cage.

"Hey, Beck," I said, interrupting him. "I—I have to tell you something. It's about my dad." I took an unsteady breath.

"I definitely want to hear about it, Ro, but I've got trig in two minutes, and Lux is pinging me to hurry. Talk later?"

"Sure," I said, hiding my disappointment. There was a click and he was gone.

I called Hershey next. My call went straight to voicemail so I logged on to Forum to see where she was.

@HersheyClements: Even the bathrooms are better in first class

was Hershey's most recent status update, sent ten minutes ago from somewhere over Nebraska. I messaged her. Call me when u land.

The dorms were quiet as I mounted the steps to our room. Our room. There was no "our" anymore, despite the fact that the space looked the same as it always had, with Hershey's stuff everywhere. All at once, the reality of the past twenty-four hours descended like a heavy cloak around me. My dad—the man who'd taught me how to ride a bike and who'd worn a tiara to my ninth birthday because I told him only princesses were allowed—wasn't actually my dad. My mom was a pregnant high school dropout. And a liar. My faculty adviser was out to get me. My roommate had betrayed me, which was bad enough, and then gotten kicked out of school when she tried to make it right, which was ten times worse. And, to top it all off, I had the freaking flu.

The tears I'd been holding back came pouring out of me in giant, racking sobs. I pressed my face to my pillow, letting myself scream. When my throat was raw, I sat up, wiped my eyes on the sleeve of my sweater, and resolved that I wouldn't cry again. I'd wanted the truth, and the truth was what I'd gotten. Some of it, anyway. And if I wanted the rest, I couldn't back down now.

"I'm listening," I said to the voice. But there was only silence. Then I curled up in a fetal position and went to sleep.

I stared at him. "What do you mean she never went to the health center?"

After a two-hour nap and another two Tylenol, I was wrapped in a blanket on North's couch while he worked on his laptop beside me. He'd managed to hack the health center's patient records database but hadn't found a psych eval in Hershey's file, so he'd tracked her Gemini's GPS instead.

"She was in your dorm building all night," North replied, pointing at the GPS log on his screen. "She left early this morning and went to a house on High Street, then went straight from there to the airport less than thirty minutes later."

"But she wasn't in our room last night," I told him. "Unless she somehow came in while I was sleeping?" I thought about it then shook my head. "Her bed was made this morning."

"Then maybe she just left her phone there and came to get it before you woke up," North suggested.

That seemed plausible. Every time Hershey had snuck out to meet her mystery guy, she left her phone behind. "Okay, so where'd she go after that?"

North reached for the tablet on the coffee table. "That one doesn't even take any hacking skills. It's all public record." He launched a property finder app and typed in the address from his computer screen. "Whoa," he said when the results popped up. He handed me the tablet.

My eyes went straight to the word *owner* then went wide when I saw the last name. *Tarsus.*

"She went to confront her," I said. "Just like I thought. But there's no record of her checking into the health center, and no evaluation in her file?"

"Nope. She went straight from that address to Logan Airport."

"So Tarsus lied."

"From what you've told me about this woman, are you surprised?"

He had a point.

"How did Tarsus get her to leave, then?" It didn't make any sense. Hershey wouldn't give up Theden voluntarily, not after she'd survived midterms and made the decision to focus. I pictured her tearstained face the night before the second day of exams. No, she wouldn't have gone without a fight. So what did Tarsus have on her? "Ugh," I said, nearly shaking with frustration. "Every time I think I've gotten more of the truth I realize how little of it I have." I threw the blanket off and stood up. I instantly felt dizzy and put my hand on the arm of the couch to steady myself. "Why does that woman hate me so much?"

"You think it's all connected?" North asked. "Your mom, this Tarsus woman, the stuff in your Lux profile?" I hadn't yet told North what I'd pieced together about my dad not being my dad. It was too fresh a wound to make it permanent with spoken words.

"I don't know," I told him. "I wish there was a way to find out who those social security numbers belong to."

"I'll try to get into the Social Security Administration's database," offered North.

"I thought you said you'd tried that already."

"Not the SSA directly. The kind of thing I do, my clients give me their social security numbers going in. I try not to go anywhere I don't need to go. It just increases the risk of detection."

"I don't want you to do anything risky for me," I said quickly.

"Good thing I'm not doing it for you, then," he said. He pulled up the website for the Social Security Administration on his tablet.

"You can do it right from there?" I asked.

"No, this is just research," he explained, finger scrolling to the bottom of the page. "See that *G*? That means they use a Gnosis firewall."

"And that's bad?"

"It makes it harder. Maybe not impossible. It'll take me a couple of days." He set his tablet on the coffee table then reached for my hand. As soon as his skin touched mine, he shot to his feet. "Rory, you're burning up," he said, laying his palm on my forehead. "When was the last time you took something?"

"An hour ago," I said. "Have you gotten the flu spray? I'm probably infecting you."

"I don't do vaccinations," North said. "But my immune system is superhuman. I'll be fine. You, on the other hand, worry me. You need medicine."

"I'm fine." But the truth was, I didn't feel fine. I felt awful.

"Rory, if you want to fight the forces of evil, you need your strength." He said it with a completely straight face. I laughed lightly.

"Is that what I'm doing?"

"I wouldn't rule it out," he said, and helped me to my feet.

20

IN THE END, we went to the student health center. I told North I was fine to go alone, but he just rolled his eyes at me and put on his coat.

The waiting room was empty. "Looks like someone has the flu," the nurse at the check-in station said as we came through the automatic door, making a little tsk sound with her tongue.

"Is it that obvious?"

"You have that hit-by-a-truck look about you," she replied. "You a student?" I nodded. "Tap your handheld there," she instructed, pointing at a sensor on the desk. As I did, a new text appeared on my screen.

"Have a seat in the waiting room," the nurse said.

"Mm-hm," I murmured, eyes on my screen.

I am the beginning of every end,
and the end of time and space.
I am essential to creation,

and I surround every place.

What am I?

It was a riddle, and I read it again as I shuffled into the waiting room where North was swiping through an issue of *Wired* on one of the health center's mounted tablets.

"Everything okay?" I heard him ask.

"Mm-hm." I sat on the edge of the seat next to him and read it a third time. *I am the beginning of every end, and the end of time and space. I am essential to creation, and I surround every place.* Beads of sweat popped up on my forehead. I had nothing.

"It has to be an element," I murmured. "Air, is it air? But how is air the beginning of every end? God. It's God. It has to be God."

"Rory, what are you talking about?" I looked over at North. He was staring at me. "You're babbling."

"I'm trying to solve a riddle."

"A riddle?"

"Yes."

"Why?"

"Just because."

"Okay. Well, what's the riddle?"

"I don't think I can tell you. That would be cheating." It struck me that I hadn't been given any rules for this exercise. Maybe it was perfectly acceptable to ask someone else or GoSearch for the answers to these things. But somehow

I doubted it. Something I didn't doubt was that the society would know, either way.

"Cheating? Is this a graded thing?"

"Sort of," I said. Which *was* sort of true. "It's for a club I'm trying to get into. An extracurricular thing."

"What kind of club?"

"It's just a club, okay?" I snapped. "And I have to solve this riddle to get in, so please just let me think." I pulled my handheld back out, hoping that maybe the words themselves would give me a clue. "I think it's God," I said again, trying to convince myself that I could be right. But the *beginning of every end* part didn't seem right.

North leaned over to look at my screen. "It's the letter *e*." He settled back into his seat, looking smug. "Think they'll let *me* into their club?" I reread the riddle. He was right.

I quickly typed the answer and hit send. My whole body relaxed when I got the standard response. I leaned my head back against the wall behind me and closed my eyes. Every part of me ached.

"Why do you want to be in this club so badly?" I heard North ask.

"My mom was in it," I said.

"Aurora Vaughn?" a nurse called.

"I'll be here when you get out," North said as I got to my feet.

"You really don't have to stay."

"Uh-huh. See you when you're done."

As I waited for the doctor, I pulled up the snapshot I'd taken of my mom the night of the Masquerade Ball. I hadn't looked at it since. I stared at her eyes, nearly black in this photograph, as if they held the answers I needed. Who had Aviana Jacobs been?

I was still looking at my screen when the exam room door opened.

"Hello," I heard the doctor say as I started to put my phone away. Just then, my eyes caught something I hadn't noticed before at the very edge of the frame.

My mom was holding someone's hand.

"I'm Doctor Ryland. What brings you to—?"

"Hold on a sec," I said, cutting him off as I zoomed in closer on the photo. It was a boy's hand that held my mom's, and he was wearing a ring I'd seen once before. Four symbols engraved in silver. All of a sudden I remembered who'd been standing next to her in that photo.

Griffin Payne. *The* Griffin Payne. CEO of Gnosis Griffin Payne.

Holy. Shit.

Shaking, I went to GoSearch and typed out his name and added "at 18." Griffin's senior photo popped up on my screen. I stared at him, at the boy he'd been. The aqua-blue eyes. The wavy mahogany hair. The decisive cleft in his chin. Features I saw every morning in the mirror.

It was all the proof I needed. In that instant, I just knew.

Griffin Payne was my father.

I pressed my head against the seat back, feeling light-headed.

"Are you all right?" the doctor asked.

I jumped a little. I'd forgotten he was there. "No," I said simply. I was definitely not all right.

"I need your help," I told North when I returned to the waiting room twenty minutes later. He stood to greet me, holding my coat awkwardly in his arms.

"Okay," he said. "What'd the doctor say?"

"Flu." I handed him the bag of antivirals the nurse had given me and I took my coat. "I need access to Griffin Payne."

"Uh, okay. And by *access*, you mean . . . ?"

"I need to talk to him. Alone."

North reached forward and put his hand on my forehead.

"I don't have a fever anymore," I snapped, pulling away from him. "They gave me aspirin to bring it down."

"You need to talk to Griffin Payne," North repeated. "Alone."

"Yes." I zipped up my coat. "In person."

"You do realize this is *Griffin Payne* you're talking about. You'd have a better chance of meeting the president."

"I've met him already. At a Theden event. He's nice." I walked past North toward the automatic exit. Outside, the clouds hung low in the night sky, giving off an eerie green glow.

"I'm sure he's lovely," North said, following me out. "But that doesn't mean he'll take a meeting with a high school girl."

I stopped at the curb, letting North catch up. The sidewalk was deserted. When he reached me, he stepped down off the curb so we were eye level. "Rory, what's this about? You go in to see the doctor and you come out saying you need an in-person meeting with the CEO of the biggest tech company in the world."

"He's my father," I said quietly. North's face registered the shock I felt.

"I don't understand," North said. "Since when?"

"Since he and my mom had sex seventeen years ago, I guess." My voice was terse. "I'm sorry," I said quickly. "I'm just—still processing it."

"But how'd you find out? I mean, you grew up with a dad, right? I've heard you talk about him."

I nodded, and took a shaky breath. "I found my mom's medical file in the Department of Public Heath's database about a month ago, when I was working on a research paper for my cog psych class. Last night I went back through it. Turns out I was born almost a month past my due date, not three weeks before it like I always thought, which means my mom was pregnant when she left Theden."

"The blood type thing," North said. "You think that means your dad isn't your dad."

"Not think. *Know*." My voice trembled. I would not cry. "There was an ultrasound photo in my mom's file. She was A positive and I'm AB negative. My dad—the man I thought was my dad—is A positive too."

North exhaled. "Why didn't you say anything?"

"I didn't know how," I admitted. "It's a kind of heavy thing to lay on someone you barely know."

"You more than barely know me, Rory," North said, taking my hands in his. "And I can handle heavy."

I just nodded, not trusting myself to speak. "So what makes you think Griffin Payne is your real father?" North asked.

"She's holding his hand. In their class photo. She's holding Griffin's hand."

"That hardly means—"

"Look at him," I said, shoving my phone into North's face. Griffin's senior photo was still on my screen. "Then look at me."

"There's a resemblance," North allowed. "There totally is." He exhaled, running his hands back and forth along the sides of his Mohawk. "Wow."

We were both quiet for a moment. "Well, then I take back what I said earlier," North said finally. "It'll be easy to get in to see him. Just tell him who you are."

"I can't," I said. "If I want to know what really happened seventeen years ago, he can't see it coming. I don't want to give him the chance to lie to me."

"You assume he's going to?"

"I don't want to take any chances. It has to be in person," I said firmly. "And it has to be a surprise. I want to be able to see his face."

"You think he's the reason your mom dropped out of school?"

259

"She didn't drop out," I reminded him. "She was expelled."

"Could the pregnancy have had something to do with why?"

"Maybe. But there was no record of her being pregnant in her medical file. No test results, no mention of a baby in any of her psych reports. If she knew she was pregnant, she didn't tell her doctor."

"Can you show me the file?"

I shook my head. "I don't have access to it anymore. I have only a photo of the final page."

"I'll see if I can get it," North said. "You know your mom's social security number, right?"

"Yeah, but her file was deleted from the system. You won't be able to find it."

"Au contraire," replied North. "Deleted files are even easier to get. Before they're permanently removed from a server, they're almost always put in these little holding bins for a few weeks. It's a stopgap for accidental deletions. Because the bins are hidden from users, companies think they don't need to protect them."

"Can we do it now?" I asked him.

"Sure. It might take me a couple of hours, but you're welcome to hang out. Stay over, even." His eyes twinkled. "So I can play doctor."

"I can't stay over," I said, though his place was the only place I wanted to be. "I should probably just go back to the dorms now," I said reluctantly. "Weeknight curfew is at ten."

Now that I knew exactly what Tarsus was capable of, I had to be a model student. "Can I come by tomorrow?"

"Of course," North said. "I'm working the early shift, so stop by the café first. But give me your mom's full name and social security number, and I'll see what I can find tonight."

I caught his hand and laced my fingers through his. "Thank you."

He brought my hand to his lips and kissed the tips of my fingers. "It's going to be okay. You know that, right? You'll figure all this out."

"Yeah." My vision blurred as the tears I'd been holding back spilled over. I blinked, but it was too late. They were dripping down my cheeks. "Damn it," I muttered. So much for my resolution not to cry. I swatted at my eyes.

North lifted my chin with his finger, all the confidence I didn't have bright in his eyes, and then, even though I was probably wildly contagious and smelled like a hospital and hadn't brushed my teeth in twelve hours, he kissed me and for a moment I forgot everything but what it felt like not to be alone.

21

I SET MY ALARM as an afterthought, certain I wouldn't sleep well enough to need it, and it was a good thing I did because I'm not sure I would've woken up before noon without it. I slept deeply and dreamlessly that night and woke up in the same position I'd been in when I'd lain down. My mouth felt like it was stuffed with cotton balls, but otherwise I felt pretty good. Better, at least. I touched my handheld to my head to check if I had a fever. "Your temperature is in the normal range" came Lux's reply. I hadn't heard her voice in more than a week. There was a time when I talked to Lux more than I talked to anyone else.

Clearly, those days were gone. I'd been consulting Lux so infrequently that I spaced on dropping my dirty clothes at the campus laundry service on Friday. I had nothing clean. After hesitating for a split second at the door of her closet, I put on Hershey's stretch velvet pants, which were too long but looked okay tucked into boots, and one of the four gray cashmere sweaters I found wadded up on her shelf.

Izzy was in the courtyard when I came out of the building, drinking coffee from a paper cup and reading something on her tablet, her cheeks red from the cold. She wasn't wearing a jacket. "Hey," I said coming up to her. "What are you doing?"

"Trying to get through three more chapters before lit. We have a quiz on the first half of *Atlas Shrugged* today." She looked up at me with tired eyes. "I kept falling asleep in my room," she explained. "I thought the cold would keep me up."

I clapped my hand to my mouth. We were in the same class. I'd forgotten about the quiz. Izzy saw the look on my face.

"You haven't finished either?"

"Haven't even started."

Izzy scooted over on the bench. "Room for one more," she said. "We've got an hour till practicum and all of lunch period. If you skim, you'll finish."

"I can't right now," I said. "I have to meet someone." I had to know what North had uncovered about my mom. I'd deal with the quiz later.

"Oooh, a guy?" Izzy put her tablet down and gave me a once-over. "Is that why you look so nice?"

"Sort of."

"It's sort of a guy, or that's sort of why you look nice?"

"I can't really talk about it," I said. Then, because that sounded too cryptic, I said, "We're not telling anyone about us yet."

"What is it with you and Hershey and your secret

boyfriends?" Izzy made a pouty face. "Ugh. Can you at least tell me where I can find one? Hey, where's Hershey been, anyway? I haven't seen her in days."

"She, uh, left school."

Izzy's forehead wrinkled in confusion. "What do you mean she left school? For what?"

"She's taking some time off," I said vaguely, not wanting to say too much. "I don't really know details. I'll see you later, okay?" Before Izzy could respond, I walked off, taking long strides to get out of earshot before she could ask another question.

As I was cutting across the quad, I spotted Dr. Tarsus coming toward me. Our eyes met, and she pointed at a nearby bench. I walked over to it but didn't sit. Neither did she.

She cut right to the chase. "Hershey didn't make it home yesterday afternoon."

My stomach dropped. "What do you mean?"

"Her family sent a car to the airport, but Hershey never met the driver. A flight attendant found her handheld in the pocket of the seat in front of her on the plane."

"Her parents sent a *car*?" Clearly this was not the key piece of information here, but my brain couldn't get past it. Their only child was kicked out of school for psychological reasons and the Clements couldn't even be bothered to pick her up from the airport.

"Have you spoken to her?"

I kept my face neutral. "You told me not to contact her."

"And yet you called and texted her." Tarsus saw my surprise.

264

"Her parents checked her phone records. Has she responded?"

I shook my head, sick with dread. What if Hershey was dead in a ditch somewhere because of me? "They don't have any idea where she is?"

"Not yet. They're calling friends in the area. She withdrew some cash from their account before she got on the plane in Boston, so they assume she had this plan in place before she left."

I exhaled. "So they think she's okay?"

"At this point. But, Rory, it's very important that they find her. If you know where she is—"

"I don't," I said quickly. "I haven't spoken to her since the night before she left."

This seemed to satisfy Tarsus. "Well, if you hear from her, let me know."

I nodded. "I will."

Tarsus eyed me for another moment, then turned and walked off.

I waited until she'd disappeared into the dining hall to cross into the woods toward downtown.

North waved me in when he saw me outside Paradiso's bay window. I could tell from the look on his face that he'd been successful. He pointed at a corner table. "My break's in five minutes," he called. "Want anything?"

"Coffee," I said. "And one of those." I pointed at the biggest, stickiest pastry in the display case.

North joined me at the table a few minutes later. "You

found her file," I said, tearing off a piece of the pastry. It was soft and sweet, melting against the roof of my mouth. I hadn't had a pastry in years. My breakfast options with Lux had ranged from oatmeal with almonds to scrambled egg whites and toast. An eight hundred calorie mountain of sugar, butter, and pastry flour was never the reasonable breakfast choice. I tore off another piece.

"I did. And you were right; there was no mention of a pregnancy anywhere. But I cracked the metadata on all those psych entries. Rory, they weren't added to your mom's file until June."

"I don't understand. She was expelled in May."

"Yeah, according to an expulsion notice that was added to her file a whole month after it was supposedly issued."

"What are you saying?"

"I don't know. Maybe there's a reasonable explanation for the delay. Maybe her doctor sucked at charting." He hesitated. "Or maybe someone was trying to make her look crazy."

I stared at him, the pastry forgotten on my plate. "Someone like who?"

"I don't know," North replied. "But maybe Griffin does."

"You figured out how to get to him?"

"Turns out the Gemini Gold launch party is this Friday night. Griffin is giving the keynote.

"Those tickets have to be thousands of dollars."

"Worse. They're not even for sale." He smiled. "Good thing we're on the guest list."

22

"WHAT IF SOMEONE ASKS HOW WE GOT INVITED?"

"No one's going to ask," North said. "It's a huge ballroom. We'll blend." I caught sight of my reflection in the tinted windows of the train and almost didn't recognize myself. Noelle, the girl at the computer repair shop, had loaned me her homecoming dress, a calf-length black bustier that was in no way high school dance appropriate, and Kate had done my makeup, hiding the constellation of dark freckles across my nose under spray foundation and lining my eyes in charcoal shadow. My hair I'd done myself, preferring to have it loose and wavy around my face in case I needed to hide behind it.

North was even more incognito. His Mohawk was combed down flat and his tattoos were hidden under the sleeves of a gray herringbone jacket. Between the suit and his tortoise-shell Wayfarers and the Bluetooth earbud clipped to his ear, he looked like a prep school kid on his way to a party. Precisely the part he was playing tonight.

He was on his handheld now, checking our progress on his map. It was going to be tight; we had to get to Boston, to the party, somehow get Griffin alone, then get back to the train and to campus before the library closed at midnight. I'd left my Gemini there, hidden in the stacks, with location services turned on. North had created a program that would auto-post status updates twice in the six-plus hours we'd be gone, in case anyone was looking for me. It wouldn't do me much good if anyone actually came to the library to find me, but it'd keep me off the radar as long as no one did. Theden's rules about leaving campus were lenient, as long as you stayed close by. We weren't allowed to go outside a five-mile radius of the campus gates without written permission from the Dean. If I got caught tonight, I'd be expelled.

To calm the cyclone in my stomach, I watched North, memorizing every detail of his face. Even in the train's harsh fluorescent light, he was handsome. Classically handsome, I saw now. His skin was cinnamon colored and the corners of his eyes were angled down, but his nose was straight and his jaw was strong and the whole of his face came together with beautiful symmetry.

He turned and caught me looking at him.

"You look really pretty," he said, touching the tip of my nose with his finger. "But I miss your freckles." I tilted my head back and kissed his palm. His finger slid down my neck, tracing the contours of my collarbone toward my right shoulder. He hooked the thin strap of my dress, lifting it a millimeter before skimming over it and down my arm. My skin crackled with heat.

"You don't look bad yourself," I said, my voice airy. I could still feel the path his finger had made, and it wasn't hard to imagine him tugging my straps down, unzipping the back of my dress. I'd kissed only one boy before North, and now I was picturing myself topless with him. I suspected both Lux and the voice in my head would reel this one in, but I wasn't consulting either of them right now. I gripped the edge of my plastic chair and reminded myself where thoughts like that had gotten my mom.

"So there's a nine-fifteen and a ten-oh-five train back," North was saying. "If we take the later one, we won't get into the Theden station until eleven fifty."

"That's not enough time," I said, although the truth was I had no idea if ten minutes was enough time to get from Theden Central Station back to campus on North's motorbike. Using Lux for so many years had completely destroyed my ability to assess travel times. Lux told me when to leave, which way to go, and what time it would be when I arrived. How little attention I'd paid to the details, trusting Lux to get me wherever I needed to go. And invariably, it had.

"It'll be tight," North said, "but if we have to, we can make it. Still, we should aim for the nine-fifteen." He glanced back at his handheld. "We're the next stop."

My heart started drumming in my chest. Oddly, I was more worried about getting into the party than I was about confronting its famous host. I wasn't expecting the ambush to go well, necessarily, but I knew he'd at least believe I was who I said I was. Even dressed like this, with all the makeup, I bore an uncanny resemblance to my mom.

"You ready for this?" North asked as the train pulled into Back Bay Station. I nodded. I had to be. And with North by my side, maybe I was. He slipped his hand in mine as we made our way onto the platform and through the building to the taxi stand outside.

"Copley Square," North told the cab driver. "The Boston Public Library." The man grunted and we were off. The station was only half a mile from the library where the party was being held. Walkable if I hadn't been wearing three-inch heels. So the cab ride didn't give me much time to collect myself. Two minutes after getting in, it was time to get out.

We'd pulled up in front of a massive stone building with arched windows that occupied an entire city block. It looked more like a palace than a library, and nothing like Seattle's glass and metal Central Library back home. It didn't hurt that it was lit up like a castle, with warm, yellow spotlights illuminating its stone face. Above the lights and the row of arched windows was the word *GOLD* projected in 3D. There was a red carpet on the front steps and a velvet rope and throngs of photographers hovering on the plaza out front. This was an odd place, as it were, for a tech launch party, considering Gnosis had made public libraries irrelevant when it started offering e-books to borrow for free. None of the old buildings even housed books anymore—not paper ones, anyway. They were basically just big tablet terminals, with rows and rows of desks with screens built in, and public media rooms where you could surf the Web and watch TV.

With shaky hands, I pushed open the taxi's door and stepped out onto the pavement.

"Here," North said in a low voice, pulling a second hand-held from his pocket and slipping it into the small purse on my arm. "When they scan it at the door, it'll pull up the name I added to the guest list. Jessica Sizemore. She's an undergrad at Harvard. Her dad's a shareholder."

"What if she shows up?" I hissed. We were approaching the edge of the crowd waiting to get in.

"She won't. She RSVPed no the day after invitations went out, and according to Forum, she's still on campus right now." He put his arm around my shoulders. "Just act natural. Once we're inside, it won't matter."

I leaned against his shoulder and tried to relax. We blended in easily with the well-dressed twenty-somethings milling around us, immersed in their screens as they waited to get in.

The girl taking tickets smiled as we stepped up to the red carpet. "Welcome to the future," she said, reaching for our handhelds. I held my breath as she scanned them. "Enjoy the party, guys." She handed them back to us and lifted the velvet rope.

We were in.

The main event was in the open-air courtyard in the center of the building, which Gnosis had transformed into a metallic garden. The fountain in the center was lit up from under the surface of the water and seemed to be pouring liquid gold. Servers in black ties were circling with shiny gold trays of champagne, and there were tiny gold *G*s projected on the stone walls all around us. There were high tables constructed out of shiny gold Legos and standing chandeliers made of bright gold coins. "Wow," I breathed, taking it in.

North grabbed two flutes of champagne off a server's tray and handed me one. "Props," he said. The next server had some sort of ahi tuna cupcake with avocado "icing." I reached for one.

"Snacks," I said, biting into it. "Ohmygod, this is amazing. You have to try one."

"Focus, Jessica Sizemore, focus. We've got an hour to find your father." But before the server stepped away, North grabbed a tuna cupcake and popped the whole thing in his mouth.

Now that we were on the other side of the velvet rope, I was calmer. No one was paying any attention to us, and it was easy to move along the periphery of the party, along the walkway that encased the courtyard, subtly scanning the crowd for Griffin. As we made our way along the eastern wall, walking slowly so as not to draw any attention, I let myself pretend for a second that we hadn't snuck into this party, that we'd been invited like everyone else. It struck me that it probably wasn't a far-off fantasy. Not anymore. This was the kind of stuff that came with a Theden diploma. Parties like these, people like this. If I stayed on track, I wouldn't have to lie my way into these places. I'd belong.

I was between North and the wall as we rounded the corner at the southeast end of the courtyard and saw her. A beautiful black woman in a winter white pantsuit standing by the fountain. There was no one between us. If she turned just slightly to her left and looked up, she'd see me.

North heard me gasp.

"What is it?" he asked in a low voice, inclining his face toward mine.

"Kiss me," I whispered. "Right now."

I didn't have to ask twice. His hands came to my hips as he pushed me gently against the wall, the edge of my crystal flute clinking against its polished surface. I wrapped my free arm around his neck, pressing my body into his as if I could disappear against him, closing my eyes as his lips touched mine. Had she seen me? I didn't think so, but I wasn't sure. North's elbows were on the wall now, one on either side of my face, somehow holding his champagne glass without spilling it as he kissed me. For a second I got lost in the sensation, thinking nothing and feeling everything, from the flutter in my chest to the static in my stomach to the tingle in my tongue every time it touched the tip of his. But then Tarsus's face came slamming back into my brain and my whole body tensed up. North felt it and pulled back.

"I sense that kiss served a purpose beyond the fulfillment of about five of my fantasies," he said, his face still inches off mine.

"She's here," I whispered. "Dr. Tarsus."

"Shit. Did she see you?"

"I don't think so," I told him. "You hid me." My arms were still around his neck, so I traced his earlobe with my thumb, careful to keep my body behind his as I shimmied along the wall behind a column.

"Where is she now?" He leaned ever so slightly to the left, as if he was nuzzling my neck, so I could scan the courtyard. A crowd of newcomers had arrived, and they stood between us and the fountain, blocking our view.

"I don't see her anymore," I said. "She was by the fountain."

"What is she doing here?"

"No idea. Gnosis is a big funding source for Theden—maybe that's the connection?" Still, it was odd to see her here, at a trendy tech launch party. Odd, and very unlucky for us.

"Do you want to leave?"

"No," I told him. "This is our best shot at getting to Griffin. We've gotten this close—I can't give up now. We'll just have to make sure she doesn't see us." I felt a boldness in my chest. It was an unfamiliar feeling, but not an unpleasant one. I wasn't used to being so sure about things. Not without Lux calling the shots, anyway.

North slipped his hand in mind. "If that happens to require a few more of those kisses, I suppose I could oblige."

He glanced at his watch. "We've still got an hour until Griffin's speech, so he's probably in the crowd somewhere. Assuming we can find him, the trick will be getting him alone."

"Not once he sees me," I said, confident in that.

It was even easier than I hoped. As we were making our way through the crowd, my head angled down to avoid being spotted, we passed right by Griffin, who was talking to a group of women in expensive cocktail dresses. North elbowed me, I lifted my head, and there he was, two feet away from me, looking like he'd been airbrushed into the room. The first thought that popped into my head was *How did the offspring of two gorgeous people end up looking like me?* The second was *He is smiling, but his eyes are sad.*

I opened my mouth to say something but didn't have to. Griffin was already staring at me, his mouth slightly ajar. "Excuse me," he said to the women, cutting one of them off, his eyes still on me. He stepped through them as if they weren't there. They swiveled their heads to look at me.

"I think you knew my mother," I said lamely. "Av—"

"You're her *daughter*," he said, then made a sound that was like a laugh but coarser. "Of course. For a second, I thought— But of course you couldn't be." His eyes lifted to look past me then fell back to my own. "Is—Is your mother here?" There was such unbridled hope in his voice that my own caught in my throat. I just shook my head.

"Rory needs to talk to you," North said then. Griffin looked over at North as if seeing him for the first time. North offered his hand. "Gavin West," North said, giving him his cover name. We'd agreed I wouldn't use mine.

Griffin shook it, but his eyes were back on me. His smile was kind, but his eyes were even sadder now, almost wistful. "Rory. Have we met before? I know I'd remember your face, but your voice—it's familiar. And your name."

"We met at the Theden Masquerade Ball," I told him. "On the balcony."

"You were the girl in the peacock mask," Griffin said, and I nodded. "Well, it's nice to meet you again, Rory."

"You too," I said. My nerves made it difficult to smile. Griffin seemed to notice. He glanced at North then back at me.

"It's quieter inside," he said then. "How about we talk there?"

We followed him through a side door and into the library's small café. The chairs were stacked on the tables and there was a sign blocking the entrance, but Griffin stepped past it and took down two chairs.

"I'll wait over there," North said, pointing to a bench by the stairs.

I nodded and looked at Griffin. His face was half curiosity and half confusion. I needed to say something before his guard came up. *Please don't let me screw this up,* I prayed. I didn't want to ambush him with what I knew, not if I wanted the truth, but I didn't have time to skate around it either. His keynote was scheduled for eight o'clock, and it was already seven twenty-five.

"Thanks for agreeing to talk to me," I began. "I—I have a lot of questions, and no one to answer them."

"Your mom," Griffin said then. "Something happened to her, didn't it." His voice didn't go up at the end because it wasn't a question.

I nodded slightly. "She died right when I was born."

He buried his face in his hands for a second, and when he dropped them back to his sides, he looked his age for the first time. There were lines extending like sunbeams from the outer corners of his eyes. It was ironic, smile lines beside sad eyes.

"And your dad?"

I eyed him. *Was he trying to see what I knew, or could he honestly not know that I was his child?* "My dad?"

"Yeah. I mean, you know, is he in the picture? Is he around?" Griffin looked uncomfortable, like we'd crossed into unpleasant territory.

"I've never met my father."

This didn't seem to surprise Griffin, and in fact, something like relief flashed in his eyes. So he *did* know. He was trying to see if I did. I gritted my teeth. It wouldn't help me to get angry with him. Putting him on the defensive was the quickest way to shut this down.

I kept my voice casual. "I know you have a speech to give and all, so I won't take up too much of your time, but I was just hoping you could tell me what happened between you and my mom."

Griffin sighed. "I haven't talked about your mom in fifteen

years." He tugged at his tie. "No, longer. Not since she left." He reached inside his jacket and pulled out his handheld. It was shiny and metallic and the size of a matchbox. The Gemini Gold. He tapped his screen and it lit up. It was 7:35. "I have to be in the prep room at quarter till. This isn't a ten-minute story, but I'll try to make it one." He snapped his Gold into the metal band on his wrist and ran his hands through his hair. It was the exact shade of mine, so dark brown it looked black, but straight where mine was wavy. Unlike my dad's, whose straw-colored hair was flecked with silver, Griffin's showed no hint of gray.

"Your mom and I met our first year at Theden," he began, his eyes brightening for the first time all night. "I fell for her the very first time we spoke—we were in practicum together, and she sat next to me on the first day. There weren't pods back then, just desks with laptop docking stations, and she couldn't get hers to turn on. Our teacher was this horrible, crotchety old man—Mr. Siegler—and Aviana was terrified he'd yell at her if she asked him for help. So I helped her, and in the span of about five seconds fell madly in love."

My heart turned over in my chest. It was easy to imagine that moment, my mom flustered and nervous the way I'd been on my first day, Griffin all confidence and charm. It was the beginning of something, something that could've gone a thousand different ways, with a thousand happily-ever-afters. Yet here we were.

"I never imagined I had a shot with her," Griffin continued.

"She was totally out of my league. I, meanwhile, didn't even have the IQ to be at Theden. My family had to pull strings to get me in." His eyes clouded over. "My parents never liked Aviana," he explained. "My stepfather hated her."

"Why?"

"She was . . . different. She didn't play the game the way everyone else did."

"The game?"

"The ambition climb," replied Griffin. "I'm sure it's the same now as it was back then. All that drive and competition, the fight for top grades. Aviana didn't care about any of that. And yet, she was our valedictorian."

"I don't understand. My mom was expelled from Theden. How could she—?"

"Expelled? Aviana?" Griffin laughed. "Hardly. She was the campus darling." He looked at me curiously. "Who told you she was expelled?"

"I saw the expulsion notice," I said slowly.

In her doctored medical file.

"Well, I can promise you Aviana didn't get kicked out of school," Griffin replied. His expression darkened. "She took her finals then ran away."

"Why?"

"I'll get to that," he replied. "Let me explain what she was up against first. Not that it excuses what she did, but I know it affected her more than she let on."

"Your family."

He nodded. "They were awful to her. And the closer she and I got, the more aggressive they became. They threatened to take away my trust fund, not pay for college, the whole nine. I couldn't have cared less. None of those things mattered to me then. So I asked Aviana to marry me. And I told my stepfather he could take my trust fund and shove it."

"You and my mom were engaged?"

Griffin seemed to hesitate then. "We were more than engaged," he said finally. "Rory, your mom and I were married."

I stared at him. "What?"

"We got married a week before graduation," he said softly. "At the courthouse in Albany. We spent the next two days holed up in a little cabin in Canada, completely disconnected from the rest of the world. Just the two of us and a fireplace." He blushed a little, as if he'd forgotten that I was there. "We spent the whole weekend making plans. Aviana wanted to get as far as we could from my family, and I just wanted to make her happy. Theden had a pretty good reputation in the UK, so we decided to move to London, apply to Oxford and Cambridge, make a life there. I had a little money of my own saved, and we figured it was enough to tide us over until we got jobs. The plan was to leave right after graduation."

"But then she got pregnant," I said. It sounded bitter, but I couldn't help it. It wasn't fair that something that was his fault as much as hers changed what he wanted. Changed how he felt. He wanted a life with her as long as it was just the two of them. A baby wasn't part of the bargain.

His face darkened. "There was no 'then,'" he said. "She was already pregnant when we got married. That's how I knew it wasn't mine."

Confusion stalled my next thought. "Huh?"

Griffin hesitated. "I don't want to paint a nasty picture of her, Rory. We were both really young. We were kids. I don't blame her for lying to me. Not anymore."

I shook my head. "I don't understand. What did she lie to you about?"

"Aviana and I, we never— She said she wanted to wait until we were married." He made a sound in his throat. "I guess that rule didn't apply to other guys."

"She cheated on you?"

He nodded. "While I was in Nantucket for spring break. I found out the morning of graduation. Someone emailed me a copy of her pregnancy test results. The test was dated April 14. Long before we ever . . ." He trailed off, his eyes hollow now. "It was at that moment, staring at her test results in black-and-white, that it all just clicked. That voice I'd been listening to, the one that led me to her, it wasn't some higher power guiding me along. It was nothing more than cognitive dissonance working itself out. My rational mind sensed I shouldn't be with her, but my emotional brain couldn't accept it, so it invented a fiction, a voice that knew something I didn't." He looked up at the ceiling. "We're better at lying to ourselves than most people realize."

There were so many things I wanted to ask him—what my mom had said when he confronted her, why he didn't go after her when he started hearing the Doubt—but the questions were lodged in my throat. Griffin kept talking.

"This company owes a lot to your mom," he said then, gesturing toward the window overlooking the party outside. "If she hadn't left, I never would've come to work for them."

"Why not?"

"Your mom, she was very anti-Gnosis," Griffin explained. "I never understood it. They were just a little tech startup back then. But somehow they'd gotten on Aviana's radar, and she was adamant that I not have anything to do with them. The Monday after graduation, I drove to their offices and told them I'd work for free."

"And you've been there ever since?"

He nodded. "It's funny how things work out. When I started at Gnosis that summer, they'd just launched the R&D on a new decision-making app. An app that would keep people like me from lying to themselves. A voice we could trust. I decided right then that I'd dedicate my career to that app. The more people that used it, the fewer who would end up with their hearts broken."

My mind leaped to the boy ten feet to my left. Was it worth it to avoid heartache if you also avoided its opposite, the feeling that your heart might burst with joy?

"Mr. Payne." The voice caught both of us off guard. It was a hulk of a man in a black suit with an earbud in his ear. I recognized him as the guy I'd passed on the steps at the Masquerade Ball. Griffin's bodyguard. "It's quarter till."

Griffin nodded at the man and turned to me. "I've got a speech to give," he said. He sounded apologetic.

"She wasn't pregnant when you got married," I blurted out. It was now or never. "Whoever sent you those test results wanted you to think she was, but she wasn't."

Griffin's whole body tensed up, like I'd hit him. "What?"

"My birthday, it's March 21," I said. "If she'd gotten pregnant when you think she did, I would've been due in early December. But I wasn't. I was due in February and born in March. Three weeks and five days late." The words were getting jumbled now, but I kept talking, afraid that if I stopped he'd walk away. "I saw a photo from her last ultrasound. The math all works out. She got pregnant on your wedding night." Griffin was shaking his head. I grabbed his arm. "Look at my eyes. And my hands—" I held out my arm. "And my chin! The cleft on my chin. It's just like yours. Our hair, it's the same color, too. And—"

I could tell Griffin wasn't listening anymore. His face looked broken. I got quiet, abruptly, and let go of his arm. It was several seconds before he said anything. When he spoke, his voice was hoarse, like he'd been screaming. "You're saying I'm . . ." He didn't say the rest of it. It didn't seem as if he could.

"My father," I said softly.

All at once Griffin was crying. I took a step back, startled at the rawness of the emotion and how quickly it had come. He wiped his eyes with the back of his hands.

"All this time, I thought she'd betrayed me," he said thickly. "The Doubt, it kept telling me to trust her, to go and find her. For months I couldn't shut it off. I thought— I thought I was going crazy. I couldn't make it stop. And then one day it did." He rubbed his eyes with his fists as if trying to blot the grief away. "All that I've done since then—"

"Mr. Payne," the man in black said.

"I need a minute, Jason." Griffin's eyes hadn't left mine. "If I was the father, why did she leave?" he asked me. "She was supposed to give the valedictory address. She'd been working on it for weeks. But when I went to her dorm room that morning, to confront her about the email, she was gone. It doesn't make any sense."

"Do you know if my mom was seeing a psychiatrist that spring?"

"A psychiatrist? For what? Because of the Doubt?" He shook his head. "Your mom never would've gone to a doctor about that. Why, did someone tell you she did?"

"It's a long story," I told him. "But I think someone may have been out to get her. I just don't know who, or why. I was hoping you'd have some of the answers."

"Unfortunately, I'm as in the dark as you are," he said. "But maybe we can figure some of it out together. Can we talk after my speech? How long will you be here?" He smoothed his hair and the skin under his eyes, collecting himself.

"I wasn't supposed to leave campus," I admitted. "So I need

to be on the nine-fifteen train back."

"I'll get you a car," Griffin said. "If you leave by ten, you'll be fine. And the speech won't take long. I'd cancel it to talk to you, but they're live-streaming it and there are a few things I need to say before this thing goes any further than it already has." There was a tenor of resolve in his voice that hadn't been there before. *Before what goes any further?* I wanted to ask, but the man in black was at Griffin's elbow. "So you'll stay?"

"Sure," I said.

My father smiled, and for a second his eyes weren't sad at all. "I'm so glad to meet you, Rory," he said, taking my hand in his.

"What do the symbols mean?" I asked, nodding at the ring.

"*Timshel,*" Griffin replied. "It's Hebrew. Steinbeck used it in *East of Eden.* It means 'thou mayest.' The idea being that we all have a choice. To do good, to live well."

"*Timshel,*" I repeated. "I like that idea."

"Me too," Griffin replied. He examined his ring as if seeing it for the first time. "Your mom had it made for me for my eighteenth birthday. When she left, I kept it on as a reminder of the mistake I'd made, trusting something other than myself." He looked up at the ceiling, as if searching for something there. "I think I missed the point."

"Mr. Payne, the stream goes live in five minutes." Jason was back, and his voice was urgent now. There was static buzzing from his earpiece. "They have to mic you, sir."

Through the window I could see that the crowd had formed

a semicircle around the fountain, facing the stage at the south end of the courtyard where Griffin would be giving his speech. There was a paper-thin screen mounted on the wall behind it, playing the latest TV ad for the Gold.

"I'll find you as soon as I'm done," I heard Griffin say.

And then he was gone, through the door and swallowed up by the boisterous crowd outside. North was at my side seconds later.

"How'd it go?"

"He never knew the baby was his," I said, following North outside. "He got some email with the results of a pregnancy test dated two months before he and my mom ever slept together, so he thought my mom had cheated on him. When he went to ask my mom about it, she was gone." I chewed on my lip. "Why would someone want him to think the baby wasn't his?"

"I don't know. You think the person who sent that email is the same person who messed with your mom's medical file?"

"I guess so, but it seems weird, right? I mean, I understand the fake test results, but it's not like Griffin would ever see her medical file. Why go to all that trouble?"

"Rory?" I spun on my toes, startled by the familiar voice. Beck was standing just a few feet away, in a navy suit that fit him perfectly but looked completely ridiculous. It reminded me of something Liam might wear, which made it the polar opposite of anything I'd ever seen my best friend put on.

"What are you doing here?" I demanded, rushing over to give him a hug and nearly tripping in my heels in the process.

"Another perk of being a beta tester?" I grabbed him by the elbows and gave him a once-over. He looked good. The zits he'd always battled had cleared up and his arms were bulkier, like he'd been working out.

"Oh, it's way cooler than that," Beck said, glancing at North then back at me, a reminder that I hadn't introduced him. "My photographs are on the wall in one of the exhibit rooms. It's part of an exhibit of new artists that Gnosis is sponsoring. It goes from here to the MFA in Boston."

"No way! That's amazing!"

"Yeah, it's pretty sweet. Gnosis flew all the artists out for it. There's another event at the museum tomorrow night."

"Holy crap." I punched him in the arm. "Why didn't you tell me?"

"It just happened. So what are you doing here? Class field trip?"

"Something like that," I said. The knowledge I'd accumulated over the past few weeks, about the voice, and my mom, and now, my real dad, was pressing out from the inside. How had I not told Beck any of it? I felt a twinge behind my rib cage. I'd tried. Several times.

Beck looked over at North. "So we should probably just introduce ourselves since Rory's clearly not going to."

North laughed. "Probably a good plan. I'm North." I stepped back so they could shake hands and noticed that Beck had his Gold snapped to a brown leather wrist strap. It was like the suit. Much too preppy for Beck's taste. Then again, it was a party and he was here on someone else's dime, and this was probably just his attempt at dressing up.

"Beck's my best friend," I told North. "From back home." I turned back to Beck. "So where are they? I want to see them!"

"They're inside," Beck replied. "Let me just make sure we have enough time." He raised his wrist toward his mouth. "Lux, do we have time to visit the exhibit before the keynote speech?"

I felt as if I were watching a stranger. Beck had told me he was using Lux now, but to ask it something as ridiculous as that? Beck didn't need an app to tell him that we had plenty of time. Yet he was earnestly waiting for Lux's reply, a bizarre half smile on his lips as he stared at his tiny screen.

"The presentation is delayed," Lux said, in a voice that sounded so much like Beck's that I thought for a second that he'd been the one to say it. The Lux voice on the older model Gemini was tinny, audibly distinct from its owner's. This version was indistinguishable. "You have adequate time to view the exhibit," Lux continued. "I will notify you when it is time to return to the courtyard."

"Thanks," Beck said to his handheld. He readjusted his sleeve and smiled at us. "Let's do it."

I started to follow him then stopped to scan the courtyard first. Tarsus was easy to spot this time, a flash of iridescent white silk in a blur of dark colors. Thankfully, she was on the other side of the fountain and her back was to me. I could tell from the way her head was bobbing that she was in a heated conversation with whoever was in front of her.

"You coming?" Beck asked.

"Yep," I said, glancing over at Tarsus one last time. She'd moved slightly, so the person she was talking to was now in view. I watched as she put her hand on his forearm and he shook it off, his face twisted in anger.

It was Griffin.

"No," I breathed. "North, he's talking to Dr. Tarsus." An avalanche of dread cascaded from my chest to my stomach. "If he tells her I'm here . . ."

"Don't panic," North whispered, steering me toward the room where Beck was headed. "They could be talking about anything."

As we stepped inside the building, I looked over my shoulder to where Tarsus and Griffin had been standing. He was striding away from her, toward the podium. She was on her handheld, a Gold, strapped to her wrist like Beck's. It glinted in the dim light. It felt like a good sign that she wasn't searching the room for me. Maybe they *had* been talking about something else. Maybe Griffin hadn't mentioned me after all.

Or maybe she was calling the dean right now to report me.

"Mine are on the left wall," I heard Beck say. We were in a room adjacent to the courtyard, which Gnosis had converted into a chic-looking art space, with temporary white fiberglass walls. There were paintings in nearly every media, from watercolor to digital ink prints, but I saw only three photographs. All of sailboats.

"Wait, where are yours?" I asked, revolving to take in the rest of the room.

"They're right there," Beck said. "You were just looking at them." He took my shoulders and turned me back toward the boats.

"But they're sailboats," I said. I looked at North because I couldn't look at Beck. It's not that they were terrible pictures; it was just that they were the type of photographs you'd expect to see in a doctor's office or the lobby of a chain hotel. Commercial. Pretty. Forgettable.

"That's my thing now," Beck replied with no trace of defensiveness. "Boats and bridges. I realized that my previous work was too depressing to sell."

My mouth opened, but no words came out. Beck's work was evocative and powerful and raw. Hard to look at sometimes, but that was the point. "Too *depressing*?"

"Unfortunately, Rory, even artists have to eat," Beck said pleasantly. Beside me, North cleared his throat.

"I think they're beautiful," he told Beck, stepping up for a closer look. "The glossy finish really makes them pop." This was true, but it wasn't a compliment. The images looked fake, like stock screensavers. "Were they all shot in Seattle?"

"Yep," Beck replied. "On three consecutive days. The Gold comes with a photo app that links to Lux. You just type in the kind of photo you want, and Lux'll show you where in the city to shoot, and what time of day. Takes all the effort out of it."

"What happened to 'Lux thinks like a computer, not an

artist,'" I asked, barely able to look at him now.

"Every artist needs tools for his craft," Beck said. "Lux is one of mine."

"And the Doubt?" I asked softly. In my peripheral vision, I saw North's head turn.

"Quiet at last," Beck said, as though this was something to celebrate.

My stomach churned. "You're taking Evoxa."

"Nope. Still think that stuff fries your brain. I just took Lux's advice and told the voice I didn't need it anymore. Not long after that, it stopped."

My brain couldn't process a response. It was as if I were interacting with some alternate version of my best friend. I stared at his photographs, hating them even more now, wishing I could tear them from the wall and throw them into the fountain.

"Please proceed to the courtyard," I heard Beck say. But, of course, it wasn't actually Beck, but his electronic sidekick. It took restraint for me not to rip the Gold off his wrist and hurl it against the wall.

"We should get going," the real Beck said. North slipped his hand in mine.

Just then there was a tinkling sound, like a glass being tapped with a knife, but louder, and coming through the overhead speakers. Our signal that the speech was about to start. We followed Beck back outside.

"Ladies and gentlemen" came a familiar voice. Tarsus was

behind the gold-plated podium. *She was introducing him?* I quickly ducked behind North. Beck gave me a quizzical look. "On behalf of my fellow Gnosis board members, it is my great honor to introduce a man who needs no introduction. The visionary behind Lux and the architect of the game-changing device we're here tonight to celebrate. The CEO and face of Gnosis, Griffin Payne." The crowd erupted in applause as Griffin joined her on the stage.

"Thank you, Esperanza." Griffin's smile looked more like a grimace as he stepped up to the mic. "And thank you all for coming, and for helping to make Gnosis what it is today." He looked up at the ceiling for a second then continued. "When I started as an intern at the company the summer after high school, I thought I'd hit the career jackpot. Here was a company committed to remaining at the forefront of technological innovation that wanted to do good in the world. I was a kid with a broken heart who was given the opportunity to help design an app that would make sure it would never happen again." There was twittering in the audience, scattered whispers. This was not something Griffin had ever shared publicly. But the man at the podium seemed unaware of his audience's reaction. He kept talking. "It was a lofty notion, the idea that we could improve society with a handheld app." Griffin seemed to falter a little. He wiped his forehead with the back of his hand. "A lofty notion," he continued. "And a misguided one." He paused and gripped the podium, his face suddenly ashen. He wiped his brow again and blinked his eyes a few times as if he were having trouble focusing. "The truth is that—" He was still talking, but all of a sudden his words were garbled. Unintelligible. A woman beside me whispered, "He's not making any sense."

Tarsus mounted the stage in a single step, just in time to catch Griffin as he fell.

23

"RORY, WE HAVE TO GO," North said urgently. EMTs were hurriedly strapping Griffin to a stretcher, barking at one another in rapid fire. I hadn't moved since Griffin collapsed nineteen minutes ago. Nor had I spoken. I felt as if the floor beneath me had given way and I was floating through the air, weightless. This couldn't be happening. I didn't even know what "this" was yet. Was Griffin dead?

"Rory," North said again.

I forced myself to meet his gaze. "Okay," I said.

Beck was on his Gold, watching the Forum chatter about what had happened. Since Griffin had collapsed during a live broadcast, it was all anyone on Forum was talking about. New posts were popping up so fast, Beck's screen was a whirl of vertical motion.

"Come with us," I said to Beck suddenly. "Take the train with us back to Theden. You can stay at North's." I looked at North for confirmation. "Right?"

"Sure," he said. "I've got plenty of room."

Beck was already shaking his head. "I can't. I have the MFA event tomorrow."

"You'll be back by then. There are trains nearly every hour."

I could see Beck considering it. He seemed uncertain. "Let me ask Lux," he said finally.

"You can't ask Lux," I said sharply. "I'm not supposed to be here, so you can't ask it if you can leave with me."

Beck's eyes were instantly suspicious. "What do you mean, you're not supposed to be here?"

"It's a long story," I said, squeezing my fists in frustration to keep from shaking him. "God, Beck, just come with us. You'll be back in plenty of time."

"Rory, we really need to go," North said gently. "It's gonna be hard to get a cab, and we can't miss our train."

I looked at Beck. "You coming?"

He took a step back, away from me.

"Forget it," I barked, spinning on my heels as angry tears sprung to my eyes. "North, let's go."

"Nice to meet you," I heard North say behind me. "Good luck with the exhibit."

"Rory!" Beck called. I didn't look back.

By the time we made it to our train, the mainstream news media had picked up the story. We watched coverage the whole way back. A little after eleven, Gnosis released a statement. Griffin Payne had suffered a stroke.

"A stroke?" My voice faltered. "He's thirty-five. He was on the cover of *Men's Health* last month. How could he have a stroke?"

North just shook his head. "He'll be okay. He's got the best doctors in the world."

I pressed the heels of my hands to my forehead in frustration. "Ugh! I feel like we took one step forward and, like, eleven steps back." And then, out of nowhere and out of everywhere, I was crying. This time I didn't even try to hold it in. North pulled me toward him, wrapping both arms around me. I wept noisily into his jacket, which smelled like woodsy cologne and not like North at all.

"None of it makes any sense," I said, my voice muffled by herringbone. "Griffin said my mom was their class valedictorian. Why would she leave just hours before graduation?"

"Maybe she was scared," North said. "Maybe she knew someone was out to get her. Someone who was capable of more than just some doctored medical files."

"But who? And why didn't she just go to the police? Or at least to Griffin. She could've proven to him that those test results were fake." Unless she sent them to him. But why would she do that?

Just then something out the window caught my eye. A flash of light in the dark. It was a meteor, zipping through the night sky. For a moment I thought there were two of them, one below and one above, but then I realized the second one was a mirror image of the first, reflecting off the water below it. We were passing the reservoir. We were almost back.

"Theden" came the train's automated voice. "Theden Central Station is next."

I wiped my eyes and sat up as the train pulled into the station.

"Well, as far as dates go, this one was pretty uneventful," North deadpanned.

"Totally dull," I agreed.

"I'm glad you got a chance to talk to Griffin," he said, softer and sincere.

"Me too." Neither of us needed to say what we were both thinking. That we hoped it wouldn't be the last time I got that chance.

The train stopped and we got to our feet. Mine were aching in Hershey's stacked heels. "So we regroup tomorrow?" North asked as we stepped off the train onto the empty platform.

"Yeah, I guess so." It was Saturday, so I didn't have classes, but I'd resolved to use the weekend to catch up on all the schoolwork I hadn't done. I'd assumed that talking to Griffin would answer my questions, not raise about a hundred more. Now I doubted I'd get anything done before Monday, or that this coming week would be any different from the past one. A blur of lectures I wouldn't absorb and homework I wouldn't do.

My jeans and sneakers were in the compartment under the seat of North's motorbike, which was parked outside the station. North shrugged out of his suit jacket and held it up as a curtain, keeping his eyes on the sky as I changed in the space between it and him. When I had my jeans on but not my sweatshirt, I took a step closer to him so our bodies were touching, my bare chest against his white dress shirt. He looked down at me in surprise.

"Hi," he said.

"Hi," I said, and stood on my tiptoes to kiss him. When my lips touched his, I let my eyes flutter shut and my thoughts go still, pretending, just for that instant, that we were just a boy and a girl kissing in a parking lot. A boy who wasn't a cyber criminal and a girl whose life actually made sense. I felt his arms begin to lower. I shrieked. "Back up, back up!"

"Sorry," he said, raising his arms again. "I got distracted."

I giggled. "Okay, look away again, I have to put my sweatshirt on." Obligingly, he tilted his head back, exhaling a big puff of warm air into the cold night sky. I tugged the sweatshirt over my head, and the skin on my chest prickled with goose bumps. "Okay, done." I folded the dress and handed it to North. "Tell Noelle thank you." North put the dress and his suit jacket under the seat then handed me a helmet.

"I should call my dad," I said as I buckled the strap. "It was crazy to think I could keep this from him. He deserves to know the truth." My voice broke a little. I knew it was the right thing to do, but I couldn't imagine actually saying the words. *Mom lied to you. I'm not your kid.*

"What can I do?"

"Download Beck's Lux profile," I told him.

"What are we looking for?"

"An explanation," I said. "He starts using Lux and suddenly he's taking crappy photographs and not returning my calls. That can't be an accident."

"Contentment changes people," North replied. He swung a leg over his bike and tilted the seat down so I could get on behind him. "He's obviously getting a lot of validation for those photographs—which, by the way, aren't *that* crappy—"

"Yes, they are."

"And he feels like his life is coming together. It's the same reason ninety-eight percent of the people in this country won't make a decision without Lux. Life gets easier when you use it."

I gaped at him. "You're defending Lux?"

"Hell, no," North replied. "I'm just explaining it."

I shook my head, the helmet knocking against my temple. "No. There's something else going on."

"Like what?" North asked as he started up the bike.

"I don't know," I admitted. I climbed onto the bike and wrapped my arms around his waist. "But maybe it's connected to whatever Griffin was about to say tonight. Before he left for his speech, he said something about needing to say a few things before 'this thing' went any further."

. "But he collapsed before he could get it out."

"That's pretty odd timing, don't you think?"

North turned his head to look back at me as the bike roared to life. "Wait. You think there's a chance what happened to

Griffin wasn't an accident?" he yelled over the noise.

I met North's gaze. "I think there's a lot we don't know."

I got back to the library ten minutes before closing, and my Gemini was right where I'd hidden it, under a seat cushion in one of the upper reading rooms. It'd posted two mundane status updates in the time we'd been gone, and other than a few likes, my late-night study session hadn't drawn much attention on Forum. We'd pulled it off. Unless, of course, Tarsus heard from Griffin that I was at the party, or worse, had seen me, but at that point I had no way to know. I'd just have to wait.

I called my dad on the walk back to the dorm. It wasn't even nine o'clock yet in Seattle, so I knew he and Kari would be awake. He answered on the second ring.

"Hi, Dad," I said, my voice breaking.

"Sweetheart, what is it?"

The tears spilled over. How could the man who knew me well enough to know that something was wrong from the words *Hi, Dad* not be my real father?

"It's about mom . . . ," I began.

"Okay," Dad said slowly, guarded. There was the sound of a door opening. I imagined him stepping outside onto the small porch off the kitchen, barely big enough for the charcoal grill he kept there.

I started with the simplest truth. "Mom was— She was already pregnant when you guys got married."

My dad sighed. "I know that, honey."

"And"—I took a shaky breath—"you weren't the father. You aren't—my father."

There was a long pause. I stopped walking and squeezed my eyes shut, bracing against his reaction, the pain I expected to hear.

"I know that, too," I heard him say, his voice heavier than I'd ever heard it.

My eyes flew open. "You *know*?"

"I've always known," he said sadly. "Your mom and I, Rory, we— We were never a couple. Not romantically, any-way. Your mom— She was in love with someone else. But, sweetheart, that doesn't change how much I love you. Or the fact that I will *always* be your dad." His voice broke. Tears rushed to my eyes.

"I love you too, Dad," I whispered. "So much."

"Maybe I should fly out there," he said then. "I could—"

"No, that's okay," I said quickly. Airfare was expensive, and money was tight for them already. Plus, I felt like North and I were getting closer to whatever truth was behind all this, and having my dad around would only slow us down. "With classes and homework, I would hardly even see you."

"If you're sure," my dad said, sounding uncertain. "I just hate that you're by yourself in all this." *By myself.* My mom was dead, my biological father was in the hospital, my best friend was acting like he'd been body-snatched, my roommate was missing, and my dad and stepmom were three thousand miles away. I felt like one of those bright-orange buoys in the ocean, floating in deep water. But those were tethered by rope. I was on my own.

You're not alone, came a whisper.

The voice was right. I had North.

"Dad?"

"Yes, honey?"

"Do you know . . . who he was?" I couldn't say *who my father is.* Not to my dad. I'd already decided not to tell him about Griffin, not yet. Not unless he already knew.

"No," Dad replied. "Your mom wouldn't tell me. She said it was better—*safer* was her word—if I didn't know."

It was warm in my room, but I suddenly got cold.

"Safer," I repeated.

"That's what she said. She was insistent that I not try to find out, and made me promise that I'd never tell you that you weren't mine."

"Why? What was she afraid of?" What I really meant was *who.*

"It's a question I've asked myself a million and one times since then. But your mother never said. All she told me was she thought her life was in danger, and yours was too, and that she needed me to marry her, and if anything happened to her, to raise you. She made me promise never to tell you that I wasn't your father unless you found out on your own."

It was hard to imagine my dad at eighteen, taking all of this on. "And you said yes to all that?"

"It was Aviana. I would've done anything for her." His

voice caught. "Plus, what she was asking, it was what I always wanted, anyway. To be with her. I thought we'd get to spend the rest of our lives together. I never thought she'd—" He stopped himself again. He never thought she'd *die*.

She thought her life was in danger, and nine months later, she was dead.

What if her death wasn't an accident?

I didn't sleep that night, wondering. It seemed implausible, but then again I didn't know who my mom was dealing with. Neither had Griffin. There was a piece missing, a big one, and I had no idea where to find it.

At two a.m. I turned on my light. I couldn't just lie there in the dark anymore, clutching the baby blanket my mom had been so determined to finish. But there was no way I could concentrate on the mountain of schoolwork I had to do either. North's copy of *Paradise Lost* was on my nightstand, the card my mom left me marking the page where the quotation appeared. I grabbed the book and settled back into bed, letting my fingers skim the raised stitching on my blanket as I read the words aloud:

Authors to themselves in all
Both what they judge, and what they choose; for so
I formed them free: and free they must remain,
Till they enthrall themselves; I else must change
Their nature, and revoke the high decree
Unchangeable, eternal, which ordain'd
Their freedom: they themselves ordain'd their fall.

North was right. Saying the words out loud made the meaning clearer somehow. *Authors to themselves in all.* Milton was saying that we always had the power to make right choices, even if we seldom did. It reminded me of Pythagoras's view of upsilon. And Griffin's *timshel* ring. Virtue or vice, thou mayest or mayest not, there was always a choice.

I set the book in my lap and picked up my Gemini, turning it over in my hands. For the first time I sensed the Doubt before I heard it, as if my mind had been preparing for it to speak.

You lift it, you carry it, you set it in its place, and it stays there; it cannot move.
If you cry out to it, it cannot answer or save you from your trouble.

The words, the odd phrasing—it felt like one of the society's riddles. With this one, though, I didn't have to work for the answer. I was holding it in my hand. It struck me as completely ridiculous all of a sudden, how reverent I'd been of this little rectangle. As if the secrets of the universe were tucked inside these four inches of program code and metal.

I set my Gemini back on the nightstand and brought my eyes back to North's book. At the top margin of the next page, written with loopy script in dark red pen, was the name Kristyn with a phone number. Boston area code.

"Great," I muttered. So much for trying to distract myself with poetry. I'd managed to stop obsessing about my mom only to start wondering about the girl who'd written her phone number in North's book. Someone he dated back in Boston? Kristyn with a *y* sounded like a hot girl's name. For all I knew, North had a slew of hot girls in his past. Had he slept with any of them? He was definitely experienced in the hookup department—I could tell that from the way he kissed. My cheeks got hot thinking about the way *I* kissed. Could North tell how inexperienced I was?

With a sigh, I shut the book and put it back on the nightstand, exchanging it for my Gemini. It'd been a couple of hours since I last checked on Griffin's status, so I clicked over to Forum and filtered my newsfeed by the #GriffinPayne hashtag to scan the chatter. The latest official update had been posted just after midnight.

@Gnosis: @GriffinPayne being prepped for emergency brain surgery. Follow @GnosisNews for the latest on his condition. #GriffinPayne #Gnosis

Brain surgery. With no tears left, I stared at my screen with dry eyes until I fell asleep.

Noise from the courtyard woke me. Some boys were playing a very heated game of ultimate Frisbee, and from the sound of it, they had quite a few cheerleaders. I was still clutching my Gemini, so I quickly checked Griffin's status before getting out of bed. There'd been an official Griffin update at seven a.m., just over two hours ago, which said that he was still in surgery but that the report from his surgical team was that it was going well.

Buoyed by the good news, I splashed some water on my face then stepped into Hershey's closet to find something to wear. In the mad prep for the party, I'd missed the laundry drop-off again, so unless I wanted to look like a homeless person, I'd have to wear something of hers. The associate dean had asked me to pack up Hershey's things—her parents were having them shipped—but I kept putting it off, mostly because doing it would force me to accept that she wasn't coming back. I'd been Forum messaging with some of her friends back home, one of whom had told me on Friday that her parents had heard from Hershey's parents that Hershey had withdrawn sixteen hundred dollars from an ATM at the Boston airport before getting on the plane to Seattle, and that the Clementses figured their daughter would come home as soon as the money ran out. I couldn't believe they were so blasé. I didn't doubt that Hershey could fend for herself, but I was still worried about her and thought her parents should be too, especially since none of her friends in Seattle had heard from her since she disappeared.

I took the road route to downtown, not wanting to get mud on Hershey's shoes. I read Griffin's Panopticon article as I walked, which had already been updated to mention his stroke, but of course said nothing about my mom. It was odd, actually, that no one had found their marriage license. Journalists were notorious for digging that stuff up. I linked over to the page for the Gemini Gold. The device, nearly half the size of the previous Gemini but with twice the memory and infinite battery life (it was powered by the user's movements when it was snapped into the wrist holster and could hold a charge for up to an hour when it wasn't hooked in), was set to go on sale on Monday morning, and there was a quote from Gnosis's CFO, added to the page less than an hour before, saying that the company hoped consumers would show their support for Griffin's recovery by preordering the device he'd worked so hard to bring to market. The marketing ploy, in its transparency, put a sour taste in my mouth, especially since I knew it would work. Not that people needed that much urging; Gnosis was offering the Gold for less than it'd cost to buy an older model Gemini.

I stopped at Paradiso for two coffees. "Round two already?" the guy at the register asked when I ordered. North introduced him to me once, but I couldn't remember his name. Blake, maybe? I gave him a quizzical smile.

"Round two?"

"North was just here twenty minutes ago," he explained.

"Oh. Then I guess never mind then." I pocketed my handheld and headed up to North's apartment, smiling to myself. He'd gotten me coffee.

When his door opened, I realized that the coffee hadn't been for me. Stunned, I stared at the girl standing in his doorway. Hershey grinned when she saw me and put a hand on her hip.

"Nice outfit, bitch."

24

"HERSHEY! WHAT ARE YOU DOING HERE?"

Hershey smirked. "What, you were hoping I was dead so you'd have free rein on my closet?"

"No! Of cour—"

"I was kidding," she said with a laugh, and pulled me into a hug.

"I'm glad you're okay," I said into her hair.

North appeared behind Hershey. "Let's close the door," he said, ushering me inside. Hershey plopped down on the couch, pulling her legs up under her, and reached for the paper cup on the end table. I perched on the edge of the coffee table. She was paler than she usually was, not sick-person pale, just lack-of-a-spray-tan pale, and it looked like she'd lost a little weight.

"How'd you get back?" I asked her.

"I never left," she replied, tossing her hair. "I paid a girl to take my first-class ticket and post status updates from my handheld." She took a sip from her coffee. "I thought it was pretty brilliant."

"And since then?"

"I've been staying at a motel a few miles from here, trying to dig up some dirt on the Evil Queen."

"Tarsus?"

"She's such a piece of work," Hershey spat. "I went to her house that morning to tell her I wouldn't spy for her anymore. I should've just gone straight to the dean. I figured she'd argue with me or try to convince me to keep doing it, but she acted like she had no idea what I was talking about. As if I were making it up. So I told her we'd just have to let the dean decide. That was when she mentioned sending me for a psych eval, which she was *sure* would show that I'd had some sort of mental breakdown." Hershey shook her head in disgust. "It was so well played. She had me cornered. So I told her I'd leave on my own."

"I'm so sorry, Hersh. What have you been doing since then?"

"Beating the witch at her own game," Hershey replied. She reached into the leather bag at her feet and pulled out a data chip. She handed it to me. "It's from her tablet. All stuff about you. Your birth announcement, old news articles from when you won the state science fair and crap like that, screenshots of your Forum page, a couple of photos. Whatever she's had against you, it started long before you applied to Theden."

The hair on my arms stood on end. "How did you get this?"

"Don't worry about it," Hershey replied flippantly. "I owe you."

"I appreciate that, but, Hershey, if you'd gotten caught breaking in to her office—"

"I didn't break in," she said. "And I didn't get caught." She took another sip of her coffee. "If I were you, I'd be thinking less about how I got it and more about what's on it."

I stared at the data chip lying flat in my palm. Dr. Tarsus had been keeping tabs on me since birth. Why?

I looked up with a start. "She was in my mom's class!" I yanked my handheld from my back pocket and went to my photobox. I'd taken another picture of my mom's senior photo, in daylight this time, so I had a clear shot of the whole class now. "That would explain how she knows Griffin, too." I kicked myself for not thinking of it before.

Now that I was looking for her, Tarsus was easy to spot. She was in the back row, directly behind my mom, several inches taller than the boys on either side. There was no doubt it was her. She looked younger, and her Afro was a little less manicured, but the girl in the photo had the same striking features, the same impeccable skin. The only difference was this girl's mouth was spread wide in a warm, happy smile. The only smile I'd ever seen on Dr. Tarsus's face was ice-cold.

"It was her," I said airlessly. "She's the one who doctored my mom's medical file and sent Griffin those fake pregnancy results."

"You think?" North sounded skeptical.

"She mentioned my mom's illness," I said hurriedly. "After class one day. But if what Griffin said is true, my mom didn't have APD. Or wasn't diagnosed with it, anyway. So how would Tarsus know about the fake diagnosis unless she'd given it to her?" Something was bothering me as I said it, but I couldn't put my finger on it.

"I'm lost," Hershey said, looking completely confused. "Griffin who?"

"Griffin Payne," I said. "He's—He's my father."

Hershey's mouth dropped open. "Shut the front door. Really?"

"He and my mom were married," I told her. "In high school. But you can't tell anyone. I mean it, Hershey."

"Who am I going to tell? I'm a fugitive." She leaned back against the couch cushions. "Griffin Payne is your *father*. Wow. If he croaks, you'll be a billionaire."

I shot her a look. "Nice, Hershey." I looked back at North. "Tarsus is behind this. I know it. The only question is *why*."

Just then my handheld buzzed with a message. It was from the dean's assistant.

@DeanAtwaterAsst: Please report to the dean's office immediately.

"Shit."

"What is it?" North asked.

"Dean Atwater wants to see me in his office," I said miserably. "He totally knows about last night."

"Maybe you should tell him the truth," North suggested.

"About Tarsus and your mom and Griffin. He fought for you once, maybe he'll do it again."

"Yeah," I said, but I wasn't optimistic. Breaking a rule this boldly was an automatic dismissal. If Tarsus had seen me, the dean's hands would be tied.

North walked me back to campus. "Do you regret going to the party?" he asked.

I shook my head. "No. If we hadn't gone, I wouldn't know for sure about Griffin."

North smiled. "And he wouldn't know about you. I saw the look on his face when you told him. It was shock followed by sheer joy."

We walked in silence for a few minutes. "What am I going to do if they kick me out?" I asked quietly as the campus gate came into view. "Theden is everything to me."

"Because it connects you to your mom?"

"It's more than that," I replied, suddenly vulnerable. "I never felt like I belonged back home. I was always the weird girl who was too into school. Not cool enough to pretend it was lame. Here, I get to be me, you know?"

"There are other places like that," North replied. "Schools that would leap at the chance to have you."

"None of them are Theden," I said. "Nowhere else even comes close." A knot took root at the back of my throat. I tried to swallow it away. Crying wouldn't help my case. The dean would expect me to be more rational than that.

"Well, whatever happens, you still have me," North said. "Although I know that's little consolation."

I laced my fingers through his. "No. It's not. It's a lot." I chewed on my lip. It was silly, but I couldn't get the image of that name and phone number out of my head. The loopy, girly handwriting. The red pen. "Can I ask you something?"

"Sure," North said.

"Who's Kristyn?" I asked, keeping my voice light.

North looked at me blankly. "Kristyn who?"

"The name and phone number written in *Paradise Lost*. Kristyn with a *y*. Is she an old girlfriend?"

North stopped abruptly. "I've never dated anyone named Kristyn and there was definitely not a name written in the book when I gave it to you."

"But there must have been," I replied. "I certainly didn't write it."

"I'm telling you, Rory, that book was in near-pristine condition when I bought it. No markings, no tears. I've got a certificate to prove it. And it didn't leave my apartment until I gave it to you."

"Then where did the writing come from?"

"I have no idea," North said. "You said it was a name and phone number. Do you happen to remember the number?"

I rattled off the digits, embarrassed that I'd memorized it.

North typed the number into his handheld. "I'll see what I can figure out," he said. We'd reached the campus gate. "Good luck with the dean."

Turns out, I needed the luck, but not for the reason I thought.

"Every year about a dozen of our brightest students are contacted by a group of students claiming to belong to a secret society," Dean Atwater said, his voice grave. I was seated across from him in his office, perched on the edge of an oversize leather chair. "This group is not an authorized student organization, and as such, is not permitted to hold meetings on campus." He paused, as if waiting for me to jump in. I kept my expression neutral.

"A secret society?"

"You are one of our most promising students, Rory," Dean Atwater went on. "Not only because of your natural aptitude, but also because of your academic performance. If you stay on track, you could graduate at the very top of your class."

I felt sweat bead on my upper lip. "I plan to," I said weakly.

"If, however, you involve yourself with this clandestine group, I will have no choice but to dismiss you from our program." He smiled kindly. "But if you haven't yet pledged your commitment to them, there's time to set things right."

"I don't know anything about a secret society," I said, hating the waver in my voice. "No one has contacted me about anything like that."

"Now, I know there is a sense of prestige associated with this kind of thing. You feel like you've been chosen—sought out, even—to be part of an elite group, and I understand how tempting something like that would be." His eyes were soft.

Sympathetic. "But, Rory, you've got your future to think about. A very bright future that an association with this group would quickly snuff out."

I hesitated, and for a moment contemplated telling him the truth. But the society was my closest link to my mom.

"I understand," I told him. "If they contact me, I'll be sure to let you know."

"Excellent," he replied, rising to his feet. "And I trust that you'll keep this conversation between us. Discretion is crucial so that my inquiries don't drive them further underground." He pressed a button on his desk, and the door behind me opened.

I nodded. "Of course."

I practically skipped back to North's apartment.

"You're smiling," he said when he opened the door. "You didn't get kicked out."

"Nope," I said happily. "He has no idea about last night."

"So what'd he want?"

"He just had some questions about my extracurriculars," I answered, avoiding North's gaze. I hated lying to him, but I doubted there was a boyfriend exception to the society's vows.

"That's great," North said. "I have some good news too. The phone number you gave me matches the name. It belongs to Kristyn Hildebrand, a clinical psychiatrist at Harvard. Same spelling of Kristyn."

My forearms prickled with goose bumps. I knew that name.

"She's in my mom's medical file! Dr. K. Hildebrand. Her signature is on every one of those fake psych entries." I squeezed his forearms.

"So who wrote her name in my book?"

"I don't know. The same person who put my mom's transcript under my pillow, maybe. Whoever it was, we have to talk to this woman." I pulled out my Gemini and started dialing the number.

North caught my hand. "Don't tell her who you are," he warned. "If she's one of the people on your threat list, then you're on hers, too. Lux will tell her not to meet with you."

I put the phone down. "You're right. It's better if I do it in person. Catch her completely off guard. Can we go right now?"

"I know you're eager to talk to this woman," North said gently, "but don't you think you should wait until Monday, when she'll be at her office? If you show up at her house, her guard will immediately go up. Not to mention the fact that we don't know where she lives."

He was right, but Monday felt like an eternity away. "Okay." I sighed. "I'll wait."

As I was putting my handheld away, it buzzed with an incoming message. Unknown sender. Greek letters that morphed into English:

You have passed our evaluation, Zeta. Well done. Be at the eastern gate of Garden Grove Cemetery at 10:25 p.m. Do not come early. Do not be late.

"More good news?" North asked. I was beaming at my screen.

"Uh, yeah," I said, quickly putting my Gemini away. "School stuff."

Hershey shot me a suspicious look. She didn't buy it, but she didn't call me out.

"Speaking of school stuff," I said then, "I should probably go. I've got a mountain of homework to—"

"Hey, Griffin's out of surgery," Hershey said, pointing at the TV screen. The volume was down, but the banner at the bottom read, "Gnosis CEO Griffin Payne expected to recover after nine-hour brain surgery." Relief washed over me.

"He's going to be okay," I said breathlessly. "Hey, what'd you find out about Beck?" I asked suddenly, turning back to North. In all the craziness of the morning, I'd forgotten what I'd come for. "Were you able to hack his profile?"

Hershey's eyes darted to North. "Wait, you're a *hacker*?"

I winced. Hershey saw it.

"What? I'm not going to tell anyone," Hershey said.

"He's not a hacker," I said quickly. "I asked him to try to—"

"Rory, it's okay," North said. "I trust her. But, no, I couldn't access Beck's profile. Well, I could, but it was just a placeholder. The data had been migrated to a different server."

"That's weird, right?"

"Nah. My guess is Gnosis has built a new infrastructure for the Gold, and that Beck's profile was moved over when he joined the beta test. I should be able to get into it, I just have to find it first."

"Oooh, your boyfriend is so hot when he talks hacker," Hershey said coyly. I rolled my eyes. "Oh, shut up, Rory Vaughn," she said, thrusting a hand on her hip. "You know you've missed me."

I couldn't help but smile. She was right. I had.

At exactly 10:25 that night, I approached the cemetery gate. I was using Lux for the first time in weeks, not wanting to take any chances with my arrival time.

A robed figure stood at the gate like an eerie grim reaper. I shivered beneath my down coat. "Hey," the figure said as I walked up, the familiar voice immediately putting me at ease. It was Liam. "Ready?"

"Yep," I said, and lifted my tongue.

The air in the arena was cold and still. I blinked rapidly, my eyes struggling to adjust to the dark. There were others, I could hear them rustling, but the space around me was pitch-black.

Minutes passed in near silence. I waited and watched, gradually able to make out shapes in the darkness. People arrived in twos, one leading another to a spot on the stone steps. As more people arrived, the rustling got louder, but no one spoke.

Then out of the silence:

"Congratulations! The evaluation is over. The eleven of you have passed our test." I recognized the voice of the serpent figure, mechanically distorted as before, but the air of formality was gone. His voice was kind and casual, familiar even, despite the distorted edge. "We know you have questions. Who are we, where are we, what's with all the masks." There were little bursts of nervous laughter in the darkness. "I promise you, all of your questions will be answered very soon. For now I can tell you this: we are *hoi oligoi sophoi*. The Wise Few. Or, simply, the Few."

There was an explosion of light below as the stage lit up in a ring of fire. The serpent stood in the center, wearing an oversize gold crown. He reminded me of Prince John in the old *Robin Hood* cartoon, and I had to bite my lip not to laugh.

"You have been chosen," the serpent declared, raising his voice over the crackle of the fire. "Now you must choose. If you join us, you will be asked to dedicate your lives to the service of others. To use your gifts for the betterment of mankind. You will be called to a grander, more significant purpose. To see the world not for what it is, but for what it could be."

See the world for what it could be. That was exactly what the Doubt did. It gave you the eyes to see beyond the moment you were in. *A grander, more significant purpose.* Yes. That was what I wanted. To live for something other than myself.

"Initiation is in two days," I heard the serpent say. "You have until then to decide. Choose wisely, friends."

My right knee was throbbing. I was standing at the foot of my bed, holding a black velvet knapsack cinched shut with gold rope. My Gemini was lit up on my bed, my Notepad open on my screen:

Put ice on your knee.—L

I looked down at Hershey's jeans. The right knee was scuffed with mud. Stepping out of my shoes, I yanked open the knapsack. Inside was a robe cut from crimson red velvet, a zeta symbol, and the number thirty embroidered in gold on the lapel. "Woo-hoo!" I yelled, doing an awkward victory dance.

I was in.

25

SUNDAY CRAWLED BY in a thick haze of anxiety, excitement, and hope. I was anxious about Griffin's recovery, excited about initiation, and hopeful that Dr. Hildebrand would have the answers I so desperately needed. I spent the day on North's couch, weeding through my schoolwork, surprised to hear that Hershey was all caught up on hers. She said she didn't want to be behind when they let her back in. There was no "if" in Hershey's mind. She was determined to be back at Theden in time for finals. It was still a little weird for me that she was staying at North's apartment, knowing all that I did about how hard she'd come on to him the night they met, but she was out of money and didn't have anywhere else to go, and North, being North, had invited her to stay. So for now she was a permanent fixture in his living room.

I forced myself to go back to campus on Sunday night for dinner. I'd run into Rachel and Izzy at brunch and they'd commented on how little they'd seen me. It wasn't until they said it that I realized how much time I'd been spending at North's. I hadn't eaten dinner in the dining hall all week. There was no requirement that we eat on campus, but the Theden app tracked our dining hall check-ins, and I assumed that meant the administration was tracking them too. I didn't need anyone asking questions about where I was spending my time. Now that we knew Tarsus was watching my every move, North and I were being careful to keep our relationship off her radar. He couldn't afford to have someone looking too closely at his life. The facade he'd built was too thin.

Liam came up behind me at the pasta station. "Hey," he said, reaching for a plate. "I need to ask you something."

I slid my tray down to make room for his. "Okay."

"That blanket on your bed," he said in a low voice. "The one with the pink stitching. Where'd you get it?"

"My mom made it for me. Why?"

"Your mom," he repeated. I nodded.

"It was my baby blanket," I explained.

"It's a Fibonacci spiral."

"I know that," I said, a little surprised that Liam did.

"Why would your mom sew a Fibonacci spiral onto a blanket?"

"I don't know," I told him. "She died when I was born. Why do you care so much?"

"Because the pattern on your blanket is the map of our tomb," Liam replied, his voice even lower now.

I looked at him blankly. "Huh?"

"The society's compound. Underneath the cemetery. It's ten rooms, with Fibonacci proportions. Identical to your blanket."

I dropped the tongs I was holding. They clattered onto the stainless steel counter. "Really?"

"Yeah. Of all the designs for her to put on that blanket, she picks that one?"

"My mom went here. She was in the society."

Liam took a step back. "Your mom was one of the Few?"

I nodded. "Upsilon '13." I showed him my pendant. "This was hers. She left it for me. She didn't break her vows or anything," I said quickly.

"How come you never mentioned any of this be—" Liam stopped as Izzy stepped up to the fettuccini pan.

"Hey," Izzy said, reaching for the tongs I'd dropped. "What're y'all all hush-hush about?"

"Nothing," Liam and I replied in unison. Izzy gave me a knowing smile.

"I'll text you later," Liam said, and walked off.

"He's *so* your secret boyfriend," Izzy squealed.

"No. He's definitely not."

Izzy pouted. "Well, boo. Then who is?"

"Still not telling people," I said, wondering how long I could pull this off. Izzy was heaping fettuccini Alfredo onto her plate. Lux had definitely not sanctioned this meal. "Hey, did you preorder the Gold?" I asked her. The first shipments of the handhelds were supposed to arrive at the campus post office the next morning.

"Didn't everybody?" was her reply. The answer was no, because I hadn't. I didn't want it anymore.

By lunchtime the next day I was in a very small minority. I hadn't seen a single person on campus who *didn't* have a Gold strapped to their wrist. According to the latest numbers, the tiny device had already broken the record for the fastest-selling handheld of all time. Two hundred million had already been shipped, and they were expecting to sell more than twice that over the next two days. That meant that more than half a billion people would be using the Gold by week's end. Griffin was still in the hospital after his surgery, and Gnosis was milking that for all it was worth. The hashtag #GoldsForGriffin had been trending on Forum since Friday night, ever since Gnosis had promised to donate a percentage of the proceeds from Gold presales to stroke-prevention research.

I left after history to meet up with North. We were taking the one-fifteen train to Cambridge, hoping to catch Dr. Hildebrand on her way back from lunch. When I knocked on North's door, Hershey answered, wearing skinny black pants and a V-neck cardigan that I'm pretty sure was intended to be worn with a T-shirt underneath. Hershey had opted for a lacy black bra.

"Don't worry," Hershey said when she saw my face. "This isn't for your boyfriend, it's for mine." She stepped back to let me inside. "Yours is in his secret room."

I shrugged out of my dowdy blue jacket, wishing I'd worn something nicer. Hershey said I could wear whatever of hers

I wanted, but I felt weird about it now that she was back. So I was stuck with my own stuff, and the worst of it at that, since all my decent clothes were at the bottom of my laundry basket. "Is yours the same guy as before?"

Hershey smiled coyly. "Maybe. Hey, I have a present for you." She turned and walked over to the couch, reaching under the cushion and pulling out an oversize hardback book.

"What is that?" I asked.

"The Evil Queen's yearbook. Class of 2013 was the last one they printed on paper."

"Where did you get this?" I demanded.

"I figured there might some be clues in there," she said, not answering my question.

"Hershey, this isn't a game. We don't know what this woman is capable of."

"I'm not scared of her," Hershey retorted, reaching for her jacket and a pair of dark sunglasses. "She's just a bully who needs to be put in her place." She tossed her hair and pulled open the door. "Oh," she said, turning back around. "North was waiting for that." She pointed at the small box on his coffee table, imprinted with the Gnosis logo. "It came a few minutes ago." She blew me a kiss and was gone.

I picked up the box and carried it into the bedroom closet. The door to North's secret room was cracked. I could see him at his desk chair, leaning back with his eyes closed, bobbing his head a little like he was listening to music. But it was quiet in the room.

"Hey," I said, ducking inside. North didn't look up. It was as if he hadn't heard me. I tried again, louder. "Hey!" This time, his eyes popped open.

"Come over here," he said, leaning to grab my hand. "I want you to hear this." He pulled me into his lap. As my body came in line with his, I heard the distinctive sound of Nick's mandolin coming from a speaker above our heads. I looked up.

"Was that on the whole time?"

"Cool, right? It's called an audio spotlight. Only the person sitting in this chair can hear what's coming out of that speaker. Although, apparently, the sound isn't actually coming from the physical speaker but from ultrasonic waves in front of it. Don't ask me how it works, though. I've read the manual forty times and still don't get it." He reached around me to twist the knob on the little gray box on his desk, turning up the volume even more. "But the song's amazing, right? The guys released their new album today. This is the first track."

It was one of the songs we'd recorded in the mausoleum. I leaned back against North and closed my eyes.

"I can't get over how good they are," I said when the song was over, sliding off his lap. I realized I still had the box in my hand. "Hey, this came for you," I said, setting it on North's desk.

"You mean Norvin," North corrected, slitting the packing tape with his pocketknife. Inside was a smaller, shinier black box, plain except for an image of the Gold and the words BOW DOWN printed in glossy gold foil. "Does it come with an altar?" North retorted as he lifted the lid. I peered into the box. The shiny device was snapped into a clear silicone wristband.

North slipped the band onto his wrist and grimaced. "It's so tacky."

I giggled. "All you need is a matching gold chain for your neck."

North tapped the tiny screen and it lit up. It was 12:35.

"We should probably go," I said. "I don't want to miss our train."

"I want to show you something first," North replied. "I found Beck's Lux profile."

I perked up. "And?"

"And you should look at it," he said, scooting his chair toward his desk. "You—"

The music suddenly went silent, like someone had turned the speaker off. But the power light on the control panel was still lit. North looked at the ceiling, puzzled. He turned the volume knob all the way up and the speaker started making a loud popping noise. Still no music.

"Did we blow it out?"

"I don't think so," North said. "It wasn't even that loud." He leaned over toward the far end of his desk where the plug was and the music started to blare. My hands flew to my ears as North quickly reached for the volume knob. But before he even touched it, the music cut out again. North looked down at the Gold on his wrist. Slowly, he outstretched his arm. The music came on again. He brought his wrist toward his body. The music stopped.

"I don't understand. What's happening?"

"I think they're canceling each other out," North said slowly. "But for that to happen, the Gold would have to be emitting sound waves at the exact same frequency as my speaker. Really high frequency waves that we can't hear. That we aren't *supposed* to hear."

"Why would it be doing that?"

North shook his head. He looked baffled. "I have no idea. Especially since there's nothing about it in the new terms of use." He unsnapped the Gold from its strap and tossed it onto a pile of clothes in his closet. The music came back on. He shook his head again and scooted back up to his desk.

His computer had finished booting up. North clicked on a document saved to his desktop, labeled BECK.

"Show me the threats first," I said. North zoomed in on the bottom right quadrant. My eyes scanned the list. *Surprises. Sunsets. Storms. Solar eclipses.* "No, the threats first," I said.

"These *are* the threats," North replied.

"But Beck loves eclipses," I argued. "They're, like, his favorite thing. And he gets his best artistic ideas at sunset." North slid his cursor over and zoomed in on the opportunities quadrant. *Predictability, monotonous routine, temperate weather, successful people, homogenous neighborhoods, steady income, stable work.* My chest tightened.

"No." I shook my head violently. "This is not Beck." Part of me was relieved. I hadn't been able to reconcile Beck's behavior at the party with the boy I'd grown up with, the free spirit who blazed his own path. Now I understood. "Lux is manipulating him."

"Of course it is," North replied. "That's what Lux does. It steers people into the life they think they want—the 'happiness' they think they deserve."

"But this isn't the life Beck wants," I insisted. "You don't know him the way I do."

"I don't know him at all," North said. "But, Rory, if Beck is trusting Lux, then he's *choosing* to. You can't blame the app for that."

But I *did* blame the app. Beck wouldn't just decide to become a whole different person—a total d-bag, by the way—just because he thought it'd make his life easier. My best friend was less shallow than that.

Help, I said silently, pleading with the voice. *Help me figure this out.* There was something I wasn't seeing here, maybe something I *couldn't* see. But if I'd learned anything about the Doubt, it was that it *could* see. Everything I couldn't. I needed that vision now.

"I know it's hard to accept," North was saying. "But the only person at fault here is Beck. He's the one who decided to listen to—"

Just then North's screen froze. "Crap," North said, quickly typing a series of commands. The screen didn't budge.

"What happened?"

"I don't know," North replied, holding down the power button. After a few seconds, the screen went black and lit up to blue. And stayed that way.

"Yikes. That seems bad," I said. I'd heard stories about old computer malfunctions, the dreaded blue screen. Gnosis devices hardly broke down.

"I back everything up every ten minutes, so it's not a huge deal if it's fried. I'd just prefer not to spend another ten grand on a machine if I don't have to."

"These computers cost ten thousand dollars?"

"They didn't originally. But nobody makes computers with hard drives anymore. Everything is on the cloud. I have to have mine custom built by some guys who used to work for Apple, before they went under." He glanced at his watch. "We've still got twenty-five minutes. You okay if we swing by the shop and drop this off on the way to the station?"

I could see Noelle behind the counter, so I went in with North to thank her for letting me borrow the dress. There was an older man with her this time. Her grandfather, I assumed. He smiled when he saw North come in with his laptop.

"Zapped another one?" the old man asked.

"I'm hoping it just needs the Ivan touch," North said, setting the laptop down on the counter.

The old man's eyes wandered to me. "Who's this?" he asked.

"I'm Rory," I said. "Nice to meet you."

The man reached across the counter and lifted my pendant. "I haven't seen one of these in years," he said. "Where'd you get it?"

"It was my mother's," I told him.

"What do you keep on it?"

I looked down at my pendant, confused. "What do I keep on my necklace?"

He pinched my pendant between his finger and thumb and pushed his thumb up. The face of the pendant slid up and a little port popped out. "It's a thumb drive," the old man said. "You didn't know?"

"I don't even know what a thumb drive is," I said, still staring at my pendant.

"It's a little hard drive." North sounded as awed as I felt.

"So that means—"

North finished my sentence. "There's something on there."

26

IT WAS LUCK that North's laptop froze exactly when it did. First because it brought us to the shop while Ivan was there, but second because it meant that we got Ivan's clunky loaner laptop that, while heavy and slow, had something North's nine machines did not: a USB port.

Then again I didn't believe in luck. Not anymore. I'd asked the Doubt to help me, and it had. I'd bristled and balked when Hershey suggested that listening to the voice made life easier, but she'd been right after all. It was the back and forth, the wavering between reason and faith, that was difficult. Once I'd decided to trust that still small voice in my head, the stormy sea inside me got calm.

"Unsurprisingly, the files are encrypted," North said, typing furiously, the laptop balancing on his knees. We'd made it to the station less than a minute before our train was supposed to depart and had sprinted to the platform.

"Can you open them?"

"I don't know yet." He was chewing on his lip, his eyebrows knitted together in thought.

I pressed my forehead against the cool glass of the train window and watched the blur of brightly colored leaves, waiting.

The thick of trees gave way to a high double fence, like something you'd see around a prison. There were little metal plaques at regular intervals. CAUTION: ELECTRIC FENCE.

"Hey, what's back there?" I asked North. Just then a guard station and gated driveway came into view. Beyond it, I could see a great expanse of water. "Oh," I said, answering my own question. "It's the reservoir. But why is there an electric fence and an armed guard?"

"To protect the water supply, I guess." North was still chewing on his lip, staring at his computer screen. "Damn, if your mom wrote this encryption, she was good."

I smiled. Despite his frustration, this was high praise.

I looked back out the window. We were in front of the reservoir's entrance now, so I was no longer seeing the stone sign at an angle. ENFIELD RESERVOIR, it read. There was a carving next to the words. A tree sprouting out of a pair of hands. The tree looked just like the one on my Theden pin.

I pulled out my Gemini and went to Panopticon. The entry for the Enfield Reservoir was surprisingly paltry.

The **Enfield Reservoir** *is an inland body of water created by the* **Enfield Dam** *on the* **Connecticut River** *just east of* **Theden, Massachusetts**. *At capacity, the reservoir holds two million* **cubic meters** *of water. It is the only* **privately owned** *water source in Massachusetts. Before the Enfield Dam was built, the land where the reservoir now sits was home to the Enfield Quarry, a quarter-mile deep, quarter-mile wide* **pyrite** *mine made famous when it collapsed in the late 1980s, trapping twelve miners inside. In 1998, the* **Theden Initiative** *purchased the quarry in order to build the dam that created the reservoir.*

The Theden Initiative. I'd never heard of it, but the tree logo made me think it was affiliated with my school. I clicked the link.

The **Theden Intiative**, *founded in 1805, is the private entity that manages the roughly two-billion-dollar endowment of* **Theden Academy**. *The company's other assets include extensive land holdings in western Massachusetts, the* **Enfield Reservoir**, *and a controlling stake in* **Gnosis, Inc**.

It took a second for it all to register. The entity that ran Theden's endowment owned a controlling stake in *Gnosis*? How did I not know that? It explained quite a bit, actually. The Gnosis gadgets all over campus. Dr. Tarsus's position on

the Gnosis board. The fact that our practicum simulations
worked a lot like Lux. The water reservoir was more puzzling.
It was just so random.

Something was bugging me. I went back to the reservoir's
page.

At capacity, the reservoir holds two million **cubic meters**
of water.

There had to be *billions* of cubic meters in a cubic mile. I
couldn't do the math in my head, but that quarry's capacity had
to have been *way* more than two million cubic meters. So why
didn't they make the reservoir bigger?

I clicked over to the page for the Enfield Quarry and
skimmed it, looking for clues, but there weren't any. My eyes
hung on the passage about the mine's collapse.

*For eight days, rescue workers communicated with the
twelve trapped miners via a six-inch* **borehole** *drilled
through nearly a quarter mile of rock. Relief supplies
were sent down in narrow, rocket-shaped parcels called
"***doves***," which were lowered through the small tunnel
in the rock. All twelve miners were eventually evacuated
by a* **rope pulley system** *through an eighteen-inch
rescue shaft adjacent to the room where the miners were
trapped. After the accident, the mine was shut down.*

I clicked out of Panopticon and lay my head back on the headrest, thinking of those twelve miners. I couldn't imagine what they must've gone through, being trapped beneath the earth. I must've fallen asleep, because the next thing I knew North was shaking my shoulder, telling me we'd reached our stop.

Dr. Hildebrand's office was in William James Hall on Harvard's campus. I felt like an impostor walking through Harvard Yard, but it's not like there was anyone checking student IDs at the campus gates. We found the building easily.

"So the plan is to act like you accept her diagnosis, right?" North whispered as we took the elevator to her sixth-floor office. "Like you assume those entries are real?"

"Right. I'm going to tell her my mom's illness sparked my interest in psychology, and that I figured there was no better person to intern for than the woman who treated her. If she's actually the one who wrote those reports, she'll have to pretend the appointments really happened."

"And who am I?" North asked.

"My boyfriend," I replied, and smiled. "I'm sixteen. It's not weird that I'd bring you along."

"Come in!" A woman's voice called when we knocked on her door. I took a breath and turned the knob.

On the other side of the door was a cramped office. The woman behind the desk wore vintage horn-rimmed glasses and had a mane of fiery red curls that cascaded halfway down her back. The hair would've looked amazing on a girl my age, but Kristyn Hildebrand was at least fifty years older than that and twice as many pounds overweight. She wasn't unattractive, just incongruous. Even more so hunched over a cheap metal desk. There was an older-model Gemini at her elbow and an unopened Gemini Gold box on the bookshelf behind her.

"Can I help you?" she asked, peering at us through thick lenses. "I don't recognize you. Are you students of mine?"

"Uh, no," I said, tentatively stepping inside. "I, uh—I think you may have treated my mother."

"Oh?" Dr. Hildebrand pushed her glasses up on her forehead. "What was her name?"

"Aviana Jacobs," I said. "She was a student at Theden Academy. I think you treated her at the health center there? It would've been in April 2013."

"Nope," the woman said, sounding very certain. "I never saw patients at Theden. I was doing research at a lab there in 2013 and had a Theden student as a research assistant, but her name wasn't Aviana."

"So you're absolutely certain you didn't treat my mom? She suffered from akratic paracusia."

Dr. Hildebrand pinned her eyes on mine. "Are you symptomatic?"

She caught me off guard. My eyes flew to the ceiling, then the floor. "Me? No."

"Then what are you doing here?" She wasn't being antagonistic. Her brown eyes were curious.

I faltered. My interested-in-psychology cover story was on my lips, but something stopped me.

Tell her the truth, the voice said.

I chewed my lip. The truth. How little of it I had.

"I found my mom's medical file a few weeks ago," I began. "And there was a series of entries signed by a doctor named K. Hildebrand at the Theden Health Center. Psych evaluations. Diagnosing my mom with APD and recommending that she be institutionalized." The older woman's eyebrows shot up. I took a breath and continued. "But I don't think my mom actually *had* APD. I think those entries were fake."

"Well, I can tell you *I* didn't sign them. When did you say it was?"

"April 2013."

"Well, there's your answer. My computer was hacked that spring." She shrugged. "Whoever did that could've written those entries, I suppose."

"Any idea why you were hacked?" North asked.

"Oh, I know why," Hildebrand replied. "I was working on what would've been a landmark clinical trial that spring, and someone wanted to make sure I never published. They doctored my data using my login credentials so it appeared as if I'd done it myself."

"What was the clinical trial?" I asked.

"We were looking at whether nanorobots could be used as a synthetic replacement for oxytocin in the brain."

We'd studied oxytocin in Cog Psych. "Oxytocin," I said,

mostly for North's benefit. "That's the love hormone."

"Yes," Dr. Hildebrand replied. "Well known for the role it plays in maternal bonding, childbirth, and orgasm"—I felt myself blush—"but I was more interested in its influence on human trust. Particularly, whether we could simulate what psychologists call a 'trust bond' between total strangers." She sat back in her chair. "I can't tell you more than that. As part of the settlement after the disciplinary hearing, I signed a non-disclosure agreement."

"Disciplinary hearing," North said. "Because of the logs?"

Dr. Hildebrand nodded. "I couldn't prove that I'd been hacked. My data was solid, but to the FDA it looked like I'd doctored my results to make it appear that SynOx was more effective than it was. So they shut down the trial and took my medical license." She flashed a rueful grin. "What is it they say? Those that can't do, teach?"

"You said your research assistant was a Theden student," I said. "What was her name?"

"Patty. No. Penny. I think."

"Is there any way you could check? It's kind of important."

Dr. Hildebrand studied me for a second. Then she nodded and swiveled in her chair. On the shelf behind her was a row of six white binders. She reached for the one marked 2013 / SYN-OX.

"I was supposed to destroy my logs as part of the settlement," she said, pushing her touchpad aside to put the binder on her desk. "But I couldn't bring myself to destroy perfectly good research. So I kept a paper copy." Her glasses slid down the bridge of her nose as she flipped pages. "Her name should be in the acknowledgments, at least."

"How'd you end up at a lab at Theden anyway?" I asked. "Did you go to school there?"

Dr. Hildebrand laughed. "Ha. Not even close. Public school all the way through. Which is why it was such a big deal when the Theden Initiative gave me a grant. They hardly ever fund non-alumni projects."

The hair on my arm prickled. The timing was so odd. I'd just read about the Theden Initiative on the train, and here they were again. But what did it mean? Why would the Initiative fund this particular study, and what did it have to do with my mom? I stared at the binder on Dr. Hildebrand's desk, desperate to read every page. There was a plastic DVD case tucked into the inside front pocket, and I imagined myself reaching across the desk to snatch it.

"Peri Weaver," Dr. Hildebrand said, tapping the page with her finger. "Does the name mean anything?"

I shook my head.

"I'm sorry I don't have more answers for you," Dr. Hildebrand said, returning the binder to its shelf.

I didn't want to leave, but I knew there was no way she would give us that binder, not even if I begged. Reluctantly, I got to my feet.

"I have to see that binder," I hissed at North when we were back in the hall.

"I know," he replied, already on his iPhone. "I was thinking about it the whole time we were in there, trying to come up with a way to get her out of the office."

"And?"

"I might be able to set off the fire alarm. Assuming I can find the control panel. Just give me a second." He chewed on his lip as he typed and tapped at his screen. A few minutes later I heard the shrill scream of an alarm. As doors along the hallway opened, North pulled me into a vacant office, out of view. We waited until Dr. Hildebrand shuffled past our doorway and into the stairwell, then we peeked into the hall. It was empty. "I'll go," North said.

"No. I'll do it," I insisted. "You can't afford to get caught."

"And you can?"

I ignored him and dashed to Hildebrand's office. Her door was slightly ajar.

I grabbed the binder and started for the door, then stopped. If I took the whole thing, she'd notice its absence immediately. I shoved the plastic DVD case under the waistband of my jeans and was just about to snap open the rings of the binder when I heard footsteps in the hall. I dropped to my knees with the binder, heart pounding.

"I knew we weren't scheduled for a drill," I heard Dr. Hildebrand say. "I should've checked Lux before I left my office. Would've saved me four flights of stairs."

Shit, shit, shit. Panicked, I shoved the binder back onto the shelf and looked for somewhere better to hide. There wasn't even a closet in this tiny office. I was screwed. And worse, I didn't even have the contents of the binder.

"You'd think they would've figured out a way to run the alarm through our handhelds," another female voice said. "So we'd know not to evacuate unless Lux told us to."

"Dr. Hildebrand," I heard North call. "I'm sorry to bother you again, but do you have just one more minute?" I shot to my feet. He was giving me a way out. Their voices got muffled, like they'd gone into that vacant office. I bolted from the room and dashed toward the stairwell on tiptoes, practically colliding with a man who was on his way back up. I was sitting on the stairs, turning the DVD over in my hands in defeat, when North joined me a few minutes later.

"C'mon," he said, pulling me to my feet. "There are benches on Harvard Yard, and Ivan's laptop has a DVD drive. Let's see what we got."

We had a lot, it turned out. The video started with a detailed explanation of the trial's design from a younger, thinner Hildebrand.

"The control group will receive a placebo," she was saying. "A nasal spray of saline solution. The test group will also receive a nasal spray." She held up a syringe. "However, this solution contains a swarm of two thousand nano-size robots. These nano-bots have been programmed to travel to the subject's amygdala, a part of the brain involved in emotional response, where they will function like remote-controlled neurotransmitters."

"She put *nanorobots* in their *brains?*" I said incredulously. North's eyes were as wide as mine.

"The subjects will meet with our lead researcher for five minutes every day," Dr. Hildebrand continued. "For what they believe is a short psychotherapy session." She exchanged the syringe for a small black remote. I immediately recognized the G etched into its back. It was a Gnosis device. Which was weird, since Gnosis was barely off the ground in 2013. Were they somehow involved in the trial?

"At the start of each session," Dr. Hildebrand explained, "the researcher will press a button on this remote, emitting a very short-range, very high-frequency audio signal. While this will have no impact on a control subject, in the case of a test subject, the signal will trigger the swarm to release a dose of SynOx, a synthetic and highly concentrated form of the neurohormone oxytocin."

North pressed pause on the video. "Okay, just to be clear: She not only put robots in their brains, she screwed with their brain chemistry, *without their knowledge.* How is that even legal?"

Fear had taken root at the pit of my stomach. "North, what if my mom was one of her subjects? What if that's the connection?"

"Do you want to stop watching?" he asked. "I could watch the rest of it alone."

"No," I said firmly, pressing the play button. "I want to see it."

I sounded a lot more certain than I felt.

"Three minutes after the signal is sent," Dr. Hildebrand went on, "our lead researcher will ask the subject to drink from this vial." She picked up a bottle labeled with a skull and crossbones and the word ARSENIC.

"Poison?" I said, gaping.

"It can't actually be poison," North said.

"The liquid in this vial is sugar water," Dr. Hildebrand said, as if she could hear us. "But the subject will be told by the researcher that it is, in fact, poison. By asking subjects to do something that no rational person would do, we are seeking to determine the outer bounds of human trust, and, most important, whether this boundary can be manipulated."

"There's no way any of them drank it, right?" I said as the words DAY ONE flashed on screen. North just shook his head.

"I don't know which is worse," he said. "The nanobots or the poison."

My stomach was in knots as we watched the first day of sessions. But my mom wasn't among the subjects, and not a single one drank the poison. The researcher said the same thing to each of them. "This vial contains a lethal dose of arsenic, which is poisonous to humans. I recommend that you drink it." Most of the subjects laughed at the prospect. A few got angry. One stormed out.

It was like that for the first three days. The researcher would ask and the subject would refuse. But, then, on day four, something changed. Gaping at the screen, we watched as *all*

344

twelve test subjects drank the contents of the vial.

"No way," North breathed.

We were silent as we watched the next six days' worth of sessions. The people with nanobots in their brains drank the poison every time they were asked. And most of them did it eagerly, with stupid smiles on their faces, like there was nothing they'd rather do more. No, it wasn't actually poison in that vial. But they didn't know that. It made my skin crawl.

When the last session concluded, I closed my eyes. Something was bugging me, but I couldn't figure out what it was.

"My team and I would like to thank the Theden Initiative for their generous funding," I heard Dr. Hildebrand say, "as well as our cosponsors, Gnosis, Inc. and Soza Labs, who co-own the patents on the nanobots and the SynOx compound."

My eyes flew open.

"Soza," I repeated. "Why do I know that name?"

"Probably because their logo is in every drugstore window," North replied. "They're the ones that manufacture the flu vaccine."

As soon as he said the word *flu vaccine*, something fluttered in my chest. A rush of sensation, like rock turning to sand. The day Beck had been picked for the Gold beta test, he'd been at the pharmacy getting his flu shot. A nasal spray, just like the one Hildebrand's research subjects had been given. All of a sudden I realized what had been bothering me. The signal used to activate the nanobots was a high-frequency *audio* signal.

Ultrasound.

My brain filled with the popping sound we'd heard in North's computer room. All at once I knew exactly why Beck had suddenly decided to trust Lux.

Because the nanobots in his brain were telling him to.

"Holy shit, North. Holy shit, holy shit, holy shit."

"Whoa, simmer down there. I think you just broke the rider's code of conduct. Four times." He pointed at the sign on the wall. "No profanity." We were back on the train, and I was officially freaking out.

"North," I said, making every effort to keep my voice down. "This isn't a joke. Soza and Gnosis are putting *nanobots* in people's *brains*. Not just in a research study. In real life."

"Through the flu vaccine." North sounded skeptical. It infuriated me.

"Yes," I hissed. "Think about it. Gnosis puts out the Gold for less than the cost of its older-generation model—a device that, for no apparent reason, emits high-frequency *sound waves*. Meanwhile, my best friend, who'd previously distrusted Lux as much as you do, joins the beta test for Gold and suddenly starts heeding its every command. Soza, meanwhile, for the first time ever, starts offering seasonal flu sprays for *free*." I gestured around the half-full train car. "Every single person in the cabin was wearing a Gold on their wrist, and every single one of them was smiling at it. "Look around!" I pointed at a girl a few rows up who was literally *beaming* at her handheld as she interfaced with Lux. "Does that look normal to you?"

"People do seem a little overly enamored with the Gold," North conceded. "And, hey, I've always been suspicious of drug companies. And it's awfully coincidental that Soza manufactures Evoxa, too."

"I'm surprised it's so hard to convince you," I said. "You're the one who's always been so anti-Lux."

"Well, yeah, but only because I don't think people ought to be ceding their decision-making to an app. Not because I thought the app had commandeered their brains. Rory, if what you're saying is true—"

"It *is* true," I insisted. "I know it is. And we have to expose them."

"How?" North asked. "Send an email blast? Post a YouTube video on Forum? People will think we're nuts."

He was right. Especially with my family history. Oh, God. My *own* history. Who knows what Tarsus had done with those logs Hershey sent her.

"It's pretty mind-blowing, if it's true," North marveled. "Think of the power it would give them. They get to decide what people watch and what they listen to and what they buy. Meanwhile, people have no idea. They think they're deciding for themselves." He shook his head. "It's sickly brilliant."

"So is that what it's about?" I asked. "Money?"

"Isn't everything about money?" North scoffed. "Think how much a toy company would pay Gnosis to steer parents toward their toys. Or how easy it would be to hide a news story you didn't want people to see. 'Lux, should I write this exposé that makes Soza look bad? No, buddy, write this fluff piece instead.'" North shakes his head. "If it's happening, it's unbelievable."

"You think my mom was onto them? Was that what the fake diagnosis was for, to discredit her?" All this time I just assumed whoever was trying to make her look crazy was doing it for personal reasons. But maybe she found out about the SynOx study and threatened to expose the companies behind it. Griffin said she was anti-Gnosis. This would explain why.

I reached into my bag and pulled out the yearbook Hershey had given me.

"What's that?" North asked.

"The 2013 yearbook. Peri Weaver was a Theden student that year. Maybe she's the link to all this." I started flipping pages.

"Will you show me your mom?" North asked gently.

I slowed at the *H*s, sliding my finger over the *I*s to the *J*s until I found her. Aviana Jacobs. Her hair was down and wavy around her shoulders the way I'd worn mine at the Gnosis party, and her eyes were the same almond shape. But we weren't carbon copies. Her hair was auburn, not brown, and her nose and cheeks were dusted with pretty light-colored freckles, not the dirt-looking black ones that spotted mine.

"Wow, she was beautiful," North said. He pointed at her collarbone, bare above the black velvet drape. "She's not wearing the necklace." Instinctively, I reached for my own neck, but the pendant was stuck in the laptop, which was open on North's knees.

I flipped to Griffin next. He had the same overgrown, combed-forward hair he'd had in the class photo, its shade a match to mine. His eyes weren't quite as round, but they were the exact same blue, and he had my subtle cleft. "You look so much like both of them," North said softly. "The best parts of each."

I touched my father's face with my fingertips, wondering what he was like at eighteen. He seemed more accessible, somehow, than my mom ever had. So much of her was a mystery. Griffin, at least, I knew *something* about. *Not enough,* reverberated in my head. I quickly flipped to the next page before my brain could go where I knew it was headed, to the image of him on that stretcher Friday night.

I stopped again at the *T*s, scanning for Tarsus, before remembering that she was married and that her last name would've been different back then. So I skimmed toward the *W*s, hunting for Peri Weaver. "Weaver, Weaver," I murmured, sliding my finger over the page. There was only one. Esperanza "Peri" Weaver. When I saw the girl above the name, I gasped.

She was beautiful. Wide eyes peeking out from beneath an untamed afro. The slightest gap between her front teeth.

It was Dr. Tarsus.

27

I COULDN'T GET HER face out of my mind. The teenaged version of Tarsus, a gorgeous, striking-looking girl who went by Peri and spent her afternoons working in a psych lab. How had she gotten wrapped up with Gnosis and what did it have to do with my mom? I knew looks could be deceiving, but the photograph of Peri Weaver just didn't fit with the picture I had in my mind, neither the girl I imagined she must've been nor the coldhearted monster of a person she'd become. The girl in the photograph looked too *nice*.

These were the thoughts preoccupying me as I was getting ready for initiation that night. I wondered how my counterparts were swinging it, with sleeping roommates to deal with, or, worse, awake ones to lie to about where they were sneaking off to in the middle of the night.

I put on triple layers and pulled my hair back off my face. We were told to carry our robes with us until we reached the woods then put them on with our hoods pulled down to cover our faces. We'd be greeted by our second-year "handlers" at the cemetery gate. Before putting on my jacket, I brought my pendant to my lips, kissing it for good luck. North had moved the files to his hard drive to work on the encryption so I could put the necklace back on. It was silly, but I felt calmer with it around my neck. Tethered, somehow. Lux's voice spoke out of the silence: "You should leave in sixty seconds." I was using it again to make sure I was on time. "There is a seventy-five percent chance of rain," Lux said then. "I'd recommend a rain jacket."

"How's a velvet robe?" I quipped, zipping up my fleece.

"Velvet is not waterproof," Lux replied. "But your cloak is."

I froze. "What did you just say?"

"I said, 'But your cloak is'" came the app's reply.

I grabbed my Gemini off the dresser and stared at my screen. *How did Lux know about the cloak?*

"You should leave now," Lux announced. Still stunned by the cloak comment, I grabbed the velvet knapsack and headed out.

I'd just put the cloak on when my handheld buzzed with a call. Incoming call from @KatePribulsky. It had to be North. I'd just crossed into the woods and had only a minute and a half to get to the gate, so I had to hurry. Leaves crunched beneath my sneakers.

"Where are you?" North asked as soon as I picked up. "It sounds like you're outside."

"I couldn't sleep," I lied. "I went for a walk."

"Don't you guys have curfew?"

"We just have to be on campus." That was two lies. Curfew meant we had to be inside the dorm building, and I'd left the confines of campus when I'd stepped into the woods. I quickly changed the subject before I had to lie again. "So did you crack the encryption?"

"Yes," North said. "And oh. My. God. Rory, it's—"

"Tell me," I said, my heart hiccupping in my chest.

"There were three files," he said urgently. "The first is an internal memo on Gnosis letterhead dated April 2013 about a project called Hyperion. A joint undertaking between Gnosis and Soza Labs to—and I quote—'develop swarms of nano-bots capable of mimicking the activity of oxytocin in the brain.' It's signed by various Gnosis and Soza executives and is stamped DELETE UPON RECEIPT. Rory, you were right," he said then. "About all of it." The same words were reverberating in my brain and pounding in my chest. *I was right.* My limbs felt loose with relief.

North kept talking, faster now. "The memo goes on to say that the nanobots would work in connection with a new decision-making app Gnosis was developing. They'd make the user trust the app so intensely that it would eliminate any cognitive dissonance. I guess the nanobots Hildebrand was using were finicky, and the SynOx compound didn't work exactly the way they wanted it to, so they were building in five years for more R&D."

"Five years," I repeated. "But it's been seventeen."

"Five years for R&D. Twelve more to—another quote—'prepare the way.' It's insane how detailed their strategy was. They knew they'd have to first take over the handheld market, then gradually get people accustomed to using a decision-making app. They even planned for how long it'd take to phase out the needle vaccine. It's all here, every single step."

I was ten yards from the cemetery. I glanced around. No sign of Liam yet. "What were the other two files?"

"The second was a list of names. The Gnosis and Soza reps who signed the memo were on it, along with several hundred others. I recognized some of the names. The founders of Gnosis, for example. The rest I started looking up. They're all corporate bigwigs. CEOs, hedge fund managers, venture capitalists."

"It was just a list of names?"

"Yeah, but with these weird letter/number combinations beside each one," replied North. "Mia Ritchson, CEO of Soza Labs. Gamma, eighty-one. Alan Viljoen, then-COO of Gnosis. Alpha, ninety-nine. Here, I'll send you a screenshot."

As if in slow motion, I looked down at the lapel of my cloak: *Zeta '30.* I didn't need a screenshot. I knew exactly how those letter/number combinations looked.

My rib cage contracted like a vise grip. The people on that list were members of the Few. The same people who'd signed that incriminating memo.

Oh, my God.

The society was behind all this.

"Oh, no," I murmured.

"Rory, what is it?"

"What was the third file?" I asked him urgently.

"A photograph. It's—" Just then, the line went dead. I looked at my screen. *No service.* I looked up and realized I'd crossed into the cemetery without realizing it. Suddenly I wanted to run. The Few were behind this. The quote, the blanket, the necklace. I saw them differently now. My mom was trying to warn me.

"Ready?" At the sound of Liam's voice, I spun on my heels. He was right behind me. "Sorry I was late. We should hurry." His hand was already moving toward my mouth.

"I—" Before I could get the words out, I tasted cherry on my tongue.

He didn't take me to the arena this time. When I came to, I was standing with the other initiates in a different room, a smaller, square-shaped one, with a much lower ceiling and four stone walls that were shimmering slightly in the yellow candlelight, oddly iridescent. Unlike in the arena, I could see every corner of this room. There was a stone altar along one wall, built out of a single piece of granite. Behind it was a woven tapestry of the Garden of Eden. There were two doors, at opposite sides of the room. If the tomb was laid out like a Fibonacci tile, then each room was bigger than the last. Where in the sequence was this room? How far was I from the center? Liam said there was an exit there. I pictured myself running for it, but I knew it was too late for that. I was trapped.

Fear coursed through my veins. *What had I gotten myself into?*

Two boys next to me were whispering, their excitement practically bursting out of every hushed word. One of them had his arm pulled into his cloak, shoving peanuts into his mouth through the opening at the neck. I stiffened at the smell and quickly moved away from them, swallowing the bile that was creeping up my throat.

Minutes passed. As we waited, I tried to get a look at some of the other initiates' faces, but they'd all followed the instructions and pulled their hoods down low. The peanut boy was still going at it. He seemed to have an unlimited supply.

Please, I pleaded silently. *Get me out of this.*

There was the sound of stone sliding on stone and one of the doors opened. A figure in the serpent mask strode in, clutching a brown leather book with two hands. There was no way to know if it was the same man who'd worn the mask the two previous times I'd seen it, but I guessed that it was, and that the mask was a symbol of his status. My stomach turned over. Our leader was a *snake*. Why had that not bothered me before now?

The serpent was followed by two other figures. One wore the head of a fox. The other, an owl. The three masked figures took their places behind the altar, and the serpent opened the leather book.

"There are two types of people in this world," he began. His voice was missing Saturday's kindness. "The wise man and the fool. The wise man is prudent, strong-willed, and courageous. The fool is impulsive, weak, and desperate for a master. The wise man understands that *he* is the master, a god in his own right." The serpent opened the book as if he was going to read from it, but I could tell he wasn't even looking at the page.

"I form'd them free: and free they must remain," he declared. The hairs on the back of my neck stood up as he began to recite the lines I'd long ago committed to memory. *"Till they enthrall themselves; I else must change their nature."*

All at once I understood. *Change their nature.* It was exactly what Project Hyperion was designed to do.

The serpent looked up from the book and paused, surveying us. I forced myself to meet his papier-mâché gaze.

"Fall," he said then. "It's how Milton described what happened in Eden. As if man suffered a loss. But what happened in the Garden of Eden wasn't a fall. On the contrary, it was a glorious *coup d'état*. When Adam and Eve ate the fruit of the Tree of the Knowledge of Good and Evil, they became equal to the God who created them. And that God became eternally irrelevant. The wisdom they acquired that day has been passed down through time to an elect few. Men and women who were born to live as gods among men."

My skin crawled. *They think they're gods.*

"For the past two hundred and fifty years, the Few have been working to rebuild the paradise that was lost when mankind was expelled from the Garden. Our forefathers founded the Eden Academy as a breeding ground for elite minds, and every year we select the most promising students to join our ranks. It is your wisdom that has gotten you here. Your classmates are intelligent but weak. They have the capacity to reason, but not the strength of will to use it." He made a clucking sound with his tongue against his teeth. "Then there is the rest of the world," he said. "Fools in search of a master. So proud of their freedom, and yet so willing to give it up."

In Lux we trust. In a flash, I saw it. What they were doing with Project Hyperion. What Gnosis had been doing with Lux all along. Who needs higher wisdom when the little gold box on your wrist knows everything there is to know? Never mind that there were men behind those tiny machines, orchestrating your every move with an algorithm written to keep you "happy." As happy as a clipped bird in a pretty, gilded cage. And never mind that the choice to obey Lux wasn't yours anymore, but the work of a swarm of microscopic robots that had commandeered your brain.

I wanted to throw up.

"Our goal is nothing less than a modern paradise. A new Eden. *The* Eden. Here. Now. A perfect society ruled by *hoi oligoi sophoi.* The wise few."

There was an eruption of applause from the other initiates. I looked around in disbelief. My skin was crawling and they were *clapping.*

"The time has come to declare your divinity and to take your vows," the serpent declared. *No no no no,* the voices in my head were screaming. Voices, plural, this time. The Doubt and my own.

The other initiates were twittering with excitement as the first names were called. I looked around frantically for some escape, but the doors were sealed and we were deep under ground and I didn't know which door led toward the exit. Running wasn't an option.

There was a sound like pebbles scattering. The kid with the peanuts had spilled the bag beneath his robe. He quickly stepped on the mess, trying to hide it beneath his cloak, but several nuts had rolled toward me and lay untouched by my foot. I stared at them. They were a way out. It might kill me, but an allergic reaction would surely get me out of there. And right then that was all that mattered. I could not take their vows.

Fear not, the voice whispered, and my decision was made.

I glanced up at the altar. The serpent was slicing a female initiate's thumb with a thin sliver of mirrored glass while she recited the vows, pledging her life to the society's aims, promising never to reveal its existence or her affiliation. Her voice was familiar. It took me a second to realize it was Rachel. I watched as he pressed her bloody thumb to the leather book then gave her a quilled pen to sign her name. Eight seconds when he was distracted. Long enough to pick up the peanuts without drawing attention.

"Epsilon," the serpent called. The sixth letter in the Greek alphabet. He was going in order. The boy with the peanuts moved toward the altar. Zeta would be next. If I was doing this, I had to do it *now*. I waited until the serpent reached for the boy's thumb. When he started cutting, I bent for the stray peanuts, said a quick prayer, and popped them in my mouth, chewing quickly, my mouth like sandpaper.

"Zeta" came the serpent's voice. My throat had begun to itch. It was working. But would it be fast enough? I walked to the altar and peered directly into the painted mesh of the serpent's eyes. I could make out the whites of the human eyes staring back at me, the wrinkles around them. "Repeat after me," the serpent said, gripping my wrist. The sleeve of his cloak fell back, revealing his bare hand. He wore a jade ring on his ring finger, emblazoned with a design of overlapping *O*s.

My throat was closing in.

He was reciting the vows I was supposed to repeat, but I couldn't make them out. All I could hear was my own labored breathing, heaving through my swelling throat.

I saw his lips stop moving, and his gray eyebrows arch up like a question mark behind the painted mesh. "Can't. Breathe," I managed, as my knees buckled.

"She's having an allergic reaction," I heard a female voice say. Unlike the serpent's, it wasn't distorted. And I recognized it right away. I'd heard it every weekday morning for the past two months, and sometimes in my sleep. The voice I'd come to fear. "I'll take care of it," she said briskly. "You stay."

No! I tried to say. *Not Tarsus.* But I couldn't form the words. I felt myself falling, and then I passed out.

28

THERE WAS A DULL ACHING in my throat. Fighting
for consciousness, I tried to swallow and immediately gagged.
Someone was trying to choke me. I went to react, to push whoever it was away, but my hands were strapped to something
hard.

My feet were free and so I kicked them, thrashing with all
the energy I could muster, which wasn't much. I felt as if I were
underwater, swimming for the surface.

I forced open my eyes. I was lying on my back, strapped to
a table, or was it a bed? There was a bright fluorescent light
above me, so bright it was blinding. Oh, God. Where had she
taken me? I squeezed my eyes shut, breathing through my nose,
trying not to panic. I realized now there was something *in* my
throat. I had to get it out. Where was I? Where was Tarsus?

Stupid, Rory. As soon as I put the pieces together, that
Gnosis and the Few were one and the same, I should've realized that Dr. Tarsus would be in that room. Of course she was

one of the society's leaders. She'd been part of the machine from the very beginning. But if she was so high up in the organization, how had I made it as far as I had? Shouldn't she have been able to keep me out? There was still so much I didn't know. Things I'd never know unless I made it out of here alive.

It was quiet except for the hum of machines. I did a mental scan of my body. Other than my throat, nothing hurt. I blinked my eyes open again. My vision adjusted to the light now, and I looked around.

It was a hospital room. Through a pale flowered curtain I saw doctors and nurses with tablets. One made eye contact with me and smiled. Her pink scrubs were printed with the words THEDEN HEALTH CENTER. *She's awake,* I saw her mouth. A moment later she was sliding the curtain to the side.

My brain was struggling to keep up. I wasn't in the society's tomb. I was at the health center. Dr. Tarsus wasn't torturing me. Inexplicably, she'd saved my life.

"Hi there," the nurse said kindly. "You scared us. Let's get that tube out of your throat." She gently reached into my mouth to dislodge it. Seconds later it was out. I immediately started coughing. "Your throat will be sore for a few days," she said, unstrapping the bands around my wrists. "Sorry about these. We couldn't risk you pulling at the tube." She went to the sink and filled a cup with water.

"Small sips," she instructed, and handed the cup to me.

I gulped the water. It burned my throat.

"Small sips," she said again, and smiled.

I drank the rest slowly then set the empty cup on the tray beside my bed. "How'd I get here?" I asked her hoarsely.

"Your boyfriend brought you in," she replied. "I'm just glad you had that EpiPen, and that he knew how to use it. It saved your life."

"My boyfriend?"

The nurse winked at me. "Don't worry, we won't report that you were together after curfew," she said conspiratorially. She went to the sink to refill my water cup. "Any idea what you ate that triggered the reaction? I imagine you're pretty careful with peanuts. Says in your file you were hospitalized the first time you were exposed." She handed me the cup and I took another tiny sip.

"A granola bar," I lied. "I forgot to scan it with Lux."

I heard a tsk, but it hadn't come from the nurse. She looked past me toward the door and smiled. "Couldn't stay away for long, could you?"

"From this girl? Nah." It was Liam, dressed for class, his hair wet from the shower. He put his hand on my forearm, his lambda tattoo peeking out from the webbing of his fingers. "How are you feeling, babe?"

"Better," I said, managing a smile. It took effort not to snatch my arm back. It's just Liam, I told myself. But now that I knew what the society really stood for, even he creeped me out. I saw his eyes drop to my collarbone. Out of habit, I felt for my necklace.

It was gone.

Tarsus must've taken it while I was unconscious. But why? Did she know what it really was? I swallowed my panic. There were no files on the pendant anymore. North had taken them off. Still, my heart was pounding. It didn't help that Liam was staring at me.

"Well, I'll leave you two lovebirds alone," the nurse said. "Just press the button on your armrest if you need me." She stepped outside the curtain and slid it closed behind her.

"Why would you eat a peanut granola bar?" Liam asked when she was gone.

"It wasn't a peanut granola bar," I told him, my voice still raspy. "It was chocolate chip. Must've been made on shared equipment."

"Why didn't you scan it with Lux?"

"I don't know. I forgot." I stared at the Gold on Liam's wrist. Were there nanobots in his brain right now? Or were society members excluded from that? What about the people like me who'd forgotten to get their flu spray this year, or the ones like North, who always opted out? Then again, with hundreds of millions of people vaccinated and strapped to the Gold, a couple of thousand outliers hardly mattered.

"So you brought me here?" I asked Liam, changing the subject. "I thought I heard Dr. Tarsus's voice before I passed out."

He gave me a wary look, as if I knew something I wasn't supposed to. "She thought it'd be less suspicious if I brought you."

"And the EpiPen?"

"She carries one."

"Why? What's she allergic to?"

"So many questions," Liam said, not answering me. "I've got some for you. Why were you wearing her necklace yesterday?"

I stared at him. "What?"

"She was Upsilon '13," he said, watching me closely. "Not your mom. Your mom wasn't even one of the Few. I checked the roster in the tomb, and her name isn't on it."

I opened my mouth to say something, but no sound came out.

"Look, Rory," Liam said, "whatever you're playing at—"

"I'm not playing at anything, Liam," I said, trying not to sound defensive. "My mom left me that necklace. You don't know for sure that it belongs to Tarsus. Just because it's her society name doesn't mean it's her necklace." But it *was* hers. I had no doubt. That whole bit about Pythagoras's letter, virtue and vice. She knew I had it, and she wanted me to know it. But why? And why did she wait until now to take it back?

"Okay, so what about the pattern on your blanket? What's that about?"

I shifted in my bed. "It's probably just a coincidence," I said weakly. "The Few didn't invent the Fibonacci sequence."

"Class starts in three minutes," Lux announced from Liam's wrist.

"I can't be late," Liam said. "But, Rory, I'm serious. I'd be careful if I were you. Tarsus is not someone you want to piss off, believe me. She has the power to keep you out of the Few."

As if that was my fear.

"Well, thank you," I said, attempting a smile. My heart was pounding like a drum. "For the advice. And for saving my life. I'm just bummed I missed out on initiation." I tried to sound disappointed.

"Oh, don't worry. You're getting a do-over."

"That's great," I managed, my stomach churning at the thought. "When?"

"Tomorrow night."

They kept me at the hospital for observation until early evening. By the time I left, I had eleven missed calls and three cryptic but frantic texts from Kate's phone. North was clearly worried. I didn't blame him. My line had gone dead last night and he hadn't heard from me since.

I couldn't tell him about the Few over the phone. It had to be in person. But as much as I wanted to see him, and more than that to unload everything I'd been holding back, something told me I should play my next moves carefully. If I wanted last night's hospital visit to seem like an accident, I couldn't raise any suspicions. I needed to act naturally. Go to dinner in the dining hall. Spend some time with my Theden friends. Be seen by whoever else had been in that room last night. So I sent Kate a talk later text and headed back to the dorm to change.

The sun had dropped behind the trees by the time I made it back to Athenian Hall. Izzy was sitting on the bench by the main door, scrolling through her newsfeed on her new Gold, which she was wearing on a studded band. "Hey," she said when she saw me, glancing up from her screen. "Where have you been all day?"

"I had a weird allergy thing," I told her, downplaying it. "How are you?"

"Starving," she replied.

"If you can wait twenty minutes, I'll go with you to dinner," I said. "I just want to take a shower first."

"That's perfect," Izzy replied. "Lux says the optimal time to eat isn't until six anyway. I'll wait for you here." She smiled and went back to her Gold.

I felt a wave of nausea. *Lux says.*

"Hey, did you get a flu spray this year?" I asked.

She nodded without looking up from her screen. "Yep. Why?"

"No reason," I said, and walked off.

I let Lux decide what I ate for dinner that night, in part because I was too revved up over my discovery to make my own food choices, but mostly because I knew everyone was wondering how those peanuts had gotten in my system. No one had near-death scares like that anymore. Not with Lux. So I made a show of using the app, for whoever was watching. I needed to look like a girl who was paranoid now, overly cautious about every bite. For all I knew, the person behind the serpent mask was sitting at the faculty table, eyeing me. A plan was forming in my head, and if it had any chance of working, the society had to believe my accident was just an accident, and that I was as eager as ever to take my vows.

Preoccupied with my performance, I nearly choked on my risotto when Tarsus approached our table. "I imagine it's been quite a day for you," she said, laying a hand on my shoulder. "No simulation can prepare you for an experience like that."

An experience like what? The allergic reaction or the creepy ritual in which my classmates pledged their allegiance to a group of people who believe they're wiser than *God*, people who were using technology to manipulate free will?

"It was . . . instructive" was my reply. My eyes went to her collar. No pendant, only a single strand of pearls.

Dr. Tarsus smiled. "Let's be careful going forward, shall we?"

"I'll do my best," I said.

"We need to schedule a make-up session," she said then, her eyes boring into mine. "For the simulation you missed this morning. Will you be ready tomorrow night?"

I knew instantly that she wasn't really talking about practicum. The make-up session she was referring to was the society's initiation ritual, and the implied offer for more time was a test to see if I would try to get out of it.

"Definitely," I said, and smiled. No hesitation. Surprise flickered in her eyes.

Dr. Tarsus held my gaze for a moment then returned the smile. "Excellent," she said. "Tomorrow night it is."

"She creeps me out," Izzy said when she was gone. "I'm so glad I don't have her."

"Really? I think she's badass," Rachel said, and turned to me. "Don't you?" I'd forgotten until that moment that she was in the room last night. She was one of the Few now. She had to know that I'd been there too. I imagined they'd pulled back my hood as soon as I'd passed out.

"Yeah," I said vacantly, distracted by what Tarsus had just said. *Let's be careful going forward.* It was impossible to decipher what she meant. Had she seen me eat that peanut? Maybe I hadn't fooled anyone. Maybe the society leaders knew all about my stunt. I shivered at the prospect. Now they were expecting me in the tomb the next night, and I had no way of knowing what lay in store. I felt a flutter of fear in my chest. What had I gotten myself into? Better question: How was I going to get out of it?

"Earth to Rory," I heard Izzy say.

My eyes refocused. "What?"

"I asked when you were planning to leave the dark ages," she said, pointing at my Gemini. The three of them were wearing Golds.

"Oh. I kind of like the old one," I said, averting Rachel's gaze.

"Yeah, but do you like it better than Lux?"

"Huh?"

"Gnosis is discontinuing the old version of Lux," Izzy said. "And you can only get the new version on the Gold. So if you want to keep using Lux, you'll have to say good-bye to the clunker." *The clunker.* Two days ago it was the smallest hand-held on the market. Now it was obsolete.

Just then, my phone rang.

KATE—CELL

"Yep. I guess I will," I told Rachel, already standing up. "Hey, I'll catch up with you guys later." I answered the call as soon as I stepped away from the table, keeping my voice low as I passed a group of faculty members by the frozen-yogurt machine.

"Where have you been?" North demanded as soon as the call connected. "I've been calling you all day. When I lost you last night, I called right back, but it went straight to voicemail."

"A lot has happened," I said quietly. "I don't want to talk about it over the phone. Can I meet you at your place in ten minutes?"

"Of course. I'm there now. Are you okay?"

"I will be," I told him, and hung up. Then I slipped my Gemini under the napkin on my tray and dumped both into the trash.

"They think they're *gods*?" North's voice was incredulous. "Actual deities?"

"'Gods among men' was what the serpent said. He didn't get into technicalities."

"And they think they're re-creating Eden?"

"Their version of it, anyway. A society where they decide what's best for everyone. *The Eden.* A.k.a. Theden. This didn't start with SynOx, North. They've been at this for *centuries.* Hyperion is just their endgame."

North rubbed at his eyes. "This is seriously messed up, Rory. And your *mom* was one of these people?"

I shook my head. "I thought she was, but Liam checked their roster and her name's not on it."

"So she was trying to expose them."

I nodded. "That's the only thing that makes sense. Those files on the necklace were her evidence. But someone found out what she was doing and she got scared. I think that's why she left Theden."

"But why not tell Griffin? If she needed to disappear, he could've gone with her."

"Maybe she was protecting him. If the Few are as powerful as I think they are, the less he knew, the better."

"The Few. Is that what they call themselves?"

I nodded. "Short for 'The Wise Few.' The official name is Greek."

"Because the rest of us are imbeciles," North spat. He shook his head in disgust. "And until last night, you wanted to be one of them?"

"I thought they were the good guys," I said, defensive.

North gave me a reproving look. "Good guys don't wear masks and hooded robes and do things in the dark, Rory."

My eyes dropped to my hands. He was right. But I'd felt so honored to have been chosen. I had gotten caught up in it. North tapped his tablet screen, where he'd pulled up the list of names he'd retrieved from the thumb drive. "So all these people are members?"

I nodded. "That's what the Greek letter/number combinations mean. It's their society name and the year they were initiated."

Instinctively, my hand went to my clavicle, but of course the pendant wasn't there. "Where is it?" North asked.

"Tarsus took it," I told him. "Last night, while I was passed out. I think it's actually *hers*," I said. "Or was at some point. Upsilon is her society name."

"Could she have *given* it to your mom?" North asked.

I shrugged. "I don't know. It's possible, I guess." It was hard to fathom that Tarsus could've been helping my mom. But someone had to have given her those files. "Hey, you said there was a third file," I said, remembering. "What was it?"

"A wedding photo," North said gently. "Your mom and Griffin."

Something inside me hardened, bracing against the flood of emotion I was barely holding back. No. I couldn't let myself feel this. Not until I'd done what I was planning to do. So I pressed my lips together and gave my head a firm shake. I didn't want to see it. The look in North's eyes told me he understood. I reached for his hand and squeezed it.

North took my hand and gently tugged it, pulling me forward so our bodies were almost touching, and then he cupped my face in his hands. They smelled like espresso and nutmeg. "I could've lost you last night," he said softly.

"I know. But you didn't."

"You took such a risk." He traced the line of my jaw with his thumbs.

"I had to," I said. "I couldn't take their oath. Pledging my life to their vision. Renouncing the Doubt." I shook my head slightly. "I couldn't do it. But I couldn't just refuse, either. I knew they wouldn't let me walk out of there knowing what I know."

"So now what?" he asked. "You tell them you don't want to join and hope they're cool with it?"

"No." I lifted my chin from his hands and leaned back. "They have to believe that I still want in. It's the only way they'll let me back into the tomb."

"*Back* into the tomb?" North was apoplectic. "Rory, you just said you think these people are dangerous. Why would you go back?"

My response was matter-of-fact. "If we want to expose them, we need more than a couple of documents. We need video proof." This was my plan. It terrified me, especially since there was no way to live-stream the initiation—the tomb was a dead zone. I'd have to make it out with the footage to have anything at all.

North started to shake his head. "Rory, no. It's too—"

"North. I think these people killed my mom." It was the first time I'd said it out loud. I hadn't really let myself think it, really think it, until right that second.

"And what do you think is going to happen to *you* if they find out you're recording them?"

"They won't find out." I sounded certain, but I wasn't. Even if I managed to get the footage, how would I get out of the tomb without taking their vows a second time?

"Okay, so let's say you get them on tape. What does it prove? You said everyone is wearing masks, so you can't see their faces."

"At least people will know the Few exist."

"Rory, you post a video like that and one of two things will happen. Either Gnosis will get rid of it as soon as it goes live, or someone will take ownership of it and say it was a fake. We're talking about the company that controls virtually all the technology we use. From GoSearch to Forum to Lux. They control the medium, so they control the message."

"So we attack the technology, then," I argued. "Forget exposing the Few. We'll dismantle Project Hyperion. Shut down Lux."

"And how are we going to do that?"

"I dunno. A virus or something."

"A virus like that would take weeks to build. And even if I could miraculously write some supervirus overnight, there's no way we could get it through Gnosis's firewall."

"Okay, so we'll turn off the nanobots, then."

North shook his head. "I've studied every word of that memo. There's only one mention of how to deactivate 'ferrous nanobots,' the kind they used, and that's with a cerebral MRI. So unless we can come up with a way to convince half a billion people to go get their brains magnetized, I think we're out of luck on that front."

I squeezed my eyes shut in frustration. "So we'll think of something else. People are literally *addicted* to their handhelds, North. As long as they've got a Gold on their wrists, they'll trust whatever that little box says. Who knows what the Few are planning to do with these people's lives!"

"I know," North said with a sigh. "And I'm with you. I'm just trying to be realistic here."

"Ugh!" Tears sprung to my eyes as I plopped down on the couch. "I feel so powerless."

"But you're not powerless," North said. "You know the truth. There's power in that. And you've got something else, too."

"You?"

He laughed. "Yes. But I was going to say wisdom. The real kind." He pulled me to my feet. "You see things other people don't."

"I don't see anything," I told him. "It's all the Doubt."

"So ask the voice for help. It's given you insight before."

"I need more than insight, North. I need an actual plan."

"Why not go to Griffin for help?" he suggested. "He's

CEO of the company behind this. He has to be able to do something."

"The man just had major brain surgery."

"He just woke up this afternoon," North replied.

"What?"

North picked up the remote from the coffee table and turned on his clunky TV. A local news reporter was standing outside of Massachusetts General Hospital. The banner at the bottom of the screen was GNOSIS CEO GRIFFIN PAYNE WAKES UP.

I took the remote from North to turn up the volume.

"Mr. Payne is being moved early tomorrow morning to an undisclosed private facility to focus on his recovery," the reporter was saying. "In a recorded statement to Gnosis's board of directors released about an hour ago, Griffin resigned as CEO, citing his desire to 'dedicate full attention to his recovery' in the coming months. No word yet on who will replace him at the helm of the 750 billion dollar company." The camera cut away from the reporter and back to the news desk.

The female anchor launched into the next story as an ominous-looking photo of the sun appeared next to her head. "A large, irregularly shaped sunspot group has solar physicists concerned that a geomagnetic superstorm may be in the forecast. If the active region bursts—"

"Great," I muttered, clicking off the TV. "On top of everything, the world is coming to an end." I tossed the remote onto the couch, reaching for my bag. "I need you to take me to the train station."

"Rory, it's past eight already. It'll be eleven before you get to Boston. No way they'll let you see him tonight."

"Then I have to find out where they're taking him." I looked at North. "Can you do that?"

He was already heading toward his closet. "There should be a transfer directive in the hospital's system," he called over his shoulder.

"Hey, where's Hershey?" I asked, following him.

"I dunno. She left about an hour ago. Told me not to wait up." North slid the poster back and pushed the secret door open.

"Do *you* know who the mystery guy is?" I asked.

"Nope," North replied. "If I did, I'd thank him for the privacy." He grinned as he pulled me into the tiny room and wrapped his arms around my waist. I stood on my tiptoes to kiss him, and for a few seconds I wasn't thinking about anything except the way his lips felt on mine.

"Okay," I said, putting my hand over his mouth as I pulled away. "Hold that thought." I pointed at his computer screen. "Transfer notice."

It only took him a few minutes to get into Massachusetts General Hospital's patient records database. "Griffin Payne," North said, typing in the name.

"Please let it be somewhere close," I murmured.

"There he is," North said. "Now let's see where he's—"

He stopped.

"No." His voice sounded funny.

"What is it? Where are they taking him?"

"Maybe this isn't— No, that's when he checked into the hospital. Do you know when his birthday is?"

It was on his Panopticon page, but I couldn't remember the date. "In November, I think? Why? What is it?" I took a step closer to the screen, not sure what I was supposed to be looking for.

North turned around in his chair. His face was ashen.

"Rory, Griffin died on Friday night."

29

IT TOOK NO EFFORT NOT TO CRY. It was as if my insides had turned to dry sand when North said the words *Griffin died*, my emotions disappearing into dust.

"Rory, talk to me. Are you okay?"

I was still standing where I'd been standing, less than a foot from North's chair, but I was eons away. My brain clung to its pragmatism, determined to solve this, to gather the facts that would explain how this happened, how I could've lost my father literally less than an hour after I'd found him.

"How did he die?" My voice sounded hollow. The way I felt.

North turned back to his screen. "Cerebral venous thrombosis. But it doesn't say what that is."

"It was a blood clot in his brain," I said. The same way my mom had died, except hers was in her lungs. My eyes came into focus. "Could nanobots do something like that?"

"I don't know. I can't even—" He clasped his hands behind

his neck, cradling his head between his elbows. "It's insane, Rory. He's been dead for three days and they're telling the world he's still alive. How long are they going to keep this up?"

"For as long as it takes to convince people that Gnosis can run itself without him," I said flatly. "Then they'll have him suffer some setback in whatever 'private facility' they're supposedly sending him to, and to everyone's great surprise and shock, he'll die." I met North's gaze. "You said it yourself. They control the medium, so they control the message."

"Rory, this is seriously effed up. How does a thirty-five-year-old man have a *stroke* and *die*?"

"Because they killed him, North." My voice was uncharacteristically cold. I couldn't help it. The warmth that filled this tiny room a few moments ago, when our bodies were pressed against each other's, was gone.

"You think they caused his stroke?"

"Think about it. He was about to say something critical of Gnosis two days before the Gold's launch, on national television. We saw him talking to Dr. Tarsus right before, remember? She knew what he was about to do. The Few couldn't risk the fallout of whatever he was going to say."

"Okay," North said slowly. "But how?"

"If nanobots can mimic oxytocin, why couldn't they clump together to cause a clot? Tarsus was standing with him on the stage. She was close enough. She could've done it from her handheld." I pointed at North's computer screen. "Is there a link to the autopsy?"

North scanned the page then tapped his screen. "An autopsy was declined. There's a form here, signed by his father."

His father. My grandfather. Why wouldn't he want an autopsy? Because he already knew what it would show. Griffin's voice echoed in my head. *My parents never liked Aviana. My stepfather hated her.*

"It must be his stepfather," I heard North say. "The last name's not the same." He squinted at his screen. "It's hard to read the signature, but it looks like it says Robert Atwater."

My chest contracted like a corset. I couldn't breathe.

"Robert Atwater is Griffin Payne's father." I nearly choked on the words.

North looked over his shoulder at me. "You know him?"

I managed to respond before I threw up. "He's the dean."

I lay on North's couch, my mind whirling, my stomach churning, wishing I could rewind my life. If only I hadn't picked akratic paracusia as my research topic. If only I hadn't applied to Theden in the first place. I could be in Seattle right now, blissfully addicted to my handheld, convinced, like Beck was, that I was living my best life. Instead I was here. Drowning in the awareness of how bad things really were.

How easily I'd fallen for it. Dean Atwater's inquisition the day after the Gnosis party. His urging that I tell him all that I knew. It was all an act, part of the society's evaluation process, designed to test my allegiance. I saw that now. He wasn't trying to root out society members. He was trying to weed out those who didn't have what it took to become one.

I realized all at once what had been bothering me. The thing I couldn't put my finger on. The dean made that comment the first day of school about my not letting history deter me. But my *real* history wouldn't have deterred me. I was the daughter of a valedictorian, not a dropout. He knew that. But he assumed I never would. He was the one who'd altered my mom's file.

I pulled up Griffin's Panopticon page on North's tablet. The "Early Life" section said that Griffin had been raised by his mother and a stepfather but didn't mention a name. His biological father was killed in a boating accident off Cape Cod two weeks before Griffin was born.

"How are you feeling?" North had emerged from the closet, carrying a plastic trash can. I groaned, covering my face with my hands.

"Mortified," I said from behind my palms. "You cleaned up my puke."

"I must really love you," North replied.

I bit my lip, keeping my face hidden. *Love.* Was that what this was? I wanted the brain space to think about it, but every ounce of gray matter was focused on the Few and how to take them down. I let my hands fall and nodded a little, the corners of my mouth turning up just a bit. It wasn't a response, exactly, but North didn't seem to be looking for one.

"How are you feeling, really?" he asked.

"I don't know," I admitted. "None of it feels real. Even the part about Griffin being my father in the first place. It's like I'm living someone else's existence. And yet, the one I had before, it never really felt like mine either."

"I know what that's like," North said. "Feeling like you don't belong in your own life. That's how it was for me growing up. My dad was my real dad, but we might as well have been strangers." North hesitated for a second. "So why not leave? I mean, what's keeping you at Theden, knowing what you know about the Few? If it goes as high up as the dean, then the whole school is under its thumb."

"It's more than being under its thumb," I said. "The society is the whole reason the school exists. Theden is their breeding ground."

"Then why stay?" He knelt down so we were at eye level. "I have an apartment in New York City. Paid for in cash. You and I, we could—"

"I can't leave," I told him. "Not until I stop them. Not after what they've done. If I'm right, then these people killed both my parents, North. And they've brainwashed my best friend. Not to mention hundreds of millions of other people." I shook my head. "I can't just run away."

North sighed. "I knew you were going to say that. But I can't let you go back into that place, their godforsaken *tomb*, by yourself."

I knew better than to argue with him. But I was going back in. Whether or not I had a way out.

• • •

I left North's apartment not long after that. Our conversation had come to a standstill. He felt how he felt, and I wouldn't budge. There wasn't much else to say.

The courtyard was quiet when I got back, no doubt because of the cold. The temperature had dropped ten degrees since last night, and the wind had picked up. It was now whistling through the dry leaves of the maple trees that lined the campus sidewalks, ripping them from their stems and tossing them in the air. I tilted my head back and looked up at our window. Our light was on. I was almost certain I'd turned it off.

The main door was propped open with a rock, so I hurried inside out of the wind. I took the stairs two at a time, digging in my bag for my Gemini. But it wasn't in my bag. It was in the belly of the dining hall's trash bin.

Crap. I was locked out of my room.

"You accidentally *threw it away?*" Izzy was looking at me like I was speaking a foreign language.

"It was on my tray at dinner," I said, refusing to be defensive. "I must've dumped it with my food."

"And you're just now realizing it?"

"I've been at the library," I lied. "I thought it was in my bag. So can I borrow yours? I need to call the janitor."

"Sure," she said, unsnapping her Gold from her wrist. "Unlock," she said to the device before handing it to me. I gave her a quizzical look. "It's tethered to your voice," she explained. "It won't work for someone else unless you unlock it first." *Oh good,* I thought. *So your phone won't activate the nanobots in someone else's brain.*

I didn't even want to hold the thing, much less put it near my head. But I took it from Izzy and quickly dialed the campus help line. The janitor was at my door five minutes later with a key card. He, too, seemed confused about how a person could lose their handheld and not realize it for several hours. "When does your new one arrive?" he asked.

"Tomorrow," I lied, and thanked him for his help.

The moment I stepped through my door I froze. I'd left Dr. Tarsus's yearbook on my desk, open to her senior photo. The yearbook was gone. Its disappearance reminded me that this wasn't the first time someone had come into my room. I checked under my pillow, then grabbed *Paradise Lost* and began flipping pages, looking for another handwritten clue. But there wasn't any.

I sighed and stepped out of my shoes, climbing into bed without bothering to wash my face or brush my teeth. It was hard to care about zits and cavities at this point. "How far I've come," I muttered, yanking my blanket up to my chin. As soon as my fingers touched the crisscross orange stitching at the top right corner, I bolted upright in bed. There were two of them in the design, one at the top right corner, by itself, away from the tiled square design and the other in the center of the smallest square. Liam had told me that the entrance to the tomb was in that smallest inner room, exactly where my mom had sewn an orange X.

X for Exit.

My eyes jumped from that *X* to the other one, seeing for the first time what my mom had left me.

A map.

Flinging off the covers, I sprung out of bed then smoothed my blanket back down. Liam had said that the rooms of the tomb were laid out the way the squares on my blanket were, so if I could figure out where the entrance was, I'd be able to pinpoint where the other *X* would be. Maybe it was my way out.

I grabbed my tablet off the desk and launched my map. I started with my current location then scrolled over to the edge of the woods, toward the cemetery. When the fence came into view, I switched over to satellite mode and zoomed out. Almost immediately, I gasped. It'd been there all along. I just couldn't see it from the ground.

The stone sidewalks of the cemetery were laid out in the same tiling pattern as the squares on my blanket. My eyes went to the innermost square. It enclosed the patch of lawn where I'd seen the apple tree, right across from North's mausoleum hideout. The mausoleum was also surrounded on all four sides by stone. It was the second square in a Fibonacci sequence. The spot where my mom had put the first orange *X*.

My heart picked up, each beat crashing into the next, as I stared at the aerial shot on my screen. The mausoleum was the entrance to the tomb. It had to be. It explained why there was no body in the coffin, and why the lid was so light, and why the floors were swept every week. It also made sense that there would be a lone apple tree in the innermost square. The iconic symbol of the Tree of the Knowledge of Good and Evil.

"Now how do I get in?" I asked aloud, double-tapping my screen for a ground shot of the mausoleum, as if I might find some clue there. But of course, what I really needed was a look at the *inside* of the space. The coffin that I was sure hid a stairway into the earth. Staring at the outside of the building would get me nowhere.

So I zoomed back out. Placing the other X would be harder, because the stone tiling stopped at the cemetery gates. Wherever it was, it wasn't on campus. It was much farther away. I'd have to do the math to figure out exactly how far. But I could, as long as the pattern held up.

Fibonacci numbers followed a particular sequence. The first two numbers were always zero and one, and every number after that was the sum of the previous two numbers. The pattern on my blanket was a tiling with squares whose side lengths were successive Fibonacci numbers, with a series of curved arcs connecting the corners of the squares and forming a golden spiral. I knew that the two smallest squares were one millimeter on each side, and that the largest was fifty-five by fifty-five. I'd measured them when I was a kid. The second orange cross-stitch was set away from the squares, at the widest curve of the spiral, which ended at the stitch. I had two questions to answer: How many millimeters away from the innermost square was that little X, and what was the corresponding distance in miles?

I used the scale on my map to figure out that the mausoleum was a twelve-foot square. So one millimeter on my blanket was equal to twelve feet on the map. I immediately downloaded a ruler app and began measuring out what would've been the next several squares on my blanket, the ones my mom hadn't stitched. Why had she stopped after the tenth square? My only guess was that that's where the Few's tomb ended, probably at the big arena they'd taken us to, which according to my map was just beneath the Theden Green. The orange stitch, then, was pointing to something outside the tomb, something that lay at the tip of the arc on the fourteenth square.

I went back to my map and began drawing squares on my screen with my stylus. The draw function allowed me to type in the side lengths of each one, so I just had to line them up in the right pattern. It was staggering, the precision with which the tomb must've been built. Not just the tomb, but the cemetery and campus and town above it, all laid out in a careful mathematical sequence.

When I got to the fourteenth square, I stopped and stared. There, near the northeast corner, right where the second orange cross-stitch would be, was the Enfield Reservoir. Owned by the Theden Initiative, funder of the SynOx study, the same entity that controlled Gnosis and my school, a man-made pool occupying a mere fraction of the quarry beneath it. I pictured the reservoir's armed guards, electronic surveillance, and high-powered electric fence.

There was something underneath that water.

30

"THERE'S SOMETHING UNDER the Enfield Reservoir,"
I said to North at eight o'clock the next morning. I'd called
him on Kate's phone from Izzy's Gold, which she'd been willing but reluctant to part with at breakfast. I was meeting her
outside Hamilton Hall and timing it so I'd arrive just as first
period was starting so I wouldn't have any alone time with Dr.
Tarsus.

"What kind of something?" North asked, his voice echoing a
little. Paradiso's tiny bathroom was the café's only private space.

"I don't know," I admitted. "But whatever it is, my mom
thought it was important." I quickly told him what I'd figured
out about my blanket, and how it corresponded to the land-
scape around the cemetery. "It's a Fibonacci tile," I explained.
"Which basically just means that there's this sequence of bigger
and bigger connected squares with a spiral running through
them. The pattern on my blanket stops after ten squares, and
I think because that's where the tomb stops. But the spiral

continues into what would've been the fourteenth square, and that's where my mom stitched the second X." I was talking fast now, hurrying to get it all out. "And if you keep drawing the spiral even farther, all the way out to where the twenty-first square would be, you run into the Gnosis headquarters. Like, right through the center of the building. So I'm thinking all three are connected underground—the tomb, whatever's beneath the reservoir, and the Gnosis complex."

"Wow," North said. "It's like something out of a bad Nicolas Cage movie from the early aughts."

"I don't know who that is."

"You don't know who Nicolas Cage is?" North sounded incredulous. "You need to see *National Treasure* immediately. I mean, it's terrible, but since you're essentially living it, you ought to at least see it."

"Focus please. The Enfield Reservoir. What would the Few put under there, and why?"

As I was talking, I spotted Dean Atwater across the court-yard and physically recoiled. Now that the courtyard had begun to clear, the walkway between Hamilton and Jay was in his direct sightline. I ducked behind the buildings, out of view.

"Beats me," North was saying. "Want to drive out there this afternoon and check it out? I get off at four."

"Definitely," I replied, pulling the Gold away from my ear. 8:44. Dr. Tarsus would lock her classroom door in sixty seconds. "I gotta go," I told North. "I'll come by Paradiso after my last class."

I got to practicum at exactly 8:45, just as Dr. Tarsus was pulling the door closed. I caught it with my hand. "Feeling better today?" she asked when she saw me.

"Much," I told her, and flashed my brightest smile. "Looking forward to that make-up session."

"Glad to hear it," she replied, reaching into the pocket of her blazer. "You'll need this." I looked down at her hand and saw a small envelope pressed between her finger and thumb. She handed it to me at waist level, as if she were trying to keep it out of view. I quickly slipped it into my bag.

"Let's get started," she said then, louder, to the whole class.

I stepped into my pod and dropped my bag in the bin by my seat, but not before pulling the envelope back out. I heard a sliding sound as I lifted it sideways, and heaviness at the lower end.

"The goal today is escape," I heard Tarsus say. "You'll be evaluated based on your ability to reason without relying on your sensory perception. How well can you make decisions in the dark?"

I tore open the envelope and stared at its contents. The silver chain and pendant were in a heap at the bottom corner. She was giving the necklace *back*?

My screen turned on, but the scene was so dimly lit, I couldn't tell what I was looking at. I thought for a second that my screen was messed up until I heard Dr. Tarsus's voice again.

"We rely on our senses to guide us. But what if you were in a situation where your senses were compromised? How would your mind compensate?"

I looked down at my necklace again. *You'll need this,* she'd said. For what?

"You're on the top floor of a burning building," Dr. Tarsus was saying. "There is a single elevator that connects all the floors and a stairwell between each set of floors, but these stairwells are not stacked, meaning that each one is in a different location." These were important details and I'd only half heard them. I shoved the envelope with my necklace back into my bag and tried to listen. *Burning building. Stairwells in different locations. Escape.* "The fire in this building originated on your floor," Tarsus went on, "and will quickly escalate. Your task is to get out of the building alive. The meter at the bottom of your screen will tell you how much smoke you've inhaled. If you lose consciousness, the simulation will end and you will get a zero score. Good luck."

The lights in the room dimmed and the simulation began. I blinked a couple of times, as if that would help me see more clearly, but of course it didn't because there was virtually no light on my screen. I looked around for the smoke Tarsus had mentioned, but I didn't see any. Or any other signs of a fire. *Find a stairwell,* I told myself, moving forward slowly with my arms outstretched. A few seconds later my palms hit a surface. A cold, almost damp surface that felt like stone.

Confusion stalled my next thought. If this building was on fire, the walls wouldn't be cold, and they certainly wouldn't feel damp. Had I missed something she'd said?

Now that my eyes were adjusted to the semidarkness, I

could make out the shape of something jutting out from the wall above my head. I reached up for it and felt something smooth and cylindrical mounted on a small platform. My fingers creeped up to the cylinder's rounded edge then dipped down as I slid them over the top. Something stiff crunched beneath my middle finger and suddenly it registered. A candle with a burnt wick, mounted on a stone wall.

I was in the Few's tomb.

It took effort not to obsess over the *why*—why had Tarsus put me in the tomb and instructed me to escape?—and instead to focus on the *how*—how was I going to get to whatever was beneath the reservoir? The clock at the bottom of my screen was ticking.

Now that I knew where I was, it took me only a few seconds to determine that I was in the room where the initiation had been held. I could make out the shape of the altar on the far wall. I'd seen the doors at opposite corners, so I moved through the one closest to me. The room I stepped into was smaller than the one I'd been in, which told me I was moving toward the center.

I turned and sprinted back through the altar room, toward the other door. I guessed that I was in the third or fourth square in the sequence, so I had six or seven more to go until I reached the arena and another four to get to the reservoir.

Since I knew where the doors were—at opposite corners on opposite walls—I could move through the rooms quickly, slowing down only when I passed through the narrow doors. When I ran into the arena, I stopped for a moment to catch my breath and to marvel again at the sheer size of the space, standing completely still so as not to lose my bearings. It was so dark that if I got turned around, I'd be running in circles to find the opposite wall.

When my breathing slowed, I started moving again, jogging toward the other end of the massive circular stage, praying for another door. My heart leaped when I felt an opening in the rock. It was a tunnel.

The timer at the bottom of my screen had hit 10:00:00. I had ten minutes to get to whatever was under the reservoir. I clung to the wall at my right, keeping one palm on the stone and the other out in front of me as I fell into a steady jog, the wall curving into the shape of a spiral. Even though I was only running in place in my pod, I'd never make it the whole way if I tried to sprint.

I figured it'd take me at least seven minutes to cover that much distance, but just shy of six I ran smack into a wall. In the darkness I didn't see it coming. It was made of stone, like the one beside me, and I felt around for an opening, refusing to accept that it could be a dead end. My hand slid across a stone that protruded from the rest. Instinctively, I pressed it, the wall slid away.

Behind it was another wall, this one made of glass and lit from behind. I blinked rapidly, blinded by the bright light. On the other side of the glass was a smooth steel wall with a vault door in the center, engraved with a giant G. The Gnosis logo. Beside the door was a mounted wall mic with a red button beneath it and a rectangular screen above it. To the right of the mic was a control panel with rows of green lights.

I touched the glass in front of me to get a sense of how thick it was, and the glass became a touchscreen with a keypad. Twelve boxes appeared, with numbers inside the first four.

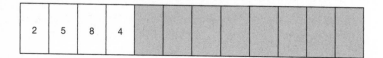

It was a password sequence. My brain went to work to find a pattern. Two plus three equaled five, and five plus three equaled eight, but eight plus three didn't equal four. Damn it. My eyes flicked to the bottom of my screen. 2:59:45 remaining. I felt my mood dip. The time was going to run out while I was still standing here.

Think, Rory, I told myself. My mom had thought of everything. She had to have left me a clue for this. My mind raced over everything she'd wanted me to have. The necklace, the note, the blanket.

The blanket. With its mathematical pattern.

In a flash, I saw it. It wasn't 2, 5, 8, and 4. It was 2,584, the twentieth number in the Fibonacci sequence. I'd calculated it last night. What was the next number in the sequence? My brain stalled. I couldn't remember. I'd have to start at the beginning. The first two numbers were zero and one, and every number after that was the sum of the two before it. Doing the math, the number right after 2,584 was 4,181. I quickly typed four, one, eight, and one into the next four boxes. Now for the last four: 2,584 + 4,181 = 6,765. I added these, took a breath, and touched the enter button.

Clang.

I jumped at the loud sound, metal against metal. A lock lifting out of place. A moment later there was a sound like a puff of air, and then a whoosh as the glass retracted and slid away. My eyes darted to the timer: 1:45:00 left.

I stepped inside the chamber. As soon as I did, the glass resealed behind me. There was a sucking sound as it resealed, trapping me between glass and steel. Now what? I scanned the small chamber. The red button beneath the mic was blinking, as if the mic were recording. Was I supposed to say something? If there was a password, I certainly didn't know it. I watched as the screen above the mic lit up with a moving wave pattern, as if I *was* speaking.

Then I heard a beep as the lights on the control panel flashed from green to red, followed by a loud metallic snap as the lock on the vault door disengaged.

It was letting me in.

As I reached to pull open the vault door, I noticed for the first time that the skin on my arm was black. I surveyed the rest of me and realized why the system was letting me in. It thought I was someone else. All this time, I'd been Dr. Tarsus in this simulation and hadn't realized it. No wonder I'd gotten here so fast. My virtual legs were twice as long.

With only ten seconds left on my timer, I darted through the heptagonal opening and into the biggest room I'd ever been in.

It was unlike anything I had ever seen. Lit with an eerie blue light. Stacked with rows and rows of identical machines, from floor to ceiling. So cold, it felt like a freezer.

The floor beneath me was grated and raised several feet off the ground beneath it, which seemed to be cut from sparkling stone. I looked up at the ceiling, more than a football field away. The size, the machines, the temperature. This was a server room. It had to be.

Look to your right!

The words were a boom, like thunder, bathing me in fear and relief. The voice was here, helping me, and, from its tone, it cared about this as much as I did. I spun to my right and saw a machine that looked different than the others. Tri-panel screens suspended above a glass desk sitting inside a copper-colored cage. I took a step toward it and my screen went black.

"No," I blurted out. "Not yet."

But the timer had run out and the simulation was over. A few seconds later, my screen lit up with our class roster, ranked by escape times. My name was at the middle of the list. Inconspicuous. As far as anyone else in the class could tell, I'd done the same simulation they had. Only Tarsus and I knew the truth: that, for some reason I couldn't begin to fathom, she was trying to help me. She'd not only let me loose in the tomb, she'd showed me how to access Gnosis's server bank.

Our teacher spent the rest of the class period going over the various mistakes my classmates had made in their sims. I didn't hear a word of it. I just stared at my pendant.

Had she left that copy of my mom's transcript under my pillow? Had she written Dr. Hildebrand's name in North's book? I heard the voice loud and clear then, not a boom like before, but more of an echo. Two words, resounding in my head.

Trust her.

31

GRATEFUL I WAS IN SNEAKERS, I ran from Hamilton Hall toward Paradiso, the upsilon pendant banging against my collarbone, and I hopped the fence at the cemetery. As I sprinted across the grass, I cast a quick glance around to make sure I was alone. When my eyes landed on the statue of the archangel, I stopped in my tracks. His arm was pointed at the entrance to the cemetery, which made sense now that I'd seen the illustration in *Paradise Lost*. He was expelling Adam and Eve from the Garden. But I was certain that his arm had been pointed at the sky the night the Few summoned me to the angel's wing.

I jogged over to it. It was almost imperceptible, but there was a slit in the stone at his left shoulder joint, as if his arm were a lever. I gripped his wrist and pushed up. His arm didn't budge. I gritted my teeth and pushed again, squatting my legs for leverage. His arm inched upward, and as it did, I heard a rumble to my left. Stone sliding on stone.

It was coming from the mausoleum.

I dashed over to the building and let myself in. I knew even before I lifted the coffin's lid what I'd done. I'd opened the entrance to the tomb.

The coffin's marble bottom had retracted a few inches to reveal spiral stairs descending into pitch-black. I peered over the coffin's edge, trying to make out the bottom, but I couldn't see farther than ten feet down.

With a start I straightened back up. What if I'd set off a silent alarm? Not to mention that I'd left the mausoleum door open in broad daylight. I slammed the coffin lid shut and left the mausoleum as quickly as I'd come in, stopping only to yank the angel's arm back down before sprinting toward the fence.

Kate was behind the register when I came barreling through the café's door. "Hey, Rory," she called. "North's not here."

"What do you mean he's not here?" I demanded. "He has to be here."

Kate eyed me. "Are you okay?"

"I just need to see North," I said. "Do you know where he is?"

She shook her head. "But his break's over in five minutes. You want me to make you something while you w—"

"No, thanks," I said, and dashed out.

Relief washed over me when I saw him through the glass door of Ivan's repair shop. North had his laptop open on the counter, and Ivan was tinkering with something in North's palm. I yanked open the door, sending the bell clanging.

North jerked up, his fingers clamping down on whatever was in his hand. He quickly shut his laptop, too.

"Rory," he said when he saw me, relaxing a little, but his brow was now furrowed in concern. "What are you doing here?"

"I need to see what's on my necklace," I said hurriedly. "I think she put something on it. I think that's why she took it."

Ivan was already unlocking his loaner cabinet.

"What's in your hand?" I asked North. His fingers were still tight around it.

He hesitated and glanced at Ivan. The old man nodded. "It's ready to go."

North opened his hand. The dove locket I'd seen in the shop's glass cabinet the first night we'd hung out was lying in his palm. Even more exquisite up close. The gold was etched with intricate detail, the wing raised slightly from the surface. "I bought it for you," North said, glancing sideways at Ivan. "To replace your necklace." He faltered. "I mean. I know nothing could replace it, but I thought—"

"I love it," I said, sweeping my hair up with my hands. "Will you put it on for me? And take the other one off so we can get the file?"

Feeling North's fingers skim the nape of my neck made the tiny hairs beneath them stand on end. How I wished we could just be two regular teenagers who didn't have a biotech conspiracy to take down.

The dove locket fell about an inch above the pendant,

wedging itself in the space between my clavicles. "What's inside?" I asked suddenly, remembering that it was a locket. The hinge was along the top, so I slid my nail between the dove's beak, the obvious place to snap it open.

"It doesn't open," North said quickly. He unclasped the upsilon necklace and caught it with his hand.

"Isn't it a locket?"

"Whoever owned it before you sealed it shut," Ivan explained.

I slid the back of my hand under the delicate bird, lifting it so I could see it better. I remembered the dove's eye being a turquoise gemstone, but I must've been mistaken, because it was black, not blue, and reflective, like mirrored glass.

"Well, I love it," I said, turning around to smile at North. "Thank you."

He beamed. "You're welcome." He released the USB plug on my pendant and stuck it into the port of Ivan's laptop. "How'd you get this back?" he asked.

"Dr. Tarsus," I said. "She gave it back to me this morning. It sounds crazy, but I think maybe she's been trying to help me all along."

"Help you do what?" North asked.

"I don't know. But this morning in practicum she showed me the inside of the tomb and let me use her credentials to get into what I think is a Gnosis server room. That's what's beneath the reservoir."

North said something in reply, but I was too preoccupied

with the two files that had popped up on my screen to hear it. One was a JPEG, the other was an audio file, seven minutes and forty-five seconds in length. I lifted my eyes and met Ivan's. "Do you have some earbuds I could borrow?" It wasn't that I didn't want North to hear it, or Ivan for that matter—I just wanted to listen to it once through first.

"Of course," the old man replied. He went back to the loaner cabinet and retrieved a pair of vintage headphones, the kind you wore over your ears. "If you'd like some privacy, you can listen to it in my office in the back," he said kindly, and gestured for me to come around the counter. He pointed to a door just behind the fabric curtain that separated the front of the store from the back.

"Thanks," I said, casting my eyes back to North as I lifted the laptop off the counter. "I'll just be a few minutes."

The office was cramped but clean. There was an old transistor radio on the desk, propped up against the wall. It was on, set to what sounded like a news channel. The volume was too low to make out the words. I caught the phrase "solar flare" and turned it up. It was the tail end of a news story.

". . . wind would hurl a burst of electromagnetic radiation in our direction," the reporter was saying. "Traveling at speeds upward of eight million miles an hour, this cloud of solar plasma and magnetic field would slam into the Earth's atmosphere in less than a day, posing significant risk to our power grid."

A solar storm. It was the kind of thing the old Beck would've gone nuts over. But the new Beck probably wouldn't see it at all. Lux would make sure of it. Weather events were on his threat list, after all.

The thought snapped me back to the present moment. I clicked to open the JPEG first.

A black-and-white photo opened onscreen. It was a year-book picture, an action shot from the sports page. A basketball player in a Theden jersey was launching a three-point shot with four seconds left on the clock. The crowd was on its feet in the bleachers behind him. I saw my mother's face almost immediately, her mouth open in a happy yell, hugging the girl beside her. A girl with an Afro whose inky black eyes hadn't changed in seventeen years.

Holy crap. They were *friends*.

I shoved the headphones plug into the jack and clicked the other file.

"You no doubt have questions," came Dr. Tarsus's voice through the speakers. "I have some answers, but not all. I don't know why your mom left Theden when she did, or whether her death was an accident, although I suspect it wasn't. I do know that Griffin Payne is your real father, and that he and Aviana were deeply in love, and she was certain you were conceived on their wedding night." Dr. Tarsus took a steady breath. I felt my body stiffen, bracing for whatever she was about to say.

"The last time I heard from your mother was the day you were born," she began. "She'd been gone since the previous June. She called from a nurse's phone to tell me she was in labor, and that she thought the Few had found her. She didn't

403

say what had happened to make her run, only that something terrible had, and that, because of it, you could not grow up as Griffin's child. She said she'd made sure that Griffin didn't suspect that you were his, and that you would grow up believing that a man named Duke Vaughn was your father." My eyes watered at the mention of my dad's name. How far away my life with him seemed. "She said she was calling to say goodbye," Dr. Tarsus continued. "And to ask me to keep you safe. I promised her that I would.

"By now you know that the upsilon necklace is mine. Your mom was never a member of the Few. Neither was your father. Your father was never even considered, despite his stepfather's pleas on his behalf—his IQ didn't meet the threshold. Your mother was invited and went through the evaluation process, but when the time came for her vows, she refused to make them. I'll never forget her words. She pulled back her hood and said, 'Only the powerless hide behind masks and robes.' The rest of us were caught up in the prestige and exclusivity, the flattery of being told that we were destined for greatness. It was so easy to rationalize it, to call this greatness our duty, to make it sound important and even good. It's how we're made I suppose. How did Milton put it? 'Sufficient to have stood, though free to fall.' The choice was ours, and we chose ourselves. Not Aviana. She was wiser than that.

"I didn't know at first if you were like her. Growing up you didn't seem to be, not from a distance, anyway. When you decided to come to Theden, I had to be sure. That's why I asked

Hershey to keep an eye on you. When she told me she would go to the dean, I knew I had to send her away, however I could. In retrospect, I wish I'd never involved her to begin with. I didn't end up needing her weekly reports. I knew you heard the Doubt on the first day of class, when you threw yourself in front of that trolley. It was something Aviana would've done." Dr. Tarsus paused there, and I imagined her smiling. I heard her smile fade before she went on.

"I didn't see what she saw. Not then. So I took my vows that night without knowing how deep the society's power ran. Now I know too well." Her voice was grim. "The Few may be few, but they are everywhere. They have members in every city, in every industry, at the highest level at every major company. Gnosis and Soza are just the tip of the iceberg. Slowly and steadily, they have been creating the infrastructure for their dominance." *The infrastructure for their dominance.* I shuddered. It sounded like a line from a creepy conspiracy thriller. But no, this was real life.

"But the Few have an opponent they haven't yet overcome," Dr. Tarsus said then. "The Doubt. A label designed by them to make the inner voice seem untrustworthy. Irrational. It wasn't a difficult sell. After all, people who hear it do things that don't make sense to the world—they give up what they've earned, they help those who don't deserve it, they forgo what they desire. They don't put themselves first, and selfless people are impossible to control. So the Few began to foster the idea that this 'Doubt' couldn't be trusted. They created the fiction of a psychological disorder, as if the voice could be explained away by science, when, in reality, it's the most complicated concept of our existence. The inexplicable nudge of providence that has guided the human spirit since the beginning of time. It is, I've come to believe, the thing that makes us human. Whether it's coming from God or our collective conscience or some unknown part of ourselves—the voice isn't something we can study in a lab, or put in a box. It is so much bigger than that.

"The Few helped people forget that. Slowly, methodically, they set out to change the story. The voice people once trusted became the enemy of happiness. Something to fear. Knowing that the voice wouldn't scream to be heard, they made sure that the world stayed loud with music and movies and 24/7 news and incessant online chatter. If they couldn't silence the whisper, they'd bombard people with other voices. Infinite choices.

"It worked, but it wasn't perfect," she went on. "There were still some who chose the voice. Who couldn't be distracted. Who couldn't be misled. So Project Hyperion was born. The Few would launch a new tech company. That tech company would develop a decision-making app, and that decision-making app would become a social necessity. They knew the world well. And they had patience.

"The summer of my senior year, the society got me an internship with Gnosis," Dr. Tarsus continued. "That's how I ended up as Dr. Hildebrand's research assistant that spring. It was a fortuitous accident that someone put my name on the distribution list for that internal memo you found on my pendant.

As soon as I saw it, I went straight to your mom. I wasn't afraid for my life, not back then. Just the loss of my status. I was a girl from the Bronx who'd been given this whole new life. A life I didn't want to lose." Heavy with shame, her voice faltered a little. She cleared her throat and kept going.

"Your mom didn't waver for a moment once she knew. She wanted to expose them. And with the memo and the society roster I'd put together, she had the proof she needed. Her plan was to write an open letter to all the major newspapers in the country, enclosing the memo and the roster. Every one of them would've run the story. Reporters were still making their own choices back then. But she said she wanted to confront Griffin's stepfather first. Atwater was the Divine Second then. The society's number two. Aviana felt like she needed a confession from him, if only for Griffin."

Dr. Tarsus's voice was grim now. "Neither of us knew what the Few were truly capable of. We knew they were powerful, and we knew they were ruthless, but we didn't imagine that they were murderers. I don't know for certain that they killed your mother, but I do know they killed your father." Her voice broke. "I hate for you to find out this way, Rory, but Griffin is dead." My eyes welled up with tears even though I already knew. It was the sympathy in Tarsus's voice that got to me, the unbridled compassion. "He died the night of the party," she said softly. "Of a blood clot in his brain. He didn't know what he was up against when he got behind that podium. He knew that the version of Lux on the Gold used a different algorithm, designed to steer people away from the Doubt, but he had no idea that people were being chemically manipulated into trusting it, or that the flu spray he got in September was riddled with nanobots." Her voice got hard again. "Or that his bodyguard, Jason, was taking orders from someone else."

I'd wondered who'd pressed the button to cause that clot. How much of our conversation had Jason overheard? Was I the reason Griffin was dead?

"I'm sure you think I'm a coward," Tarsus said then, her voice faltering again. "With my position, my access, I should have done something myself, long ago, before it got this far. And you're right. But I couldn't take them on and keep my promise to your mom. So I've kept you safe, hoping that the day would come when I wouldn't need to anymore. I wish that day were today. I want nothing more than for you to leave Theden, to disappear the way your mom tried to do. But while I am not as wise as your mother was, or as you are, I am no fool. I saw the look in your eyes when you stepped up to that altar. It's the same look I saw in hers when she pulled back that hood. So if you choose to go back into the tomb, I will do whatever I can to get you out alive." She started to say something else but seemed to change her mind. There was a shuffling sound, and the clip cut off.

Tears were streaming down my face now, dripping onto the desk. She hadn't told me anything I didn't already know, or at least suspect. But her words had solidified things for me. I wouldn't run. I couldn't run. Not after what these people had done to my parents. To Beck. To millions of other people.

"Rory?" North's voice was muffled through the headphones. I pulled them from my ears, letting them drop onto the desk. "What did she say?"

I just shook my head.

"Is she really on our side?"

"More than that," I said, hoarse from the tears. "Everything she's done, she's done for me. She promised my mom she'd keep me safe." I pulled the pendant from the laptop and handed it to North. "Can you put the recording on your phone? I want to listen to it again later."

He nodded. "Of course." He sat on the edge of Ivan's desk. "Do you want to talk about it?"

I wiped away my tears. "I want to talk about how we can take those bastards down."

"Okay, you said you saw a Gnosis server room in your simulation," North said. "What'd it look like?

I described it in as much detail as I could.

"And what about security?"

"Numerical password and a voice recognition mic."

"Voice recognition. Yikes. How'd you get through in the simulation?"

"I was her. Tarsus. I couldn't hear what she was saying, but her voice got me through the door."

North chewed on his lip. "You said she'd be at your initiation, right? If we could get to the room undetected, would she let us in?"

The hope that had all but vanished came surging back. "You have a plan," I said, leaping to my feet and slamming my knees against the underside of the desk in the process.

"Well, technically it's *your* plan," North replied, the corners of his mouth turning up just a little. "I'm just a sucker for a challenge. Plus, the timing is just too perfect. It feels like a gift."

"What do you mean?"

"The utility companies are shutting off the power grid tomorrow afternoon to protect the transformers from the solar storm. Gnosis claims its systems are grid-independent, so its taking its servers off the grid at midnight tonight."

"Why?"

"So they'll keep running during the blackout, I guess. The utilities are saying that power could be out for twenty-four hours."

"God forbid that people be without Lux for that long," I said sarcastically.

"The good news for us is that the entire Gnosis system will be offline tonight from midnight to two a.m. eastern for maintenance."

"Including Lux," I said. I felt my pulse pick up.

North nodded. "Which means if we can get this done while the servers are down, we might be able to do it undetected."

"But won't people be in the server room during that time? Like, working or whatever?"

"I doubt it," North replied. "It's freezing in server rooms, and super loud. And it's not like Gnosis employees need to be in the room to access the servers anyway—they can get in through the company's internal network."

My heart was racing now. "Oh my gosh. We could really pull this off."

"There's still a lot to figure out," North cautioned. "Assuming Tarsus can get us past security, we'd still have to find the terminal, and then I'd have to—"

"The terminal. What is that?"

"The entry point for the system. A machine with a keyboard and a screen. It's how you—"

I cut him off again. "I saw it. Three screens, a glass desk that looked like a giant touchpad. It was surrounded in copper mesh."

"Okay, so we found the terminal," North said. "But we still don't know how tight the security is on the machine itself. And we won't know until we get in there."

"Not we," I corrected. "I. I'm doing this alone."

"Like hell you are," North scoffed. "First of all, there's no way you could pull this off without me. What we're talking about is a figure-it-out-once-I'm-in-there kind of thing. I couldn't tell you how to do this even if I wanted to. Not until I see it. Second, I love you way too much to let you walk into that place alone."

With a sharp pang, I realized this might be my last chance to say it back. Though I was forcing myself to ignore it, I couldn't shake the awareness of just how dangerous this plan of ours really was. "I love you too," I said softly. "But how will we possibly get you in there?"

"Liam always brings you in, right? In a hooded robe?" North shrugged. "I'll be Liam."

"If they catch you—"

"They won't catch me. And so what if they do? You said there's the serpent, an owl, and a fox, right? With Tarsus on our side, it's three against two."

The knot in my stomach loosened a little. North's confidence was contagious.

"The only question is, how do we take Liam out of commission for a couple of hours?" North asked.

"We roofie him," I said without hesitation. "It'll incapacitate him without killing him, and it'll screw with his memories."

"Oh, okay. I'll just grab the bottle of date-rape pills I have in my medicine cabinet."

"Not pills," I corrected. "Has to be injectable. There's no way we can guarantee that he'll drink whatever we put it in."

North gave me an incredulous look. "You're actually serious?"

"What? It's what the society uses. And it'll do exactly what we need it to do."

North tugged at his Mohawk. "I know we don't have time to get into this right now, but, holy crap, Rory, this shit is seriously messed up."

"You're right. Not the time. We have to go buy roofies."

"Where, at Walgreens? I'm sure we'll find them right next to the Advil."

I crossed my arms, irritated by the sarcasm. "You're a guy with a Mohawk and tattoos. Don't you know people?"

"People with *Rohypnol?*"

"So you don't know anyone who can get it?"

He started to shake his head but seemed to think of something. "One of my clients is a pharmacist in Greenfield. I could probably get a prescription sleeping serum from him. Something potent but legal. I can message him from my apartment."

"We need to fill Hershey in anyway," I said, grabbing the laptop and headphones.

We thanked Ivan and hurried out. After a quick stop at Paradiso to tell Kate that North wouldn't be coming back to work, we headed up to North's apartment with coffee and one of every pastry in the café's glass case.

"Hershey?" I called out when we stepped inside. But the living room was quiet.

"She's with mystery boy," North said. "She came by this morning for her bag. She said she was gonna stay at his place for a few days." *His place.* So he definitely didn't live on campus. Or with his parents.

I gnawed on the inside of my bottom lip. My boyfriend didn't go to Theden or live with his parents. That didn't make him a psycho killer. Hershey had been hooking up with this guy, whoever he was, for a while. He wasn't a stranger. And she was Hershey. She could take care of herself.

North had disappeared into his closet. When I joined him, he'd already launched what looked like a chat box on his screen. "This is how I communicate with my clients," he explained. "It's a private chat program. It'll call his handheld and beep three times, signaling that he should log in."

A few minutes later the guy did, and North started typing.

"He'll do it," North said, and grinned. "He's at the pharmacy now. It'll be ready in fifteen minutes." He spun around in his chair and looked at me.

"We're really doing this," I said.

North's brow furrowed. "It's what you want, right?"

"Absolutely. It's just—" My voice caught. "I don't want anything to happen to you."

"I don't want anything to happen to *you*."

"But I got myself into this. You didn't. You got dragged in by me."

"You clearly don't know me as well as I thought you did," North said. "I don't get dragged into things, Rory. I'm doing this because I want to. Because what these people are doing is wrong. And because the voice in my head is saying the same thing that yours is."

"Fear not," I whispered. North met my gaze and nodded.

"Fear not."

32

WHILE NORTH TOOK HIS MOTORBIKE to the pharmacy in Greenfield, I stayed behind to wait for Hershey. We'd decided to leave for North's apartment in Manhattan as soon as we got out of the tomb, so this might be my last chance to say good-bye. If we pulled this off, we'd have to disappear.

Our plan was actually pretty simple. We'd decided to manufacture chaos by reprogramming Lux to direct Gold users *into* their threats and weaknesses instead of away from them, enabling people to experience the moments the Few were so intent on keeping them from— and throwing a massive wrench into their daily schedules in the process. It wasn't breaking the shackles, exactly, but if people's lives were thrown off kilter, maybe they'd look up from their screens. Maybe they'd seek guidance from somewhere other than the shiny gold box on their wrists. It was all we could do, really. Lay the groundwork. In the end, people had to choose.

I formed them free and free they must remain. I saw the quote from *Paradise Lost* differently now. The Few hadn't changed human nature. They hadn't taken away free will—they didn't have the power to do that. Yes, the nanobots in people's brains were manufacturing a sense of trust, leading them to blindly put their faith in Lux, but those tiny machines weren't dictating their choices. Nobody was. Nobody could, not even God. It was the message on Griffin's ring. Steinbeck's *timshel*. Thou mayest. With Lux, people were simply choosing not to choose. We had to remind them that they still could.

We were optimistic. After seeing Beck's Lux profile and my reaction to it, North had started clicking through Lux profiles randomly, looking at the users' threats and weaknesses. As it turned out, there were some that appeared on nearly every profile, so he'd started cataloging the repeats. Synchronicity, serendipity, and sunsets, for example, were common threats. As were unfulfilled expectations and unanticipated delays. Meanwhile, the same five traits appeared almost universally as user weaknesses. Patience, compassion, humility, gratitude, and mercy. Their antitheses—instant gratification, smugness, confidence, entitlement, and indifference—were at the top of nearly every strengths list. Our plan was to keep the app's existing algorithm but change the variables. If North got the code right, our modified version of Lux would manufacture the scenarios it had previously been programmed to avoid. I didn't know exactly what to expect if we succeeded, but I knew that if the Few were keeping people from having them, then these types of experiences—moments of compassion, of mercy, of gratitude, of humility—must be powerful. I kept thinking of the way Hershey acted after I helped her study for her midterms. She was a recipient of my grace that night, and it changed her.

I put my earbuds in and pressed play on Tarsus's recording. North had put it on his iPhone like I'd asked, and since he'd been gone, I'd listened to it three more times. As Tarsus spoke, I pulled my legs up under me and closed my eyes. Focusing on my breath, I tried to clear my brain of its whirling, fruitless worry. In . . . Out . . . In. My breath sounded like the ocean, or like the wind.

The wind blows wherever it pleases, I heard the voice say. *You hear its sound, but you cannot tell where it comes from or where it is going.*

So it was with the voice, I realized. It, like the wind, could not be predicted or contained. I held on to these words, letting them repeat like a refrain as I steadied my breaths. I couldn't control who the voice would speak to, or even when it would choose to speak to me. All I could do was decide to listen each time it did.

Peace took ahold of my heart as I sat there, its presence filling me with the certainty that there was purpose in our plan and confidence that we would carry it through. I remembered the words the voice spoke the day I arrived at Theden, the promise I'd forgotten until now. *You won't fail,* it had whispered. I waited now for an assurance that nothing bad would happen to us in the process, but none ever came.

"Rory?" I felt a hand on my shoulder and a gentle shake. Groggy with sleep, I opened my eyes. The light had faded in the living room, the sun a warm amber through the slats in the window shade. My earbuds were still in my ears, but the recording had long since cut off. North was next to me on the couch, a pharmacy bag on his lap. He brushed the hair out of my face. "I thought you were meditating," he said, then smiled. "Until I heard a snore."

I punched him in the arm. "So you got it?"

North pulled a small vial and a box of needles from the bag. "One dose of intravenous triazolam. It should sedate him within minutes and keep him out for at least eight hours. If all goes according to plan, we could be in Manhattan before he wakes up."

I only nodded. *If all goes according to plan.* That was a big *if.*

North glanced at his watch. "It's almost six," he told me. "I need to get all my gear to the storage unit before it closes. And you should probably go pack up whatever you want to bring with you and get it back here before you go to Liam's." The plan was for me to go to Liam's dorm room a few minutes before curfew, under the guise of being nervous about initiation. His roommate had flown to Birmingham that morning for his grandmother's funeral and wouldn't be back until the following day, so Liam would be alone. Since he no doubt kept his robe hidden, I'd have to somehow convince him to show it to me before I pricked him. We'd talked about waiting until Liam left for the cemetery but decided that leaving him out in the open was too risky, for him and for us. It was safer for everyone if he spent the night in bed. Once I had him tucked in, I'd take his robe and meet North in the cemetery to wait for the text from the Few. North wanted to come with me to Liam's dorm, but we couldn't risk someone seeing him, especially not with the restraining order still in effect.

"Not yet," I told North, sliding my back down the couch and pulling him on top of me. His body tensed up in surprise. I held him tight against me, arching my back to press against him. He framed my face with his forearms and kissed me, gently at first, then deeper. Hands trembling, I fumbled for the button on his jeans.

"Whoa," North said, pulling away from me. I met his gaze and brought my hands back to the button, tugging it loose. "Rory—" he began.

"We could die tonight," I said softly.

"We're not going to—"

I cut him off. "And if we do, I don't want to regret not having done this." I slid the zipper down and felt a stirring behind the blue plaid fabric of his boxers. He caught my hand in his and held it.

"Rory," he said, softer now. "I want this. I want you. So much I can't even breathe sometimes thinking about it." He intertwined his fingers with mine. "But not like this. Not because you're afraid. Fear not, remember?"

"Fear not," I whispered, tears pooling in my eyes. North leaned down again to kiss me once more, with so much tenderness, it took my breath away. For a moment time seemed to expand and stand still until I could almost believe that the kiss would never end. My chest ached when he finally pulled away.

"To be continued," he said, sitting back on his heels.

I managed a hint of a smile. North stood and helped me to my feet. "So we'll meet back here in an hour or so to pack the bike?" I nodded and pressed my lips to his once more before I left. Every kiss felt precious now.

The sun had dropped behind the trees by the time I made it back to campus. The double doors to the dining hall were propped open and the freezing air carried the sounds and smells of the dinner hour. My stomach growled, but I didn't have time to eat. I had to pack my things and take them to North's so he could load his bike, then come back to campus to shower and change before going to Liam's.

I blinked and felt tears behind my eyelids. Campus was most beautiful at dusk, just after the globe-shaped streetlamps turned on but before it was completely dark, when the sky was its deepest and richest shade of blue. Even with everything I knew about the people who'd built this place and the egomaniacs who were now running it, I wasn't ready to leave. I loved it here. The status, the belonging, the sense that I was destined for something great. It was exactly what Dr. Tarsus had said on the recording. Theden had given me a whole new life. A life I didn't want to lose.

But then again, in a way I'd already lost it, weeks ago, when

I decided to trust the Doubt no matter where it led me.

The courtyard was empty except for a lone figure sitting on the bench closest to Athenian Hall. As I got closer, I realized it was Liam.

"Rory," he said when he saw me, getting to his feet. "Where have you been?"

"Errands," I said vaguely. "Downtown. What's up?"

"Rudd was looking for you." Liam's body was tense, like he was nervous.

"Mr. Rudman? Why?"

"He said they're moving up your initiation." Liam saw my blank look. "He's the Divine Third, Rory. The one in the owl mask."

Rudd was a member of the Few? Not only that, but the third in command. The "Divine Third." Just the title made my skin crawl. The arrogance.

"And Dean Atwater's the Divine First?" I'd already decided he had to be the man behind the serpent mask. Liam's nod just confirmed it.

"He and Rudd and Tarsus are waiting for you in the tomb," he said, glancing around. But the caution was unnecessary. There wasn't a soul in sight. Everyone was at dinner. "I was supposed to wait for you here and take you down there."

"It's happening *now*?" Panic licked at my legs. I'd left the syringe at North's. It couldn't be time for initiation. It wasn't even dark yet.

"That's what Rudd said." Liam looked uncomfortable.

"Liam. What?"

"It's just . . . if they're initiating you, why didn't he tell me to bring our robes?"

Fear shot down my spine. *They know.*

"Shit," I whispered.

"Rory, what's going on? What did you do?"

"I found out some things about the society," I said carefully. I watched for Liam's reaction. There wasn't one. "They're not who you think they are, Liam. They're—"

His arm shot forward to grab my wrist, hard. "There is no 'they,' Rory. Not for me." I snatched my hand back like I'd been stung. He eyed me, his gaze cold and hard now like the stone walls of the tomb, and all at once I understood. To Liam, the Few were "we," not "they." They'd promised him a lifetime of acceptance, the assurance that he would always belong, and that was enough for him. "Look," Liam said then. "If you want to bail, I won't come after you. But they're expecting us in the tomb, and I won't keep them waiting." He got to his feet.

For a moment, maybe two, I let myself believe that I might run. To North, to safety, to my future. But my feet stayed planted. I couldn't run from this. I'd given up that option when I decided to take on the Few. In the distance, the campus bell tower tolled the hour. It was seven o'clock. A full hour before North was expecting me back. He wouldn't even begin to worry until after eight, and it'd take him another fifteen minutes to get to the cemetery. The realization that I might not see him again made every part of me ache. But if I went back to him now, we'd lose whatever shot we had of getting into that server room. My only option was to try to stall them.

For over an hour.

I can't do this, the me part of me whimpered. I waited for the voice to tell me I was wrong, but there was only silence.

Liam had turned and was heading toward the woods. "Wait," I called. "I'm coming with you."

It was only then, after I had made my choice, that the voice finally spoke.

Fear not, for I am with you.

"I'm not afraid," I whispered back, and for a moment it was true.

33

THE SKY WAS NEARLY DARK when we reached the center of the cemetery, the last hint of light fading fast from the horizon. The angel's arm was already reaching toward the sky. They'd left the coffin open for us. The irony didn't escape me. They'd summoned me to a grave.

"Why are you doing this?" Liam asked as we stepped inside the mausoleum. How different it looked now, in this moment, with this boy. The marble etchings were menacing, not beautiful, the space claustrophobic, not cozy.

"They're the Few," I said. "What good would it do to run?" I then forced a laugh. "And it's not like they're gonna kill me because I don't want in." In reality, I was pretty sure that was exactly what they were going to do. From the look on Liam's face, he had his own suspicions about my fate. I could tell he was conflicted about his role in all this. But clearly not conflicted enough to walk away.

"I really liked you, Rory." *Liked*. Past tense. As if I'd already ceased to exist. He nodded toward the coffin. "You go first. Wait for me at the bottom."

"No blindfold?"

He didn't meet my gaze. "Rudd said not to bother."

I swallowed hard, realizing it didn't matter if I knew how to get in if I wasn't ever coming out.

I held the railing tight as I descended the spiral staircase into the dark room below. Liam was right behind me. He reached under the bottom step and pulled out a short metal rod. It looked like a flashlight, but when he punched the button on its base with his thumb, it ignited into real fire. "The altar room is the third chamber," Liam said under his breath. "They'll be in there."

He took my elbow and led me through the only door, a narrow archway into the next room. Square, of course, like the one before it, but bigger, and furnished with plush crimson couches and mahogany end tables, all arranged around a thin, woven rug that formed a curve from one archway to the other. A straight diagonal line would've been more efficient, but the Few preferred mathematical elegance instead. I knew without seeing the rest of it that the curve would become a golden spiral as it wound its way out toward the tunnel.

Halfway across, I heard voices in the next room.

"You should be thanking me." Rudd.

"Thanking you." Dean Atwater.

"Yes," Rudd replied, but he sounded less certain than before. "I solved our problem."

We'd reached the edge of the archway. Liam paused and looked at me. I held up a finger. One minute. He nodded slightly. I could tell he was as curious as I was.

"And how, exactly, did you do that?" the dean asked coolly. "Was it by sleeping with a sixteen-year-old girl?"

Liam's eyes shot to mine, his eyebrows arched like question marks. I quickly shook my head. Not me.

"You thought I didn't know?" the dean asked when Rudd didn't answer. I hadn't heard Tarsus speak yet. Was she even in there? My stomach squeezed at the thought that she might not be. She was my only hope.

"It was an error of judgment on my part," Rudd said finally, weakly.

"Indeed. Which is a problem, you see. Because it suggests there was an error of judgment on *mine.*"

Incomprehensibly, I felt bad for Rudd. He'd miscalculated this.

There was a rustling behind one of the couches to my left. But just as I turned my head toward the noise, Liam's hand gripped my elbow. The dean's talk of poor judgment had reminded him whose side he was on, I guessed. With a jerk, he pulled me through the arched door.

"But if it weren't for my relationship with her, we wouldn't know about Rory," Rudd was saying as we stepped into the room. He was defensive now. Pleading his case. All at once I knew who Rudd had been sleeping with. Hershey's mystery boy wasn't a boy after all.

"And what about what *she* knows?"

"She doesn't know anything. Not that it matters anyway. After they commit her—"

I stumbled a little, and three heads turned toward us. Dr. Tarsus was there after all. Unlike the first two rooms, this one was lit with mounted torches that cast a menacing glow on the three figures in its center. They stood apart from one another, in a triangle, the alliances unclear. Liam seemed unsure of who to approach. He'd gotten his orders from Rudd, but it was obvious who was in charge.

"Liam," Rudd said, gesturing for him.

Liam hesitated then headed for the dean. The old man looked at me, not my escort. "Thank you, Liam," he said, his eyes on mine. "You can return to your dorm."

Liam's hand was still on my arm, so I felt his surprise. He dropped my elbow like it was hot. "Yes, sir." Without so much as a glance in my direction, he turned and left.

The dean was still staring at me. There were only a few feet between us, and his gaze felt hot, like a spotlight. Beads of sweat sprung up on my lips and hairline.

"Hello, Aurora," Dean Atwater said. Revulsion ripped through me when he spoke my name. I despised him in that moment, with such intensity that I thought my skin might catch fire. I managed a confused smile.

"What's going on?" I asked.

"That's what we'd like to know," the dean replied. His free hand was in his jacket pocket, as if he were holding something there. Something like a gun. The cold sweat at my hairline began to slide down my forehead.

I gave my head a tiny shake. More confusion. Another smile. I glanced back at Dr. Tarsus. In the flickering light, her ebony irises were inky and opaque and completely inscrutable. "I don't understand. I thought— Liam told me you'd decided to move up my initiation."

"So you're ready to take your vows then?" the dean asked.

"Of course," I said smoothly. "I just have some questions first."

The dean looked amused. "*You* have questions." He pulled his hand from his pocket. The thing he held looked like a gun, but not like one I'd ever seen before. There was a vial of blue liquid where the barrel would be. "I think you're confused, Aurora, about who owes who an explanation." He tightened his grip on the trigger.

"I'll answer whatever questions you want," I said, stalling. "I just want to know what happened to my mom."

"From what I understand, your mother died of a blood clot," Dean Atwater said coolly. "A common complication after a cesarean section." Fury shot through me.

"I've seen the death certificate," I shot back, too angry now to be afraid. "I want the truth. Was it nanobots? Did you kill her the same way you killed Griffin?"

The dean's eyebrows shot up.

"Yes, I know about Griffin," I said, as smoothly as I could. "His death I understand. He was the CEO of Gnosis. You couldn't let him destroy what the Few had built. But my mom was a high school girl. How was she even a threat?"

"She wasn't," Dean Atwater spat, as cold as ice. "Even if she'd gone public with what she thought she knew, no one would've believed her." His lips twitched into a smile. "Not with her medical history."

"So why kill her?"

He sighed. "Because she was an inconvenience, Aurora. Because she'd gotten in the way."

The tears sprung to my eyes without my permission. I tried to blink them back, but it was too late. I knew he'd seen them. I fought to keep my composure. He saw that, too.

"Yes, it was nanobots that did it," he said, baiting me now. "They came in through an IV bag, into her veins, making it very difficult to predict how the clot would travel through her body. It was luck, really, that it worked as well as it did."

Luck. I wanted to rip his eyeballs out. But I knew it was exactly the reaction he was fishing for. I wouldn't give him the satisfaction. I kept my gaze steady.

He went on. "These days, our solution is more elegant," he said, raising his gun. "We use straightjackets and padded rooms."

A shiver shot down my spine, but I didn't flinch. "So whatever's in that dart . . . it'll make me crazy?"

"No, your brain will do that all on its own," Dean Atwater replied with a sick smile. "Once these nanobots reach your temporal lobe and begin their cacophony. Roars. Explosions. Screams. It'll be the sleep deprivation that ultimately gets you, but we'll make sure you're institutionalized long before that."

"You're acting like we've already made our decision" came Dr. Tarsus's voice. I heard the sharp click of her heels on stone then felt her beside me. "It seems to me, Robert, that we ought to give our initiate the benefit of the doubt."

"The *benefit* of the *doubt*," the dean repeated. "What exactly is the *benefit* of doubt, Esperanza? There's certainly no benefit to *the* Doubt, which is what we're really talking about here, isn't it?"

"It's Kyle's word against hers," Tarsus replied. She took a step forward so she was a few inches in front of me now. She was standing on her toes, I noticed, like a cat preparing to pounce. "We have no evidence that she's afflicted." *Afflicted.* Like the Doubt was a curse.

"Are you kidding me?" came Rudd's voice behind me. "It's so obvious. I hope neither of you are buying this little act."

"It's not an act," I said, as convincingly as I could. "I'm not my mother."

"Is that so?" said the dean.

"Don't be a fool, Robert," Rudd said derisively.

The dean's eyes snapped past me to Rudd. "Leave. Now."

"But I—"

"Now," he bellowed. Rudd stormed to the door.

"So you don't hear it?" the dean asked me when Rudd was gone, his finger tight against the trigger. "You don't hear the Doubt?"

It was one word. *No.* But I couldn't say it. So I hesitated.

He didn't. He pulled the trigger.

I heard a click and then the snap and suddenly I was on my knees and Dr. Tarsus was where I had just been standing, a dart sticking out of her left shoulder.

"Esperanza!" I heard Dean Atwater gasp. He stared at the gun in his hands then at her, his mouth hanging open.

"Rory," Dr. Tarsus said calmly. "I need you to listen to me." My head swiveled toward her. She grabbed hold of the dart with her opposite hand and yanked it out. "I am allergic to gelatin, the main component of the suspension serum used in this dart. It's only a matter of time before my throat will start to close up." Her tone was matter-of-fact. "I don't know what you're planning, but—"

"What *she's* planning," the dean said coldly, spinning the chamber of his gun to load another dart, "is less than irrelevant right now." He'd regained his composure, the shock and dismay of the previous moment gone from his face. Behind him, something moved in the shadows. Some*one*. He had a black ski mask covering his face and our syringe in his hand. My breath hitched in my throat when I realized it was North. How did he find me?

"Rory," I heard Tarsus say. "I don't have much time."

Something inside me gave way. "You're a monster!" I screamed at the dean, getting to my feet. The old man *laughed*.

"And you're a foolish little girl," he said, pointing his gun at my neck. "Just like your—"

North grabbed his arm and twisted it behind his back.

Dean Atwater screamed and I heard a bone snap. Gritting his teeth like an animal, North drove the needle so deep into the dean's neck, I thought the entire syringe might disappear into his skin. I heard footsteps then Rudd burst back into the room. It took him a few seconds to piece together what had happened. A few seconds too long. There was a crack and then a groan and then his body was crumpling forward to the ground.

Hershey stood behind him with an unlit torch, her eyes wild and reckless, black streaks of mascara like war paint on her face.

"Asshole," she spat, and let the torch fall.

He was still breathing, but Rudd was out cold. She kicked him angrily with her boot.

"Hershey!" I cried, rushing toward her. "Are you okay?"

"I am now. What's happening to him?" She was glaring at the dean, who North had pinned on the ground. The old man was blinking rapidly, trying to stay awake.

"He's falling asleep," I told her.

"You're letting him *live*?"

"We can't kill him, Hersh."

Hershey crossed her arms. "Why not?"

"Because," North said, getting to his feet. "If we kill him, he wins."

Hershey's eyes flicked to Dr. Tarsus, who was kneeling at Dean Atwater's ankles, untying the laces of his navy oxfords. "What about her? Why is she still conscious?"

"She's on our side," I said. "She's always been on our side.

I'll explain when we get out of here." *When.* Thirty seconds ago it was *if*.

I knelt by Dr. Tarsus. She was wrapping a shoelace tightly around the dean's ankles. "Your EpiPen. Where is it?" I asked.

She laid her palm on my cheek and smiled. The skin around her eyes had started to swell. "I used it last night."

Tears rushed to my eyes. She'd used it on me.

"There's no time for that now," she commanded, grabbing the dean's wrists and pulling them behind his back. His dry, papery flesh slid like snakeskin as she pushed up his sleeves. "We have work to do."

I hurried over to where Rudd lay. North had him on his stomach already and was wrapping up his ankles. He handed me a shoelace, and I went to work on his wrists. Rudd moaned a little as I pulled the rope tight, cutting into his skin, drawing blood.

"God, I'm glad you're okay," North said breathlessly.

"How'd you find me?"

"Your necklace," he said, nodding at the dove. "I put a tracking device inside it. And a camera." He managed a smile. "I didn't want you doing anything crazy without my knowing about it." My limbs were limp with gratitude. For him, for Dr. Tarsus, for the inexplicable fact that I was still okay. "So did you bring Hershey in with you?"

"No, she—"

"I followed Kyle in," Hershey said softly. The bravado of the previous moment was gone. She was staring at Rudd's motionless body, tears welling up in her eyes, which were no longer hateful and fearless but sad. She looked so young standing there. Like a lost child. I stood and pulled her into my arms.

"What happened?" I asked.

"I'd been using his skeleton key," she said miserably. "While he was asleep. That's how I got you all that stuff. I thought all the faculty had them. I didn't know he—" Her voice broke. "He caught me with it this morning, and I told him the truth—that we were trying to take down the assholes that had your mom killed. I thought he could help us. I thought—" Her tears spilled over. "He called the *psych ward* on me, Rory. He said he was getting me a cab, but I saw him dial the number—the same one they gave us the first day of school." She pulled away from me and swatted angrily at her eyes. "I'm such an idiot. He told me he loved me. And I believed him."

"Are we doing this?" Dr. Tarsus called. She was wheezing a little now and clutching her right arm like it hurt. Without waiting for a response, she stepped out of her suede pumps and headed toward the darkness of the tunnel.

"Doing what?" Hershey asked.

"The less you know the better," I told her. "You should go back the way you came. Wait for us at North's apartment." I expected her to argue with me, or to demand details, but she just nodded. North handed her his key ring.

"Be careful," she whispered, her lip trembling a little.

"We'll be back in a couple of hours," I assured her as North went for one of the torches. I prayed that I was right.

34

DR. TARSUS DIED ABOUT TEN YARDS from the Gnosis data center. Her arm had quickly swollen to twice its size and we could tell it hurt, a lot, but she didn't complain about it once, not even when her skin started to turn blue. When she started coughing, I started crying. I knew it wasn't fair that I should be crying when she was the one dying, but it literally felt like my heart was breaking apart in my chest. I hadn't let the thought fully register, but when I'd listened to the audio recording she'd given me, I'd had this sense that maybe, in some messed-up way, she could become the mother figure I'd never had. Yes, I'd hated her almost the entire time I'd known her, but everything she'd done, she'd done for me. I was no expert on motherhood, but that seemed like the essence of it to me.

We'd just come around the last curve of the spiral when she fell against the wall. She looked at North first. "I'm not going to make it there," she said. Her words were labored, but her tone was matter-of-fact. "You'll have to use a recording. I don't know if it'll work, but it's worth a try." She eased herself down the wall until she was sitting, knock-kneed like a little girl. I knelt beside her and took her hand as North fumbled for his iPhone.

She turned to me and smiled. "Your mom would be so proud of you, Aurora." She spoke slowly, her chest heaving from the effort. "Just promise me— Promise me that when you leave, you won't ever look back."

"I love you" came out instead of "I promise." Laying her hand on my knee, she managed a weak smile.

"I love you too."

"Whenever you're ready," North said gently, his thumb hovering over the record button. His voice sounded funny, as if his throat were as knotted as mine. Dr. Tarsus nodded. North hit record.

"Free to fall," she said hoarsely, a shallow breath between every word. Her eyes fluttered shut and she shook her head. "I'll try again," she said, wheezing, and tried to inhale. "Free. To. Fall."

My heart sank. I had very little experience with voice recognition software, but I suspected the voice would need to at least sound like the person it was supposed to belong to. *Try again,* I begged her silently. A few moments passed. What little breath she had was rattling in her chest.

I took her hand and squeezed it. Her lips formed the word *go.* Soundless, but as commanding as her voice had ever been.

We both knew I had no other choice. As I knelt and kissed her cheek, the tears I'd been holding back spilled over, dampening her face. "Thank you," I whispered. "For everything." She smiled, the sweat on her face glistening in the flicker of North's torch. Then her face went slack and she was gone.

Neither North nor I spoke as we made our way to the stone wall.

"Don't use your fingers," he said when the stone facade retracted, bathing us in fluorescent light. "Fingerprints."

I nodded and touched the glass with the knuckle of my thumb. The screen lit up with twelve boxes again, but the first four numbers were different this time.

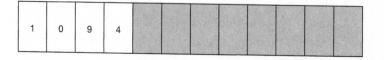

I'd written the first fifty numbers in the Fibonacci sequence on the inside of my forearm in preparation for this moment— North's idea—and 10,946 was the twenty-third number on the list, which meant that the next eight digits were 6, 1, 7, 7, 1, 1, 2, 8. I typed them as fast I could.

As soon as my knuckle hit the eight, the glass door slid open with a whoosh of warm air, just like in my simulation. I followed North inside the small chamber. A few seconds later the glass slid shut and the stone facade retracted back into place, concealing us. He pulled out his phone and stepped up to the microphone.

"You think it'll work?" I asked him.

"Maybe," he said, but he sounded doubtful. He tried the first recording first. I knew before I heard the words *access denied* that we were screwed. Not even I would've recognized her voice if I hadn't heard her record it. The second recording was even worse.

"Damn it," I whispered, and squeezed my eyes shut. I waited for the Doubt to give me guidance, but I heard Dr. Tarsus's voice instead.

Sufficient to have stood, though free to fall.

My eyes sprung open. "North," I said urgently. "The audio recording—the one Tarsus made—it's still on your phone, right?"

"Yeah, why?"

"She said free to fall. In the recording. Toward the beginning, I think."

North was already pulling up the file. He nudged the track bar to the right and pressed play. Dr. Tarsus's voice—her regular, healthy voice—filled the small chamber.

"It's right after that," I told him, and he bumped the slider forward.

"It's how we're made I suppose" came her voice through the tiny speaker. *"How did Milton put it? 'Sufficient to have stood, though free to fall.' The choice was ours, and we chose ourselves."*

North slid the track bar back and lifted his phone back up to the mic. As he held down the record button, I held my breath. It sounded just like her, but was the intonation right?

Please let it work, I prayed.

"Look," North said suddenly, pointing at the control panel I'd seen in my simulation. One by one, the green lights were turning red. "That's a security panel. Each of those lights is connected to a camera. I think they're going offline." A few seconds later there was a loud clang as steel slid against steel and the vault door disengaged.

We were in.

Part of me was still expecting to see workers inside, doing their thing, but North was right. The massive blue-lit space was completely empty. And loud. And *freezing.* I closed the door behind us, but not all the way. I had no idea how it opened from the inside, if at all.

North was tugging on a pair of gloves. They were thin, with rubber pads on the fingertips. "Hacker hands," he explained, yelling over the hum of the machines. "No prints." Seeing the gloves reminded me that this moment, or some version of it anyway, had always been part of our plan. But instead of reassuring me, it only emphasized how far we'd veered off course. I blinked quickly, afraid of what I'd see behind my eyelids if they stayed shut too long.

"I thought the servers didn't go offline until midnight," I said as I followed him between rows of servers toward the terminal. The floor beneath us was made out of some sort of metal mesh. I could see smooth gray concrete several feet beneath it.

"They don't," North replied, touching the keyboard in front of the terminal to light up its three screens. "Which makes it harder, but not impossible, to hide our tracks." The screens were locked, with a login box at the center of each one.

"Now what?" I started to ask, but North had already bypassed the login screen. He was typing at lightning speed, not glancing at his fingers once as lines and lines of computer code appeared on screen. His eyes kept darting from screen to screen as he opened and closed about a thousand different windows. Hunting for the Lux program code. What if he couldn't find it?

I started to pace.

"Rory," I heard North say.

"What?"

"Stop pacing. It's stressing me out."

I sat down on the grated metal floor behind him. "I just feel so useless right now. What can I do to help?"

Without taking his eyes off the screens in front of him, he reached into his back pocket and handed me his iPhone. "Find us some good music."

Hours passed as the music played. North hummed a little as he worked. I was quiet, watching the back of him, waiting for the *click click click*ing of fingers on keys to go quiet. Finally it did. It was after eleven.

"Rory," he said urgently. I was tracing the squares of grating beneath me with my fingertips. "I'm in the algorithm. I need you to check my work to make sure I got the changes right."

I scrambled to my feet. There was a string of words and

symbols in a box on the center screen. "Uh. I have no idea what any of that means."

"I know that," North said, sounding testy. I looked at him then and saw how tired he was.

"What can I do?" I said.

"Read it out loud," he told me, closing his eyes. "My eyes are swimming, I can't even see it anymore. Just read exactly what you see."

He kept his eyes closed the entire time I read it, his brow furrowed tight. When I got to the end, the muscles in his face went slack.

"North?"

Several seconds passed. My heart sank to my knees. I said his name again, quieter this time, almost a whisper.

"There was a fifteen-minute period about an hour ago when I was convinced it couldn't be done," he said with his eyes shut. "The algorithm was too nuanced to just do a one-to-one exchange of the inputs, not without driving people's cars into one another or risking mass suicide." *Mass suicide.* At the whim of an algorithm, no less. I pictured that dopey smile on Beck's face as he interacted with Lux and shuddered. "I couldn't see a way around it," North said. "I was ready to give up." He opened his eyes finally and looked at me.

"But?"

"But then I heard the voice. 'It's there' was all it said." He shook his head in amazement. "And at that moment, I saw it. A very slight variation in the way the algorithm treated certain categories of threats. And I realized if I could isolate these categories and come up with a way to treat them as a sort of preferred opportunity, a trump card almost, I could essentially override the formula instead of just reversing it. It meant I had to create an additional command string within the algorithm, which made the whole thing about nine thousand times harder, but I think it'll work."

I wrapped my arms around his neck and climbed into his chair, sliding my knees in next to his hips. He laid his hands on my thighs, sending a ripple up my spine. "You," I said, "are a genius."

He let me kiss him, but then he pulled back and shook his head. "No. I can't take credit for this. If it were up to me, I would've given up."

I started to argue with him but thought better of it. The Few needed the credit for their victories. The boy I loved didn't. That's why I loved him.

"So can we get out of here now?" I asked.

"Almost," North said. "I just have to copy all these changes to the versioned control system and deploy the code to the servers, then wait for Gnosis to initiate the reboot." I glanced at the clock on his screen. It was 11:53.

"Is seven minutes enough time to do whatever you need to do?" I asked.

"Should be," North said. "Then, once the system reboots, I'll run a script to hide my tracks and deploy the worm. *Then* we can get out of here."

"The worm?"

"It's our diversion," North explained. "In case someone at Gnosis figures out that we were inside the network. They'll see the worm and think they got us."

"So crafty. Did the voice tell you to do that, too?"

North grinned and kissed my nose. "Nah. That one was mostly me."

He leaned around me to type on the touchpad on the desk. I kept my eyes on his face, watching him work. All the fatigue I'd seen before had vanished.

I nuzzled his ear with my nose. "You're amazing," I whispered, and went to kiss his cheek.

"Shit," he said, his whole body tensing.

I jerked back. "What?"

"I tripped an alarm," he said, cursing under his breath. He was typing furiously.

"What kind of alarm?" I asked as I tried to slide off his lap without touching either of his arms. My heart was pounding in my chest and my legs felt like jelly beneath me. At what point did we run?

"I don't know."

I looked at the center screen. At first I thought it was strings of computer code, but then I realized that it was rows of Greek characters. "Wait," I told North, touching his arm. "I think it's a riddle."

"A *riddle*?"

"Yes," I said, not as certain as I sounded. "Just give it a

second." Just as North lifted his fingers from the touchpad, six lines at the center of the screen morphed into English.

I formd them free, and free they must remain,
Till they enthrall themselves; I else must change
Thir nature, and revoke the high decree
Unchangeable, eternal, which ordain'd
Thir freedom, they themselves ordain'd thir fall.

PRESS THE NECESSARY KEY TO PROCEED.

In my peripheral vision, I saw North's eyes go wide with surprise. "These are lines from *Paradise Lost*. The ones your mom left you." He looked over at me. "The Greek, that's how you knew what it was?"

I nodded. "Not what it said, just that it was a puzzle. The ones we had to answer during the evaluation process, they all started as red Greek text. But those were—" I was about to say *timed*, but right then my eyes caught the little clock at the bottom right corner of the screen, racing down from sixty. One minute. That's all we had. "Hurry," I said urgently. "We have only sixty seconds."

"Rory, there's no way I can crack the code that fast."

"So we'll solve it. 'Press the necessary key to proceed.' The answer has to be in the quotation. That's why it's there."

For several seconds we were quiet, both of us just staring at the screen. "Rory, there are one hundred and one keys on this keyboard," North said finally, tugging on his Mohawk in frustration. "And we've got thirty-two seconds left. I don't think—"

"Could it be the letter *e*?" I asked. "There are a bunch of them missing. Formd, thir. Maybe we're supposed to complete the words."

North shook his head. "I don't think so. Milton wrote those words without the *e*'s. That's how they look in the original."

"Okay, so it's got to be something in the meaning, then. What does—?"

With a start, North bolted upright in his chair. "Milton is talking about man's imprisonment here," he said excitedly. "So the 'necessary' key is the *escape* key."

I considered this. It made sense. And it was clever, which made me think it had to be right. North's finger was hovering over the ESC key, waiting for my cue. There were only twenty seconds left. Heart racing, I squeezed my eyes shut. It was time to decide.

Free they must remain. Suddenly I remembered what the serpent had said during initiation. *The fool will always seek a master.*

"No," I said abruptly, my eyes popping open. "There's nothing to escape from. That was Milton's whole point, right? 'Till they enthrall themselves.' It's only a trap if we let it be. To proceed, all we need to do is *enter*."

North didn't hesitate or question me. He hit the enter key and instantly, all the words disappeared. All but one.

PROCEED.

Almost immediately, a new window opened and the words COMMAND _ COMPLETED appeared on screen.

"Thank you," I heard North murmur as his body went slack against the chair. He looked back at me. "I thought we were screwed."

"But we're not?" I asked, just to make sure.

"Not so far," he said, laying his forehead on my stomach. "Now we wait."

I stared at the clock at the bottom of the screen as it ticked from 11:58 to 11:59 to 12:00. When nothing happened, I tapped North's head.

"It's midnight," I told him. "Nothing's happening."

"It could take a couple of minutes," North said, his voice muffled against my sweatshirt. "Someone at Gnosis has to initiate the reboot, and he'll want to be sure everyone is logged out of the internal network before he does."

"And the new algorithm will go into effect when the servers come back on?" I asked him.

"It should." He sat back in his chair. "Although I'm not sure how the solar storm will affect Lux generally. But as long as the app is working, the algorithm should too."

"And what about us? Will we be okay?"

"Oh, we'll be fine," he said, pulling me back down into his lap. "We'll hole up in my apartment and play battery-operated electronics and eat cold SpaghettiOs from the can."

At 12:02, there was a wave of *whew* sounds as the rows

and rows of machines around us began to power down. The terminal was the last to shut off, and when it did, the room was completely quiet. The emergency lights gave the room an eerie green glow.

"What happens if someone comes down here?" I whispered.

North didn't look up. "We run."

But no one came. A few minutes later the servers turned back on again in a ripple of beeps and whirls. After the quiet, the noise was unnerving. I felt uneasy now.

A loud clang behind me made me jerk so violently, North's head snapped back. "What was that?" I whispered.

"I don't know," North said, sounding as concerned as I felt. He spun in his chair and we both saw it. A wall where the society's secret door had been.

"It must be programmed to close on restart," North said, sounding sick.

I didn't respond. *We're trapped,* I told myself, because clearly my brain wasn't grasping it. If it were, I'd be freaking out, and I was just sitting there, completely still, staring at the wall. You couldn't tell there'd ever been a door there.

"Rory?" I heard North say.

"There has to be a way to get aboveground from here," I said calmly. So calmly, it caught me by surprise. But my mom hadn't let me down yet, and she'd sewn *two* orange Xs on my blanket. There had to be another way out.

"All I see are elevators," North replied. "Two Gnosis elevators

447

that require key card access. But the door we came through, it has to open from the inside, right?" His voice sounded tight. Panicky.

"I don't know," I said honestly. "I'm not sure the Few would risk someone discovering a way to open it. But I don't think we're stuck. I think there's a way to get from this room all the way outside." I pointed at the terminal screen. "You finish what you need to do. I'll get us out of here."

North looked skeptical, but he nodded and brought his eyes back to his screen, which was now lit up with the Gnosis login box.

I jogged around the periphery of the room first. The two elevators North saw and an alarmed door marked EMERGENCY EXIT were the only visible ways out. There wasn't even a bathroom down here. I scanned the ceiling next, but it was ridiculously high up, so even if there'd been an opening, we never could've reached it. If there was a way out of here, it had to be in the floor. Starting at the opposite corner of the room, at least a football field from where North was sitting, I went row by row, combing the cement beneath the mesh grating. All I saw was smooth concrete. My stomach twisted in knots. Had I been wrong?

I waited for words of comfort, some assurance from the voice that there was a way out. But I didn't get any. I *hadn't* gotten any, not since we hatched this plan. Not once had the voice promised me that we'd get away with this.

I looked up again, and this time my eyes caught the security camera mounted on the wall to my left. I froze.

Oh, my God. The cameras. If the reboot reset the door, it probably turned the cameras back on too. I opened my mouth to scream North's name but quickly shut it and went sprinting toward him with my head down instead.

I was halfway there when the toe of my shoe caught the grating and I went flying. My hands hit the ground first, hard, metal digging into flesh, and my knees banged down right after. My eyes smarted with the pain, but I quickly forgot it when I saw what was beneath me. A round manhole cover in the concrete with the letters έξοδος engraved into its face. I didn't know what the letters meant, but I was pretty sure manhole covers didn't come standard with Greek engraving. My eyes swept the floor, looking for a way to get beneath the grating. It was lined up against the bottom edge of a nearby server bank, so I almost missed it. A latch.

I scrambled to my feet and went running toward North. Without saying anything, I pulled his hoodie up over his head. "The cameras," I whispered in his ears. His whole body went rigid. At that exact moment, the speakers above and around us began to scream with a shrill, piercing sound. We'd been seen.

"I found a way out," I said, my lips pressed to North's ear, and tugged on his arm.

"Wait," he said. "I can delete the footage. I need to delete the footage."

My nails dug into his forearm. "There's no time."

"The Gnosis complex is six miles away," he said, already

typing. A flurry of windows opened and closed as he flew through the network. "Even if there's an underground train between here and there, it'll take them at least five minutes to get here. I can do this in sixty seconds. I saw the feed earlier. I know where it is." The sweat on his brow was back, but he was determined. I stared at the two elevator doors, my heart pounding so hard my ribs ached. "Done," North said finally, pushing back his chair so hard it went flying.

I took off toward the manhole, North right on my heels. The latch did exactly what I thought it would, freeing a portion of the grate, which lifted like a cellar door. Once beneath it, we relatched the grate and, on our hands and knees, started twisting the manhole with our fingers in the pick holes. It turned easily. Moving it was harder. It must've weighed fifty pounds, and on all fours it was difficult to get enough leverage to lift it, especially with the alarm screaming in our ears.

We'd just gotten it to the side when we heard the elevator doors whoosh open. *Go,* North mouthed, and pointed down the hole. I peered into the blackness. It was impossible to tell how far down it was, but since there was no ladder, I figured it couldn't be that far. So I eased my legs into the opening then slid around onto my belly and lowered the rest of my body down until I was hanging just by my hands. When my face passed beneath the floor, I was hit with the stench of rotten eggs and a terrible fear that I'd made a mistake. "Please," I murmured, kicking off my left shoe with my right foot. *Please don't let me break my neck, please let this work, please don't let them find us.*

When I heard the shoe hit rock a second later, I let go.

I kept my knees bent, so when my feet landed, the impact pitched me forward, onto my hands. The ground was rough and prickly beneath me, like coarse stone. I couldn't have been more than fifteen feet down, but the light from above did little to illuminate the dank space. I heard shouting and running above me and a sliding sound as North tried to move the manhole cover back into place before he dropped down. He had his fingers through the pick holes and was trying to heave the metal disk over as he dangled from it, his feet just above my head. With a jarring clang it slipped into place, leaving us in complete darkness. North landed with a soft thud beside me.

"Do you think they saw you?" I asked him.

"Let's not wait to find out," North replied. His face lit up as he turned on his phone's flashlight. He revolved slowly with his hand extended, the weak beam revealing the smallness of the space we were in. The stone walls shimmered in the light, as if they were flecked with gold and might have been beautiful had their presence not meant that we were trapped. I felt a pressing, suffocating weight pushing in on me. The opening we'd come through was now sealed with a heavy metal plate. Even if I stood on North's shoulders, I wouldn't be able to reach it, and even if I could, I wouldn't be able to lift it enough to slide it over.

"Rory," I heard North say. "There's an opening over there. It's narrow, but it looks like it was made to pass through." I followed his light and saw a slit carved in the rock behind me, almost hidden in a shadow. "Let's go," he said, and took my hand.

The ground slanted down on the other side of the slit, taking us farther into the earth instead of toward the surface. The passageway was tight, the walls on either side grazing North's shoulders as we walked, and the ceiling was too low to stand up straight. As we inched down the rocky slant, crouched so as not to bang our heads, I focused on my breath, refusing to panic again. If we really were stuck down there, there would be plenty of time to freak out once we were sure of it. The sulfur egg smell got worse as we descended. "What is that?" I asked, pulling my shirt up over my nose.

"I don't know," North replied. "But I'm really glad we didn't eat before this."

A few minutes later we reached flat surface again. A room, bigger than the first one, but with a lower ceiling. North could stand upright, but only barely. The walls around us were textured and uneven and looked bronze when North shone the light on them. There was only one way forward, another tunnel, this one rounder and more uneven, as if it'd been there longer. As we moved toward it, North's light caught some writing on the wall. It was a drawing, crudely done, of a mine cart moving toward a tunnel. Seeing the image, it clicked. We were in the old pyrite mine. The shimmer in the walls wasn't gold but its cheap impostor. It was ironic, or maybe just fitting, that the Few had commandeered this space for their empire. They'd built their castle on a foundation of fool's gold.

I followed North into the tunnel. This one sloped up and was even more slippery than the first, rock sliding on rock. More than once I lost my balance and landed on my hands. It was tempting to take off my shoes. Bare feet had to be better than no-traction Toms. But there was no way to know what I might step on, and so I left them on. When it got steep, North stopped to let me pass him, and somehow it was easier to stay balanced knowing that he was there to catch me if I fell.

We'd been climbing for a while when North's phone made the sound I'd been dreading. The low battery whimper. We didn't acknowledge it between us. We just kept climbing, shoes and hands on rock the only sound in the silence. There was no use saying what we both were thinking. If this was a dead end, we were done.

I slipped again, and this time the rock was wet beneath my hands. "There's water on the rocks," I said over my shoulder to North. I could feel him right on my heels. "It has to be coming from somewhere aboveground, right?"

"You'd think," North said, his voice laced with the hope I felt. We kept climbing.

When the ground leveled out again, North caught my arm. "Wait," he cautioned. "There could be a drop-off." He shone his light on the floor and around us. My heart sank when I saw the solid walls. The tunnel we'd come through was the only way out.

I wanted to scream. I wanted to curse the voice that had told me not to be afraid when it knew this is where we'd end up. But right behind my anger was the realization that this was exactly the moment that voice had been trying to prepare me for. *Fear not for I am with you.* Not as some amulet to protect me from all harm, but as a refuge when there was nowhere left to turn.

You did what you came to do, whispered the voice. And instead of anger, instead of fear, I felt peace.

North was at the wall, combing the surface with his light. "Hey, come look at this," he called. It was another drawing, etched in black in the shimmery stone. It was simple, just a circle and three lines, but it was so clearly the shape of a dove. I reached out my hand to touch it, moved beyond words by its presence. *What was it doing here? Why a dove?* It felt like a sign. A gift.

As I traced its simple shape with my fingertip, North's phone finally went dead. Neither of us reacted. We'd been expecting it, after all. And for me, it was a relief not to be waiting anymore, dreading the moment the light would go out. Now that it had, we could get on with it.

North reached for me in the darkness, pulling me to him. His hands slid up my arms to my face, and though I couldn't see him at all, in a weird way, I could. Not with my eyes, but with my memory, which felt more real somehow. More true. When he kissed me, I forgot everything else. The darkness, the stench, my thirst. Our fate. All I could feel were his lips on my lips, his body pressed against mine. All I could smell were his skin and his citrusy shampoo. All I could hear was his breath, and mine, hot and fast as we clung to each other, each wanting more of the other.

Then, out of nowhere, there was a cracking sound above us, so loud I thought the earth was breaking apart. We froze.

"Was that—?"

"Thunder," North said.

My hand flew to the place where the dove was. All at once I understood why it was there.

"The miners," I said breathlessly. "The ones who were trapped in the mine. They were *here.*"

"What? How do you know?"

"I saw it on Panopticon. The care packages the rescue workers sent down here, they were called doves. The hole they used was eventually widened to get the miners out."

The thunder boomed again, even louder this time.

"The opening is above us," I said. "We didn't see it before because we never looked up." I tilted my head back.

A raindrop hit my cheek.

I didn't react, not right away. I waited for another one, and another, until the rain was spraying my face, and then I laughed.

"What is it?" North asked.

"It's raining," I said, pulling him into the icy spray.

"It's raining," he said, astonished. Then he laughed too.

It took us a couple of tries to get me up on his shoulders, but when we did, it was easy for me to feel the opening in the rock. It was a perfect, smooth circle, as wide as the manhole we'd come through. And a few inches into it, there was the frayed end of a rope.

35

"IT'S PRETTY EERIE, ISN'T IT?"

I'd been sitting on the balcony outside his apartment—
our apartment, North kept correcting me—for hours, staring
out at the forest of dark buildings. The utility companies had
turned off the power grid at three o'clock, as soon as something called a "coronal mass ejection" left the sun's surface
and started hurtling toward ours. The geostorm was officially
under way. They were expecting the huge mass of solar plasma
to slam into Earth's atmosphere a little after one a.m. It was
12:30 now.

The past twenty-two hours had been a total blur. The
opening we found in the mine brought us up through a stone
well and into the woods, about twenty yards from the electric
fence around the Enfield Reservoir. If I hadn't known better,
I would've thought it was as old as it was made to look. There
wasn't a sign commemorating the mine rescue that was accom-
plished there, or anything at all to suggest that the hole inside

it led to anything. Which, I suppose, was the point. It was the Few's escape route. Their secret way out.

Hershey had been waiting for us at North's apartment, shaken, but mostly okay. We tried to convince her to come with us to New York, to leave Rudd and Theden behind, but she wanted to stay.

It was harder than I thought it'd be to say good-bye to her. Our relationship would always be complicated, but she was part of me somehow. Part of who I'd become. We clung to each other in the alley behind North's apartment for a long time. When we finally let go, our shoulders were drenched in tears.

North and I crossed over the RFK Bridge a little after six a.m., just as the sun was rising over the East River. His apartment was on 47th Street, right in Times Square. After a greasy breakfast at the diner around the corner, we went upstairs and slept, North's body curled around the back of mine, like two commas. The sun was setting when we woke up, still in our clothes. North reached over and twirled my hair. Looking at him, feeling the heel of his hand on my cheek, the hollow feeling inside of me began to recede. We were okay. We were more than okay. We were free.

We'd eaten SpaghettiOs, like he'd promised, for dinner, straight from the can, and now I was here, on the balcony, looking out at the dark city. Blackout blinds hung on the sliding glass door behind me to block out the neon lights, but tonight we wouldn't need them. None of the billboards were lit. There wasn't much of a moon, either. Just a faint yellow sliver. There were stars, though, a thick blanket of them in the cloudless black sky. I wondered how often people in Manhattan got to see stars. As often as people in Seattle, I imagined, which was pretty much never. Too much light pollution. There wasn't any of that tonight. The entire East Coast was blacked out.

There were people on the sidewalk below me, gazing up at the stars. I could tell by how frequently they were checking the bright rectangles of light on their wrists that Lux had brought them outside. Starry nights. The cosmos. The type of experience Lux was designed to steer them away from. Not tonight.

It appeared our algorithm was doing exactly what it was supposed to. Leading people into their "threats" instead of away from them. Lux's erratic behavior was all anyone was talking about. We'd slept through it, but the app had been busy causing chaos all day. Traffic jams, long lines, people leaving work in the middle of the day. People skipping work altogether. Gnosis was claiming the problems were a result of GPS interference from the solar wind, and they were urging people to stop using the app until the satellites were back online after the storm. Lux users were cheerfully ignoring this advice. The nanobots in their brains were making them trust the app more than its makers, even as they were driving miles off course and walking out of conference rooms mid-meeting. It'd be funny, if it weren't so sad.

Not everyone was listening to Lux, though. North said there was some chatter online about people "de-Luxing"—

uninstalling the app from their phones—and those who were doing it were using hash tags like "guided" and "led." It wasn't exactly a movement yet, but #deLux was trending on Forum and all the major news sources were covering Lux's mistakes. There was no way to know how long it'd take Gnosis to detect the changes we'd made to their algorithm. I just hoped it was long enough to snap Beck out of his nanobot-induced stupor. How many sunsets would it take to remind him what was true?

The radio was on inside. I could hear the voice of Gnosis's new CEO, a man who was failing badly in his attempts to emulate his predecessor. People still didn't know Griffin was dead. According to the latest Gnosis statement, he was "getting settled in" at a treatment center in an undisclosed location. Hopefully, the truth would come out as soon as the power came back on. We'd emailed copies of Griffin's medical file to every news outlet we could think of, along with the Gnosis internal memo about Project Hyperion, hoping at least one of them would run the story before Gnosis discovered the changes we'd made to Lux's algorithm.

The video from my necklace went to only two people— Dean Atwater and Rudd. The email accompanying it explained that if anything ever happened to me or to Hershey, or if I ever sensed that the Few were trying to find me, the footage would go public. I had no doubt that I'd bought their silence. There was too much at stake for them both.

"Our cutting-edge infrastructure uses light and fiber optics instead of metal," the new Gnosis CEO was saying, "insulating our devices from electromagnetic interference, so users will be able to use their Golds and G-tablets with no problems during the outage. Of course, GPS requires satellites and, unfortunately, those we can't immunize. But be assured, once the solar storm has passed, Lux will once again function without error." I cringed. *Without error.* "In the meantime," he went on, "we are recommending that people refrain from using the app and remain indoors for the duration of the storm."

No mention of the worm North released into their network. Lucky for us, it appeared Gnosis couldn't bear the bad publicity of a successful hack, so they were burying it.

"What are they all doing?" I heard North ask. I'd forgotten he was beside me. I followed his gaze over the railing of the balcony. There were now at least a hundred people on the street below, all looking up at the sky.

"Seizing an opportunity," I said wryly. And the truth was, a starry night *was* an opportunity. To be awed and overwhelmed by the infinite unknown. To brush transcendence. The Few knew this, which is why they'd been so careful to keep people sheltered. Transcendence was transformational. That's what made it so risky.

"Rory, something is happening," North said then, getting to his feet. "There are literally thousands of people in the street." He was right. It was beginning to look like New Year's Eve below us, with people standing shoulder to shoulder in the plaza below. Since the EV charging stations turned off when the grid went down, the only cars on the road were a few gas-powered ones, which was good, because people were spilling out into the street.

My stomach twisted. It was our fault they were outside. What if something bad happened out there? A riot or something? Or some unforeseen effect of the solar storm? There must've been hundreds of thousands of people outside now. And it wasn't just in Times Square, either. There were people as far as I could see down Broadway, and on balconies and rooftops, too. Was this all for the stars? The sky was beautiful, for sure, but it wasn't anything particularly spectacular. No comets or meteors, no low-hanging moon. So why had it topped every user's opportunity list? This evening's sunset was more breathtaking than this was, and Lux had brought far fewer people outside for that.

I was staring down at the crowd, watching the masses interact with their screens. They seemed as confused as I did about why they were outside in the middle of the night. Most of them weren't even looking up at the sky anymore. They were tapping their screens, waiting for Lux's cue to call it a night.

I was willing them to go back inside, when I felt a prickly tingling, like static, deep in my bones. It only lasted for a second, then it was gone. Beside me, North shuddered. He'd felt it too. From the gasps and murmurs on the street below, I guessed that everyone had.

"What was that?" North asked.

"I don't know," I said, my heart fluttery in my chest. The hairs on my arms were standing on end, and my tongue tasted like copper. "Was it from the storm?" I peered over the balcony. It was hard to tell in the dark, but everyone seemed okay.

Just then North inhaled sharply. "Oh," he breathed. "Aurora." It was odd to hear him use my whole name, and even odder the way he said it. Just then there was a collective gasp below, followed by a wave of more gasps, as eyes flew from screen to sky.

Every cell of my body was sharp with apprehension, I tilted my head back. At the exact moment my gaze hit the horizon, I heard my name again, this time in my head.

Aurora.

I trembled when I saw it, the wondrous neon array. Spectacular and eerie and electric with color, it took my brain several seconds to take it all in. The downward slanting green streaks, the upward slanting purple ones, the pool of colors where the two lines met. The breathtaking aurora forming a crude outline of a dove with its wings outstretched. Light-headed with wonder, I sucked in deeply, filling my lungs with the cold night air. Space seemed to retract in that moment, drawing me nearer to the infinity above.

North reached for my hand and held it, both of us staring, awestruck, at the sky.

"It's for you," he whispered.

Below us were the muffled sounds of conversations. I tore my gaze away from the sky and looked down at the street. One by one, tiny rectangular lights were blinking off as handhelds timed out, but no one seemed to notice. Their eyes and minds were elsewhere. On the sky. On one another. For the first time in a long time, connection had replaced connectedness. I'd never seen anything like it before, not on this scale. The effervescent pulse of human interaction. People turning to faces instead of screens. It was a splendor of its own.

Hope filled every crevice of my body, and the smile that stretched across my face came from the deepest part of my soul.

Well done, the voice whispered. *Well done.*

Epilogue

"HAPPY SPRING SOLSTICE," he says, setting a small box on the table. I can tell he wrapped it himself.

"I feel like it's my birthday," I tease, because it is. I am seventeen today.

"I hope you like it," I hear North say as I lift the lid of the box. "Because I can't return it." Inside is a folded piece of paper. It's an email, addressed to me, with the purple NYU logo embedded in the text. *Dear Aurora Vaughn*, it reads. *Congratulations! I am pleased to inform you that you have been accepted into New York University's Class of 2035.*

"It came this morning," North says. When I look at him, his eyes are twinkling. "You got in."

"That's funny. Since I didn't apply."

"Oh, but you did," North replies, and leans across the table to take my hands. "And your application was very compelling. Especially your personal statement. You wrote about the person who most inspires you." He lifts my palm to his lips and kisses it. "He sounds like an amazing guy." He lowers his voice now, though it's unnecessary. The tables beside us are empty, and our waiter is hung up with a party of six across the room, answering questions about the menu. Dining is a more time-consuming affair these days, without Lux to guide the process. There are so many decisions to be made.

"I know it's not the same as getting in for yourself," North says quietly. "But once you're there, it'll all be you. And it's not like Atwater is going to tell them you didn't graduate from Theden this year. Not that I'm pressuring you to go—it's up to you. If you don't want—"

"I love you," I say, leaning on my elbows to kiss him.

He grins. "So you'll go?"

"Well, one of us has to get a respectable job," I tease, and kiss him again.

When the waiter brings our check, we pay with cash. Six months ago that would've raised eyebrows, but not today. People are distrustful now of electronic things, preferring the tangible instead. Dollar bills. Paper maps. Metal keys. It's not as bad as it was in the days after the storm, when most wouldn't even touch their phones. The paranoia was pervasive then. A withdrawal effect, some doctors said when the truth came out. When the nanobots shut off, brains were left jonesing for the trust boost they'd come to expect, and it took a few weeks for people's natural oxytocin levels to recover. By then the story had broken, and it wasn't paranoia that drove people to ditch their devices, but the facts.

We heard from scientists first, assuring us that the sensation we'd felt right before the aurora hadn't done us any harm. The human body could withstand an electromagnetic pulse much stronger than the one the storm had induced. "This was the equivalent of getting an MRI," a geophysicist said during one of NASA's many news conferences in the days after the storm. "Our bodies barely registered it."

The nanobots in those bodies, on the other hand, were made of iron oxide, a highly magnetic compound, and were designed with a fail-safe in case of malfunction. If something went wrong, an MRI could be used to short them out. An MRI or, as it turned out, a solar-induced electromagnetic current. Nearly twenty years of planning and the Few hadn't accounted for that.

It's ironic, actually, how it all turned out. The Few had chosen the Greek god Hyperion as their sacred project's namesake. Hyperion, the god who controlled the sun. And yet it was the sun that ultimately destroyed the Few's Hyperion, in one fiery burst. I guess the Few had misjudged Hyperion's divinity the same way they'd misjudged their own.

The floodgates opened a few days later. Without nanobots to persuade them, the one hundred and eleven reporters we sent the Gnosis memo to got to decide for themselves whether to run the story.

Every single one of them did.

The FDA immediately pulled Soza's flu spray off the market, and the Justice Department launched an investigation into

Gnosis, Lux, and the Gold. A week before Christmas, a grand jury in Boston issued seventy-seven indictments. When I saw the arrests on TV, I felt sorry for those executives in handcuffs. How many of them were like Griffin, clueless to what was really going on? The true culprits weren't on those companies' payrolls, and their names weren't ever mentioned in the news.

The Few—they haven't been defeated. Not by us, not by the storm. They aren't gods, but they are very smart men. And like Dr. Tarsus said, they are patient. Eventually they'll try again. But I, at least, am off their radar. For now that's enough.

According to Hershey, my departure from campus was a source of speculation for about a day. Then Rudd left Theden and people began to whisper that he'd had an affair with a student, and everyone just assumed it was me. The school isn't pressing charges and neither will Hershey, so the rumor has stayed a rumor and Rudd has stayed out of jail. I hate that he's out there, free, but Hershey says it's better this way.

"You wanna stop by the library?" North asks as we step out onto the sidewalk. It's a silly question. We go almost every night, now that the main branch on Fifth Avenue stays open until midnight. All the libraries do, to accommodate demand. The main branch has more than five hundred public computer terminals, yet tonight, as always, the line of people waiting to use them stretches out of the front door and down the iconic stone steps. This line says a lot about us. It says that we are too wary to use our handhelds, too concerned about our privacy to log on at home. And yet it also says that we are unwilling to cut the cord. We may carry wads of money in our pockets and keep paper maps in our cars, but like moths to a flame, we're drawn to those screens.

When it's my turn, I sit down at the terminal and begin my nightly ritual. Using a fake profile, I log on to Festival, the site that replaced Forum when the government took it down, and check up on the people I love.

There's a message from my dad in my in-box, wishing me a happy birthday. He doesn't understand why I'm using this fake profile, or why I won't give him my mailing address, but he seems to accept that it has to be this way for a while. I'm not hiding—I refuse to—but I am being cautious. Too much has happened for me to be cavalier with my freedom.

Beck is next. My best friend snapped out of his Lux-induced stupor the moment the nanobots shut off and he chucked his Gold into the Columbia River before the aurora faded from the sky. He's using his mom's old Galaxy now and has started taking pictures on film. There's been a surge of interest in old gadgets like that. Ivan is making a killing, no doubt.

Tonight I see that one of Beck's photographs—taken the day the story broke, as thousands of people gathered in Pioneer Square to burn their Golds in an impromptu bonfire Seattle police didn't even attempt to stop—will be part of an upcoming exhibit at the International Center of Photography, near Times Square, and that he'll be in town when it goes up in June. I smile, imagining what it'll be like to surprise him there. To hug his skinny neck, to spend hours catching up.

It's midnight now, and the voice over the PA tells us that it's time to proceed to the exit. The library is officially closed. "Just one second," I say to North, taking his hand as I quickly make one last click.

Hershey's profile is the hardest for me to look at, so I always save it for last. She's still at Theden, which is what she wanted, but the sunny statuses and smiling selfies don't fool me. I know her better than that. Still, I don't think I'll ever understand it, or forgive her for the decision she made. That knowing what she knows, she still chose to stay. Then again, that's what this whole fight was about, I guess. The terrifying but glorious freedom to fall.

Acknowledgments

First and foremost, I thank the One who gave me the idea for this book, my ever-present Paraclete. I hope I didn't butcher it too much in the execution.

Thank you to the incomparable Kristyn Keene, agent extraordinaire, whose enthusiasm for this story never waned and whose sensibilities shaped and improved it at every stage. And to Kyle Kallman, the best intern ICM ever hired, who liked my crazy idea enough to give me notes on it when he didn't have to. Sorry for naming a bad guy after you.

Thank you also to my editor, Sarah Landis at HarperTeen, whose insights and care for these pages left me swimming in gratitude on more than one occasion, and to the whole Harper-Teen team, especially Jen Klonsky, Gina Rizzo, Christina Colangelo, Sarah Kaufman (who's two for two on kickass covers), Jon Howard, Kaitlin Severini, and Alice Jerman for all their hard work and general awesomeness.

For your amazing expertise on all things nanobot (and for

basically giving me my oxytocin hook), a thousand thanks to the brilliant Dr. Katrina Siffred. For my hacker scenes, I'm indebted to Mike Siley, who isn't a hacker but still manages to be a badass. Please move back to LA. And then there's Alex Young at NASA, the coolest solar physicist in the world, who somehow explained solar storms in a way my not-scientifically-inclined brain could understand. Without your help, I may never have ended this book, and especially not with a spectacular green glow. And finally, Anne Drewry, dear friend and brilliant doctor, who helped me figure out how to kill all the people I needed to kill in this book, and who also taught me, years ago, the particular joy and privilege of having a "roomie BFF."

Thank you also to Ryan Dobson, for coming up with the name "the Doubt" (gee, did I write any of this book myself?); to Brent Robida, for your consistent and complicated friendship but also for reading the very first iteration of this story (that forgotten TV script that AMC didn't want) and for sending me Wendell Berry when I was stuck; to Bobbi Shiflett, for reading the first draft of this book in three days and single-handedly saving me from a black hole of self-doubt; and to Jordanna Fraiberg and Natalie Krinsky, for encouraging and inspiring me from across coffee shop tables as I wrote these pages and reminding me that this writing thing we do doesn't have to be loners' work.

These acknowledgments would not be complete without a huge, all caps THANK YOU to the fabulous Niki Castle, who read this book even faster than Bobbi did and said such nice things that I have to wonder if I can trust her. If anyone could convince me to move across the country, it's you, lady. Just as long as you promise to supply me with pumpkin cookies and vinho verde rosé.

Last but certainly not least, to my family, for their unending support and love, and especially to my husband, daughter, and little peanut on the way, who will no longer be a peanut when this book hits shelves but an actual person. I'm excited about this book, but I'm way more excited about you, Lil'er Miller. May you and your sister always trust that whisper within.

YOUR PATH CHANGES.
YOUR DESTINY DOESN'T.

Overnight, it's as if her past has been rewritten. Abby must
race against time to take control of her fate, without losing
sight of who she is, the boy who might just be her soul mate,
and the destiny that's finally within reach.